Fallen Descent

Meg Castro

Bohlander House Press
Dover, NJ

First published 2017
By Meg Castro
Bohlander House Press, Dover NJ

ISBN: 9780998651804
ISBN: 099865180X
Library of Congress Control Number: 2017902000
Bohlander House Press, Dover, NEW JERSEY

This book is dedicated to my husband.
He had to put up with all the demons that I battled while working on this book.

Prologue

REDEMPTION. IN THE dictionary it means to be saved from evil, error, or sin. For the faithful it means being forgiven for any transgression they have committed in their mortal shell. For Ana Gerfallen it meant redeeming her family so they would no longer be cursed. Most thirty year olds didn't have to worry about their families' salvation, but then most people aren't descendants of Johann Faust, the man who sold his soul to the devil in order to gain ultimate knowledge of the world. To most of the world, Johann Faust was a literary character made famous by Goethe and Marlowe. But for Ana, his story was very real, for her family was still paying the price for his foolishness.

There were times when Ana wondered if he had known it would curse his family for five hundred years would he still have signed the contract? Not that it mattered, "What if's" didn't change things. Instead of spending her mandatory two week vacations relaxing somewhere tropical, she was helping to restore a medieval monastery outside of Salzburg, Austria with her brother and cousin. They were searching for clues that might help end the curse.

"If you hit the wall any harder the whole place will come down," Sam Gerfallen, her cousin, stated sarcastically.

Ana stopped and took off her goggles, pulling the bandana down from her mouth. "If you're worried about the foundation don't hand me a sledgehammer and say destroy," Ana pointed out.

"Don't you need a break?" Sam asked seriously. "You've been attacking that wall for over an hour now."

"I'm good," Ana promised. She paused, leaning on the sledge hammer, watching Sam as he sipped his coffee. "You want to help? Or you going to watch me do the hard work?"

"Yeah. I'll help, I'm done in the bathroom anyway," Sam admitted. He had been tiling the bathroom at the other end of the abbey. "Toby should be done painting the last room in the groundskeeper cottage."

"Hard to believe that after two years the cottage is finally done," Ana answered. Her brother and cousin had bought the property two years ago and were still renovating the buildings on it.

"You and me both," Sam replied. "It will be nice to have one building completely done, and not just any building but the one we actually live in."

He pulled on goggles and a bandana. They counted to ten and both began attacking the stubborn wall in the main room of the old abbey. Rock music blared in the background as they hit the wall at the same time. The wall was a puzzle to Sam because from the outside of the building there was a room that should be right behind this wall. The problem was they had yet to find a door into the room. They had ripped the boards off the exterior windows only to find that they were boarded up on the inside as well. Now with the foundation strengthened and confirmation that this was not a load bearing wall, they could finally bring it down.

They counted to ten again and swung their hammers together. Ana's went completely through, almost sending her through the wall. Sam cursed and grabbed her by the waist before she fell into the mess.

"Holy shit," Ana grasped as she sat down on the ground. Dust was everywhere, including all over her, Sam grabbed her a bottle of water. He handed it to her and grabbed a clean cloth to wipe the dust off of her.

"You hurt?" he asked turning a portable ventilation fan to high.

"I think I'm good," Ana answered as she looked at her arms. They heard the front doors slam open.

Toby Gerfallen came running into the room. "I heard the crash," Toby stated as he crouched down next to his sister. "What happened?"

"Ana decided to throw herself through the wall," Sam stated as he looked over her arms.

"You helped," Ana reminded him.

"No blood, so that's a good sign," Sam noted ignoring her comment as he examined her arms. "A few minor scratches but nothing major."

"There's a door," Toby noted as he looked through the whole. "It's old."

"I love how his concern for me vanishes the moment he sees something old," Ana pointed out. "This whole place is old!"

Toby flipped her the finger as he studied the old door. "You're fine, besides this is huge."

Sam helped Ana get up, then they joined Toby at the large hole they had made. Behind the wall they were taking down was another one, this one had a mural on it and an old wooden door. Both had been concealed by the outer wall. Sam studied the plans he had for the building.

"This probably leads to the room we can't get to but can see from outside," Toby realized.

"Everyone, grab a mask and a hammer," Sam instructed with excitement in his voice. "The rest of this false wall needs to come down."

It took two hours to pull the wall down. Once they cleared out the debris they stared at what they had found. A wall had been built in front of an older wall. The purpose to it was only a guess - it was to conceal whatever was behind the door. Sam, an art restorer, got them what they needed to clean the dust off the older wall. They turned on the scaffolding lights as the daylight began to fade.

"Alright religious and art scholars, what do we have?" Ana inquired. Unlike her brother and cousin, her degree was in psychology.

"You don't just wall up over something like this," Toby pointed out in awe. He ran a gloved hand over the mural amazed at how well preserved it was. "You don't cover up this work of art."

"You do if you're hiding something," Sam stated.

"So what is it?" Ana asked. She knew she had to keep them on task, Sam was a well known art restorer who focused on architecture of old buildings, whereas Toby was a historian specializing in the Medieval to Renaissance era. Something like this wall could mean losing them for days.

Toby walked to the mural studying it more closely. "If I'm right, it's Judas as he betrays Jesus to the Romans," Toby began. "It's a scene that is popularly portrayed, but you do find it from time to time in churches or religious dwellings. It was used to remind us of our sins, of the ultimate betrayal."

"It's early renaissance in style," Sam added as he looked at the wall. "The place was built in the more gothic era but this wall was added later. So it would make sense that the mural would also be from a later time period."

"In an abbey that was once rumored to be owned by Faust it seems fitting to have Judas appear now and again don't you think?" Ana inquired with the hint of a smile.

"The question is what's behind it. A hidden lab?" Sam suggested with a hint of amusement. "A hidden library, even."

"Or dead bodies," Toby added. His sister and cousin both looked at him. "What? You know how many times bodies have been walled up so they could be forgotten about?"

"Before you tell us, let's get on respirators and coveralls," Sam instructed. "I'll grab my air monitor and camera. Ana grab some flashlights."

Once they were suited up and had their gear, Sam tried the old knob but it didn't budge. Toby went to kick the door but Sam glared at him. "You are not kicking down a five hundred year old door," Sam informed him.

Ana rolled her eyes at them and reached for the knob. Before her hand could actually touch it the door slowly opened. "And now we will hear some organ music from a horror movie," she whispered. Turning on her flashlight she nudged the door open wider.

"Good thing you're no virgin otherwise we would all be in trouble," Sam joked and got an elbow in the ribs from Toby.

Ana ignored them as she entered the room that time had forgotten. Cobwebs covered everything as she looked around the space. Her flashlight caught a glimmer of something on the floor, she headed toward the center of the room and kneeled down. Using her gloved hand, she brushed the centuries of dust away from a spot on the floor as she looked at what lay before she sat back on her heels.

"Holy shit," she whispered as she brushed away more of the dust.

"What is it?" Sam asked walking over to her.

"The zodiac symbols," Ana replied. "They're inlayed with gold into the floor. A perfect circle in the center of the room."

"There are cabinets back here that are filled with things," Toby called from the corner of the room.

Sam looked at Ana, excitement flashed in both of their eyes. This discovery was huge, it was what they had been hoping to find. The hidden lab of Johann Faust, the man who sold his soul to the devil for ultimate knowledge. By doing so, he had cursed all those who came after him. Ana was the oldest by a year which meant the family curse had fallen on her shoulders. Sam always felt that it should have fallen to him after his father committed suicide. For his father was the oldest of three brothers. But it had gone to Ana. Sam vowed to help her fight the curse, to find away to break it.

"We found it," Sam whispered as he pulled her in for a hug.

"We need to be sure," Ana stated not wanting to get her hopes up but there was excitement in her voice. "We can't rush this, we need to take our time with this room."

Sam nodded and took a deep breath. "We clean, and while we clean we catalogue what we find," he replied going into his work mode. "Cabinets should be last to open because we don't know what's in them. I want to get blackout drapes for the windows before we pull the boards off."

"Guys," Toby called over to them. He had been trying to get their attention for a few minutes. "GUYS!!!"

"What?" They both exclaimed at the same time.

"Come here, you need to see this," Toby answered.

Toby just shook his head at the two of them. They were always like that when they were together, finishing each other's sentences, knowing what the other was going to say before they did. The two walked over to where he was standing in front of a section of wall. Shining his lantern he highlighted a portion of the wall for them to see. There, over the faded wall, colored letters were written in both Latin and an older form of German all over the wall.

"He made notes on the wall," Toby stated pointing at the writing on the walls. "This isn't the only section either. There are also formulae, as well, some scratched out, other's circled."

The three looked at each other before they each began to examine other parts of the walls in the room. Where there weren't bookcases or cabinets, notes were scrawled over the surface. Sam grabbed his camera and began taking pictures of everything while Ana just took in everything that was staring at them. It was then she saw the gilded mirror hanging above the fireplace. She stepped back in horror as that night from almost ten years ago came slamming back into her mind.

She was handcuffed to the fourposter bed, her clothes had been removed leaving her in her underwear and bra. Ana studied the room, refusing to let fear overwhelm her. It was a huge master suite with antique furniture all around. The bed was made of solid oak which meant she couldn't break it if she tried. Drapes were pulled back from the sides giving her full view of the room. There was a sitting area in front of the bed with a red victorian couch sitting across from the fireplace and two two Queen Anne chairs flanking it.

Above the mantle was a hideous gilded mirror with cherubs peering over the corners of the frame. The mirror part of the frame was new as it hadn't tarnished with age. Ana did note that there were no windows and only one door to the room. When the door swung open she refused to curl up instead she watched as the man approached. He wore an all white suit with a black silk dress shirt underneath. His hair was dark blonde that curled slightly at the ends, his skin tan, and his eyes saw everything.

"I thought you would still be asleep," he stated.

"I'm awake," Ana replied.

"You aren't going to ask what I want?"

"It's pretty obvious what you want since I'm chained to a bed," she answered.

He laughed at her response. "Oh we are going to have fun together," he declared. "You are unlike any of your other ancestors." Ana arched an eyebrow and narrowed her eyes. "What do you mean?"

"You mean you haven't figured out who I am yet?" He inquired with a chuckle. "Is your brain telling you all the tales you were told are just that, tales. That there can't be any truth to them."

Ana didn't say anything as she watched him. He couldn't possibly know anything about her family. They had crossed the oceans in the early 1800's to get away from what was known as the family curse. They had changed their name hoping it would give them a fresh start. It hadn't. Bad luck still plagued the Gerfallen's.

"Bad luck?" he inquired. "I love the excuses that rational minds come up with to explain what can't be explained in mundane terms."

"Look, I think I'm not who you think I am," Ana began. "You apparently think you know me, know my family."

He smiled as he approached the bed and sat on the edge. He ran a finger over the inside of her foot and smiled wider when she pulled her foot back. "Oh sweet Analiese," he whispered. "It is far easier to believe that your uncle killed himself because he was weak then to believe the devil pushed him toward it. It is much easier to think that the dreams that haunt you around your birthday are just the way your mind copes with another year passing. Because to think that the Devil was whispering to you, entering your dreams, knowing your thoughts would be a true nightmare, wouldn't it?"

Ana couldn't say anything. He shrugged out of his coat and moved closer to her. "They are wrong, all this time they blame the devil or Lucifer, thinking they are the same person," he whispered in her ear. "But they are wrong for they were not the one that was gypped out of a soul."

"No," she whispered.

"Let me introduce myself, though I believe you already know my name," he began using a line for a song he actually liked. "I am Mephistopheles, the right hand of Satan."

Ana sat at the kitchen in the cottage with a tea mug nestled in her hand. Toby sat across from her with one of his hands resting on hers. Sam was at the stove making a late dinner. She wasn't sure how she got to the table, she remembered the room, then seeing the mirror.

"The mirror," she whispered. Sam turned from the stove and took a sip from his beer bottle.

"I sent a picture to Jules," Toby said gently. "She confirmed what we already figured out. It's the mirror from the night he attacked."

Ana nodded. It was her senior year of college, the week before finals and a group of friends and her went out. They were smart, never drinking from drinks that had been ordered for them. They had gone to a bar that handed out bracelets to groups so that the bouncers knew they all left together. But outsmarting the devil or one of his minions was near impossible.

But Jules, or Juliana Vijelens, was her best friend and had been since elementary school. Jules knew the moment that Meph, as they called him, took her.

Somehow Jules had been able to follow the "slime trail," as she calls it. It was Jules that saved Ana from being raped. Later in the ER with Jules and Sam they all realized that the warnings, the stories, they had all been true. Later, they all vowed to end it so that no other generations had to deal with it.

"We can destroy it," Sam told her. He was speaking about the mirror, bringing her back to the present.

"No," Ana answered, shaking her head. She surprised even herself when she said no. "I want to see why it's so special. Why it's here and why there was another one in Boston."

"Alright," Toby agreed. "We will add it to list of things to study."

"I should call Jules," Ana realized. "She's going to be frantic if I don't."
"You got ten minutes before dinner is ready," Sam warned her.

She nodded and slid out from the table. Ana headed up the narrow stairs to the second floor. There was one bath for the three bedrooms upstairs. Thankfully Sam had been grouting the new bathroom they put in on the main floor. Grabbing yoga pants and a Yankee's t-shirt she headed into the bathroom and stripped out of her dust covered clothes. The water washed away the fogginess that came with the memory, it helped relax her, and soothed aching muscles. Once she was clean and calmer she stepped out and dried off. Getting dressed, she headed into the guest bedroom and called Jules on her office line.

"Dr. Vijelens, how may I help you?" Jules asked when she picked.

"So Doc, I found this weird mirror and it so messed with my mind," Ana stated in an exaggerated accent.

"Oh my god," Jules couldn't help but chuckle. She walked over and closed her office door. "How are you?"

"I took a shower, it helped calm me down," Ana admitted. "I told them I didn't want to destroy it. I want to know why it's here."

"I agree," Jules replied. "I don't know if Sam told you, but from his picture, I noticed that the glass is discolored in the one in your abbey. It's not new, like the one in Boston had been."

"I didn't really study it too much," Ana answered. "Just seeing it was enough to send me back. Anyway did they tell you about the room?'

"Inlays in the floor of the zodiac and writing on the walls," Jules summed up. "Sam told me. I told him I could fly out if you want a second pair of hands."

"You mean both of us be gone from Bohlander House?"

"I know," Jules sighed. "And with all the drama that is going on here I think it would look bad if I left."

"How are things there?"

"Jenna is under constant watch," Jules answered. "Luke is here everyday along with Helen and Jill. Carl isn't answering any calls."

"Cassie sent me a text about the fight that Jenna tried to pick with her," Ana replied. "What else has happened?"

"Jenna has been cutting school so her parole officer, Luke, and the principal are pouring over security footage to see how she is doing it, since Terry walks her into the front office each day and signs her in."

"Do I need to come back?"

"No," Jules assured her. "Luke has Judge Harrison updated on the situation, there is going to be a hearing next week but it's nothing we need you here for. She's violating her deal by cutting school so you are fine where you are."

"If that changes let me know," Ana informed her.

"Cassie is bunking in the carriage house with me," Jules replied. "So that has helped somewhat."

"I should have brought her with me." Ana sighed thinking of the the thirteen year old girl she had legal custody of.

"She didn't want to go because she would miss rehearsals and school," Jules reminded her. "She knows you are coming back, so relax."

Ana heard Sam calling up to her. "Dinner is ready, but give Cassie hugs and tell everyone I miss them."

She hung up and headed back down the stairs. "So how are things?" Toby asked.

"The same," Ana answered.

"And my niece?" Toby inquired.

"Amazing," Ana said with a smile. "She's keeping Jules company in the carriage house."

"You know mom gets such pride in what you do with the house," Toby replied. "And then brags about my degrees."

Ana just chuckled. Bohlander House was where Ana worked and lived. It was a home for at-risk teens that focused not just on giving them a safe place to live but also working with them, getting them ready for the real world. Giving them a chance at life. Cassie Clark was the youngest of the teens and, as of last year, was Ana's adopted daughter. While Ana was thirty and Cassie was 13, Ana needed to intervene when Cassie's mother showed up. It ended up with Ana adopting Cassie.

"You know I'm really their favorite," Sam stated as he set the chicken on the table.

"That's only because they didn't have to raise you," Toby pointed out.

Chapter I

THE PHONE CALL came a week later. During lunch in Salzburg, Ana got the call from her boss Luke Gray, the lawyer for Jenna was demanding she be there in person. This meant a lot of scrambling to get Ana from Austria to New York City with less that twenty four hours notice. Toby and Sam called every person they knew, calling in favors until finally Ana had an itinerary that would have her landing at JFK at 10a.m. the following day. While Toby, Sam, and she scrambled to get her packed and to the airport, Luke uploaded all the information she was going to need, including her own personal notes and files.

Instead of spending a few days relaxing from the labor intensive renovations at the abbey, Ana was on a plane catching up on notes about what she had missed in the week since she had been gone. It all centered around Jenna Douglas. Jenna had first come to the attention of Second Chances, the firm that Ana and Jules worked for, almost a year ago. The teenager had been recommended by the juvenile court system to be reviewed as a potential candidate for Bohlander House, as well as one of the drug programs that Second Chances offered. Since Luke headed the drug program and Ana was one of the program's counselors, they had both been called in from the beginning of the Jenna's case. That fact Ana lived and worked at Bohlander House so she would be able to see if the teen met the criteria.

From the moment of introduction it was clear that Jenna was going to be a tough case. For six months Ana and Luke talked to every person who had been involved with Jenna; parole officers, advocates, teachers, friends, family. No one knew what caused her to go down this path of self-destruction. Her parents were middle class, she lived in a decent neighborhood near Coney Island. They were a happy family, the marriage was strong.

What became clear was Jenna liked things that came easy and didn't require work. She had been told since she was born that she was beautiful, her parent's were offered contracts to model her but fear of pedophiles had them turning their backs. It was something that Jenna had resented when she learned she could have been a model. The downhill slide had started with sex when she was thirteen, her parents walked-in on her seducing the babysitter. Then the drugs started, then the selling her body for drugs. They had tried everything and she would act the part, then go back to the same old thing the minute she was home.

In a session with Ana, Jenna had become angry and hostile at the suggestion she would need to work hard to clean up. That this wasn't a program she could just sit back and let others do the work. She would need to be part of the house, try at school, go to meetings, and therapy sessions. That if she endangered the other teens living at the house she would be removed. Jenna wanted none of it, but she knew she didn't want to go to Juvie. In her mind, Bohlander House and its programs were her key. But she didn't want to do the work that would be required of her. Luke and Ana refused to sign off on her being accepted.

Then two weeks later Jenna showed up with Carl Olsen, he was the head of Bohlander House. He told her a judge signed off on her being here so they had to take her. He left the teen on the doorsteps. For the two months that she had been at the house all she had done was create drama and turmoil. Now she was claiming it had all been on them, that they had created a hostile environment for her.

When the pilot informed them they would be landing, Ana put away her tablet and notes. She prepared for landing, making sure she had everything ready for customs. She didn't have anything to declare so that would speed things along. Once through the process, she headed to the international arrivals gate and spotted Luke standing there with two steaming to-go cups of coffee. He didn't say a word when he handed her one. He took her suitcase and led her to the garage. Luke was in what they referred to as his court attire. Gray suit, with a white dress shirt underneath, then some kind of stripe tie for color as opposed to his casual attire he wore around the office.   It was a far contrast from her faded jeans and purple t-shirt.

"The judge was notified that if you were to appear it would be in jeans because of travel," Luke informed her as he loaded her suitcase into the trunk of his car. "He was fine with it."

"You mean Harrison caved in on something?" Ana asked shocked.

Judge Harrison ran a strict courtroom. You showed up properly dressed to his room and if you couldn't afford to then he would pay for a suit or dress that was appropriate. You would also get a lecture about appearances and moving forward in life you needed at least one good suit or dress. Ana slid into the passenger side of the car and stretched for a moment.

"He knows the circumstances, he knows that you are literally coming right from the airport," Luke replied. He glanced over at her and smiled. "You ready?"

"Alright, hit me," Ana said. She had enough caffeine by now, she could have an actual conversation. "Start from the beginning, Jules and Cassie only covered the surface of it."

"As usual, when you or Jules are gone, both Jill and Helen alternated between staying at the house," Luke began. "From the first night, Jenna was trying to get her way. She tried to tell Jill that she got special treatment because she came from rougher circumstances."

Ana almost snorted at that. "That went over well, I'm sure," she commented.

"With Helen she played the victim card, no one understood her, we were all so strict and mean," Luke continued. "Needless to say, she didn't get far with either of them."

"I can only imagine."

"Shit started hitting the fan when we realized she wasn't going to school," Luke went on. "With you gone, the school notified Jules that Jenna was skipping classes. Jules called Terry to confirm what the school was saying. They had video of him walking with her, Brett, and Karen to the front door each day. But after she was signed-in and escorted to homeroom she vanished."

"Great, so she's violating parole," Ana replied.

"It gets worse," Luke warned.

"How much worse?"Ana closed her eyes and sipped her coffee.

"We found heroin on her last night and fresh track marks."

Ana almost spit out her coffee, once she was done coughing she looked at Luke. "That's violation of the contract that everyone signs. You bring drugs into the house and you are done."

"I know," Luke replied. He wrote the rules so he knew very well what was in them. "From what we have been told, Carl's lawyer contracted the court because he feared for Jenna's safety. One of their complaints is that the staff ignored Jenna, using what happened with her attendance at school as proof. They are also claiming that because you're now Cassie's guardian you are no longer objective with the other kids."

"So now we are all being dragged into court because Carl is being an ass."

"I think she's seduced him into thinking she is innocent and that he is her savior," Luke admitted despite the idea sickening him. "I also think he buys her version of her life as opposed to what is real."

Ana looked at Luke. "That's revolting, he's old enough to be her grandfather."

"We are having him looked into as we speak," Luke answered. His jaw was clenched as he spoke, he still couldn't believe that they had to investigate one of their own. "There have been other things that Jill and Helen have noticed, we were hoping to deal with it more quietly but with this we can't."

"I'm sorry," Ana whispered.

Luke, Jill, and Helen had started Second Chances from an idea they had come up with as undergrads. They poured everything they had into it including a failed first marriage, life savings, etc. In the first few years the firm had been funded by credit cards, because they truly believed in helping everyone, including those who couldn't afford therapy. Twenty years later, with a variety of government grants and foundation support, it was the place to go with the difficult case, because it didn't matter what you could pay they would take you and work it out later. They ran two non-profits as well. Their Drug Rehab program in Long Island and Bohlander House where Ana worked and lived.

"The three of us went yesterday," Luke informed her. "It's how we learned what the lawyer was going to pull. Terry was the first one on the stand this morning and then Jules was following him."

Luke's phone rang and he took the call. Ana replayed all the information that Luke had told her while he talked on the phone. When he hung up he looked at Ana. "Jules is on the stand now," he told her.

"Anything I should know before I go in?" Ana asked.

"The lawyer that Carl got for Jenna is brutal and has been warned on several occasions already to ask questions pertaining to the case."

"Why is Carl getting her a lawyer?" Ana asked. "I mean why isn't the court appointing one for her?"

"That is one of the many questions that we have to ask him in our meeting with him," Luke replied. "We have a lot of questions in regards to his involvement with Jenna."

"He has never shown an interest in any of the kids like he has with Jenna," Ana noted.

"I know and that doesn't sit well with me."

"Great," Ana sighed as she drank her coffee. "Jet lag, a pissed off Judge, and a mad dog lawyer. It's going to be a great day."

They drove the rest of the way in silence, Luke pulled up in front of the courthouse and Ana hopped out with her wallet and phone while Luke went to park the car. She went through security and found Jill O'Keer pacing outside the courtroom. Jill saw Ana and gasped as she walked over to hug her.

"I can't believe you got here in time," Jill stated. Jill was head of the Crisis Intervention section of Second Chances. She was Jules' boss and helped out at the house two weekends a month to give them a break.

"Neither can I," Ana admitted.

"The bailiff is going to let me know when they call your name. Jules is still on the stand but they were finishing up when I stepped out to wait," Jill told her. "So drink your coffee while you can."

Luke came through security and joined them. "How's it going?"

"I think Terry's was the funniest when her lawyer stated that he had tried to seduce her," Jill replied. She was referring to Terry Wilkes who was the male counterpart to Jules and Ana at the house. "Terry just looked at the lawyer and then at the judge and said, 'Your honor, I'm gay. If you wish, you can contact my boyfriend, a detective in the NYPD, and have it verified. But trust me women, especially children, do nothing for me. Harrison congratulated him on his boy-friend and dismissed the claim."

"So expect anything?" Ana guessed.

"Yes," Jill answered.

The door cracked open and a bailiff poked his head out. "Ma'am they are about to call Dr. Gerfallen to the stand. Is she here?"

"I am," Ana replied. Taking a deep breath she walked into the courtroom with Jill and Luke flanking her.

"Ah, Dr. Gerfallen you were able to get a flight," Judge Harrison stated.

"I was, please excuse my appearance today," Ana replied. "Dr. Gray brought me straight from the airport and I brought no court clothes with me on vacation."

"Dr. Gray already explained the situation to me," Judge Harrison assured her. "I will wave my rule on proper attire for you. Please have a seat, I am sure you are exhausted from your travels."

The lawyer who Carl had hired for Jenna looked shocked as Ana took the oath and then sat. "Did Dr. Gray fill you in on why we are here?" Judge Harrison inquired.

"We are here to discuss the placement of Miss Douglas as well as her treatment while she was at Bohlander House," Ana stated.

"Mr. Lloyd, I suggest you tread lightly with Dr. Gerfallen," the judge warned. "She has crossed the Atlantic to get here today on very short notice. I would hate for her trip to be wasted because I have to warn you once again about your courtroom behavior."

"Of course, your honor," James Lloyd said with a nod. He then focused on Ana. "Dr. Gerfallan, I can say for most of us, that we are surprised you cut your vacation short to attend court."

Ana said nothing and sipped the water that had been placed in front of her. Unlike the courtroom of television's, this one had two long tables and folding chairs behind them. The judge sat at a raised stand and the witness sat in a chair off to his right. This was a modern styled courtroom that was normally used for adoptions, custody hearings and non felony drug cases. The lawyer spoke from his table not from a podium in the center of the floor.

"Questions, Mr. Lloyd," Judge Harrison reminded him.

"Of course," James replied. "Dr. Gerfallen, going on vacation in early late April seems odd when you live in a house full of kids. Do you find this to really be the proper time to go away, especially to Europe?"

The Judge went to speak but Ana held her hand up. "I'll answer it," Ana said. She smiled politely at the lawyer. "Every six months those that work at Bohlander House and at our Drug Rehab facility are required to take a two week vacation. This is to help prevent burnout, to help us be able to recharge our batteries. The vacations are rotated so that only one of us is gone at a time."

"And your's is April?"

"Yes," Ana replied. "Dr. Vijelens goes in March and Dr. Wyles is January. The destination is our choice."

"And you chose Europe? That's expensive."

"My brother and cousin purchased property outside of Salzburg, I go for two weeks and help with rehabbing it," Ana explained. "So as long as one is willing to pay for their own flight and lift a hammer, room and board is free."

"I'm sorry we took you away from that," James stated. "Are you in contact with the house while on vacation?"

"The intent is for us not be but we are usually in communication with someone from the house," Ana admitted. "Julianna and I are best friends so I talked to her frequently while gone. Which is normal for us anyway."

"And what of Dr. Wyles?"

"A few times, Terry called to let me know that one of the teenagers needed a form signed and he wanted to know if I had a copy of it," Ana recalled. "I am in charge of forms and schedules so he figured it was easier to call and ask me then try to find them in my office."

"Who called you to tell you that you were needed here?" James inquired.

"That would be Luke."

"And did he tell you that you had to be here?"

"I didn't give him the chance, I told him I would let him know my flight information."

"So you volunteered?"

"Mr. Lloyd, is there a point to all of these questions about her vacation and whether or not she was told to come back?" Judge Harrison inquired. "You have yet to mention why we are even here. I suggest you get to the point of the matter."

"Very well, Dr. Gerfallen how early were you brought into Miss Douglas' case?"

"Immediately," Ana answered.

"And why is that?"

"Miss Douglas was presented to us as a potential drug patient," Ana explained. "Since I am a Drug Rehab Counselor and live at Bohlander House I was brought in from the start."

"And your interactions with Miss. Douglas, when did those start?"

"Within forty eight hours of us receiving the call that she might be a potential candidate."

"Over the course of the entry process what were your thoughts on Miss Douglas?"

"She was resistant to any treatment program that was presented to her, she was argumentative, anything that resulted in a change in her lifestyle was met with defiance," Ana summed up.

"In your report on why she was not a candidate you stated she was violent," James stated. "Why do you say that?"

Ana knew that she couldn't bring up Jenna's violent outbursts toward her younger sibling, so she went with what she herself had witnessed. "Because when I was going over what would be expected of her, as a resident in Bohlander House, she launched herself across the table, spit at me, and then tried to punch me."

"And you did nothing to cause her to react in away?"

"I told her she could live in a gilded age mansion, go to the best schools in the city, have a new chance at life if she agreed to follow the program and the court orders that would go with it," Ana answered. "So no, I don't think I did anything to warrant that reaction."

"I see," James replied. He shuffled some papers. "After Jenna was brought to the house she states that she was treated unfairly, she was secluded from the rest of the teenagers that lived in the house, could only take meals in her room. In her statement, Jenna states because she did not get along with your ward the house turned against her. What do you say?"

"The claims are false," Ana said simply.

"Do you care to elaborate?"

"What would you like me to elaborate on?" Ana inquired before answering. "Jenna shared a room with one other female. The female we placed her with is a warm individual who tries to make friends with everyone. The female often tried to get Jenna to partake in group activities, but Jenna refused. Her claim that she only ate in her room is also false, no one is allowed to eat in their rooms. She had chores just like everyone else, therapy sessions to attend like the rest of the residents."

"And what of your ward?"

"My ward is a bubbly thirteen year old girl who sings opera," Ana stated. "When her few attempts to Jenna were thwarted with insults, my ward stayed away from her. Her behavior toward my ward, unfortunately was common behavior with each member of the house, including the adults."

"Then this is a lie on her part?"

"Your client has been known to make grand stories about her life that have been proven false on numerous occasions," Ana reminded him.

"Do you have proof of those apparent lies?"

"It's all in her file," Ana pointed out to him. "You will see that she was diagnosed as pathological liar."

James just looked at her, then at the files where he had made some notes. "Can you explain why you feel she is not a candidate for the program?"

"We have a waiting list a mile long to get into our program," Ana explained. "Each candidate is interviewed several times, as well as, every adult involved with them. We look at every aspect of their lives, school records, medical records, juvenile records. They are going to be living with other teenagers, we need to make sure that those that are accepted into the program are willing to work and live with others."

"And you feel Jenna did not fit those qualifications?"

"From our first interview she was hostile," Ana answered. "That can be common, so we continued, but with each interview she got more argumentative. We showed every program she could be a part of and she threw the papers off the table and just stared at us."

"What about your inability to get her to school which is being used against her as a violation of her parole?"

"Let me explain this to you," Ana began as she leaned forward. "Jenna went to a school that two of our other students attended. Which means each morning Dr. Wylkes would load the three residents into a van with another one who attended a school close- by. He would drop the one student off first then bring the three to their school. He would then escort Jenna to the front office where he would be met with a security officer. Once Jenna was signed-in the security officer would then escort Jenna to her homeroom. She was to be escorted to each class by an officer."

"And you will throw her out for cutting one day?"

"In her parole it states that failure to attend school for the entire length of the school day without an excused note would warrant her removal from the program and the house," Ana recited.

"You realize that by removing her from your program she will be forced to go to Juvenile Detention Center?"

"We are not forcing her to go there," Ana corrected him. "Jenna knew her parole agreement, she knew the risks. She knew what would happen if she cut school and brought drugs into the house. She ignored the warnings and did so anyway. Jenna has done this to herself."

"You seem alright with the house failing her."

"No, I am not alright with failing her," Ana answered. "Her failing is a reminder that we can't help everyone. Some individuals choose to continue on their destructive path. The house is like any treatment program, there are some that it doesn't work for. In the fifty teenagers that have come through the doors since it opened ten years ago there have only been four teens that did not graduate from it. They were each sent back to the courts. We knew from the beginning that this program was not a match for her, that is why the three of us and Dr. Gray stated such in our findings."

"But you took her in any way?"

"We took her in because Carl Olsen showed up with her and a signed court order from another judge, the moment she was in the house he left without so much as a goodbye," Ana stated.

"What did you do upon her arrival? Her statement reads that she was ignored and left to figure things out."

"We got her into an vo-technical academy that several of our students attend," Ana explained. "We assigned her a room, then took her shopping for school uniform and proper clothes for a sixteen year old. We went over the chore list, we figured out her day for her to see her probation officer, her NA meeting, and her therapists. We had her to a doctor for a proper physical. We did the big welcome dinner that we do for every new arrival."

"And now you wash your hands of her?"

"And now we move forward with the knowledge that we can't save everyone," Ana corrected him once again. "We will learn from her time with us, but we also understand that we can only save those who want to be saved. Who want a second chance at life."

Chapter 2

AFTER ANA'S COURT appearance, she spent another three days in meetings with judges, lawyers, and people from the house. Luke, Helen, and Jill also were there with her and by Saturday they were all exhausted. Jules found Ana in her bedroom where Cassie was filling her in on all the school gossip. Cassie was an opera phenom and was attending Juilliard. So Ana was getting updated on all the drama at rehearsals for their end of the year recitals.

"I don't mean to intrude," Jules began as she entered with a smile. Like everyone in the house she was in comfortable clothes: yoga pants and a tank. Her blonde hair was pulled back and she wore no make up.

"You are never intruding, Aunt Jules," Cassie said dancing around the room.

Ana and Jules lived in the carriage house that was connected to the main house. The mansion had once been a stunning gilded age manor for some banker and his wife. Second Chances bought it when the property went up for auction and transformed the upper west side location back to it's glory days while modernizing it. Rooms they didn't need, like the smoking lounge, were done away with and made into larger bedrooms or other rooms. It could house up to twenty teenagers and up to eight adults. More if it was an emergency. It currently housed four adults and fifteen teenagers.

"Is it time for the meeting?" Ana asked. She looked at the clock and saw that it was.

"Terry and Martha are getting everyone into the kitchen," Jules told her. Since coming back, Jules and Ana had no time to talk about the discoveries made in Austria. She was hoping tonight, after the meeting, they would be able to.

"Then off we go," Ana said as she got off the bed.

Cassie skipped in front of them as they headed to the main floor. The connecting door was through their kitchen and opened into the mudroom off of the large kitchen in the main house. It was a commercial grade kitchen with high-end appliances, but they had gone with soft color cabinets and countertops with a large central island that could sit eight. The breakfast nook could fit another ten. The walls were a soft yellow that helped brighten the room.

Martha, their house keeper and keeper of sanity, stood in front of the double ovens checking on the food. Usually, Martha spent Friday to Sunday at her son's place in Long Island but, given the circumstances, she chose to stay and help.

Everyone was talking as they filed into the room each grabbing their usual spot amongst the island or table. No one sat on the counters, not when Martha was in the room otherwise they would get swatted gently by a wooden spoon. Since this was the same woman who let them go into the cookie jar no one dared to test her. Ana let out a whistle and then waited for everyone to stop talking. It only took a few moments before everyone settled down.

"Alright, I'm starting with the biggest concern you all have," Ana began. "The house is not closing, you are all not being sent away. So take a deep breathe and relax."

Brushing a strand of hair out of her face she continued. "Mr. Olsen has been suspended without pay until the investigation into his involvement with Jenna is done," Ana explained. "As to the new head of our program, we don't know yet, but Luke is going through possible candidates. Until then he will be filling in. Any questions on that front?"

"Is he still in charge of the rehab as well?" one of the boys asked. There were seven boys and eight girls at the moment. Two of them were also in the outpatient rehab program for drugs.

"Yes, thankfully his wife loves you guys and knows this is important," Ana said with a smile. "As for you guys, nothing changes. Same schedules as before."

The teens began to relax a bit. "Alright now for all the legal shit," Ana replied. They did occasionally curse in front of the kids. Part of the role the house played wasn't just keeping them out of trouble but teaching them how to function in the world outside the front door. "Jenna attempted to stir up a lot of trouble for us. Thankfully, our obsession with detail has helped us in the court.

Judge Harrison is having the judge, who signed-off on the initial order to bring Jenna here, placed under judicial review as well, because he was going to refuse to approve the order the following day. So the court is going to be looking into how Jenna ended up here after we all said no."

"So you guys aren't in trouble," Dennis Kay asked. He was the oldest and would be graduating in June.

"No," Ana assured them all. "Now look, with the investigation, some people from Child Protective Services are going to be coming to the house. It's just like when we are thinking about taking in another teen. They are coming to look at what we do, how we are doing, and in this case is there any improvements. They are going to talk to you about Jenna and Carl. Be honest. Tell them how you feel. All I ask is try to keep the cursing and insults to a minimum. If you want to do the interviews in pairs that's fine just let Terry, Jules or me know and we will arrange it."

"The interviews are happening here," Terry added. "So it's not going to be out of the house. They also want to see how we are getting back to normal after this. Like Ana said, no one is in trouble here. Second Chances, the House, it's all fine."

"So nothing changes?" Cassie asked.

"Well one thing is changing," Ana admitted. "Until the investigations are resolved I am going to be working from the carriage house. I will try to leave a sign on the connecting door when I have a client, so just try to remember if I'm normally at the office it means I'm probably working, so bother Terry, Jules, or Martha."

"So in other words, we are still stuck with all of you," Jules stated. "And you are all stuck with us."

"What would have happened though if they closed the house?" Dennis asked.

Ana looked at Terry and Jules, they both nodded. "Luke, Jill, and Helen came up with a plan if that were to happen," Ana informed them. "What would happen is the three of them and possibly myself, Terry and Jules, would do what we did with Cassie. We take on personal guardianship of each of you. Since this house is owned by Second Chances we would still live here but some adjustments would be made into living arrangements and how things were run here. So, were that ever to happen, none of this group, right here in front of me, would be sent back to where you were. Unless that is what you wanted."

"Unlike the rehab, this is a privately owned house that happens to be the address of a non-profit organization," Terry explained. He had been on board since the conception of the idea. "Luke didn't want to take a chance with a state owned property, it might get sold if there was a budget cut. If he owned the building, ran it as a non-profit that worked with the services of the state then that fear would no longer be relevant. All the money that went into the renovations were done by private funding."

"So we would be able to stay no matter what," one of the newer kids realized. "Even if Bohlander House was technically closed we could still stay."

"Yes," Ana answered. "Like Jules said we are all stuck with each other."

Later, after curfew and everyone was upstairs where they should be, Jules found Ana outside on the back porch. She handed her a glass of wine then sat down next to her. Neither spoke for a few minutes as they sipped the wine.

"So how was Austria?" Jules finally inquired.

"You should see the lab, Jules, it's stunning," Ana answered recalling all the detail of it. "The inlay on the floor, it takes your breath away when you realize that it's gold. Then there's his actual handwriting all over the walls."

"So it's Faust's legendary lab?"

"Yes," Ana said with confidence. "We took the mirror down to study it and found a false back to it. Do you know what was there?"

"I don't even know what to think, so just tell me," Jules replied.

"His journal, Jules," Ana replied still amazed at what they had found. "We found his fucking journal. He titled it *Absolute Knowledge*. I thought Toby was going to die when he translated the title and first page."

"The two of them have to be like kids in a candy store," Jules realized, she could just picture Sam and Toby getting all excited over what they had found. "Sam with all the art history stuff and then your brother with all the notes."

"I don't think they've even realized that I'm gone," Ana admitted with a chuckle. "But do you realize what this means?"

"That maybe our next vacation could be somewhere tropical, with umbrella's in our drinks," Jules suggested.

"I was going to say that we could actually win this," Ana pointed out. "But I like your thought better."

Jules laughed. "Did you do anything fun while there?"

"We did go to Stonehenge for Beltane," Ana answered.

"And you are only telling me this now?" Jules yelled. "You went? Was it amazing? How did you get invites?"

"Sam and Toby know people, they got us invites, and it was amazing," Ana recalled. "Watching the sun come up, the procession, everything, it was just so spiritual and feeling at peace."

"I hate you so much," Jules declared.

"No you don't," Ana laughed.

Jules just shook her head smiling and looked at Ana. "Do you remember how we met?"

"I shared my lunch with you in first grade because you didn't like the sandwich your mom sent," Ana recalled. "It was the best lunch share ever."

"I don't know what I would have done without you, your family," Jules admitted. "You guys took me in when my mom bailed, going so far as to legally petition to be my guardians. No one ever looked down on me, your entire family just accepted me from day one. Not many would do that."

"Yea well, we understand that one person shouldn't be punished because of the actions of their parent or family," Ana answered.

"I also want you to know that I'm here, I'm not going anywhere," Jules told her. "I get what we are up against. I understand what's at stake. After all this shit with Carl and Jenna I don't want you beating yourself up, blaming yourself that you somehow brought this on to the house."

"Why would I think that?"

"Because I know you and I know when things like this happen you wonder if it's the devil playing tricks on you, testing you," Jules replied.

Ana went to argue but stopped and just sipped her wine. "It was a brief thought that I quickly dismissed," Ana admitted.

"Good," Jules answered. She finished her wine. "Alright I should head in."

"You're sure you don't want me taking the weekend shift?" Ana asked. Jules and Ana alternated weekends staying in the main house because usually Martha wasn't here for the weekends.

"You are dead on your feet, between jet lag and court, you need sleep," Jules argued. "Most of the girls were settled in their TV room watching a movie, some had already turned into their rooms for the night."

"Alright, if you're sure," Ana answered.

"Technically you should still be Austria so go to bed, soak in a bath, do yoga," Jules suggested. "Relax and sleep."

"What does relax mean again?"

Jules just laughed as she walked back into the main house. Ana stayed on the porch finishing her wine. The one aspect about her friendship with Jules was it started out of innocence and childhood magic. It had nothing to do with the dark cloud that had loomed over her family. Jules was the one bright light that Ana had always been able to count on. When she needed her the most, Jules appeared like an avenging angel. They had been there for each other in their most darkest moments, when Jules had been abandoned by her mother at the age of twelve, Ana had rode on her bike in the middle of the night to get her. When her parents woke up the next morning and saw Jules at the breakfast table they didn't say anything, just went through their normal routine.

Now they worked together, lived together, and helped those that needed the stability and normalcy that everyone deserved. In truth, Ana wouldn't change anything. Her soul might be damned but her life was blessed.

Chapter 3

THE FOLLOWING MORNING Ana was sitting at the kitchen table with Jules while Terry refilled their coffee mugs. Martha was out running errands and everyone was at school. Luke had given the three of them a reprieve from coming into the office in midtown. Appointments and meetings had been moved or rescheduled letting the three of them focus on the house.

"So you found a hidden room that is filled with alchemy equipment and notes?" Terry asked as he sat back down. "Sam and Toby have to be going nuts."

"If I hear another argument of the formula for the philosopher's stone I might scream," Ana confessed.   Terry knew about the monastery in Austria, about what her brother and cousin did. She just downplayed the whole Faust angle of it.

"I would love to see the place," Terry admitted.

"You just want to ogle Sam as he swings a hammer," Jules corrected.

Terry laughed. "Well yea, he's hot," Terry answered and Ana just rolled her eyes. "But he also knows his stuff. I mean look at what he did with this place and he wasn't even finished with his training yet when his company got the contract for here."

Jules sipped her coffee then looked at the binder that was the schedule for the house. One wall of the kitchen was painted in chalkboard paint. It held a huge monthly calendar that was large enough to fit everyone's chores, appointments, and activities. Everyone had their own color or shade so that it was easy to figure out who went where and when. Ana was keeper of the actual schedule.

"Alright so what do we have?" Jules asked.

"Three weeks before Memorial Day," Ana pointed out. "So that means games, practices, and the potential for holiday weekend tournaments. Dennis' coach said that he can stay with his family if their team makes the tournament. A few parents of teammates have offered to take one or two as well so we are good there. The one thing that will get crazy is Cassie's schedule."

"Right, any word on that yet," Jules inquired.

"Her vocal coach is hoping to have some draft by the holiday," Ana answered. "But at least two days a week at Lincoln Center is practice. She's going to try and see if she can work her times out to be the same as Dennis' practice so that he can pick her up on the way home."

Terry drummed his fingers on the table. "I've been thinking about everything," he admitted. "Maybe we need to rethink our roles at the house and at Second Chances."

"What do you mean?" Ana asked.

"When the house started there were five teens," Terry explained. "We could easily handle five teens, their schedules, and put in three to four days at the office. And that was when you had two males and two females plus a housekeeper who came once a day. Now we have one male, two females, a live in housekeeper, and fifteen teenagers, and Cassie. And we still have our commitments at the office."

"It is a lot," Jules admitted.

"You're not thinking of leaving?" Ana asked.

"God, no," Terry answered. "And that's part of what I've been thinking about. The house works because for the last four years it's been us. The first six years it was me and then who ever thought they could handle this life style. I love what I do, I love the kids. The thing is, I know I can get a better paying job somewhere else but it's not going to be this."

"Your right," Ana agreed. "I think about five, ten years down the line and I'm still here."

"Same here," Jules replied. "I mean I know we are living rent free and in a to-die- for location. But it's also what we do here, I love it."

"I think we need to think of a plan that involves us being permanent here and having an office that is closer to us," Terry suggested. "It would allow us more flexibility and we would have more time at the house."

"That isn't a bad idea," Ana admitted. "We could also put in more office hours if it's closer to us."

"We will also need a plan about when we find our significant others," Jules warned. "I mean, the kids are all cool with Alex."

"That's why I bring this up, we want to move in together but he knows I'm not giving up the kids," Terry replied. "His lease isn't up until the end of September so we have time to figure this out. But Jules is right, we need to figure out how to introduce this to the teens. They need to see healthy relationships, but at the same time we have to be careful who we bring home."

"Simple, we have Alex run a background check on anyone we want to bring to the house," Ana replied. "If our date doesn't understand the reason then they aren't worth introducing to the kids."

"That actually will help weeding out the losers," Jules realized. "Look, let's think about it and then over Memorial Day weekend, when we have less kids around we can really hash out our ideas. But now isn't a bad time to think about it because we are getting a new director."

"Hence the other reason I brought it up," Terry replied.

They heard the loud front door bell. "I'll get it," Ana stated. "You two behave while I'm gone."

Ana brushed a dark curl behind her ear as she headed to the front door. Looking through the peephole she saw it was Luke. Usually he used the back door that led into the kitchen. Opening it she smiled at him, then noticed the tall gentleman standing next to him. He had dark blonde hair that curled at the nape of his neck, he was wearing dark jeans and a blue polo shirt, sunglasses shielded his eyes.

"Hi," Luke said kissing her on the cheek. "Ana, this is my friend Dr. Erik Astrium."

"Hi," Ana replied shaking Erik's hand. She raised an eyebrow at Luke, this was a surprise visit. "What's up?"

"Are Jules and Terry here?" Luke asked.

"We're in the kitchen going over the schedule for the rest of the month," Ana answered.

She let them enter, then closed the door, setting the alarm as she did. Luke knew his way around the place so he headed straight for the kitchen. Erik was looking around the grand entrance way. There was a formal office off to the left of the foyer, then to the right would have been a drawing room that was now a small living room with leather furniture. He noted the large archway that led into a music room with piano, a harp, and other instruments.

"We have eight musicians and yes one of them can play the harp," Ana answered his unasked questions. "Everyone thinks it's odd we have a formal living room and music room but when someone is practicing there are always kids sprawled on the furniture listening as they do homework."

"Formal can also be functional," Erik pointed out as he noted that a lot of the old details of the house had been kept when they rehabbed the place.

"Terry knows the most about what was done," Ana told him, noting how he was studying the architecture. "He's been with Bohlander House since it's conception."

Erik just nodded as he followed Ana. He noted that she looked small compared to his 6'5 frame, but she was also curvy. Her hair was almost black and curly, it was her eyes that captivated him. They were like a whiskey color brown. He noticed they headed into a large dining room that could fit easily thirty people. Instead of one huge table they had set up tables throughout the room that could also be put together to make one large table. A large fireplace was on one wall with an old mirror above it.

"They found the fireplace when they were restoring the room, it had been closed up behind a wall," Ana told him. She looked around the room, the walls were painted a light green and it had silver accents. "We don't use this room much, mostly for birthdays, and celebrations."

"Where do you all eat then?" Erik asked looking around the large space.

Ana smiled holding out her hands pointing to the large butler's pantry that connected the dining room to the large kitchen. Erik walked through the small room and then stopped at the kitchen. It was enormous but he could tell this was the heart of the home. Three refrigerators were covered with tests, papers, and magnets. He saw Luke was pouring himself coffee from the coffee bar area of the kitchen.

"Do you want a mug?" Luke asked Erik.

"Sure," Erik agreed as he looked around.

Luke poured another mug and handed it to Erik. "Alright, so formal introductions," Luke began. "Dr. Erik Astrium these are: Dr. Analiese Gerfallen, Dr. Juliana Vijelens, and Dr. Terrence Wyles. Ana is our Drug Rehab counselor, Jules handles crisis intervention, and Terry deals with family drama. Terry has been here for ten years, Jules and Ana are here four years."

"You're part of Heroes Reborn," Terry realized. He had worked with the non-profit a few times.

"Yes," Erik answered as he took a seat next to Luke at the table.

"So what are the three of us missing," Jules inquired as she saw the look that past between Luke and Erik.

Luke looked at Erik who nodded. "Erik knows about what has been going on with Carl," Luke explained. "A month ago Helen, Jill, and I met with Erik to discuss him joining us as our fourth partner and replacing Carl. He started Heroes Reborn for some of the same reasons the three of us started Second Chances. He saw veteran's struggling, and being one himself, he created a veteran's group with some army buddies that has grown into an amazing thing."

"Veteran's and at-risk teens are very different," Terry pointed out.

"They are," Erik agreed. "And I'm not leaving my group behind. When I was approached it was more about brainstorming a lot of different options and paths. I've been friends with Luke for fifteen years, I have watched what you guys have done here, and it's amazing. You have my respect. Not a lot of people would want to raise fifteen teens let alone fifteen teens who have lived through hell already."

"So why are you here?" Ana asked.

"I agreed to join Second Chances and consider overseeing Bohlander house on two conditions," Erik informed them. "The first was that Heroes Reborn becomes part of the family of programs. This protects my creation from being bought out by a bigger company who might not be interested in helping the community. Also my friends and I can still run it without giving up anything."

"And the second?" Ana inquired.

"That the kids and the three of you have to agree to me being the director," Erik answered. He watched surprise flash across the three faces. "None of us want a repeat of Carl and in order to ensure that doesn't happen we all need to get to know each other. I get to know the kids, see how the house works, and even meet Martha. It also allows for you to learn about me and we see if we can work together. Because unlike Carl, I'm not going to sit off in the shadows. If I'm going to be in charge, then I want to be involved."

Terry looked at Jules and Ana before he spoke. "We talked about some of the things we wanted to change and this was one of them," Terry admitted. "Whoever became in charge would have to spend time with us, the kids, see how we work before it was official. We can't put the kids through another situation like the one with Jenna and Carl."

"Alright, what do you want to change?" Erik asked delving right into the conversation.

Luke slowly stood up. "I think this is where I take my leave," Luke admitted. He looked at Erik. "Call me later and let me know how this goes. Ana, is Sam able to talk or is he still in discovery mode?"

"Try calling him around dinner time their time, which is about now," Ana suggested. "He might bore you with details."

"I'll keep that in mind," Luke laughed and headed out the back door.

"Sam?" Erik inquired.

"My cousin Sam is his cousin as well," Ana answered. "Sam's mom is Luke's actual cousin."

"Shit, now I know who you are," Erik realized. "I didn't put it together because you are always mentioned along with Sam and I'm guessing Toby is your brother."

"The three musketeers," Jules commented and laughed when Ana elbowed her.

"And that makes you the childhood friend that the Gerfallans adopted," Erik stated.

"That's me," Jules answered. "The favorite child." Her statement made Ana roll her eyes.

"And no one has any connection to me," Terry pointed out with a smile. "How do you know Luke?"

"Our path's crossed when I just started Hero's," Erik answered. "Luke was called in to consult on a vet who had become a drug addict. He was willing to do the drug rehab but had heard my name and called me to consult as well."

From there they talked and planned for almost two hours. When Martha returned from errands she was introduced and joined the conversation. She added insight that the other's hadn't thought of and Erik listened just as closely to her as he did the three psychologists. As it neared the time that the teens would be heading home, Erik got up to leave.

"I'm going to want to meet with each of you individually," Erik answered. "Not here, and not at my office. It won't be an interview, more of hanging out and getting to know each other."

"We can work that out," Ana agreed. "I will warn you, with Memorial Day coming, things get a bit hectic so if you give us a list of dates we can try to work around them."

"Alright, I will take a look at my dates and send them to..." Erik paused. "Who should I send them to?"

Jules, Terry, and Martha pointed at Ana. "She's the schedule keeper," Jules admitted. "So send her the dates and we'll go from there."

"Sounds good," Erik agreed. "Can I leave through the back door or is that only for family and friends?"

"We'll let you leave through it today," Terry answered. "But screw up and it's only the front door for you."

Erik chuckled and headed out the door. They waited until he was at his car before anyone spoke. Jules was watching Ana carefully while Terry filled Martha in on what she had missed.

"Did anyone else notice his eyes kept wandering back to Ana?" Terry inquired with a hint of a smile.

Ana rolled her eyes. "It's true, even my stunning beauty didn't keep his attention," Jules joked, smiling at Ana.

"You two can plot all you want but I am going to go pick up Cassie," Ana decided.

"Oh, and plot we will," Terry warned.

Ana just shook her head as she went out to back door. They were fortunate that they had a nice size courtyard in the back where they had a grill, picnic tables, even a basketball hoop. The City had allowed them to use the connecting alley for parking of the school vans, for a fee that was cheap considering the price of parking in the city. Ana walked down the alley and onto the street. Lincoln Center was a few blocks walk from the house. She could used the fresh air to clear her head. Erik seemed genuine, he was smart, and not bad to look at it. It was hard to ignore the reaction she had to him, but with everything going on in her life getting into a relationship, especially with a person who could be your boss, was low on the list.

Her thoughts strayed to the journal page that Toby had translated. He had sent it to her last night and she fell asleep reading it. Which was not a wise decision, her dreams were a mess of alchemy lab experiments, parts of Marlowe's Faust, and then her dancing in a field of flowers. The goods news was she didn't sense the Devil being anywhere near her dreams. With her birthday in June this was when he usually started to show his face again. Shoving her hands in her jeans pockets, she followed the crowd to Juilliard. She was so deep in thought she didn't realize she was being watched.

When she arrived at the school the kids were just being let out and Cassie ran to her giving her a big hug. Cassie didn't care about what others thought, she was still excited that she had a guardian that loved her unconditionally. Cassie skipped alongside Ana as she filled her in on the school day. Ana listened, laughing at some of the stories. Cassie had a way of brightening up anyone's day or mood. She was always moving, smiling, or humming. They were an interesting pair: a thirty year old raven haired female with pale skin and a spunky thirteen year old with frizzy curls that were currently purple in color, and caramel colored skin. But they were a unit and it was obvious to anyone who saw them.

Chapter 4

THE VIOLIN MUSIC *that was playing was tranquil as Ana slowly awoke. She lay on a black leather couch. Sitting up her hair fell over her left shoulder, she wore a strapless gown of deep red that fell to the floor. Looking around, the decor was modern: all metal, glass, leather, and smooth surfaces. The walls were a faint gray with hints of color in the abstract paintings that hung on the wall.*

Ana stood up and knew where she was. It had been nearly a year since her last visit here. She walked through the living room toward the dining room with its black Asian styled dining table and chairs. Splashes of red and orange were found in the decor. The man who sat at the head of the table drank from an old goblet.

"You are awake," he stated.

"I am," Ana answered and took her seat at the table.

Mephistopheles, in his human form, was a breathtaking work of art. He stood at six foot, he wasn't all muscle but there was no softness to his body, his hair was dark blonde with a slight curl close to the temples. His eyes were most striking, for they were a true deep blue. And they could bore into your soul, though when angered they would flash red, showing his true nature.

"How are your dear brother and cousin? Still chasing for what isn't there?" Mephistopheles inquired.

"Still convinced you are going to win after five centuries?" Ana returned.

Mephistopheles pretended to act hurt by her words. "Your words wound, my dear."

"If that's the case then die."

He clapped his hands as he laughed. Tortured souls filed into the room with serving plates, they proceeded one by one to place the dishes onto the long table. Ana watched knowing if she closed her eyes he would order them to wait until she opened them. She hated this, seeing the souls of the damned. There was nothing she could do for them and he knew it made her feel helpless.

"Do they remind you of the teens you so tirelessly work with?" He inquired sipping his wine. "I do think it is amazing what you are trying to do with them, trying to change their destiny. It's as if you are trying to save them when it's already too late."

Ana looked at a painting off to her right. It hung above a fireplace, she realized that she had never seen it before. She stood up from her chair walking toward the oil painting. This was from the renaissance, Sam would be drooling over this. There was so much emotion that came from the painting. It was an angel standing on the edge of a storm cloud, the night sky was pitch black, no stars to shine any light into the darkness. The angels hair was just as black and ran in waves down his back and shoulders blending into the sky. His wings started off as white at the tops, but as your eyes followed them down the painting the feathers began to change until the very tips of the wings disappeared into the blackness. In the clenched fist of the angel was a dagger, the tip dripped blood onto the gray storm cloud. Ana studied the angel closely, it was then that she noticed where the wing met the left shoulder blade was an incision that looked fresh, as if it had just been done.

"Amazing isn't it," Mephistopheles asked as he walked to stand next to her.

"It's stunning," Ana whispered. Her hands wanted to reach out and stroke the feathers of the wings. Each one painted in detail so that no two were the same. "There is such beauty in it."

"Most would be drawn to the darkness, all they would see is their own fate," Mephistopheles stated. "But there is beauty hidden there."

"The artist?"

"They all blend together that I can't be sure," he said with a shrug. "But I can tell you the subject."

"A portrait of you?"

His eyes flashed red as he laughed bitterly. "I never wore wings," he informed her. "I was born already damned."

Ana watched as he filled a wine glass for her. "I promise no Hades Rules apply," he assured her, sounding as if he was tired. "If you eat or drink anything tonight they will not be held against you."

It was a rare offer, so Ana accepted the glass and drank the red wine he poured for her. "The subject is Lucifer, or the Morning Star, "Mephistopheles informed her. "It is said to be painted just before he took the leap from Heaven."

"Yet there is a dagger in his hand, there is an incision above his one wing?" Ana pointed out.

"He was always a dark soul," he replied, a hint of jealousy in his voice. "He was God's chosen, and he bore a heavy burden by being so. He did the work that the holy books don't talk of. The artist is showing that torment, will I bleed if I cut myself, and if I bleed can I survive the fall that should kill me."

"You don't like him," Ana realized.

"He's a bloody spoiled sport," Mephistopheles told her and headed back to the table. "He has rules, morals, he doesn't like tricks, he doesn't like using deceit when trying to get souls."

"He must despise you as well," Ana stated looking at the demon who stood next to her. "You excel at trickery and bribery."

Mephistopheles laughed and raised a glass to her. "You have far exceeded my expectations," he confessed. "To think we could sit here and discuss a painting as if we are two normal people is amazing."

"You can't have my soul," she reminded him.

"And there you go and ruin the moment," he sighed.

Ana woke dripping in sweat. She could still taste the wine and smell the scents of the room. She sighed as she rolled out of bed for there was never going back to sleep after a dream with Mephistopheles. One of the few ways she could shake the effects from a dream like that was a run. With how early it was she would have time for a run through Central Park and be back with plenty of time to shower and get ready for work. Ana had to go into the midtown office today so that she could meet with some of her clients who would be allowed to have sessions at the carriage house.

When she got back to the house from her run she felt better, more stable. After showering and changing she helped get all the residents into vans. Once everyone was where they were supposed to be Ana headed to the subway. Terry's idea of having their own office space closer to them became more and more appealing as she took a crowded subway to the Roosevelt Hospital stop. Jules was coming in later so they could head home together.

It was going to be a day filled with appointments, she would have little chance to dwell on the dream. There were a few files that Luke needed her to go over for patients he might want her to take on over the summer after they graduated from rehab. She took notes, then looked at her last sessions with her patients before she had gone on vacation. When her favorite patient arrived Ana smiled and nodded to the petite blonde and the teen with the bright blue liberty spikes.

"Hey, Jeremy," Ana greeted the seventeen year old.

"Hey, Doc," Jeremy answered with a smile.

"Can I talk to Laurie first," Ana asked. The teen nodded putting his earbuds back in.

Laurie was his step-mom and was also a trauma nurse. Ana closed the door behind Laurie and they both sat down. "Relax," Ana replied when she saw Laurie get nervous. "He's doing great. I got off the phone with his coach at school, starting in the fall he will be free and clear."

"Ok, I got nervous that something had happened," Laurie answered letting out a breath of relief. "What's up?"

"I know that Carl's lawyer contacted you and tried to have you talk bad against the firm," Ana stated. "So I want to apologize for that."

"You have no need to apologize for someone else's stupidity," Laurie replied. "We actually sent a notarized letter to the judge, as well as to Dr. Gray about you. Stating that if those teens in the house were as lucky as our son is to have you in their lives, then they will do amazing things with this second chance. You don't just believe everyone deserves a second chance, you show them they deserve it and teach them how to grasp it."

Ana sat speechless for a moment. "Thank you," Ana answered softly. She then took a deep breath. "Anyway, as a result of all this craziness, I am going to be seeing patients from my home. So our next session after Memorial Day is going to be there, as will all the others after, until further notice."

"I will make a note on our calendar," Laurie replied.

They got up and Laurie left the office and Jeremy came in. Gone was the angry teen who was bent on self-destruction. Now stood a laid back teen who was learning how to cope with the stress of teenage life. His spikes added to his height as he sat in the chair that Laurie had entered.

"I'm not in trouble right?" Jeremy asked shoving his earbuds in his jean pockets.

"Should you be?" Ana inquired with a smile as she took her seat.

"Nah, I'm perfect, we all know that," Jeremy laughed.

Ana shook her head smiling. "I was just letting Laurie know that sessions are moving to my place for the time being," Ana told him.

"You aren't in trouble are you?" Jeremy asked concerned.

"No, it's more precaution," Ana assured him. "We thought it might be a good idea to have one of us at the house everyday until the legal drama blows away."

"And you got chosen," Jeremey stated.

"Well you know, I am the best," Ana teased.

"I was kind of worried about you after dad got off the phone with that asshole lawyer," Jeremy admitted. "Never saw my dad so mad at someone who was a stranger. Him and mom wrote a pretty awesome letter. Asked for my input as well."

"You are still stuck with me, my dear," Ana promised him.

"Good, because dude, I'm going to be a senior next year," Jeremy reminded her. "And who the hell is going to get me through that craziness if it's not you?"

Ana laughed. The rest of the session went smoothly. Jeremy had some concerns about parties over the summer. "What are you worried about?" Ana asked.

"Temptation," Jeremy sighed. "Cara's pretty awesome, she has no problems not going to parties."

"But?"

Jeremy let out a long sigh as he leaned forward, resting his elbows on his knees. "What if she's just saying that but really wants to go to them?"

"Have you told her she could go with her friends?" Ana inquired.

"Yea, she said she'll think about it," Jeremy answered with a long sigh. "I just don't get it. The whole going to parties to get drunk and act stupid. They see me everyday in the hallways, they know I ODed on drugs twice, that I was in rehab, that I see a shrink. I'm the perfect example of being stupid. Yet they still go and party and act stupid."

Ana tapped her pen on her desk as an idea came. "Jeremy, have you ever told your story?"

"What do you mean? Like my friends know, and other people know parts of it," Jeremy answered. He studied her for a moment. "You have an idea."

"First, I want you to think about it, talk to your parents, including your other mom, as well as Clara," Ana stated first. "Think about giving a talk to your school before it lets out for the summer. Tell them about you, what led up to you doing drugs, your downfall, Laurie finding you, then your brother. About Rehab. Everything. Maybe if they actually heard the tale, with all the gory details, they'll get it. Maybe it will help them battle their own temptations."

Jeremy looked at her. "Have you ever been tempted?"

"Every day of my life," Ana admitted. Jeremy looked at her. "I have family demons that are hard to ignore. And at one point I drank a lot to try and ignore them, when I realized the direction I was headed I stopped. Now I keep it to just wine and no more than two glasses. We all face temptations. Some people can ignore it, others, like us, stumble but are able to get back up and learn to ignore it. And others keep going back for more."

"If I did this, would you come?" Jeremy asked her.

"Yes," Ana said without hesitation. "And Jeremy, if Clara says it's okay missing the parties then believe her. She's pretty incredible."

"Still don't know why she's with me," Jeremy chuckled.

The buzzer sounded meaning their session was over. "Still doing burgers with Laurie?"

"Hell yea," Jeremy stated. "Hated these nights at first now I look forward to them."

"So does she," Ana answered. "Alright get out of here."

Jeremy headed out of the office leaving the door open so that people knew she was done with appointments. He was always her last one of the day, at first it was because he had been her toughest kid, now it was because he was one of her favorites. As she finished up, Jules knocked on the open door.

"You ready?" Jules asked.

"I am," Ana answered grabbing her backpack. "How was your day?"

"Spent half the day with the sex crime unit so you know it was awesome," Jules admitted.

"Want to grab a quick dinner on the way home?" Ana inquired as they headed out of the office.

"And leave Terry and Martha to fend on their own?" Jules asked. "Invoke our one time a month girl's dinner?"

An hour later, the two were seated in the back of one of their favorite spots. It was in Greenwich village and it embraced the buildings lurid past. "Flappers" had once been a speakeasy and also rumored to be a brothel on the upper floors. Now it was a great tavern that had it's waitresses dressing as flappers and the waiters dressed as the mafia. Once a month they held a theme night and would do murder mystery's as well. You could eat casual or eat upstairs in a more intimate setting. For Jules and Ana they got a back corner booth out of the way of the crowd on the main floor.

Once they placed their order the waiter left leaving them alone with their glass of wine each. "The more and more I think about it the more I like Terry's idea," Jules sighed. "Our own practice of sorts that is closer to home."

"You okay?" Ana asked. Jules looked tired and worn.

"Just that there shouldn't be eight year old victims," Jules answered and sipped her wine. "I love what I do, but getting called into these unit's, they destroy me."

"And you're thinking if we have our own space you could limit that more, working with them more after the fact," Ana stated.

"Pretty much," Jules answered. "Which then makes me think that I'm a horrible person because I'm saying that I won't be there for the victims right when it happens."

"But you also have to think about your own sanity," Ana pointed out.

"True," Jules agreed. Their appetizer was served. "So how about you? You were out earlier this morning than usual."

Ana didn't say anything as she bit into a loaded potato. "I had a dream."

Jules arched an eyebrow as her green eyes stared at Ana. "A dream?"

"We were at his place, dinner, champagne, the whole deal," Ana explained. She didn't need to explain who 'he' was. "But I saw this painting and it took my breath away."

"Who was it of?"

"Lucifer," Ana admitted. She took another bite of the potato. "He looked so tortured, so mortal. All the colors eventually blended into black but it stole all my attention and Meph didn't like that."

"You would think he'd be okay with it," Jules answered.

"I get the feeling they don't get along," Ana replied. "He said something that has me wondering about some things."

"Like what?"

"That he wasn't born with wings," Ana stated. Jules just stared at her. "That Lucifer was born with them but that Meph was already born cursed. I wrote it all up and emailed it to Sam and Toby."

Jules tapped her finger on the table. "Angels are born with wings," Jules replied. "But Meph is saying that he wasn't born with them, so you could take the leap and theorize he was never an angel."

"We always thought you could track him because he was an angel," Ana whispered. Jules saw angels, she could communicate with them, interact with them.

"I also shot blue lights from hands when in the same room with him and that has never happened before," Jules pointed out. "So perhaps that is another connection that we didn't see before."

Ana ran a hand through her hair. "You know, Jay asked me about temptation, today."

Jay was what she called Jeremy when she was out in public. Jules went to ask something but their dinner arrived. For a few minutes they were quiet as they ate their burgers. Then Jules sipped her wine and looked at Ana. "What about temptation?"

"If I've ever been tempted," Ana answered. "I was honest, told him everyday. And it's true. Some days, like this morning, are harder to keep fighting. And then I meet with Jeremy and I remember everything I'm fighting for. I just can't wait for the day when I don't have to keep fighting him. When my thoughts, my dream are all my own. When I don't have to second guess everything that has happened because it could be some trick."

Chapter 5

WEDNESDAY WAS ONE of the few days that Cassie got home at a regular time. With everything going on Ana postponed her morning run to be after school so that Cassie could join him. The stress of rehearsals and what happened with Jenna were weighing on the usually perky teen. While Cassie was still seeing her own therapist, Ana thought a run through the park might be good for both of them. Though in Cassie's case, she skipped more than she actually ran. The teen weaved from topic to topic with little warning but Ana was able to keep up as they jogged.

"I mean seriously who tries to seduce the gay guy," Cassie stated. "It's no secret, not with Alex at the the house almost everyday. I mean really, she was such a bitch."

They were back to Jenna. Ana didn't say a word as Cassie jogged backwards so she could face Ana. "I mean like it was disgusting," Cassie continued. "First off no teen should be hitting on a guy in their thirties, that's just old, and second like the dude has a partner. That is so like off limit's."

"So people in their thirties are old," Ana stated trying not to laugh as they slowed to a walk. They had finished their lap and were leaving the park.

"Well maybe not like old old, but still old," Cassie decided. "But, Ana, I mean she like totally tried to seduce him and then he says no and what does she do but try to flip it around on him. That's like psycho."

"She has problems," Ana agreed.

"Yea but the things is she likes her problems," Cassie informed Ana as they stopped at the red light. "She likes that she can use them as an excuse for why she does fu…, I mean messed up things. If she doesn't get help then she's not special anymore."

"You think that's it?"

Cassie rolled her eyes at Ana. "She likes how she feels when she's on drugs, and she likes sex," Cassie stated. "She told me that. The drugs make her feel free and the sex helps her forget shit. I told her there were other ways and she just laughed. Told me I was naive and grew up sheltered."

"This is the fight I missed," Ana inquired.

"Well yea," Cassie sighed. "Dennis was on us like from that moment, he caught me around the waist afraid I was going claw her eyes out."

"Were you?"

"You can give me some credit, you know," Cassie replied. "I was so not screwing up my mortal life by letting her get to me."

"I'm glad to know that the threat of being grounded for all eternity works," Ana commented with a chuckle.

"She is so not worth that," Cassie agreed.

"You've come a long way, my little padawan," Ana said putting an arm around her.

"Star Trek, right?" Cassie joked laughing as Ana pretended to sound injured. "You are so easy to tease!"

Ana just shook her head as they neared the house. She spotted Erik talking to Jules on the front porch. "Who's the hunk?" Cassie asked as they got closer.

"That would be Dr. Erik Astrium," Ana informed her. "He is temporarily in charge of the House and could become permanent."

"Well he's already better looking than Carl," Cassie pointed out.

"Behave," Ana warned as they approached the house.

"Hello," Erik replied as he saw them. "This must be Cassie?"

"I am," Cassie said and shook the hand he offered. "Ana said you're gonna be the guy in charge of us?"

"That's the plan," Erik answered. "But I want us all to agree on it. So I'm gonna be coming by to get to know you guys, hang out, see all the craziness that happens behind the doors."

"If you aren't running for your life after twenty minutes I'll be impressed," Cassie admitted.

"Homework," Ana stated.

Csasie rolled her eyes. "You are no fun."

"You're right, I'm not," Ana agreed. "You can use my office if you want quiet or to blast your music."

Cassie nodded as she skipped up the stairs. "I guess I should go run herd on homework," Jules sighed.

Erik and Ana watched her head into the house. Ana motioned at the stairs. "Why don't you step into my office and tell me what brings you here today?"

Erik chuckled as he sat next to her on the concrete steps. "This is a beautiful street," he commented. "How do they feel about the House?"

"At first there was uncertainty, a lot of neighborhood meetings, Terry knows more about that because he went to them," Ana admitted. "By the time Jules and I signed-on it was respected and they really embrace the kids who come here. The teens shovel snow, help with groceries, they even baby sit. It's good all around."

"The teens benefit from being part of a community that cares about them and the community benefit by helping others and being more diverse."

"Very true," Ana agreed. "So why are you here?"

"I was checking out a property that Hero's wants to buy," he admitted. "Since I was a few blocks over I thought I would stop by."

"Well it's a typical Friday night which means no Martha until Sunday night," Ana answered. "So that means it's Taco night."

"I can't even imagine the meal planning that goes into this place," Erik replied.

"It's feeding a small army," Ana replied with a smile. "So how was the building?"

"It has a lot of potential," Erik answered. "It's eight stories. The first three floors are offices and storefronts. Then there are two or three apartments on the upper floors and then two basement apartments. The apartments have to be inspected and redone before we could let anyone live in them, but like I saw potential."

"Terry, Jules, and I have been thinking of talking to Luke about letting us open a branch in this area," Ana informed him. Erki turned and looked at her. "That way we can be more flexible with hours and aren't always running to midtown. In theory, it should take like twenty minutes but it can be an hour each way or more."

"I'm commuting from the Village to Long Island four days a week, I get it," Erik replied. "I'll keep you posted on what we plan to do. But if you want space there is more than enough at this place. I'm checking out another one next week if one of you want to come with me?"

"I'll look at our schedules, this week coming is packed, and the next week is a short week, so things get a bit crazy around here," she admitted.

"Speaking of schedules," Erik began taking a deep breath. He wasn't sure why he was nervous all of a sudden. "I was thinking since you are kind of the house leader that I should start with you."

"Tomorrow is my actual night off," Ana informed him. "Otherwise we will have to figure out something during the week and that could be tough."

"I can do tomorrow," Erik agreed. "My weekends are pretty free unless I'm at the center."

"No life either," Ana smiled.

"None," Erik said with a smile. "I'll pick you up here for 7, we'll grab dinner?"

"That would be fine."

"Good," Erik replied. He ran a hand over his hair. "I guess I should actually head home now."

"You could come in and experience taco night." The invitation came out of nowhere.

Erik turned and looked at her. "Would that be okay with them?"

"Be prepared for twenty questions coming from fifteen sources and you should be fine," Ana assured him. She noticed something shimmer just off to the side of Erik's shoulder. It was odd but it was gone in a second so she ignored it.

"Then I accept."

Ana stood up and headed for the front door. When she opened the door she heard chairs moving from the living room and the office, which meant eyes were watching her while she had been outside. Shaking her head she motioned for Erik to follow.

"I'll introduce you to the horde before dinner," she replied.

Chapter 6

THE FOLLOWING EVENING, Ana stood in front of her mirror. Cassie and Jules were both sprawled on her bed commenting on her outfits for tonight. Why she was so nervous was a mystery to her, this was a business dinner. Not a date. Ana settled on a black jersey knit dress that showcased her curves but didn't reveal too much. She kept her makeup simple, pulling her hair into a quick twist. For jewelry, she went with a three strand necklace that had a clear quartz with pale crystals around it hanging from the shortest strand, the middle strand was of hematite beads, with the longest strand being another clear quartz, it was all done in an antique gold finish. She paired it with pearl studs and a simple gold bracelet. It made the simple cotton black dress look more elegant.

"Why am I nervous?" Ana asked Jules.

"Because he's hot and has a brain," Cassie suggested with a shrug. Ana shot her a pointed look.

"I'm agreeing with her," Jules informed Ana. "I also will add, that you rarely put yourself out there. I think he scares you a bit because he is already getting you out of your comfort zone."

Jules phone vibrated while Ana packed her small clutch with essentials. "Erik has arrived and is being questioned by the boys," Jules said with a smile as she read the message that Terry had just sent her.

"I guess we should go save him," Ana answered. "Alright, I can do this."

Cassie went ahead of them, Jules laid a hand on Ana's shoulder. "I know that this a business dinner, at the same time you should take this as a chance to just socialize, get to know someone, make a friend," Jules told Ana. "It doesn't have to be dating or sleeping with him. But it might be nice to get to know someone that is new."

"I'm not the only one who doesn't date," Ana pointed out.

"I know," Jules replied. " But Terry's right. These kids look to us as role models, and we've been so focused on their healing, that we put ourselves on hold. The kids need to see healthy relationships, see the ups and downs, see that arguments are okay, that affection isn't to be a power trip."

"I know," Ana sighed. "I'll have fun."

"Good because that means it buys me some time," Jules joked.

"I hate you so much," Ana informed her. Jules just laughed as they headed through the door that connected them to the main house.

Ana had to bite back the smile as she watched a room full of teenage boys grill a man in his thirties. Giving Eric credit, he took each question serious as they made sure he was aware of the house rules and what time she needed to be back. Ana cleared her throat and they all turned to face the doorway. Erik stood up and stared at her for a moment as she took in the charcoal dress pants and navy blue dress shirt.

"You look amazing," Erik said as nerves fluttered his stomach. The realization this could be more than just a business dinner was being harder to ignore.

"So do you," Ana agreed. She then looked at the teens. "Don't drive the adults crazy."

They all rolled their eyes as Erik and Ana headed out the front door. She saw his luxury sedan parked in front and raised an eyebrow as she slid into the passenger seat. Mellow jazz came on as he pulled into the street. Neither spoke as he drove, it was a comfortable silence.

"How'd they do?" Ana asked turning to look at Erik.

He chuckled. "They did awesome, they were respectful but also wanted me to know that they were watching," Erik informed her. "It says a lot about what you guys have been able to do with them."

"I don't know how much Luke has told you," Ana began. "Terry's been in a relationship for almost two years. Alex's a great guy and he is over almost every other day. He always tries to spend the weekends with us. He goes to games, helps mentor. His entire precinct is really hands-on with the kids."

"So they are seeing what a healthy relationship looks like," Erik realized. He was also impressed that the group of teens were okay with Terry dating a guy. "And they are cool with him being gay?"

"Any issues are dealt with respectfully," Ana admitted. "One of the newer boys wasn't cool with it. Terry and he had several conversations about it. About stereotypes. He let him ask any type of questions and he answered them. They worked out an agreement that he would let the kid know when Alex was coming over and if he wanted to take some boys to another part of the house that was fine."

"Respectful and understanding," Erik stated. "You want them to be comfortable. To know this is their house as well and that their feelings matter."

"Two months later we found him and Alex shooting hoops out back, he told Alex more in that game about his life then most of us could get out of him," Ana replied. "Now you would never know he had any issues with it."

"It shows them that they didn't have to fear someone who is different, something they probably aren't used to."

"It's a good learning experience because Terry is really comfortable with who he is," Ana admitted. She noted they were heading toward Little Italy.

Erik found a spot a few blocks from their destination. Ana inhaled as she took in all the smells of Little Italy and Chinatown. "We need to bring the kids down here more than we do," Ana realized. "We get so caught up in schedules and stuff that we forget about things like this."

"Let me know if you do, I know some people who would be glad to have you take over their restaurant, fill it with regulars," Erik told her.

"That would be awesome," Ana admitted.

They arrived at a cute restaurant in heart of Little Italy. "Ah, Mister Erik," the host said when he spotted Erik approaching him. "We have your table ready for you. Good evening, ma'am."

He picked two menus and showed them toward the back of the room. Ana noted some of the people waiting at the door looking annoyed that they were ushered right in and didn't have to wait. They were seated in a corner away from the buzz of the main part of the place. Once the host had them seated he returned to his podium.

"You can't get reservations here," Ana pointed out.

"I helped their son out a year back," Erik told her. "So I can pretty much get a table when I want. Though usually it's in the kitchen or at the bar."

"Don't take a lot of dates here," Ana commented.

"Never," Erik admitted and smiled at her. Their waiter arrived and Erik ordered a bottle of Riesling. When the waiter left. "I figure with all the time you have spent in Austria you would like a nice Riesling."

"It's my favorite," Ana agreed. "So should we do the business stuff now?"

"And then let this play out as a date perhaps?" Erik asked and she laughed as she nodded. "Alright, so why don't we start with Cassie."

Ana took a sip of water as bread and dipping oils were brought to the table. "Where do I even start," Ana stated and let out a sigh. "She came to us during mine and Jules first year there. She was eight going on nine. We don't take kids that young because they have a better shot at foster care or a relative taking them."

"But you took her," Erik noted.

Their wine came and he sampled it before agreeing. The waiter smiled at them both. "Joe is here tonight," the waiter informed Erik. "Would you like him to surprise you or would you both like to order?"

Erik looked at Ana. "It's up to you, everything on the menu is amazing."

Ana folded the menu smiling at the waiter. "Surprise us."

"Very well, I will let him know," the waiter answered and vanished to the kitchen.

"Joe is the son, I take it," Ana guessed.

"He is," Erik confirmed. "Afghanistan, three tours. Came back and couldn't deal with the quiet. The staff at Hero's, we would come here for quick business dinners, his dad caught me on the way out and asked me to talk his son. He didn't want to leave the house, couldn't make it to the sidewalk without reliving something that he saw in war. So I met him at their place."

"Wow," Ana whispered.

"He's a great kid, he is going to culinary school, and it's amazing," Erik agreed.

"They were lucky to know you," Ana stated and Erik blushed as he looked away for a moment.

"The same could be said about you and the kids," Erik pointed out. She smiled shyly at that and they raised their wine glasses and took a sip. "So Cassie. You guys made the exception for her?"

"Alex and his partner came to our house at close to midnight with this tiny girl who was soaking wet," Ana recalled. "She was cursing up a storm. Martha was able to get her to calm down enough to go take a warm shower and change into warm clothes. While Martha tended to Cassie, Alex informed us that she had been assaulted by her mom's boyfriend. The mom was high on drugs. The boyfriend took off, they didn't want to risk bringing her to the precinct or Juvie in case he showed up."

"Shit," Erik replied as he ran a hand through his hair.

"So we took her," Ana replied. "It was going to be temporary, give her a place to stay until social services could find her a home."

"You guys changed your mind though."

"She started skipping everywhere about a week into staying with us, then we heard her sing," Ana remembered with a smile. "She has this voice that is amazing, even at 9 it floored us. And we knew that if we let her go that voice, that talent wouldn't be nurtured. We talked to her, to her officer, the judge for her case. We all agreed that the house would be perfect for her. At the time the closest person to her age was fourteen so we moved her into the carriage house until we got younger teens."

"How did she become yours?" Erik asked. He had read Cassie's file but he wanted to hear it from Ana. To hear why a thirty year old single female would adopt a thirteen year old girl.

Ana let out a long sigh and took a sip of wine before answering. "Her mom made a plea deal when she was arrested," Ana explained. "Two years jail, if she attended their NA meetings and then probation. She could have supervised visits with Cassie and perhaps weekends if she was able to show that she was clean, had a stable job, and a safe home."

"Seems reasonable, I'm sure child endangerment was part of the charges against her," Erik realized.

"Among others," Ana agreed. "Cassie hated going to see her mom. It took days sometimes weeks for her to recover from a visit. So it was agreed she would visit for holidays and that was it. Then about a year ago her mom is released from jail and on probation, like planned. She was able to get a job at a beauty parlor in Harlem. She was going to meetings doing good so she petitioned for visitations to start up again."

"There was an issue with housing," Erik guessed. "You didn't list it with what she did getting out."

"Living alone in NYC is costly, the judge knew this, so in the agreement was that her roommates would also have to be clean and not a threat to Cassie," Ana answered. "One of her mom's new roommates is on the sex offenders list. Needless to say judge refused for any house visitations. Mom flipped out. A week later I get a call from Juilliard that this woman was waiting outside the school entrance. They were worried it was Cassie's mom. So I told them to call the cops and that I would be there. Luke came with me and we met Alex there. They let us in the back entrance, we got Cassie out of there without the mom knowing. We went right to the judge to go over options. Guardianship was one of them. We let Cassie choose."

"Two questions," Erik stated. "Juilliard? And why You?"

"Cassie goes to their academy," Ana answered and smiled with pride at his shock. "We keep all the schools names out of the reports for security purposes. But yes, my little punk is an all star opera singer."

"Cassie who skips and has electric blue hair?" Erik inquired laughing. "I love it. Oh my god, she will be a super star."

"I know," Ana agreed. "And why me? Well that's a funny story."

She paused when a sample platter of appetizers was brought out to them. "This looks amazing," Ana replied studying the tapas dishes that had been set out before them. "I can not wait for dinner."

"I will let him know," The waiter replied.

The waiter left and Ana filled Erik in on why Cassie chose her to adopt her. He laughed at what the teenager had said to the judge. After that they talked a bit more about the house and the other kids. How the three of them managed to not go crazy, that they each got a night off each week. Erik was impressed with how involved Luke, Jill, and Helen were. When their main course was served they were silent for a few minutes as they selected from the tapas that Joe had created. Erik talked a bit about his military background, how Heroes Reborn was created. Ana talked about Toby, Sam, and her other cousins.

When dessert came out, they talked about what they liked to do when not working. They both skied and liked movies. When the meal was over and the bill paid, Erik stood up and took her hand. They went to the kitchen where he introduced Ana to Joe. Joe was really easy going and had Ana laughing at a joke. Hand-in-hand, they walked to his car and both slid into the car. The traffic was light as he made his way uptown.

He pulled into the small driveway in front of the carriage house and looked over at Ana. "Next date will be a real date with no business portion," Erik promised.

Ana smiled. "Sounds like a plan."

They climbed out of the car, taking her hand Erik walked her up to the front door of the main house. Even if this had been a business dinner, like it was supposed to be, Erik knew he would have to walk Ana to the door. There would be teens inside making sure he was playing by the rules, and he also wanted to show them it's what you do. Ana paused in front of the door.

"You know there's an audience," Ana informed him quietly.

"I know," Erik replied. "Does it bother you?"

Ana shook her head and for a moment she thought she saw him glow. He bent down and kissed her planning for it to be a light and simple kiss. But when their lips touched he felt electricity jolt through his body, he knew she felt it too because she gasped. He deepened the kiss a bit before pulling back.

"I'll call you to set up our next date," Erik promised. "Just remember I'm stopping by on Monday to go over lists and schedules."

"We'll be here," Ana replied. She smiled softly before turning and heading inside.

Erik let out a breath as he watched her close the door. Shoving his hands in his pockets he headed to his car adding a cold shower on the list of things to do when he got home. Tonight had not gone as planned, his attraction to Ana had only increased as he learned more about her. And that could be a problem. His phone vibrated and he glanced at the screen wondering if it was Ana. When he saw the name it was a reminder of his other life.

It's Mike. We have a problem, someone broke into the vault.
Which Vault? Erik typed back at a stop light.
The one containing the Faust line.

Erik cursed as he ran a hand through his hair. Life could never be simple, as guilt came over him. He was going to have to tell Ana everything before they went any further in their relationship.

Chapter 7

ANA WAS FINISHING her morning run through Central Park when her phone rang. She saw it was Toby, she sent him a quick text that she would call him when she got back to the house. Her mind was still confused over Erik. The dinner had been amazing, at some point it had gone from business meeting to date and she wasn't sure how that happened. But it seemed to have surprised him as well. She wasn't sure how she felt about it, technically he was her boss but that wasn't the problem. There was something about him that she couldn't explain.

The house was quiet when she entered it, it usually was on Sunday mornings. No games or meets, so everyone slept in. Sunday mornings were fend for yourself in the morning unless someone felt like making breakfast for everyone. Ana headed into the carriage house and took a quick shower before changing into lounge pants and a t-shirt. Closing her bedroom door, which meant privacy, she called her brother.

"You rang?" She inquired when he picked up.

"How was the date?"

"It was a business meeting," Ana lied.

"You are a horrible liar," Toby pointed out. "And no I am not calling to drill you on the guy but I want to ask you more about your dream. I just want to clarify some things that you said."

"Did you find something in the journal?" Ana asked as she lounged on her bed. She took out her dream notebook. She kept all records of anything to do with Mephistopheles in the book.

"I might, which is why I need to ask you some questions first."

"You are so annoying," Ana informed him. "What do you want to know?"

"He told you that he wasn't born an angel," Toby stated.

"No he said he wasn't born with wings, that he was already born damned," Ana corrected.

"And is that different?"

"Well, I asked our resident Angel expert," Ana replied.

"And what did Jules say," Toby inquired. He knew that Jules could see and communicate with Angels.

"Every being, in theory, is born pure," Ana began. "Demons are the exception. They are born out of chaos and hate."

"So he was born a demon."

"Damned is different then chaos," Ana pointed out. "She's wondering if he was supposed to be born an angel but something happened and changed that. So instead of being an angel he became something that wasn't an angel or a full demon."

"Making him hate all angels, even those who fell," Toby theorized. "It would explain a lot."

"That was what I was thinking as well. All the other Angels, even those who fell have wings, yet he was born without them," Ana theorized.

"Sam wants to know more about the painting."

"It was beautiful," Ana recalled. "It was haunting, you felt sorry for the subject, like he didn't have a choice in what was going to happen."

"What else?"

"Renaissance, definitely in the style of the masters," Ana replied. "It was stunning. The detail of the hair and the wings eventually blending into the night sky."

"You said there was a wound on Lucifer," Toby recalled. He was watching as Sam did a rough sketch based on what she was describing to them.

"His left shoulder, where his wing met his shoulder blade," Ana answered. "Meph said it was self-inflicted."

"But you don't think so," Toby stated.

"I think someone else inflicted it but we only see the aftermath," Ana replied. "Like a moment just after the first fight but before the major battle."

"You said he spoke about who Lucifer was to the heavens."

"According to what Meph told me, Lucifer is not Satan," Ana began.

"That's not a new theory," Toby stated. "Scholars have argued that our understanding of Satan and of Lucifer is based off a misunderstanding of texts in the third centuries."

"What else have you got?" Ana inquired. She didn't mind when her brother went into historian mode as she called it. His recall of information had always amazed her.

"He was the first born of God," Toby recalled. "Often referred to as the light bearer. Some old religious text state that all souls of humanity come from Lucifer, this was before he fell of course."

"And the reason for the fall?"

"Well see that is the interesting part," Toby admitted. "For how important Satan and Lucifer is to Christian ideology there isn't a whole lot of them in the Bible. The reason for the fall is pure speculation. Most agree that it had something to do with Lucifer's pride."

Ana thought over what Toby had told her, comparing it to what Meph had said in her dream. "That fits with what he was telling me," Ana stated. "Meph confirmed that Lucifer was the first born. According to Meph, he always was a dark soul, that he was asked to do things that only he could do. Eventually, it got to him and that is why he chose to fall to earth."

"What things were he asked to do?"

"This wasn't an interview," Ana reminded her brother. "He didn't go into details, just that Lucifer would be asked to do things so that balance could be maintained."

"But he confirmed that he was the first born?"

Ana had to roll her eyes, knowing that her brother was geeking out at the moment. "Yes, he stated that Lucifer was the first born."

"Shit, Ana, this is huge," Toby replied. He took a deep breath to calm himself. "What else did he say, you said he mentioned how he was actually born?"

"Not how he was born, but what he was supposed to be," Ana corrected. She ran a hand through her hair. "It was weird how he said it, maybe you and Sam will have more luck into understanding it."

"Sam wanted to make sure that you said it right before we looked into it," Toby answered. "He told you that he was supposed to be born an angel?"

"But something happened before he was born, something that changed him," Ana explained. "Meph said that he was born damned and because of that he was born without wings."

"No explanation into what he meant?"

Ana snorted at the question. "You really think he would tell me even if I asked for more detail?"

"True," Toby sighed. "Alright, I'll start looking into divine beings that are born out of damnation. Sam is going to look at some artistic masters to see if he could find one that is similar in the style."

"Now it's your turn to talk," Ana informed her brother. "Any progress with the journal that we found?

"It's rough," Toby admitted. "Sam called- in one of his contacts at the Vatican to help with some translations."

"Brother Thomas?" Ana asked. Brother Thomas worked at the Vatican Library, he specialized in demonology, as well as, one of Sam's close friends. With the exception of Jules, he was the only non-family member who knew about their family curse.

"So far we have the first part of the first page translated," Toby answered. "It's a slow process but Faust is already trying to expand upon the alchemical formula. If it can create gold and immortality then in his mind it can also expand the mind. He believes that the creation made between the joinings of the two chemicals can be altered to open up new pathways."

"What kind of pathways?"

"To other worlds."

"Like the astral plane?"

"That is one of our thoughts," Toby answered. "But he also starts talking about creating a formula that could erase sin."

"What do you mean?"

"Well that's the part we are having trouble with," Toby admitted. "His other theory is that if it can create immortality, can it also create a re-birth? Wash away any transgression we faced in our mortal shell so that in our immortal shell we will be pure."

"That's insane," Ana pointed out.

"But it also explains why Faust might have thought he could beat the devil at his game," Toby replied. "And it could be why Meph targeted him. If it could work on him would he be granted wings?"

"That's crazy."

Ana heard Sam yell something at Toby. "Alright I will let you two get back to being dorks," Ana replied. "I have to start waking up the kids."

"Before I go, how's my favorite niece?"

"Her recital is in a few weeks," Ana replied. "Her schedule is crazy with rehearsal and therapy but we are getting by. She talks to mom and dad every other night before bed time. They are thinking of coming up for it."

"Yea they mentioned about a trip up north," Toby recalled. Their parents had retired to South Carolina after Toby had finished undergrad. "Mom's nervous with it being close to your birthday."

"I know." The one thing that Ana hated most about the curse was how it isolated her from her family as her birthday grew closer. Meph picked up his tormenting of her the closer they got to her birthday, the more family that was around her the worse it got.

"You're going to videotape the performance right?" Toby asked bringing them back to the recital.

"I'll send it to you that night then you can call her the following day to tell her how brilliant she is," Ana promised him.

"You are going to bring her next time you come, right?" Toby inquired. The whole Gerfallen clan had descended on the group home for Christmas so that they could spend it with Cassie and Ana, as well as spoil the other kids. But that was almost six months ago.

"I am, either later in the summer or one of the school breaks," Ana replied. The intercom that linked the two houses beeped and Terry was asking for reinforcements. "I'll talk to you later."

Ana hung up with her brother and headed out of her bedroom. She could hear Jules walking around in her bedroom. Heading down the stairs she took the connector door into the main house. It had been an extra butler pantry that the servants had used to store extra supplies, now it was a mud room that joined the two houses and gave a back entrance to the courtyard behind the house. The large kitchen was already filled with the smells of coffee. Terry poured her a mug before going back to the mixer.

"Pancakes?" Ana asked. Making pancakes was no easy task with the amount of people present at breakfast.

"Waffles, they can make their own," Terry corrected. "It's about time you showed up. I thought the horde was going to descend any minute and I would be ripped apart."

Ana rolled her eyes at him as she helped him with the batter. The kitchen had industrial appliances that one would find in a restaurant but still managed to hold the warmth of a home. A huge island, that could fit six easily, sat in the center of the room with a stove top and separate sink. By the row of windows was a kitchen table with bench seating so that if they wanted they could all hang out in the kitchen. The walls had been done in a soft silvery blue, with light wood cabinets, and recycled glass countertops.

"What do you need me to do?" Ana asked.

"Tell me what you think of our illustrious new leader," Terry suggested. "Besides that he's hot and has brains."

Ana chuckled as she sipped her coffee. "He read Cassie's files, and I mean read them," Ana replied.

Terry looked up from his batter. "She has one of the thickest files," Terry pointed out.

"And he knew things that you don't pick up from a quick scan," Ana stated. She leaned against the counter that was their schedule and message center. "He's motivated, he wants to help others, he's determined."

"And he's charming," Terry added and got a glare from Ana. "So did he ask you out on a real date before or after the kiss?"

"Were you all at the windows last night?" Ana asked him. He just chuckled as he started to turn on the row of waffle irons he had plugged in. Ana got out the stack of plates and set them up by each iron. "Besides he's our boss."

"No Luke, Jill, and Helen are our bosses," Terry corrected. "Erik is just overseeing the house and making sure we don't kill each other in the process.

He doesn't sign our paychecks nor will he be doing our evaluations. Now, if you were at Heroes Reborn that might be a bit more complicated."

"I'm changing the topic: Memorial Day weekend," Ana warned him. "It's in two weeks. Which means three days at the office and then four days off with the kids. Any plans?"

"At last count, only five are going to be here the whole time," Terry stated. "Brett will be with his brothers, we have a few going on a band trip, and the rest are listed behind you."

Ana turned and looked at the schedule. "I have to go into the office for the next two Tuesdays so I can do some paperwork and meet with Jeremey before which we switch to here," Ana informed him.

"Then I'll see about working from here on those two days because I know Jules is also in the office for at least this Tuesday," Terry replied.

"We talking about me?" Jules asked as she entered the room. She sniffed the air and sighed. "Waffles."

"Yes to both," Ana replied. Jules grabbed a mug and filled it with coffee. "Your office schedule, Terry said you'll be there on Tuesday?" Ana asked.

"Yes, I have a new consult that week," Jules answered. "So we can leave together and then Luke won't freak about us leaving all alone."

"This is my worry, once we enter June things get crazy," Terry confessed as he put one bowl a side and started the next. "Between final games, Cassie's recital, I don't know how we are going to manage. I don't think it's fair to leave all that to just you and Martha."

Ana looked over the calendar that had been filled in for May and June. "We are going to have to sit down and figure out who is doing what. Erik knows about us wanting our own office space so he would like one of us to go with him when he checks out another place."

"Alright we can do that," Jules and Terry agreed.

"A lot of the activities start winding down after Memorial Day, so it's really just getting through until then," Jules pointed out.

The swing door opened and in came a bunch of kids. "Waffles, so grab the batter and make your own," Terry informed the kids. He handed the bigger of the mixing bowls to one of the oldest boys.

"We should wait until Martha is back tonight before we hash anything out," Jules replied. "And maybe Terry and I alternate days off so that it's not just you and Martha."

They heard the thunder of footsteps. "And here comes the rest," Ana said with a smile. It might be crazy, and loud, but the four of them wouldn't change a thing about it.

"And that ends that conversation," Terry stated as the rest of the horde came in through the doors.

The kitchen was filled with noise as kids talked and laughed while they waited for their turn at the waffle machines. Jules, Terry, and Ana watched from the island smiling as the teens got their breakfast together.

Chapter 8

ERIK HAD CLEARED it with Ana, Terry, and Jules before he came over Friday night. They were going to order pizzas and have a low key night, which was needed. The kids were still nervous about him coming over to hang out with them. They were used to Carl and how he hated every moment he spent in the house or with them. Which is why the adults thought it would be good for the kids to see that Erik was different.

When Erik knocked on the carriage house door it was Jules that answered. She smiled at him and for a moment, he realized he was slightly afraid of the blonde. That smile could fool anyone into thinking they were safe but it was the glint in her eyes that told him he might be in trouble. He followed her into the small entryway of the carriage house.

"Alright, why am I in trouble?" Erik asked as he studied how Jules was looking at him.

"You hurt her in anyway I will kill you," Jules informed him. "Because we all know that it wasn't just a business dinner. It might have started out as one but it became something else."

"I know," Erik answered. "I don't want to hurt her."

Jules narrowed her eyes for a moment because she thought he shivered for a brief second. "I am going to give you a piece of advice about Ana," Jules stated.

"Why?"

"I did some research on you," Jules informed him and saw wariness flash in the them. "What I read, what Luke has told me, I've decided that I like you and respect what you are doing. Instead of leaving a good idea on the table you built something amazing out of it."

"Thank you," Erik replied not sure what to think.

"Ana has seen some things that no one should," Jules hinted. "Because of that she doesn't trust easy. When around the kids she is more at ease, more relaxed. But for some reason, with you she is at ease. I want you to push her, make her open up, she has a lot on her plate and she needs someone to help her keep it all in perspective, and if she seems distracted then she probably is, just go with it."

"Is this your approval speech?" Erik inquired.

"No, this is my 'don't fuck up' speech because if you do then fifteen teens are going to rip you to shreds and hide the pieces," Jules said with a sunny smile.

"Are you done scaring him?" Ana asked coming down the stairs with Cassie behind her. "Because if you are then let's head over because a riot over what toppings is about to occur."

They headed into the kitchen and then went through the connecting passage into the main house kitchen where Terry was trying to keep the peace. Erik watched as Ana whistled with her fingers and the whole room went silent and looked at her.

"Terry to the stove, Jules by the message center, and Erik go to the arch," Ana instructed. "Those in favor of Pepperoni go to Terry, Cheese come to me, Sausage go to Jules, and anything weird go to Erik."

Two went to open their mouths but shut it when they caught Ana's look. "Those are the four options, so be a teenager and get in line," Ana stated. They went to protest and she just raised an eyebrow at them. "Did I make that a question? Because I didn't, so get in line."

Sulking, the teens headed into one of the four lines. Ana counted up the number of kids in each line. "Alright four cheese pies, two pepperoni, and two sausage," Ana told Terry who was calling in the order. "Add four large house salads and one caesar for our weirdo who doesn't like pizza. Those who wanted something weird on top you get first pick next time. Now go so we adults can have two minutes of peace and quiet."

Erik just stared at her in amazement as Terry chuckled."She's small but fierce," Terry warned.

Erik looked around as the kids filtered in and out of the kitchen. Now that the pizza was ordered they were figuring on what to do until the food came. "What's the success rate here?"

"Four including Jenna," Terry answered. He had been at the house the longest and their first to break the trust rule was soon after it had opened. "We had one break the rule in the first six months of the house. Then another a few years later, and Jenna was the last. So in eight years: fifty kids who have come through here and only four were kicked out because they broke the honor system."

"That is pretty impressive," Erik stated. "Explain the honor system?"

"It's pretty simple," Terry replied. "At the moment four kids here are in drug treatment, six are here because their home lives were dangerous, and three are here to avoid Juvie. They all know that if they bring drugs or alcohol into the house it's a one way ticket out of here. We don't search their rooms unless they give us cause. We respect their privacy as long as they respect the rules."

"Are there any room searches?" Erik asked.

Ana nodded. "Those are scheduled by the probation officers," Ana answered. "They come while the kids are in school, they come with the dogs. Once every other month they come on a surprise visit."

"Terry said four are in here for drugs, do you see them as well?" Erik asked Ana.

"No," Ana replied. "They see either Luke or the other counselors. We felt that if I treated them while they were in here it could be a conflict of interest."

"But you work with them until they come here?"

"I work with their impatient programs to help ease them into outpatient treatment," Ana explained. "I also help with selecting which programs they should be put into as well as being a coordinator with the families."

"How many do you see?"

"I have five full time patients," Ana answered.

"None of us treat the kids that live here," Terry added. "As Ana said, when Luke and I started to really hash this out we felt it would be a conflict. But we do work with their counselors. We let them know if something is going on, if the kids told us something. The kids know that we pass the information on."

"That makes sense," Erik agreed. He looked around the house. "How often do you do pizza night?"

"Not as often as they want," Terry answered.

"If it was up to the boys this would be every night," Jules chuckled.

"One of the local pizza places donates the pizza, the owner has been real supportive. They have also hired a bunch of our kids over the years," Ana explained. "Actually, three of them are renting the apartment above his place. One is in the kitchen with him, another is a driver while he goes to college and the third is an apprentice to become an electrician."

"We figure they all need a break after the Jenna fiasco, so pizza night usually means a night off from studying, therapies, we even had a parole officer reschedule because she knew this was more important," Ana explained. "We try to do it once every two months, sometimes more than that depending on what's going on and how many are in the house."

"It's a good thing," Erik told them. "Let's them be free of everything for a night, they can just be teenagers."

They went into the family room where some residents were watching a movie on the TV above the fireplace, another group were playing video games in one of the corners with headphones on. The rest were on tablets reading, Erik was impressed with how at ease the kids were, how they had their own little groups, and how they interacted with each other. It wasn't perfect, there were some kids that seemed a bit tense around others but if comments were made they were dealt with by the older teens before an adult needed to handle it.

"What do you think?" Ana asked coming to stand by him.

He put an arm around her without noticing and just looked around. "It's amazing," Erik admitted. "They're at ease, there's respect, and they feel safe here."

"Yea, it's a good thing right now," Ana agreed. "Jenna shook some things up, we had fights, screaming matches, and lots of tears. Now we are all getting back to our 'normal'."

"Does it always work?"

"No, sometimes we get a mix that don't work well together," Ana admitted. "We try to adapt, try to see if we can work with it, to teach them what to do when we don't get along. It's a fine line though of keeping it under control and also not adding more stress to those that have been here awhile."

"I've read the court documents on Jenna," Erik informed her, she narrowed her eyes at him. "Relax, none of you did anything wrong. I still don't understand how she got here with you all saying 'No'."

"That is a question for Carl," Ana replied. "Judge Harrison was not the one that signed off on it. They are looking into the judge that did because it undermines what we are all trying to do here."

"How does the selection occur?" Erik asked.

"Usually by the courts, a welfare agent, the police," Jules explained joining them. "They will send names to Luke, Jill, or Helen. The three of them would look through the cases, then narrow the list down. If the candidate falls into one of the areas that the three of us treat then we meet with them early on."

"With most of the kids we are pretty involved from the beginning," Ana added. "If we're not, then we get the name and read through the notes. We interview potential candidates and anyone involved with them. Then it's majority rule. So the fact that we all voted 'no' but Carl put her here says a lot."

"Do the kids get a say?" Erik wondered.

"We talk to them about it but they should have more of a say then they do," Ana answered. "It's one of the things that they want us to change is that they're say counts somehow."

"That is something we can work on," Erik agreed.

The front door bell rang and Cassie got up with Dennis following her. When they heard Cassie squeal, Ana walked into the large entrance and smiled. Cassie was engulfed in a huge hug by one of their recent graduates. Allan Ortiz was swinging her around in a circle while the teen giggled. He spotted Ana and smiled as he set Cassie down. Allan walked over and gave her a hug too then he noted Erik.

"Who's the new guy?" Allan asked.

"I'm Erik," Erik said holding out his hand. "I'm taking over for Carl."

"About time someone did," Allan said. He looked at Dennis. "Want to help with the pies?"

"Sure," Dennis replied. Allan handed Cassie the bag with the salads then the two headed outside.

Cassie took the bag into the kitchen while yelling the pizza was here. "Welcome to chaos," Ana warned.

An hour later the pizza's were set out and most were on to their second slice, the salad's were gone, as were three bottles of soda. The adults were mixed in with the teenagers as they talked about things. Erik found out that Allan, who stayed for dinner, had graduated from high school last year and was now in pre-med at SUNY in Manhattan. He worked at the pizza place making deliveries because it worked around his crazy schedule.

"How are the two knuckleheads you live with?" Terry asked.

"Derek is dating this nice girl, Bill and I keep telling her she deserves someone better than his sorry ass," Allen laughed. "Bill is almost done with his apprenticeship."

Terry looked at Erik and smiled. "Allan here, on his first day five years ago told me that no one was going to change him, that he was fine, and hard work was for losers."

"And now you're pre-med?" Erik asked with a smile.

"And loving every minute of it," Allan admitted. "They showed me a better path."

"Yeah, well the three of you missed the drama," Dennis replied. "Jenna."

"Yea, I heard," Allen said setting his slice down. "Look, some people don't want the chance we get here. They don't think they deserve this chance."

One of the other kids snorted at that. "Nah, she liked using her body to get her way."

Allen smacked the kid upside the head. "No one likes using their body that way, she somehow was taught that it was alright to cheapen herself by manipulating other's," Allen informed the kid. "We all come here with baggage, with shit we saw, with things that we need to get past. Shit, my own dad taught me how to shoot up and which veins were better."

"Yea but you got better," Dennis reminded him.

"I got better because Luke and Doc got to me in time," Allen said as he smiled at Ana. "Jenna wasn't that lucky. No one got to her in time, so she thinks her only choices are the one's that she knows. She thinks the life she is living is the one she deserves, doesn't matter what her home life was like, that she had parents who loved her, what matters was what she thought she deserved."

Ana got up walked over to Allen and kissed him on the cheek. He blushed as she did. "Stop Doc, just speaking the truth here," Allen chuckled.

"I know," Ana replied. She looked at Erik. "You wouldn't know it but this kid was almost the death of Luke and me."

"Then I guess you do good work," Erik answered with a smile.

"Let me guess you were a perfect angel," Dennis said to Erik.

Erik almost choked on his beer from laughing. "Not really," Erik answered. "I was the rebel in my family."

"How bad?" One of the teens asked.

"I was kicked out of my home because I chose helping a friend over what my father wanted me to do," Erik answered. They all looked at him. "It took awhile for us to mend our relationship. But for it took the Army to really straighten me up."

"How many tours?" Brett asked. He had an uncle who served, an uncle who would have taken him and his brothers in but he was deployed. So he worked with the foster family and saw them when he was back.

"Three, two in Afghanistan and one in Iraq," Erik replied. "I came back different, there is now way you can come back the same."

"Do you have nightmares?" one of the kids asked.

Erik nodded. "Still wake up screaming sometimes. Still hear bombs exploding when there aren't any, not a fan of crowded places. I started Heroes Reborn to help other's like me. Help them find their place, their normal."

"So you aren't just a pretty boy," Terry joked which had the kids all cracking up.

"Aww, you think I'm pretty?" Erik joked back surprising the teens and making them laugh even harder.

Erik helped with curfew making sure all the boys were up on the third floor and that the girls were on the second floor. With Martha at her sons, Jules was staying on the second floor for the night. Cassie chose to stay with the girls so Erik walked with Ana to the Carriage house. They sat out on the back steps.

"You okay?" Erik asked Ana. She had been quiet for part of the night.

She looked over at him and smiled softly. "Just enjoyed watching you interact with all of them," Ana replied. "The way you opened up, that you weren't afraid to show them a side of you. They won't say it but it means a lot to them when an adult does that."

"I'm honored you guys let me into this little glimpse of your life," Erik told her. Watching her in action, seeing her with the teenagers, how she was with Cassie, it made him want to spend more time with her. "I get that your life is crazy."

"But?" Ana asked eyeing him with a smile.

"I want to spend time with you that is just us, even if it's like this," Erik told her. He pushed a curl back behind her ear. "What are you thinking?"

She smiled at him. "For the first time in a long time I feel like I'm finally in control of my life," she smiled.

"Which means?"

"This," Ana whispered. Laying a hand on the side of his face she leaned in and kissed him.

Erik wrapped his arm around her pulling her closer as he deepened the kiss. His other hand ran up her back and he felt her sigh as she rested a hand on his chest. He whispered her name as they came up for air then he found her mouth again as she leaned into him. He didn't want to go fast with her, she was different from every other being he had ever been with. This he didn't want to rush but savor. He felt his phone vibrate in a morse code vibration.

"Shit," Erik mumbled as he grabbed his cell and saw the message. "I have to go, new patient isn't handling things well."

"Go," Ana replied. He bent down and kissed her. "Text when you can."

"I will," he promised running a frustrated hand through his hair. He bent down one more time and kissed her. "I gotta go."

Ana knew she had a goofy smile on her face as she watched him head to his car. He was already on his cell phone as he slid into the driver seat. When a wine glass was placed in her hand she looked up and saw Jules there with a smile on her face as well.

"They all like him," Jules informed her as she sat next to her best friend since first grade. "And they all approve of you seeing him socially."

"I hate all of you," Ana informed her as she sipped the wine. "How's Cassie?"

"Passed out a sleep listening to Opera," Jules answered. "So?"

"He's different," Ana stated. "Even if it's just a fling, I'll take it. And if it's more then I'll take that as well."

"You mean like actually date someone longer than two weeks?"

"I don't know, Jules, since finding the room and the journal I feel in control. Like for the first time I really believe we can do this."

Jules looked at her. "You didn't think we could?"

Ana sipped her wine before answering. "I hoped we could, I dreamed we could, but no honestly I didn't think we would ever be this close."

"Did you doubt?" Jules asked surprised to hear this.

Ana nodded. "It's hard not to when you have Meph breathing down your neck every day."

"So why not tell us?"

"Because you all needed to believe we could do this," Ana answered.

"Ana," Jules sighed. It was a heavy burden her friend carried and she felt bad that perhaps they added to it by wanting to find a way to end it.

"You don't get it," Ana said quietly. "What it's like. He's always there but yet he's not. When I walk by a mirror or a window I fear what I will see."

"How often do you see him?"

"At least once a day now," Ana told her. "A quick glance in a mirror or window and then he's gone making me wonder if I really saw him. A breeze blows by and I hear him call my name in that way he does. He's even in my dreams, hidden but he's there."

"Do Sam or Toby know how bad it is?"

Ana shook her head. "Until we found this journal I honestly thought we would never find a clue, now I'm hopeful. And hope, it's an amazing thing to feel Jules."

Standing up, Ana looked up at the night sky. "I wonder what it's like to look up at the stars and see them for just stars and the magnificence that they are instead of wondering if there was a hidden clue somewhere up there in the cosmos."

Jules said nothing as she watched Ana head back into the carriage house. Letting out a long sigh she took out her cell phone and called someone.

"It's late," Sam grumbled as he answered.

"She sees him everywhere," Jules stated.

"How bad?"

"She never thought we would get this for," Jules informed him. "That it's hard for her to be positive when he is constantly there."

"Shit," Sam grumbled. "We are translating the journal but it's rough. He mixes a whole bunch of languages."

"We need to hurry."

"We are, just keep her positive."

Chapter 9

THE TUESDAY BEFORE Memorial Day weekend Ana was scheduled to sit down with James Lloyd, Luke, and the firm's lawyer Matt Zèle. The meeting was to go over information found by the court and the investigators assigned to the case. Ana was dreading the meeting, causing her dreams to be dark and disturbing. For the meeting she went with a dark navy blue skirt suit, wearing a gray shell under the fitted jacket. She and Jules took the subway toward midtown where the main offices of Second Chances were. Luke and Matt were waiting for them when they arrived.

"We are set up in the main conference room," Luke told her.

She nodded following the two men toward the room. James wasn't there yet so it allowed the three of them to talk before he showed up. "I have gone over everything," Matt began as they sat down. "Honestly, there is nothing that Lloyd can do without raising more suspicion on Carl. I'm not even sure why this hasn't been tossed out."

"What are we looking at?" Luke asked.

"For you guys it's all positive," Matt assured them. "Glowing accolades from past patients, families, as well as, law enforcement that rave about what you do. So Second Chances, as well as, all of you individually are clear there. The problems are for Carl and Jenna, which are separate issues entirely. I will say that since arriving in Juvie, Jenna seems to be showing signs that she now understands the situation she is in. Now that could change but it will be monitored."

The intercom buzzed. "Dr. Gray, Mr. Lloyd is here," their receptionist informed them.

"I'll come and get him, Ruth," Luke stated. "I'll be right back."

Matt and Ana nodded. "I told Luke this in his office so I'm telling you it now," Matt began. "I don't know why Lloyd wants this meeting. It's a last ditch attempt at something, what that is I don't know. So expect anything and you don't have to answer questions if you don't want too. This is supposed to be a meeting to end this nonsense."

"Thanks for the warning."

The door opened and Luke ushered Matt into the room. Matt stood up and shook hands with James and they took their seats on opposite ends of the table. Ana sat with Luke at the one end of the table.

"Did you receive all the information that my office sent over to you?" Matt asked James.

"Yes, I received it towards the end of last week," James confirmed.

"I was hoping it would get to you with time to review it," Matt replied. He looked at Luke and Ana. "Alright, so let's begin. If it is alright with everyone we will be recording this meeting."

Everyone gave their consent, Matt pressed record on his tablet. "We are here to discuss, and in hopes, come to a conclusion that will benefit Juvenile JD. In attendance is James Lloyd who represent the juvenile. For Second Chances and Bohlander House we have Dr. Luke Gray and Dr. Analiese Gerfallen. I, Matt Zèle, represent Second Chances as their legal representative in this matter. We will start with the explanation of reports gathered by Social Services, Second Chances, Officer Ortiz, as well as, court notes from Judge Harrison."

"What of Judge Colsen?" James inquired. "He was the judge that signed off on Miss Douglas going to Bohlander House?"

"He is also under investigation for that incident, as well as, three others so his notes were invalidated by Superior Court Judge Harrison," Matt explained. "Judge Harrison stated in his file that the petition should not be signed off, that he agreed with Dr. Gray and Dr. Gerfallen on Jenna not being fit for the house. Colsen is being investigated for why he ignored the order, as well as, all the evidence showing the poor fit.""

James wrote that down on his legal pad. "I reviewed the documents and was a bit concerned by what were in them," James admitted as he began to lay out his discussion.

"What particular items brought you concern?" Matt inquired.

"To be honest, all of them," James answered. "Not one document seemed to side with Jenna. While most had a few positive things to say about her, all the reports were filled with negativity. There were reasons to each of her claims, one specialist calling the child a pathological liar, another believed she was borderline sociopath."

"The reports are concerning," Matt agreed. He looked at Luke signaling him to take over. "Dr. Gray would you care to answer his concerns."

Luke nodded and folded his hands on the table. "Very early on in our review of Jenna we noted there were some signs of severe mental illness," Luke began. "You will see that in each of our reports the concern we had. Along with her drug use, her promiscuity, and her disregard for taking blame, we believed she would be a dangerous fit at Bohlander house. Her violent outburst towards Dr. Gerfallen showed us that she was not a suitable candidate for our program."

"And how do you decide such a thing?" James asked.

Matt answered. "When the idea of the House was being developed we sat down with child advocates, court representatives, and others on qualifications regarding acceptance into the program," Matt explained. "What we would need in candidates to be able to live in the house and red flags that would make a candidate ineligible for the program. Violence was one of the big red flags, as well as, severe mental illnesses that could put others in danger. All the reports concerning Miss Douglas show that she falls into those two categories. Along with her resistance to the idea of help, her dislike of authority, it all made it clear that this was not the program or setting for her."

"And if parents or an individual were to pay for her to stay there?" James inquired.

"We don't take payment to accept a child, especially when they do not fit our criteria," Luke answered. "We have to remember that there are other people living at the house and think of their welfare as well. It is a very hard line we walk regarding who do we take and who do we turn away because we do feel like we are letting them down when we don't take them."

James made a few notes. "Then you don't take individuals with severe mental illness?"

"We will take them if they are non-violent," Luke clarified. "Miss Douglas did not fit that category."

"Yet you seem to overlook violent mental illnesses that fall within your employees family," James noted.

"Can you clarify that statement?" Matt inquired as he shot a quick look to Luke and Ana.

"Mr. Olsen has raised concerned over Dr. Gerfallen's employment and position at Bohlander House," James explained.

"How so?" Luke asked leaning forward. "This is the first this had ever been mentioned."

"It is a first for me as well," Matt stated. "Dr. Gerfallen's appropriateness has not been brought to the attention of the court or to any of us in any other communications."

"Yes, well we didn't want to have to use it unless we have to," James answered. "Carl feels that gross misconduct has been used against Miss Douglas, while it has been overlooked when in regards to Dr. Gerfallen."

"And what are these gross misconducts that Dr. Gerfallen has committed?" Luke asked. He shot a look at Ana who had gone very still in her seat. If he didn't know her so well, he would think she was handling this very well. But he knew that on the inside she was shaking.

"It's not so much what she herself has done but the warnings that one can find in her family's background," James explained. "I mean if you flip through her family tree it is riddled with suicides, relatives diagnosed with severe delusions, as well as, self mutilation."

"Many families have histories of mental illnesses," Luke replied. "It is why many of us go into the field. Because we know someone close to us that suffered and we want to help, for some we are the sufferers and still want to help others so they can lead a somewhat normal life."

"So these don't seem like red flags to you?" James inquired. "Because I have to be honest, they do concern myself and Mr. Olsen as to whether Dr. Gerfallen is a good candidate for the program."

"Really, because I see them as a testament to how strong of a person Dr. Gerfallen, that she is able to look these tragedies in the face and use them as motivations to help others," Luke argued. "The court also did not see it as a concern when they allowed her to adopt a young teen last year and they were very thorough in their study of Dr. Gerfallen as a candidate."

"Dr. Gerfallen, what do you say of all this?" James inquired.

Ana stared at him for a moment, thinking of what she could say. "When I was thirteen I walked into my uncle's workshop and found him," Ana said in a clear voice. "I saw what a bullet can do to a head at close range. It's not something anyone should see let alone a thirteen year old. I watched as grief tried to swallow my family, as we tried to come to terms with his suicide. I was so angry at him for so many years. I saw it as the easy way out, a selfish act, how could he think we would be better off without him in our lives? As I've matured, I've realized that where he was at that time must have been so horrific that he thought death was the only peace he could find. While I still think he was wrong, I understand why he would think that. I've seen it in my patients, and because I have seen it first hand I was able to get them the help they needed. His death has helped me save more lives. You see it as a red flag, I see it as a way of showing others the will to live. That their life can continue not end."

The room was silent. "Mental Illness is not an excuse nor should it be a red flag," Ana continued. "It should be something that can be discussed without eyerolls, without lawyers trying to use it against someone. We all have struggles, whether is't addiction, financial, physical health, and we are always there to help and support those individuals. So why should we scorn the very people that need us the most? Why should my uncle be used in a way to show I am unworthy? He is dead, put there by the demons that haunted his mind, you using him as reason as to why I am unfit is slander to his legacy."

"That was well said," Matt replied in a soft voice. He was impressed with her composure because he was ready to punch the other lawyer. "Mr. Lloyd are there any actual allegations against Dr. Gerfallen?"

"I will withdraw the complaint," James stated. "I will be frank though, Mr. Olsen would like Miss Douglas back in the house. If you agree then these allegations go away."

"We won't," Matt replied. "And if you use these allegations against the firm or any person employed, getting treatment, received treatment, then Mr. Olsen and yourself will be facing charges of invasion of privacy, as well as, character assassination. And I am sure Mr. Olsen has enough on his plate already with his own charges against him, such as embezzlement, relations with a minor, child endangerment, just to name a few."

"Then I guess we are done," James stated. He nodded to them as he cleaned up his paperwork.

"Very well," Matt replied. "I will be sending a copy of this to Judge Harrison, just so he is updated."

James stopped for a moment then turned to look at Matt. "Do what you believe is best."

The three watched him walk out of the room and Matt turned off the recording. Luke hit the intercom. "Ruth, I want security to follow Mr. Lloyd out of the building and then report back to me when he is gone," Luke informed her.

"Of course," Ruth replied.

Luke then looked at Ana. "You have the rest of the week off," he informed her. "Call Sam, run in Central Park, I don't care what just get away from this."

"Shit, if I had known that bastard was going to pull that I would never have asked Ana to be here," Matt said pacing the room. He looked at Ana. "I don't even know what to say to you. Shit, I am letting Harrison know right away that they are definitely up to something."

"Maybe I should go on leave," Ana whispered. "I can rent a place for a few months but not be part…"

"NO!" Matt and Luke both exclaimed. Matt looked at Ana. "No. You are not to let them make you a victim of their games. You have done nothing wrong, you are integral to Bohlander House, to your patients, and to this firm. You are not the problem."

"Carl can do the same to any of us and he most likely will," Luke added. "None of us come from perfect backgrounds and he knows that. I'm not telling you to take the rest of the week off because I think you are unfit, I'm telling you to take the rest of the week off because I know you are re-living the day you found Joe. And I am going to be following shortly after you leave because I'm stuck with that image as well."

Ana nodded. "I'm going to go to my office and get my bag then let Ruth know about any phone calls," Ana replied.

"Don't leave after that," Luke instructed. "I want to talk to you before you head out."

Ana agreed, then headed out of the room. Luke hit the intercom button for Jules' office. "You are done for the day," Luke informed her. "Work from the house, I need you there with Ana."

"What happened?" Jules asked.

"The asshole brought up Joe," Luke said trying to wipe the vision out of his mind. "I'm going to be heading out shortly. But he made her walk down that road again."

"I'll grab the files I need," Jules promised.

Ana walked into her office and was hit by the first wave of grief. Everything she had worked for, fought for, seemed on the verge of slipping away from her. Grabbing what she would need, she then made a list for Ruth and instruction to forward calls to her home office phone number. She would start setting up the remote link this week. Walking into the reception area she handed Ruth the list.

"Let Luke know I had to run to the bathroom," Ana told Ruth.

In truth, a migraine had begun to form and she needed a moment to collect herself. She headed down to one of the bathrooms that not many people used and walked in. No one was in there, so she walked over to the water stained porcelain sink. Ana looked at herself in the mirror. There were dark circles under her eyes, which also seemed dull. The last few weeks her dreams had become truly disturbing. There were times when she would wake up and she wasn't sure where she was. Turning the faucet on, she splashed some water on her face and closed her eyes. A few deep breaths and she would be okay.

"Are you sure about being okay?" A deep voice asked. "Because I am a bit concerned about your mental health these days."

Ana wanted to scream when she heard the voice. She didn't want to open her eyes because she knew what she would see. He would be there in the reflection of the mirror but nowhere else. Anyone who came into the room would just see her standing before the mirror, if they looked in the mirror all they would see would be her. They wouldn't see her tormentor lurking in the mirror. Mephistopheles only existed in her nightmares.

"You know you really should think about getting some help for these issues you have," Meph stated. "I mean what would people say if they learned you see things that aren't there."

"He's not here," Ana reminded herself quietly.

"Tsk, tsk, and now we are talking to ourselves," he said in a concerned tone. "But I get it. I mean there is so much pressure on you from all facets of your life. You're family, work, friends. They all want something from you. And poor Uncle Joe is being used to cast doubt on his only niece."

Ana's eyes flew open and she stared at him. Today he wore a red suit with a black shirt and a matching red cuban hat, he smiled at her. "Did you persuade him to do that?" Ana whispered in a voice filled with anger.

Meph laughed at the question. "Persuade who? Your uncle, to end his sorry existence or the Lawyer, to bring up skeletons from your past?"

Ana closed her eyes when a skeleton appeared next to Meph. "Sorry, too soon?" he asked. "Alright, I'm sorry, the skeleton was a low blow. I apologize."

Ana raised an eyebrow at him not believing his last statement. "You wound me with your distrust in me," Meph feigned being hurt by her words. "Though I am also flattered that you think I have so much time that I spend it on targeting that distasteful lawyer."

Ana said nothing, letting him continue. "I am the voice and physical incarnation of the devil," he reminded her. "I do his bidding, I do his will. Which means that I am a very busy individual."

"Then leave me alone, that should help free up some of your time," Ana suggested.

"You know, Analiese, you really do hurt me at times," he informed her. "I mean here I have tried to help you, tried to ease some of your burden but you rebuke me at each turn."

Ana's hands gripped both sides of the sink. She couldn't deal with this right now, her head was starting to pound because he was trying to play games with her mind and all she wanted to do was scream. But she knew he wanted her to lose control, it would be a win in his book that he was able to get to her. After all these years since she turned eighteen he was starting to get her to crack.

"For once, can't you just leave me alone," Ana whispered. "Just let me be?"

His eyes flared red as he stared at her. "I am owed a soul!" Meph growled. "A soul that comes from your bloodline. A soul I was tricked out of because of your ancestor Faust. If you want to hate someone hate him, hate the god for taking him from my grasp! Do you think I like having to hunt your line with each generation? Do you think I enjoy this?"

Ana laughed bitterly. "Don't pull the 'this isn't my fault' line!" Ana yelled. "Don't paint yourself as the victim!"

"Oh why are you the victim?"

"I'm a survivor," Ana corrected. "I won't let you make me the victim."

"And what have I ever done to you that was so bad?"

"You tried to rape me!"

Meph snorted. "You wanted it."

She heard glass shattering and then saw her hand in the mirror that she had just punched. A gasp came from the doorway, Ana turned and saw Jules standing there. Ana didn't say a word instead she just walked past Jules. She ignored her phone that was buzzing in her pants pockets, ignored the pain in her hand as she hurried down the stairs to the entrance of the building. Hailing a taxi, she gave him an address.

Chapter 10

ERIK WAS ON the phone when he heard the doorbell ring. He headed down the stairs heading into the foyer as he promised Luke that if he saw Ana he would call. He looked through an old spy hole, then informed Luke before hanging up that he found Ana. Opening the door, Ana stood there looking so fragile that a gentle gust of wind could break her. Without saying a word he guided her inside. He noted her bleeding hand after she had entered his home.

"Come on," Erik said gently pulling her toward the stairs.

Ana didn't even pay attention to the layout of the brownstone as he guided her upstairs and into a bathroom. He slipped out of the room for a minute then came back with a stack of things. There were fresh towels, a plastic bag, tape, and women's clothes. Ana raised her eyebrows at the clothing.

"My half brother and his wife also stay here when they are in town, some of Miri's things are here," Erik explained. "She's a little taller than you. I'm going to wrap your hand in the bag, then take a shower, change into her clothes, and come downstairs."

Ana nodded and he stepped back out of the bathroom. She locked the door then turned the shower on as hot as it would go. Stripping out of the suit, that she now wanted to burn, she stepped into the shower and just let the water pour over her. She rested her head against the cool tile of the shower and let the tears mingle with the water. When the sobs subsided, Ana washed her hair and body hoping it would rid her of all the bad memories. When she was done she turned the water off, stepping out she dried herself off in a big fluffy towel. Dressing in the borrowed clothes she shoved her suit into the trash bin. She could never wear it again.

Stepping out of the bathroom Ana was now able to pay attention to the place. It was simple elegance, with blues and greens done in light hues. Art works was mixed with family photo's. She saw one of Erik standing with a taller man and a shorter woman in front of the pyramids. The other man had long wavy black hair and beard, his skin was darker than Erik's. The woman went up to Erik's shoulders, she had chestnut color hair with beautiful green eyes. She was beaming as she stood between the two men, which Ana couldn't blame her. They were both gorgeous.

Heading downstairs she looked around the rooms until she found Erik in the kitchen. It was a bright and open space with a back patio beyond the french doors. The french doors were open letting the breeze come in as he set a tea kettle on the stove. Erik turned and smiled at Ana motioning to the island that separated the kitchen from the large dining room.

"There used to be a butlers pantry but when Azza and I took over the place we knocked it down, we aren't as formal as our dad is," Erik explained. "The place has been in the family since it was built."

"I was wondering how you could afford such a place in the village," Ana admitted.

"It is one of the few perks of our dad's family influence," Erik answered with a shrug. He walked over and took her hand, she had removed the bag after the shower. She winced as he examined it. "Let me get my pack."

He walked to the hall closet and grabbed an Army green pack with a red cross on it. Bringing it to the island he opened it up and got some of the supplies out that he would need. "I don't think you need stitches."

"I punched a mirror," Ana admitted.

"I'll look for shards of glass as well," Erik stated. "And before you ask, I was a field medic, so yes, I know what I'm doing. I actually am a physician, but after my tours I couldn't go back to it."

Ana said nothing as she watched him exam her hand. He laid out a gauze pad and placed the small shards of glass on it. A few of the deeper cuts he butterfly stitched then he wrapped her hand.

"Keep it above your heart for today and tomorrow," Erik advised. "When you bathe, use a plastic bag to cover it. If it starts bleeding through the bandages call me and I'll stitch them close. But I don't think I need too."

"Thanks," Ana replied. "I should call Luke and Jules."

"They already know, I was on the phone with Luke when you arrived," Erik told her. He checked the water then poured it into a ceramic teapot. "My other brother, his mom always says that tea helps heal the soul and comfort those who are lost."

"She sounds wise," Ana stated.

"She is," Erik agreed. "When her crew would bicker over who was her favorite she would inform them that I was because she didn't have to birth me or diaper me."

Ana laughed. "My mom says the same thing about Jules."

Erik set two mugs down on the island then brought the teapot over. He poured them each some of the fragrant tea. "Miri is a tea snob so this is one of her blends," Erik informed her.

Ana took the honey that was on the island and added a dollop of it to her tea then took a sip. She let out a sigh as the warm liquid seemed to drown her troubles. "I should show you our tea cabinet the next time you are over," Ana realized. Erik looked at her. "If one of the kid's is having trouble sleeping we either have tea or hot chocolate in the kitchen."

"Then you know it works," Erik replied.

She didn't say anything as she took another sip of her tea. Taking a deep breath she began to talk. "My family is tight," Ana began. "My dad and his oldest brother lived on the same street. Which meant my brother, my three cousins, and I were a complete unit. We ran in and out of each other houses from the moment we could walk."

"And you're the oldest?"

"There are 8 cousins in total, not only am I the oldest but I'm the only girl," Ana replied with a smile. "Sam is ten months younger than me. Then Toby, my brother, is about three years younger than me."

"Were you guys trouble?"

"My mom and Aunt will say we were inquisitive in our pursuits of the neighborhood," Ana stated with a twinkle in her eyes as she remembered her childhood. "Aunt Tash is amazing. Not just because she had three boys but Uncle

Joe suffered from severe depression. The whole family supported him, we tried everything."

Erik stayed silent as she took another sip of the tea. When she spoke her tone was different, more neutral. "When I was thirteen we were playing pirates," Ana recalled. "And of course we needed more weapons so I ran to Uncle Joe's workshop where he would let us use scrap wood for swords. He had a rule that as long as none of the machines were on we could run in and grab a piece, otherwise we would have to flick the light switch outside so he would know we were around."

"Smart man," Erik noted.

"He was amazing, so talented in his wood crafts," Ana said sadly. "I didn't hear any noise so I ran in and time stopped. I don't remember screaming, I don't remember crawling through the saw dust. I remember Luke pulling me from Uncle Joe, trying to shield me from seeing all of it, but I had already seen it all. Uncle Joe had gotten tired of facing his demons and killed himself with a gun to the temple."

"Shit," Erik mumbled. He knew what a bullet could do to the human body, he had seen it in war, in the patients he used to treat in the ER.

"Before you ask, my Aunt Tash is Luke's cousin," Ana explained. "He lived with them during college and grad school to cut back on the costs. He heard my scream and came running, yelling at the boys to call the cops and stay out of the shed."

"Did they listen?"

"Only because Sam realized what happened and kept them at the house," Ana answered. She used her good hand to run a hand through her hair trying to see if she could pull it back with one hand.

"Here," Erik said taking the hair band from her. He stood up and ran his fingers through her curling hair. Quickly he twisted it into a coil then wrapped the band around it. "I have two nieces who like Uncle Erik to play hair dresser with," Erik explained. Ana chuckled a bit.

Instead of sitting back down he went to the fridge and pulled out some cheeses and then grabbed a box of crackers and a knife. Ana sliced a piece of cheddar and bit into it. It was a simple task but it helped focus her. "Today we were meeting with Carl's lawyer," Ana informed him.

"I remember you and Luke both mentioning it," Erik recalled. "I take it that the meeting didn't go well."

"Carl has questions about whether or not I am a fit candidate to be in the house because suicide runs in my family," Ana admitted.

"Carl needs to worry about his own legal troubles instead of trying to stir the pot," Erik stated. He looked at Ana also understanding what that statement from the lawyer would me. "His questions meant that you and Luke had to relive that day entirely."

Ana nodded. "Luke told me to go home, to relax, to focus on what I have," Ana replied. "I went to the bathroom after getting my things and this migraine was forming. All this self-doubt just came crashing down on me. I know it's stress, I know it's from dealing with the Jenna fall-out, but it just got to this point where I couldn't keep it in. So I punched a mirror."

"Better the mirror than a person," Erik pointed out.

Once again Ana chuckled. "That is very true. That would have looked great, after the meeting I get an assault charge," Ana realized. "Carl would love that."

"We all have shit in our past," Erik told her. "And now Luke and Matt know that Carl is going to try, that he is going to stir up our past. He's pissed that he was caught so he is lashing out at those he could hurt the most."

"There are other moments in my life that they could have chosen, I'm not sure I should be relieved that they chose uncle Joe and not college,"Ana admitted. Then realized what she had said.

"You want to talk about it?" Erik knew about Uncle Joe but he was unaware of anything major happening in her senior year of college.

"Might as well," Ana sighed. She had already told him more about her past than any other guy of interest. "Jules and I went to undergrad in Boston. Right before finales our senior year we found out that we got into Columbia for their psych program, it was a combination masters and doctoral program. Hard to get into but we did it. So the week before finals a group of us decided we were going to have one last night out. Jules picked this bar that had this night-out package. Everyone in the group got a colored wristband, this let security know we were part of the group and couldn't leave without the rest of the group. Our DD got her own color and free non-alcoholic drinks for the entire night."

"Smart bar," Erik stated.

"It was a great place," Ana agreed. "Anyway we got all glammed up, short skirts, tight dresses, heels, red lipstick. We were having such a blast. There was this guy at the bar who had been watching me all night. He was dressed all in black, and just watched. He gave me the creeps so I stayed away from him. Anyway, he managed somehow to slip something into my drink. I knew the moment I sipped it that something was off. He managed to get me out of there before security could react. He brought me back to this overly decorated apartment in the center of Boston.It was really over the top. I woke up in my underwear on his bed. I realized that this was the guy who had been stalking me on and off since I was 18."

Erik didn't know what to say, so he said nothing, he reached out a hand on hers. "Then Jules came barging in, followed by the police," Ana assured him. "I was rushed to the hospital, Sam met us there. You know everyone looks at you like you're damaged, like it's your fault that this happened, that maybe you shouldn't haven't worn that tight black dress."

"It wasn't your fault, you should be able to wear whatever the hell you want," Erik argued. He kept his anger in check so that he didn't scare her. "It's men who need to learn what no means, that what a woman wears is not an invitation to be an asshole."

Ana stared at him. She leaned over and kissed him gently on the lips. "You are amazing," Ana whispered and kissed him again.

"I can say the same about you," Erik told her. He brushed a kiss along her temple. "Is the guy in jail?"

She shook her head. "He escaped, somehow managed to slip away. And every now and then as I get close to my birthday he contacts me," she admitted. "And don't worry. Alex has a folder of all the messages. It also includes the police report filed that night he tried to rape me. He's determined to find him and arrest him."

"You have to be one of the strongest people I have ever met," Erik informed her. "Instead of being bitter, or resentful, you keep going, you keep believing in hope and the good in people. It astounds me."

"You don't think people are good?"

"My belief in mankind waivers from time to time," Erik admitted. "Usually when my PTSD starts flaring up."

He took a deep breath this time. Getting up, he walked into the living room with the overstuffed leather furniture and sat in his favorite chair. Ana followed him and sat down on the couch across from him.

"We were going home in two weeks, we had all gotten the official word that morning," Erik remembered. "So we were doing routine stuff at that point. No missions to flush out caves or check out a name. Just simple patrols. That simple patrol ended in an IED going off under the Humvee in front of us which set off two more. I woke up in a Humvee with dead buddies. It was burning and I could smell gas. Then I heard Scott screaming from the Humvee in front of ours. I don't know how but I smashed the window, crawled out. Managed to get Scott free and one other kid. Scott was the worst of us so we pulled him a good distance away. The kid found my pack while I kept Scott alert. We didn't get evacuated until nightfall. By then we had gotten most of the bodies out before the cars exploded, we kept vigil on Scott, while waiting for the enemy to come."

"And Scott?"

"Scott lives at our rehab facility in Long Island," Erik stated. "He lost both legs. The Kid, whose name is actually Carlos but we still call him Kid, is our lead Physical Therapists."

"So they're the buddies who helped form Hero's."

"When you survive twelve hours in the desert with a bunch dead bodies, a wounded pal, limited ammo, you form a bond that nothing can break," Erik admitted. He looked at her. "Similar to your bond with Luke."

Ana nodded looking out the windows. Erik watched her for a few moments. "Let's get out of here," Erik suggested. "Let's explore the Village like tourists? Take a day off from all of this. Do you have to be back to get Cassie?"

"Jules can get her," Ana replied.

Chapter 11

It was close to nine that night by the time Erik dropped Ana back off at the house. There had been a moment at the door when she almost asked him to stay the night when he almost wanted too. But she needed to know the truth about who he was before she took things that far. Then Jules came to the door as if she had been watching from one of the windows. Jules looked concerned but was just relieved that Ana was okay. She had been surprised that Ana had told him about her stalker.

He watched them both enter the house before heading back to his car. It had been a nice afternoon, Ana was bright, funny, and down to earth. She had seen a lot of things in her life but she tried to keep it all from weighing her down. Erik pulled into his garage and headed up to his office. Picking up the old rotary phone he dialed a number, he didn't need to worry about office hours. In some places, time was just a concept.

"The office of Michael and Gabriel, how may I help you?" A female answered on the second ring.

"I need to talk to Michael," Erik stated. He wondered what happened to the last secretary and wondered how two Archangels could go through so many secretaries.

"You and every other being," she replied sounding bored by his request. "Who may I ask is calling?"

Smiling because this would be fun, he used one of his four names. "Lucifer."

There was silence on the other end, he would have chuckled if he wasn't furious that someone had messed up big time. The receptionist spoke quickly. "Of course, right away, I will get him immediately, your highness."

Erik waited a few moments before anyone picked off. "You had to scare her didn't you," Michael inquired as he picked up his end of the phone. "I did put you're mortal name down on the 'contact me immediately if he calls' list. You didn't have to give one of your other names."

"She's new?" Erik inquired.

"And we had just gotten her trained," Michael sighed as he leaned back in his chair. "Now she'll probably want to be reassigned. So thanks."

"Hey got to get some kicks in while I can," Erik answered. "Besides, I can't be the scariest being that has come around looking for you."

"I am going to take a guess and say this isn't a social call?"

"Can you pull her files?" Erik asked. He didn't need to give Michael whose name he meant. Michael knew, it was he, who in his glorious angel form, came down to Erik's home and informed him it was time.

"Sure," Michael said for he heard the edge in his friend's voice. "What's wrong and what am I looking for?"

"Who was watching her during her senior year of College?"

"Alright give me a moment," Michael replied as he entered the information into the system. He was one of the few that loved technology, it made his life a lot easier. Otherwise, he would have to be pouring through paper files to find this information. "While I'm looking, you can me tell what's wrong?"

"Mephistopheles tried to rape her when she was twenty one. "

There was silence on the other end. Michael was rarely silent and when he was it was never for a good reason. "How could we not know that?" Michael asked, fighting the urge to punch something.

"Are you sure we didn't know?" Erik inquired. He hated to even ask the question, to doubt his closest friend.

"You know better than to ask that," Michael was pissed. "If we had known you would have been sent immediately, not nine years later."

"Mike, I had to ask the questions, you know that," Erik replied.

"It doesn't mean that I have to like that you had to ask the question," Michael stated.

"Find anything yet?" Erik asked as he heard Michael mumbling under his breath. Then he stopped.

"Well, I'll be damned."

Erik had to chuckle. Out of all the Heavenly beings Michael rarely cursed, it was actually Gabriel that had the foul mouth, which always seemed to surprise people when he did. "Any luck?"

"I can't access her files for that year," Michael stated in disbelief. "Which is impossible, I can access anyone's file."

"What about Peter, would he have higher access?"

"No, he lost his access to case files after the whole Hendrix snafu," Michael answered. "We still haven't forgiven him for that mistake. Erik, this is bad."

"I know."

"If I send more agents, Meph will get suspicious and that is the last thing we want," Michael told him.

"I just thought of something, try pulling the file of Julianna Vijelens, she's Ana's best friend and was there that night. She actually was able to stop the rape from happening," Erik suggested.

"It still doesn't solve the problem of Ana's file being locked, but it might give us information we need for the moment," Michael agreed. "Anything else I should know about?"

"Got punched by a patient."

That had Michael laughing. "Mortal life is making you slow, old friend."

"Nah, I let him punch me, it was the only way for them to see the kind of help he needs," Erik answered.

"Well that is interesting," Michael stated as he found something

"What's interesting?" Erik asked.

"Vijelens is actually Vigilance," Michael answered. He was mumbling as he read through the file.

"Like one of the virtues?"

"Yes. Now shut up and let me read."

Erik waited as Michael read through the file. He could hear his friend reading, picturing him slouched over the computer with his face inches from the screen. "Well, shit, it's here. Well in some form anyway, but it's all here."

What does it say?"

"I hope you're sitting down because this is big," Michael replied as he let out a whistle. "Julianna indeed rescued her childhood friend, whose name just happens to be blacked out. The friend was abducted from a bar and Julianna was able to track them, then rescue her friend from the assailant. Cops are called to said location, again the address is blacked out, but he vanishes while the friend is loaded into an ambulance."

"How did two mortals defeat Satan's physical embodiment?"

"You know that when we are in mortal form we can be hurt," Michael reminded him. "But this is the more interesting part."

"Such as?"

"Julianna was able to use the energy around him and throw him across the room with a ball of pure energy," Michael answered. "A talent only us Archangels can do."

"And the four of us don't have have any offspring, so that's impossible," Erik pointed out.

"I need to look into this. This is the secure line right?"

"I'm home in the Village."

"I'll call you back when I learn more."

"Thanks."

"Don't, I still owe you for taking the Fall," Michael said in a serious tone. "We all do."

"I did what had to be done," Erik said. He hated when Michael got sentimental and brought up what he had done.

"I know, but for once I wish you could stop having to pay for our mistakes."

Chapter 12

ANA MET LUKE the following day in Central Park. While Ana looked around at the tourists, Luke ordered them coffee from a stand. Once they had their coffees in hand, they headed to one of the more secluded spots in the park. It was a gorgeous day, one that reminded you about the goods things there were in life. Sitting on one of the benches by an old oak tree, they took in the scenery around them for a few moments before talking.

"I talked to everyone last night," Luke informed her. Soon after Uncle Joe had died, Luke created a phone chain amongst the family. It would keep everyone informed if something was going on. Then after Ana's attack, it was a way for all of the cousins to stay in touch and alert each other to new discoveries.

"How is everyone?" Ana asked. The closer they got to her birthday the more she pulled back from her family, worried that she could place them in danger.

"Cautious, Nick and Eli leave tomorrow for Austria, they had already planned the trip, now they are glad because they can help with research on what you have learned," Luke answered. Nick and Eli were Sam's younger brothers.

Ana just nodded as she sipped her coffee. She still looked a little pale, her hand was bandaged as well. "How's Erik?" Luke asked changing topics.

"Good, did he tell you he got punched by a patient the day before?" Ana inquired.

"It's rare when he let's one actually get a punch in," Luke admitted. "When I called to tell him to keep an eye out for you, he told me he was home because the patient punched him."

They both fell silent for a few moments. "So are you two dating?"

"I think so," Ana replied nervously. She ran a hand through her hair then looked at Luke. "Is this going to be an issue?"

"He doesn't sign any of your paychecks and when it's time for your review we'll have Jill or Helen do it," Luke replied. He never did her evaluation because they were related in a weird way and he never wanted that to become an issue. "Don't put your life on hold because Carl is being an ass. Of course, if Erik breaks your heart I'm kicking his ass."

"That I would like to see," Ana admitted laughing.

Luke chuckled. She was definitely back to her normal self and if Erik was part of the reason then he would take that. "So what's up?" Luke inquired bringing them back to why they were meeting in the park. "Why the meeting in the park?"

"It's about what happened yesterday," Ana began. "Jules said the mirror wasn't broken. But I punched it, it broke, it cut me. Erik took pieces out of my cuts."

"I know," Luke sighed. He had been on the phone earlier with Erik. "Jules said she felt HIM there."

"And that's what I want to talk to you about," Ana told him. Luke had seen first hand where the family curse could lead. He watched as everyone's worst fear came to life when it became clear that it was passed onto Ana.

"Did he give more information away?" Luke asked. Sam had filled him in on what they had learned so far.

"I think he's behind this whole Carl and Jenna drama," Ana admitted. "Like his twisting their desires into obsessions, making them think they can get away with this, because he would know that it would be an indirect attack against me."

"Let you know that you aren't even safe at work," Luke realized. He ran a hand through his hair and watched as a runner ran by them. "You know when Joe died we all hoped that was the end. That this nightmare we had been living would be done and over with. That maybe Joe's death would free your generation from all of this insanity."

"Part of us wanted to believe it was all stories," Ana admitted with a sad laugh. "That they were just family stories to scare us. Even after Uncle Joe died, we didn't think it was connected."

"You guys were so young," Luke told her. "How could you think it was connected?"

"You know Sam wishes it was him that had the curse."

Luke nodded. "Your dad wondered if it would be him," Luke replied. Ana looked at him surprised. "After Joe died, your dad and Uncle Charlie began to really delve into your family history. There are only three other times since the 1500's that a female was born first in the family. The first was born in 1620 and she died at ten. The next was in the 1700's and she died at sixteen in childbirth. Same for the third who was born in 1802. Your dad and Charlie were wondering if only males were targeted."

"Is that why they trained both Sam and I because they weren't sure?" Ana asked. By training, it was defense training, meditating, yoga, and a whole lot of reading about biblical lore.

"They didn't want to take the chance that their theory was wrong and you were left defenseless," Luke replied.

"I have to admit it was nice to have a partner in crime," Ana told him. "That I wasn't the only one going through it all."

"I think they realized that as well, which was why when the other's wanted to join they didn't see the harm," Luke replied. "I don't know if you know this. But Joe wasn't supposed to tell your Dad or Charlie anything about the curse being real. Joe knew he couldn't do it on his own, he saw the isolation of it as one of the reasons ancestors went crazy. They made an agreement that when they had kids they wouldn't hide it from them."

Ana let out a long sigh. "It is nice to know I have my own army, that I'm not alone in this," Ana admitted. "It does piss-off Meph that I'm not alone, that I have people to turn to."

Luke rested a hand on hers. "You're not alone," he assured her.

Ana said nothing. It was hard to explain what it was like for her. She chose a career that would allow her to focus on something other than the curse. Each day she got up, she lived her life, some days she acted out the part, while other days she truly embraced the day to the fullest. The curse was always there though, even on the good days. A quick glimpse in a mirror or window would reveal Meph watching. The moment she spotted him he would vanish from view making her wonder sometimes if she really saw him or was it just her imagination.

"You said that Meph made it seem like he was pulling strings with Carl and Jenna?"

Ana nodded. "He didn't come out and say it but he was really trying to redirect me, trying to do the whole he's a victim and if one of us would just give him our soul willingly this would all be over."

"I'm going to tell Matt that your stalker could be manipulating Carl or the lawyer," Luke suggested. "I'll give him Alex's information and they can talk."

"I told Erik."

Luke turned and stared at her not sure he understood what she was saying. "I'm sorry, you did what?"

"Well, I left out Jules being able to track Meph because she can do that with angels and demons, and I left out the shooting ball of energy from her hands," Ana answered. "But I told him about that night. About finding Uncle Joe."

"Wow."

"I know, I still can't believe I did," Ana agreed, still amazed that she had told him. "He told me what happened on his last tour."

"Again I'm speechless. It took me five years of knowing him before he told me about what happened."

"He's different."

"He breaks your heart I beat him up," Luke repeated. "He's a good a guy. Solid, loyal, has a temper when people betray him, doesn't tolerate stupidity. He's seen a lot, been through alot, and doesn't put up with bull shit."

"He gets that I'm a single mom to a teen and wants to include her in our relationship."

Luke laid a hand on Ana's shoulder. "He sounds like a keeper."

"And you don't think that's dangerous because of my life right now," Ana pointed out.

"Erik is different, I think you will find an ally in him."

Ana raised an eyebrow at him. "You mean tell him who my stalker actually is?"

"He won't think you are crazy."

She snorted at that. "That's hard to believe, because I think I'm crazy sometimes."

"He saw your hand, he picked shards of glass out of it, even though the mirror never broke."

"Seeing and believing are two different things," Ana pointed out.

"True, but not giving him a chance to believe is not being fair to him," Luke argued.

"You know I really don't like you sometimes," Ana informed him.

Luke chuckled. "You all say that when I'm right and you want me to be wrong."

"And this is why, because you get all annoying," Ana told him. She sighed and finished her coffee. "Alright I guess I should get back to the house."

"I'll head back with you, help get the after school rush over with," Luke decided. "Then I have to head out, I have a dinner meeting."

"Sounds like a plan," Ana agreed.

It was close to four by the time Luke took his seat at the back pub table. The tavern was located near Battery Park, it was one of the oldest buildings in the city. The pub had become a place Erik and he would meet when they needed to talk about things. He was the first one there and was seated at the table that had been marked reserved. Luke placed his order and waited, Erik arrived a few minutes later heading straight for his table. The people in line for a table didn't seem happy that Erik and Luke had been seated right away while they had to wait.

"Benefits to being old," Luke stated as Erik took a seat.

"Perks to being ancient," Erik corrected. When the waitress came, he ordered the house ale and a burger. She nodded and headed back to the kitchen to put his order in. "So I'm guessing this has to deal with Ana."

"I'm going to tell you what I told her," Luke informed him. "You need to tell her who you are, just like I told her to tell you who her stalker is."

"I've been planning on telling her," Erik admitted and stared at the painting behind Luke. "It's not an easy thing to tell, but I also can't lie to her."

"Good," Luke replied. "I should also tell you if you break her heart I'll kill you."

"I would deserve it," Erik agreed, he didn't point out that a mortal would have a tough time killing an angel. "So was that the only thing?"

"The mirror she punched, it never broke."

Erik stared at him confused for a moment. "What do you mean it never broke?" Erik asked. "I pulled mirror shards out of her cuts. I butterfly stitched them closed."

"I know, she still had the bandage on today and showed me them," Luke replied. "But I checked the bathroom out with Jules. Jules knew that Meph had been there, she heard the mirror shatter, she watched as shards flew. Yet the mirror was there, perfectly intact. There were no shards on the floor or anywhere else."

Erik leaned back in his chair. He thanked the waitress when their drinks were brought. "He warped realities," Erik theorized tapping a finger on his glass. "He created a mirror for her to punch but left the real one intact so that when she sees it she would doubt what she did."

"Can he do that?"

"Yes, but not around mortals," Erik answered. "We aren't supposed to use our abilities when mortals are around. Even Demons are limited in what they are allowed to do, it's why they mess with dreams and thoughts."

"No one is around when people are sleeping," Luke noted at how that made sense. "Can he get in trouble for it?"

"It's a minor offense, a slap on the wrist," Erik replied. "But if he builds up enough minor offenses then yes a trial could be called and he would have some form of punishment."

"What about on your end?"

Erik smiled. "I like how you don't count me in the same group with Meph."

"You aren't a demon," Luke answered simply.

Erik sipped his ale before he answered. The way that Luke was able to look past his sins, see him for who he was and not be afraid was what solidified their friendship. "Well, some things have come up that are alarming," Erik admitted. "Her file has been altered, and a week ago someone tried to break into her family's vault. Mike is looking into it, see if he can connect the dot's, find a path. I also have him looking at Carl and Jenna."

"Ana thinks that Meph might have influenced them."

"It's a theory I've been tossing around as well," Erik admitted. "Twist their desires until they act on it. He can do that and not get in trouble for it because it falls under the weak minded category."

"And it's all just one big coincidence that it's related to one of Faust' descendents." Luke turned to look around at the tavern's wood work, at the businessmen who came here for a drink after a day at the office.

"You got that look on your face like you are going to ask me a lot of questions," Erik stated.

"Just thinking about the event's you've seen, the lives you've lived," Luke commented. "Anyway, I take it that strong coincidences and wild theories won't persuade the powers-that-be that Meph is wrong."

"Not to the extent we want him to be," Erik answered. The door to the tavern opened and Erik watched the patrons enter. They were laughing at something, he smiled sadly at the friends he lost because they were no longer here. "Meph underestimates human's. It's his weakness. He won't think you will be able to defeat him."

"I have a question," Luke began. "One that no one has been able to answer."

"Alright what is it."

"You look at her family history and almost every firstborn male that didn't die in war, or in an accident, died from suicide," Luke began. "Why haven't those counted?"

"Under normal circumstance they would," Erik answered. For when he was down below it was one of his jobs to judge the suicides. "Johann willingly signed his soul over to Meph. The contract stated that upon his mortal death his soul would be Meph's. Because of the interference of my father, Meph never got that soul."

"I know that part," Luke reminded Erik.

"I know," Erik said patiently. " Johann willingly signed his soul over, Meph can only take a willing soul. In this case, when Joe took his own life it was to get away from Meph, to end the torment. Same with the others in her family, it was a way to get away from him. He needs the person to verbally agree without influence, without coercion that upon their death their soul is his."

Luke thought about it. "That makes sense," he realized, it was messed-up but it made sense. "It's been driving us crazy for years over why they don't count."

"They would under normal circumstances but when you are talking about a soul owed because of a contract, you have to adhere to the contract."

"I love how you guys are as bound to contracts as we are," Luke chuckled. "As Shakespeare said 'When law can do no right, Let it be lawful that law bar no wrong:

Law cannot give my child his kingdom here, For he that holds his kingdom holds the law.'"

"Figured you would have gone for the 'let's kill all the lawyers' line."

"Nah, *King John* doesn't get quoted enough."

Luke's phone vibrated. He checked it and saw it was his wife. "That was the reminder of bedtime routine in an hour."

"Then go see to the babes," Erik stated. He smiled sadly at Luke. "Regardless of what happens I will protect her."

"I know," Luke replied. He worried how far Erik would go to protect Ana.

Chapter 13

JEREMY WAS LOOKING around Ana's home office. She shared it with Jules, they had agreed on a silvery blue for the walls with gray stained wood for furniture. There were old custom built- in's that were crammed with books and journals. Pictures and diplomas hung on the wall space where there were no shelves. Two leather chairs sat at angles across from the fireplace while an old secretary desk sat in the one corner with a leather computer chair.

"Between me and Cassie, who dyes their hair more?" Jeremy asked, noting the young teens frequent change of hair colors in pictures. He was now sporting neon green.

"Right now you are in the lead, she's like the electric blue she's got going at the moment," Ana admitted. "Her vocal teacher is hoping for a tamer color as we approach her recital."

"She could do navy blue, it would blend well with her natural color," Jeremy answered.

"That or a deep red, she's undecided," Ana replied. "So are we going to talk about Memorial Day weekend?"

Jeremy had called her on Monday asking if he could come in on Tuesday instead of his usual day. She had okayed it with Laurie and his dad, Ana was surprised that Jeremy had arrived by himself. Ana could tell that he was agitated with how he was pacing her office.

"We went to the family cabin over the break," Jeremy replied.

"For the big family gathering?"

"Yeah," Jeremy said and shifted in his seat. They had missed it last year because of his recovery. He had told them all to go without him but they insisted on staying because it had been his last week at the rehab facility and they were going to have a graduation picnic.

Ana raised an eyebrow. She could tell that something was bothering him. "What's wrong?"

The teen ran a hand through his neon blue hair. "No hiding shit from you," he laughed. It was impossible to keep anything from Ana, she always found out what was wrong.

"I know, so what is it?"

"Dad had a fight with one of his brother's about wanting to make the gathering dry," Jeremy replied. "I told him it was fine, that alcohol wasn't my thing. That seeing a bottle wasn't going to send me on my path toward destruction again."

"What did your dad say?" She was always amazed at how down to earth Jeremy could be about his addiction.

"He said that it wasn't me he was worried about," Jeremy recalled. "He was worried that his brother might have one too many and start calling me out on my drug issues. Dad was worried that him or Laurie might punch him. I told him I know a good therapist to help with the anger issues."

Ana had to laugh at that, Jeremy had a way of making everyone at ease about his addiction. "What did your dad say to that?"

"He did that annoying parent thing where he got all quiet then hugged me after which he told me I was going to be okay."

"Oh no, he actually hugged you, heaven forbid," Ana said sarcastically.

Jeremy laughed this time and rubbed his nose. "Anyway I just know you feel weird when my shit interferes with their shit."

"Kid, let me tell you this: you are their son. They are always going to put you and your shit in front of theirs. They are always going to be awkward and annoying because they are your parents."

"You're old, do your parents still annoy you?"

Ana pretended to be wounded at the 'old' comment. "And I say you're my favorite," she tisked. Then brought up the photo of her mom pointing the finger at the screen. " I got this at four p.m. today. If my mother hasn't gotten a text, email, or phone call by three p.m. everyday she will send out the national guard to find out why my brother or I haven't call her."

"Isn't your brother in Austria?"

"Doesn't excuse him," Ana answered with a chuckle. "So yes, they are still annoying and awkward."

Jeremy fell silent again and sat in one of the chairs. "I've been having nightmares."

"About?"

"Crazy shit," Jeremy answered and ran a hand through his spiky hair. "Sometimes it's the night Laurie found me choking on my vomit. Except she's laughing and pointing at me. Then it's me walking into my bedroom and my youngest brother is lying there with a hundred needles sticking in him. Sometimes it's like I'm falling through this dark hole and all these voices are yelling at me or laughing. I even fell out of bed one night."

"What's your stress level right now? I know we touched upon it before the break but remind me."

"Classes are winding down so it's gearing up for finals," Jeremy answered. He then smiled shyly. "My principal is going to be calling you in a day or two. He really loves the idea of me talking to the school. He wants to talk to you about the whole thing before he goes to the board."

"Is that stressing you out?"

"Actually, after I told him I wanted to do this I was more relieved. I don't think I realized how many stories there are circulating about me from last year," Jeremy admitted. "Once I started asking my friends about it they were telling me all these crazy stories. Now it's like I get to set the record straight. Tell them the gritty truth and if they want to believe the crazier tales that's their issue."

"So it's nightmares and an Uncle being an ass," Ana surmised.

"Pretty much."

"Did said uncle get drunk and say shit?

"He didn't need to get drunk, he wouldn't let me near his kids because they might catch my addiction," Jeremy stated. "Jake laughed and told him you can't catch addiction, then asked if he was stupid."

"Baby brothers do come in handy from time to time," Ana admitted. "I use mine for heavy lifting."

"I mean that was like the only time that he made a comment directly at me and when Gram found out she smacked him upside the head so that kind of made it worth it," Jeremy chuckled.

"I need to meet Gram," Ana decided. She loved the stories about Jeremy's grandmother.

"She's a riot, dyed her hair blue because she wanted to know what the big deal is about it and now is planning purple for her next color," Jeremy told her.

Ana laughed at that. "So talk to me, what do you think of all of this?"

"Have you ever felt like life is testing you? Like it wants to see if you are really sure about your path, like it'll tempt you and torment you with your past, seeing if it can stop you," Jeremy asked.

"Yes, and it always annoyed me, so I would try harder to prove that I can do this," Ana answered. "With every obstacle you have overcome you can get through anything. Looking back at our past is not a bad thing. To ignore it though is. We grow just as much from our trials as we do from mistakes. But that's only if we let ourselves deal with them."

"I just can't shake the dreams," Jeremy admitted. "It's like they stay in my head and they can't get out."

"Then write them down," Ana suggested and he snorted at that. "I'm serious. I have always been plagued by nightmares. So I started a dream journal back in high school, not to analyze their meaning, but to just put them somewhere that wasn't in my mind. As I wrote them down it allowed me to deconstruct them. The next time I would have it, it wouldn't be as scary anymore."

"Back in rehab they had us make a check on our hand for every time we got a craving, we would count them up at the end of the day and record it," Jeremy recalled. "I thought they were crazy. Then when the number started to get smaller, when my hand and arm weren't covered in checks I began to realize that it was to show how we were improving."

"Sometimes as we write it down we start to realize what's behind it," Ana replied. "We might be able to find a pattern and prepare ourselves. I hate public speaking so when I have to I know the nightmares are going to come. I prepare,

I do yoga, I make tea before bed. I read a book. Something that takes my mind off of it."

"I could give it a shot," Jeremy answered. "It's better than not doing anything."

"Exactly."

They talked for the rest of the hour about things he could do before bed to help calm him down. When he left, Ana headed right for the main house. It would be dinner time rush, she could hear Martha telling a few of the kids what they needed to do. Every teen had chores to do throughout the week. One of those chores was helping Martha in the kitchen for dinner. Either they helped cook or cleaned up the dishes as she cooked. Ana heard soft music coming from the radio that Martha kept in the kitchen. Dennis was stirring something on the stove while two others on kitchen duty for the night were at the sink.

"What are we having?" Ana asked. Then she inhaled and almost drooled. "You did not!"

"The butcher sent us some extra ground beef and sausages," Martha answered with a shrug. "So with everyone being busy today I had some time so I decided to make my spaghetti and meatballs."

Ana walked over and hugged the woman, who just laughed. "I'm teaching Dennis how to make it," Martha added.

"You are going to impress future dates with this," Ana informed him.

He just grinned as she headed out of the house. What had once been the enormous ballroom was now the family room. It was set up into four main sections, a large television hung over the mantel of the fireplace. Leather furniture formed a U in front of the fireplace. In the farthest corner were four computer tables that made a square where the teens could work on homework or play games. In another corner was a smaller tv and two game systems. If the TV was on than ear phones had to be worn and cursing and yelling had to be to a minimum. The fourth section was a reading nook that could sit about ten. In the center of the room was a huge farm table where they would do puzzles, board games, and spread out homework.

Jules was working with three kids by the computers. She looked up when Ana came in. "This is more your area," Jules said to her. "History."

"I'll take a look," Ana replied. "But that means you get the math issues for the night."

"Deal," Jules agreed. "Did you smell what Martha is making?"

"I did," Ana answered as she looked at the computer screens. "History review packets?"

"I have USII, Jess and Kia have World history," Brett informed her.

"Ok, Jess and Kia work together," Ana suggested. "If one has the answer but the others doesn't, tell them, then show them where you found it. If you both don't know, highlight it. Let me work with Brett and help him."

The girls nodded and Ana pulled up a chair next to Brett to help him with his work. They worked like that for a good half hour before Martha came in and called them all to dinner. Books were closed, games saved, the television was turned off, and all cell phones were slid into pockets. Any that came out during dinner were lost for three days. A day got added for each repeat offense.

They all sat in the dining room for dinner. The dining room was the original size, it had been built to seat up to a hundred people and was right off the ballroom. For them, it was perfect because it gave them space to either eat at the large table that sat twenty or at the smaller tables that sat up to six. Tonight they all went for the large table and were silent as they dived into the pasta and sauce.

Chapter 14

WITH ALL THE craziness that had been going on since the beginning of May and then Memorial Day weekend, Jules was finally meeting up with Erik for their talk. Terry had met with Erik to look at offices and at the bar one time, but Jules had been working a case with the police so her schedule had been a bit more crazy. They had scheduled a lunch meeting and Jules headed back to the house to change from work before meeting him. Ana was in her bedroom doing yoga, so after Jules changed she headed into Ana's room.

"I think Erik is an angel," Ana stated as Jules came through the doorway.

Jules froze for a minute as she comprehended the question. "What do you mean he glows?" Jules asked as she watched Ana go through her yoga routine. Jules had noticed it once while he had been to the house, but thought it had been the light from the window.

"I mean there is this faint halo-like glow around his head," Ana stated as she moved into an upward facing dog position. "I saw it once around taco night then again the day I broke the mirror. When we kissed I felt this shimmer around us, it was amazing, like wings embracing us."

"Well the good news would be that if it is indeed a halo then he's not a demon," Jules replied. She got a glare from Ana. "I was being serious, actually."

"So what, he's my Guardian Angel?"

"They are not supposed to make contact with their charges," Jules reminded her. "Look, if he has a halo then he's an angel. Which, as your birthday approaches, it might be nice to have one hanging around."

Ana moved into a sitting position and looked at Jules. "And how would I even start that conversation - 'hey, I noticed you have a halo and by-the-way, that stalker I mentioned is the devil, think you can help?'"

"It is straight to the point," Jules replied. She got another dirty look from Ana. "Look, I'm meeting him for lunch today to go over my role at the house. I'll take a peek at him and see what I see."

"And if he notices?"

"Then we both know the other's secret," Jules answered with a shrug.

Ana stayed sitting up from her sit-ups that she had just started. "Juliana, only my family knows about you and your gift with angels. You would tell him?"

"You told him about your stalker and I also agree with Luke that you should tell him the whole truth," Jules pointed out. "Now what are your plans for the day?"

"Video call with my brother, he wants me to look at some paintings to see if they look similar to the one in my dream," Ana replied. "Then I'll help Martha tackle homework as the kids come back from school. We have three final papers that are due at the end of the week."

"Better you than me," Jules admitted. "I should get going and meet up with Erik. By the way, are angels good kissers?"

Ana flipped her off, causing Jules to laugh as she headed out of Ana's bedroom. Grabbing her work satchel she headed down the stairs and through the door that led into the main house. Martha was in the kitchen working on the list of chores, groceries, and meals for the week. Mondays were always a bit crazy at the house as it was the first day of the week and getting everyone off on time was all-hands-on-deck which is why none of them had office hours on Mondays.

"Ana is in her room, she has a call with her brother, otherwise she is all yours," Jules told Martha.

"I'll make sure she takes it easy," Martha promised. "You have the lunch meeting with tall and dreamy?"

"Yes, I should be back before the horde returns from school," Jules replied. "What about the boys?"

"Terry has the meeting at the science academy with the school social worker," Martha recalled. "Cassie is staying after to prepare for her finals, Dennis is going to pick her up on his way back from practice. So everyone will be here for dinner."

"Sounds good, call if you need me to grab anything on my way back," Jules told her as she headed for the back door.

Her meeting with Eric was at *Flappers*. It took her about twenty minutes to get there and she found Erik waiting for her outside the doors. He was wearing dark jeans and a t-shirt, the wind had tossed his dark blonde hair around.

"Hey," Jules said as she walked toward him.

"I got a table waiting for us," Erik replied as he held the door open for her. "How's Ana?"

"She is finally listening to Luke and Matt and not worrying about other people," Jules replied. She liked how he asked about Ana first. "Her hand is also on the mend so that's good but then Martha is watching her like a hawk."

"Martha is not someone I wouldn't want to mess with, " Erik replied as the hostess led them to their table. It was still relatively quiet as the lunch rush had yet to start.

Jules noted how Erik wasn't even aware that the hostess was checking him out. "What about you? How's the eye, Ana said you got punched by a patient?"

"Better," Erik said with a chuckle. "It's one of the few times I let someone get the best of me."

"Yea, I don't see that happening often," Jules agreed. The waitress came and they both ordered drinks and an appetizer sampler.

"So tell me, Jules, what do you do for the house?" Erik asked leaning back in the chair. He studied the blonde across from him, she had gone with a navy blue wrap dress and had her hair up in a ponytail.

She chuckled. "I am the task master," Jules answered. "Ana is in charge of the schedule and I make sure that it's implemented."

"And during the summer?"

"Keep everyone busy so no one kills each other," she replied with a smile. "I'm also the person the company's charities contact about wanting to help us."

"You get a lot of help from other places?" Erik asked. He had read everything on the house and knew that a lot of different companies in the city helped out with donations, discounts on products and other assistance..

"Every summer we take the whole group on vacation," Jules informed him and watched his eyes go wide. "Luke and some of the others will join us to help and Martha always comes with her two sons and their families. That's where the companies and charities come in handy."

"What's the biggest donation you have gotten?"

"Last summer we took them for two weeks to the most magical place on earth, all paid for by the Mouse himself," Jules recalled with a bright smile. "Fifteen teenagers, who have seen hell, all complaining that it was a little kids trip. Then the minute we were through the gates they all became little kids. It was amazing."

Their appetizer came and Jules took a mozzarella stick. "We know we could be making a ton of money somewhere else," Jules informed Erik. "When we each signed-on part of the draw was free housing. We could pay-off student loans and then look for a better paying job."

"What changed?" Erik asked.

"Fifteen teenagers gathering around Mickey with silly mouse ear hats on each of them, all grinning from ear to ear, finally being able to be a kid," Jules answered. "It's those moments that make us realize what we are doing at the house matters. We are giving these kids a chance that many don't get. Watching them go from closed off and angry to being free and thriving, no pay check can top that."

"That tells me all I need to know about what you guys do," Erik admitted. Terry signed- on because he could finish out his psychiatric degree and live rent free. Then he stayed because he was making huge strides with a patient and now he couldn't see himself anywhere else.

"Don't get me wrong, there are days when we want to rip our hair out, or want to throw in the towel," Jules told him. "But the thing is, as a parent you can't just quit, and that's what we are to these kids."

They both were quiet as they ate some of the appetizer and Jules studied Erik as they ate. It was quick, a second, some might have thought it was the bar's lighting, but it was there if you knew what to look for. There it was just, above his head, it was gone in a second and Jules knew it meant that Ana was right. There was a faint halo glow over his head and then a faint outline of wings. She pushed a bit just to see if he was friend or foe, because sometimes you couldn't be sure. Erik all of a sudden looked up and stared at her. Jules gasped as if someone slammed a mental door closed, none had ever caught her before.

"I...I'm sorry," Jules whispered. She didn't know what else to do or say.

"How did you know?" Erik asked, his tone completely neutral. He needed to be careful, when a mortal saw an Angel things could get weird.

"I... I didn't," Jules answered.

"So you probe everyone just to see?" Erik inquired folding his arms across his chest.

Jules shook her head biting her lip nervously. "Ana saw a glimmer when you were over for taco night," Jules explained. "She thought it was a perhaps a trick of the light."

"But you went in my head so therefore she thinks differently?"

"When she came to your place, she saw it again," Jules replied. "Saw the outline of wings."

Erik let out a sigh as he folded his hands together on the table. "Does the idea scare her?"

Jules laughed at the question. "Obviously you don't know Ana," Jules replied with a chuckle.

"Then enlighten me," Erik suggested. He was still warring with himself over his attraction to Ana. As an angel relationships with mortals were advised against, they weren't prohibited, but strongly discouraged.

"You, being who you are won't scare her," Jules answered. "The knowledge that you aren't a creation of the one below is a relief to her. You have brought something into her life and she knows that. She's already different when you are around."

"What do you mean?" Erik asked. This wasn't going as he planned.

"She's always on guard, always trying to be the strongest, trying to keep all of us safe."

Erik raised an eyebrow in question.

"Before her stalker abducted her, Ana was carefree. She truly believed in the good there is in this world. I'm not going to say she was all rainbow and sunshine but she believed in hope, believed in good," Jules explained, she looked at Erik. "You know who her stalker is?"

Erik nodded so she continued. "Unlike other relatives, Ana could actually shut him out of her mind. The only times when it becomes hard for her is when she is over stressed or we get close to her birthday. She could ignore him and send him flying with a casual thought."

"That's impressive," Erik admitted.

"The attack changed her, changed all of us."

"That night is not told in detail anywhere," Erik informed her. "The only mention of it occurring is without names and attached to your file."

Jules closed her eyes and saw it all over again. "It was a moment. She was on the dance floor with this guy that had been bothering us all night. As I watched them dance, all of sudden I knew what he was. I saw it in the edges around him and then he looked up and smiled at me. He stopped time, froze me to my spot, then when time started again she was gone."

She paused and sipped the water before starting up again. "I followed his trail, it felt like thick sludge and it stunk of rotten eggs," Jules recalled. "I followed it all the way to this stunning old apartment building. I don't know how I got through the front doors but there I was in front of his apartment door and I knew it was right. I opened the door with a simple burst of energy and walked toward the bedroom door. He was still partially dressed but she was chained to the bed. The drugs had worn off and she was fighting him every way she could. He turned and saw me and I don't know how I did it but I threw him across the room. Got the cuffs off of her, grabbed a shirt and wrapped her in it."

Erik laid a hand on hers, he wasn't sure if she knew she had been crying. Jules looked up at him as he pushed some calming energy her way. "Do you know what it's like to walk into a room and see someone who is like a sister to you about to be raped by her nightmare?"

"I do," Erik said gently. Doubt showed in her eyes. "I left my post to rescue a friend because her nightmare had found her, had taken her, but when I arrived it was too late he had raped her. It destroyed her, changed her, altered her entire being. So yes, I know the helpless feeling, the guilt that you could have done something different, I know what it's like to watch as they fall apart."

"Since that night she is always on guard, she won't look in mirrors, or a window reflection for fear of who might appear there," Jules told him. "She never knows when he is going to appear, whether in her dreams or in the mirror when she's brushing her teeth. Wondering if her thoughts are her own or are they his. It's psychological warfare twenty-four hours a day, every day of the week."

"Most would break under that strain," Erik commented. He tried to recover from his own trip down memory lane and it felt like a gentle breeze in comparison. Jules smiled at him.

"Ana is not most people," Jules stated.

"That is true." He looked at her. "How do you do it?"

"The best way to explain it is I can use the energy that comes from your kind and manipulate it," Jules answered. "If there are none around then I can't do anything. The more there are, the more power they have, then the more I have."

"I have never heard of anything like that," Erik informed her.

Jules looked at him again. "So which one are you?"

"What do you mean?" Erik asked. That question could go many different ways.

"You're older than most that are down here," Jules answered. He raised an eyebrow in question. "Most can't hide their 'accessories' as well as you do. Which means you have had a while to practice blending in. You also noticed me reaching out to you."

Erik chuckled at her summary of him. "But you can't tell who we are?"

"I can if they let me, I can figure out what kind, and the name sometimes," Jules replied. "You, however, are hard to read."

Erik sipped his drink and studied Jules. None of this was in her file but then as Michael and he had learned there was a lot missing from her and Ana's file. "I'm a Seraphim."

Jules just stared at him as if she wasn't sure if she heard him correctly. Erik wasn't just an angel he was of the highest rank of angel. There were only four

Seraphims, they had four faces, six sets of wings. They were so revered that when in their fiery serpent form no other divine being could look at them.

Erik watched her as he she let his words sink in, she wanted to ask which one he was. She shook her head. "That is for you to tell Ana."

"Jules, I planned on telling her it all from the moment I met her," Erik assured her. "I can't hide who I am from her."

Chapter 15

CASSIE WAS SKIPPING in front of Erik and Ana as they walked back from dinner. Erik had surprised both of them at Juilliard, picking them up after Cassie's practice and taking them to dinner. Ana introduced Erik to Cassie's vocal coach Dana who seemed impressed when Erik asked about what they were doing to ensure they weren't damaging vocal chords. Ana hoped Erik missed the thumbs up she got as they walked away from the pick-up area. Dinner was full of conversations centered around Cassie which the teen loved. Now they were going for ice cream.

"Does she ever walk?" Erik inquired as he held Ana's hand.

"Not really, I think in school she even forgets to walk in the hallways," Ana answered with a smile. "They started having her give tours this year to prospective students because she's a ball of energy and so excited about being there."

"The other's won't be upset that I took Cassie out," Erik asked.

Ana shook her head. "They know we are dating and Dennis was worried that Cassie wouldn't be included," Ana admitted. "They know that the two of us are a package deal and most of them know what it's like to be ignored by a parent's significant other."

"So I'm showing them that I acknowledge that you come with a kid and that I am including her as well."

"And relieving their fears that she'd be forgotten."

"Good to know."

They ordered ice cream while Cassie ordered a milkshake. As they walked back Cassie began to sing one of her pieces for her recital. Erik was blown away how she just started singing, he noted how people stopped, watching the young girl as she continued to skip.

"Her voice could make angels weep," Erik stated.

"Coming from you that says a lot," Ana replied before thinking. "I mean…"

"We need to talk," Erik finished.

Ana nodded. When they reached the house, they walked in the front door. Cassie skipped to the back room to hang with everyone before curfew. Erik and Ana joined them, Erik got dragged into a video game with four of the boys while Ana helped go over a history paper. Their conversation was going to have to wait until after everyone was in bed. At 9:30 the process of getting everyone upstairs to their floors began. Then at ten it was curfew check to make sure they were all where they should be. Jules had bed check at 11 so she stayed in the main house letting Erik and Ana head to the carriage house so they could talk.

Entering the smaller kitchen Ana went to the fridge and pulled out a wine bottle. She grabbed two glasses from the cabinet and poured them both a glass of wine. Instead of sitting at the island she headed into the living room where she curled up on the oversized chair. Erik took the couch holding the wine glass in his hand.

"I've never had this conversation before," he realized.

"Are you going to be breaking rules?"

Erik laughed at the questions. "I've been breaking them since I was born," Erik admitted. "Even more so since I met you."

"How?"

"Relationships between my kind and humans has never been a celebrated idea," Erik answered. "Flirting, sleeping with, that's fine, but to date, to wonder about your future with that person, that isn't really encouraged."

"And you wonder about our future?" Ana asked in a soft voice.

"I do, but I worry that when you know who I am this might end," Erik confessed.

"Erik, my stalker is Mephistopheles, trust me when I say not much surprises me," Ana admitted. She studied him waiting for the reaction but none came and that made her nervous. "And by your lack of reaction you knew already?"

"This is hard to explain," Erik began. "And I need you to hear it all out before you ask questions."

"Alright," Ana agreed. She was worried about what he might say, that their relationship was a farce, a means to get close to her, to test her. "Just answer me this: is what we have fake?"

"No," Erik whispered and he went to her on his knees. "No. What we have is real and I will be in trouble for our relationship, for what I feel for you, for letting this happen. But I can't stop what is going on between us and i don't want to."

"Okay," Ana replied letting out the breath she had been holding. "Than tell me your story and I'll tell you mine after."

He sat back on the couch and sipped the wine. "I am a Seraphim." Erik watched Ana's eyes go wide. "What do you know of us?"

"There are four, each to represent the winds, you surround the throne of God," Ana recalled. "So which one are you?"

"There are actually five," Erik corrected her. "Though the fifth is often overlooked. You can blame that on bad press, I guess."

"And you are the fifth?"

"I was actually the first," Erik answered. "The first born child of God, born at morning light. I was named for the morning star, I was the agent of divine providence, the laborer of ages."

"You did what no one else could do," Ana recalled from her dream with Meph. Erik looked at her with surprise. "I had a dream a few weeks back. I was with Meph, as we call him, there this huge painting of Lucifer. It was hauntingly beautiful, you were wounded, Meph told me it was self inflicted. That you had tried to cut your wings off, that you had to be the agent of God that corrected mistakes."

"You don't believe that I tried to cut off my wings?"

"No. The wound would have been at an odd angle for you if you had tried," Ana stated. "The placing of the dagger has me thinking it was done to you, then the attacker fled dropping the knife at your feet."

"How long have you known?"

"That you were Angel, almost from our first meeting," Ana admitted. "But I didn't know who you were or what kind. That's Jules talent."

"In this dream with Meph what else did he say?"

"That he hated you, hated all angels, but especially you," Ana replied. "He told me that he was born already sinned, therefore, he could never have wings."

"There was an old belief that if you cut off the wings of an angel and placed them on your back you would be blessed with their powers," Erik explained to her. "The more powerful the angel the more power you got. Meph never liked me because I was unlike the other Angels. I had a father and a mother. God and Venus. I wasn't just born out of peace and hope. He hated that. I had wings, my father proclaimed me highest of all the others. Meph was created to counter a mistake, to balance the world."

"So he attacked you, because if he was to have a pair of angel wings, they couldn't just be anyone's, they had to be yours," Ana realized.

"The thing is you can't cut our wings off," Erik informed her. "They begin to heal immediately. They are a part of us, a part of who we are. They are more than a limb and therefore can't be removed."

"If you're Lucifer why are you here?" Ana inquired.

"We each take turn with living a hundred years on earth," Erik explained.

"Who are we?" Ana asked forgetting her promise to not ask questions.

"The four seraphs and the four Dukes of Hell. We rotate always making sure there is one angel and one duke to keep the balance," Erik answered. "This is my hundred years to roam the world. Erik has always been my mortal name. As a seraph we have four names, three are angel names, and the fourth is a mortal name."

Ana was silent as she digested all of this. "The reason that I am here a bit longer than the hundred years has to do with your family, with Meph," Erik continued. "I might be a Duke of Hell but I am an Angel first. I took the fall to fix a mistake that I made. I left my post allowing Meph and his army to attack St. Peter's gates. I left because of one of Meph's deceits."

"If you hadn't taken the fall?"

"Then all my friends who fought with me would have been punished as well," Eric answered. "If I took the fall, then I took full responsibility, sparing them the burden of guilt or punishment." "It didn't matter that Meph tricked all of you?"

"We should have known better," Eric replied. He was repeating what he had been told when he asked the same question.

"Right, like my ancestor should have known better than to deal with him," Ana pointed out.

"A willing soul is a willing soul," Erik answered. He held up his hand. "I'm telling you what I was told. I willingly went, knowing the risk to my post just as Johann willingly signed his soul away knowing what could happen." "You said you are here because of Johann, so how do you tie into this? I know you are mentioned being there in the plays and other works of literature."

"I wasn't there," Erik replied. "When Meph was up here wreaking havoc during the 1500s, I was in Hell dealing with the aftermath of his actions. And yes, I'm a bit annoyed that he was here at the height of the Renaissance and I was stuck in Hell."

"I wasn't going to point that out," Ana said trying not to smile at his annoyance.

"As I was saying, I had nothing to do with the contract," Erik answered. "I was never into the selling of souls or tormenting the innocent. Meph excels at both, which you know."

"All too well," Ana agreed.

"I'm here because there are times when I am asked to fix mistakes," Erik continued. "When I am back to protecting Divine Providence, back to being the Morning Star. I was asked to watch over you last year. To just watch because you are nearing your thirtieth year of life. I was to report back anything that showed Meph was breaking the rules. Then things happened, Luke offered to buy Hero's, I met you, and here we are. And Luke knows who I am by-the-way."

"So what happens now, I mean you have to be breaking more than one rule being with me?"

"Since Michael and I wrote the rulebook, I know I'm breaking more than one rule," Erik admitted and watched her eyes go wide at Michael's name. "You react to his but not mine. You should be running for the hills not, sipping wine with me."

"Most of what is written about you is from literature," Ana pointed out. "If you read the old scriptures than you would know you are referred to as the light bringer, the morning star. There is no mention that you are Satan, only that you fell and that reason wasn't stated. But I guess a war between demons and angels wouldn't be told."

"No it wouldn't," Erik agreed. He looked at her in awe. "You are the most incredible person I have ever met."

"That I take as a huge compliment," Ana said with a smile. She got up and sat next to him on the couch. "So what now?"

"Michael is looking into some odd things on his end," Erik told her. "The night of your attack was never written down in your file. I had to have him look in Jules' file, where it's a brief mention, but no names or place. There was also an attempted break-in in your family's vault. So someone is trying to do something. I also sent him the mirror shards and told him about how the mirror was not broken at all."

"When I was in Austria we found what we believe is Johann's lab," Ana told him. He stared at her in surprise. "Follow me."

She led him up to her bedroom where she grabbed her laptop. Opening it she pulled up her file on Meph. She handed him the laptop so he could look at all the pictures of the room. He was silent as he analyzed each picture, memorizing the details.

"He wrote on the walls," Erik noted as he studied each of the pictures.

"Sam and Toby are trying to translate it, but it's rough," Ana admitted.

"I can do it," Erik told her. "It will take some time but I know the code he is using."

"That would amazing," Ana replied, sitting next to him on her bed. "We found his journal as well. I have Toby's notes on the file, I can download them for you."

"Copy the whole file," Erik told her. "Then I can look over it and see if I notice things you guys missed."

"I can do that," Ana agreed.

He handed her the laptop and stood up. "I should head out," Erik realized as he saw the time. "Give you some time to decompress from everything I told you."

Ana took his hand keeping him from leaving. "Stay."

Erik looked at her warily, not sure where she was going. She stood up and cupped his face with her hand. "Stay the night," she whispered before reaching up and kissing him.

Jules came down the stairs the next morning and found Ana humming in their kitchen. Coffee was going and something was baking in the oven. Jules raised an eyebrow in question as she poured herself a mug of coffee. It had been a while since Ana was grinning like a fool or humming under her breath.

"You had sex," Jules realized.

"I'm dating Lucifer," Ana answered and laughed when Jules choked on her coffee.

"And sleeping with him too apparently," Jules said recovering from the shock of which Seraph he was. "So what are you making?"

"I'm heating up waffles from the other day," Ana told her. "I'm gonna bring the tray over when they are done. You want to head over and make sure chaos has started."

It was close to 6:30 am. "Yea I'll let Martha know you're bringing over a tray," Jules told her.

They heard footsteps coming down the stairs and Jules grinned as Erik appeared. He looked nervous at first. "Good morning, Erik," Jules stated with a knowing grin. "Did you sleep well?"

"Go, or no waffles for you!" Ana warned her best friend.

"You are no fun," Jules replied, as she headed to the connecting door.

Ana couldn't help but laugh at Erik's face. He had showered and changed back into his clothes from last night. "Good morning," Ana replied as she kissed him.

"Good morning," Erik answered as he kissed her back. When they parted he ran a hand up her back. "I need to head out. I have an early meeting and I want to change before I go to it."

"I'll text you if anything weird happens, or if I'm bored and want to make you blush," Ana answered with a smile. It was fun to make him blush.

"You are evil," Erik informed her. He took a sip of her coffee before kissing her nose. "I'll call or text when I get a chance and we'll figure out tonight."

"Sounds good," Ana answered as he headed out their back door. The oven dinged so she got the pot holders and took the tray.

Heading through the connecting door she could already hear the grumpiness of teens coming from the big kitchen. Martha took the tray from her and set it in the center of the island almost instantly erasing the grumpiness. Terry was studying Ana from his corner of the kitchen, he was drinking his coffee.

"You are perky this morning," Terry noted with a grin.

"I slept good and already got in some yoga," Ana stated.

"I bet you did," Terry replied as he smiled into his mug.

The teens looked between her and Terry knowing they were missing something but also understanding that they didn't want to know what it was. As the kids filtered in and out, Ana filled the to-go mugs of coffee for Jules, Terry, and herself.

"Science academy, tech school, and Juilliard with me," Ana called grabbing the keys to one of the vans. "Jules has Arts, Private and local. Terry gets the rest of you. You want a ride get in line, otherwise you walk."

Everyone was off to grab their backpacks. Ana got her six students and they headed out the back to the van. Sliding open the side door she counted heads as they entered, each taking a seat they had claimed from day one. Dennis got the passenger seat because he was the biggest and the first to drop off.

"Kia, Jess, Tim, and Brett," Ana called as she got into the driver seat. "Terry will be pick you guys up. Cassie, Dennis is going to come get you after practice today. I have a phone conference I couldnt reschedule, so wait for him." "Yes ma'am!" They chorused. She just rolled her eyes and pulled out onto the street.

Chapter 16

Ana stood in the back of the auditorium with Laurie, Jack, Luke, and the Principal of Jeremy's school. Their school resource office was finishing up going over the statistics, the numbers of drug abuse amongst teenagers. The students knew that someone was going to be speaking to them but they didn't know who it was.

"I know most of you have tuned me out," Grant went on. "You look at the numbers and that's it, they are just numbers. You can say 'that isn't me' and go on listening to your music thinking we don't see the ear buds."

There were some murmurs and a shuffling in the seats. "So we have brought you a face to the numbers," Grant informed them. "He is a junior in high school, will be a senior next year. He isn't doing this because it's part of his parole, or court obligation. He is doing this because he hears what is said in the hallways, he hears the jokes, the brushing it off. He wants to do something to change that."

Grant nodded to the side of the stage then gathered his things. "You will behave," Grant warned them.

Ana watched as the students whispered to each other. Laurie clutched her arm when the curtains to the side move and Jeremy stepped out shaking hands with Grant. The whispers stopped instantly, a hush fell over the crowd as they realized who their speaker was. Grant said something to make Jeremy laugh then patted him on the back as Jeremy headed to the podium.

Jeremy sat his bottle of water on it then looked out at the crowd. "For those of you who haven't taken the honors junior English quiz, choose the second essay," Jeremy began. The crowd laughed and his English teacher held up a thumbs up. "It's the easiest one to "bs" your way through."

The tension was broken as Jeremy sipped his water. "So I came up with this crazy idea to talk to you guys," Jeremy informed them. "I kind of did a rough outline about what I wanted to talk about, I hounded my friends about what I should focus on and what we are all sick of hearing. So I'm going to start with some background."

With the hand held clicker, Jeremy walked them through his childhood, his parent's divorce, his dad meeting Laurie, and his brothers. In the pictures you could see the changes in him, the happy kid becoming serious and withdrawn. He froze the eighth grade graduation picture.

"That night was the first night I tried to kill myself," Jeremy informed them, shocking everyone in the crowd. "My biological mother didn't come to my graduation, I had told her it was fine, but it wasn't. I told her what she wanted to hear, not what I wanted to say. In my head it was easier than admitting what I felt. We are taught that feelings are for wusses, that we should be numb, we should be these robots that feel nothing. I thought I was weak, I thought I wasn't worth the air I breathed. When I woke up I hated myself even more because I couldn't even get killing myself right."

From there he moved to his freshman year where he was struggling to find his voice, to find out who he was. "The first drug I tried wasn't pot," Jeremy informed them. "It was crack. Then it was whatever prescription drugs I could find at my house. Which was hard because my step-mom, she's a nurse, so all the good shit is locked up. I moved onto heroin. God that stuff made me forget everything, it was great. Then I would come off of it and wish I was dead. So I would do more to not get that feeling. I don't know how I became an addict, because like you I never thought it would happen to me. All I know was that I couldn't handle what I was feeling. There was no slow path, it was instant. You tell yourself that this time, this time is going to be it, then in the morning I'm going to get clean. Then you wake up and you are in so much pain from the drug wearing off that all you want is the drug."

He paused to sip his water. "It sucks," he stated. "I wouldn't wish it on my worst enemy. I came from a good home, parents who were involved in my life, a stepmom who loved me. It wasn't my home life that was broken, I was broken."

Jeremy gave them time for the words to sink in and he showed a picture of him at the start of freshman year and then a picture in the spring of freshman year. The transformation was amazing. There were gasps as his own classmates saw what had been in front of all of them.

"Three days after the picture on the right, Laurie, my step-mom, got off early from her shift as an ER nurse," Jeremy informed them. "It was a slow night and my youngest brother had the flu so they let her leave early. She checked on Brad, than my other brother, then me. I never knew that my parent's still checked on me at night. I always thought the idea was stupid, why would you want to check on your sleeping kid? But it saved my life."

He then brought up a series of graphic photos that Laurie had taken to show him what it looked like. "Laurie found me choking on my own vomit, I was overdosing in my sleep," Jeremy explained.

"She went into nurse mode, taking pictures to show the police and EMT's, documenting my heart rate, my temperature. She went with me in the ambulance, while my dad dropped my brothers off at our neighbors. They had to pump my stomach because I ingested well above the lethal limit of heroin. I was told that if she hadn't checked on me at that moment, that in another five minutes I would have been dead."

The next series of photos were from his first stab at rehab. "I hated rehab," Jeremy stated. "Not because I was away from friends and family but because I couldn't do drugs. I never thought anything was worse than coming down from a high but shit, I was wrong. Detoxing is the worst thing ever. How many of you have had the flu or pneumonia?"

More than half the auditorium raised their hands. "Times that by a hundred and that's a fraction of what it feels like," Jeremy told them. "The whole time I was at that place I lied about everything. Did whatever it took to get the hell out of there. I really thought that I had fooled everyone, but they knew. No one told me, but everyone knew that I was doing whatever I had to in order to get out. So if you think that you are tricking them, you aren't."

He paused and brought up a few more photo's before sophomore year. There were blurred out faces in them, Ana watched as some students shifted uneasily in their chairs recognizing themselves in the photos. "I hope these make you uncomfortable," Jeremy admitted. "Because that's how close you are to becoming a statistic. If you're uncomfortable, good, because it means you know it's wrong. If your not, than we need to talk because you are going down a very bad path."

He then brought up a video. "Watch this and then we will talk."

The video was brutal. It was from his second overdose, from when his youngest brother found him. Laurie videotaped it because she wanted to show him what he had done. Now the school was watching as the EMT's worked on him, they allowed Laurie in the OR, as they pumped his stomach, worked on him as his heart failed. By the end of the video you could hear crying, sniffling, but that was it.

"I woke up three days later to learn that my ten year old brother had found me," Jeremy said his voice cracking for the first time. "He knew what to do, he knew to put me on my side and call Laurie or our dad. He knew because his oldest brother is an addict and our parents taught them what to do because they knew I hadn't gotten better. So you know what it's like to know that your baby brother found you like that? That he saved you? That he could have walked in on your dead body?"

Instead of giving everyone a moment he moved on. "I got a choice the day I woke up: I could keep doing drugs but I would never be allowed back in my house or I could get help and actually get help. Before I was allowed to make my choice Laurie and my dad made me watch that video. I wanted to believe it was someone else, that it wasn't me, it would be easier to think that. But I couldn't, it was then that it all hit me and for the first time in years I cried. And shit it felt amazing."

Ana sat with Jeremy and his parents at a table in a diner. They had gone to lunch after his assembly, he would be heading back to the school to talk to the underclassman. Jeremy's dad had his arm around him and just kept looking at him with so much pride. Laurie and Ana just beamed.

"You were amazing," Ana told him.

"I'm going to take the pictures out from the summer when I do other schools," Jeremy told her. "But the Board agreed that they needed to stay in there for today. Several of them recognized their own kids, or friends of their children."

"It's a wake up call," Laurie stated. "They have the information now, we can hope they chose to use it and get help."

"How do you feel?" Anas asked him.

Jeremy smiled. "Amazing. I feel amazing."

Chapter 17

SEVERAL DAYS LATER, Cassie had finished with rehearsals for her end of the year recital. It was close to five, there were a few of them waiting for rides so they hung outside of the school entrance while their teachers were inside going over schedules. The bench near the door was empty so Cassie headed over to it, Dennis had sent her a reminder text that he was picking her up after practice. Taking out a book she had been reading she waited for him to get here. Cassie ignored the feeling of being watched, this was the city and tourists were always watching the locals. Plus tour groups liked to stop in front of the school because it was by Lincoln Center. She didn't say a word when the man in the elegant suit sat next to her.

"It's nice to see the youth reading instead of being on their phones," the man replied. Noting that the other three teens were on their phone barely aware that he was on the bench.

Cassie bit back her comeback and kept reading, silently wishing for Dennis to hurry up. Turning the page she noted the man watching her carefully. He gave her the creeps, there was something that was off about him. She noted the expensive black suit that he wore, the silk red shirt seemed odd since it was in the 80's today. He wore a black fedora with a red feather stuck behind the white band. He was coordinated. Though his cologne smelled like something from a Catholic church.

"Do you go to this school? I hear it's hard to get into," he commented. "But with a lot of practice you can get in."

"It's the halfway point between my boyfriend's practice and my karate lesson," Cassie answered as she kept reading, trying not to groan at the lame joke that he tried to hide within the statement.

"A little young to be dating?"

"Look, mister, I just want to read my book in peace," Cassie replied looking at the man. For a moment she thought his eyes turned red. She sat up straighter looking at him, wondering if she knew him. He looked like the kind of creep her mom would have associated with, like the one that her mom would always make her go to the neighbors when he came over. The air around him seemed to shimmer and this time the other three teens noticed him. One of them was motioning to the teachers inside.

"Cassandra!"

She heard her real name called and saw Erik walking toward her. In all her life she had never been more relieved than to see him coming toward her. He had taken her and Ana out the other night, when Ana had gone to the bathroom he asked if it was okay that they were seeing each other. Erik explained that she was important to him because she was important to Ana. It made her feel good about him, about them.

"Erik," Cassie said trying not to sound scared or surprised.

"Dan is running late, so I told him I would come and get you," Erik told her making sure not to use Dennis' real name. He noted the man that was sitting next to Cassie then spotted one of the teachers on the phone with a careful eye on the stranger. Erik nodded to the woman he had met yesterday when he was with Ana picking up Cassie and she nodded back. "You all set?"

"Yea, I'm good," Cassie agreed. She wanted distance between them and the man that gave her the creeps.

Erik nodded to the man who was watching him closely then took her arm in his and they headed back down the street. A black sedan was parked and still running at the corner, Erik opened the passenger door and told her to get in. Cassie glady slid into the car and locked the door before she buckled her seat belt. She didn't like that her heart was racing or how scared she felt.

Erik climbed in then hit the phone button on his steering wheel. "Jeff, we need to reschedule," Erik said when a male answered. "An emergency came up with Cassie, so I'm not going to be free tonight."

"Take care of the kid, we told you that the teens are more important," Jeff answered. "We can handle things here. I'll let Scott and Carlos know. Let us know if you need anything."

Erik hung up the phone and pulled the car into the traffic. He looked over at Cassie. "You alright?"

"If you hadn't come when you did I don't know what would have happened," Cassie admitted. "I mean in this the city weird stuff happens all the time to people. But that guy, he was beyond creepy."

"I'm just glad I was nearby," Erik replied. He hit the phone button again and Ana answered. "I picked her up so we are on our way home. We're gonna come into the carriage house."

"What's wrong?" Ana asked as she told someone to stop yelling. "The school just called, said there was a stranger and that your timing was perfect."

"Will explain when we get there," Erik replied. He hung up and looked at the teen, she looked so tiny and scared. Two words he would never use to describe Cassie.

"How'd you know?" Cassie asked him as he pulled away from the curb.

"I didn't," he answered and that troubled him. "Ana called me while I was on my way to a business dinner nearby. Dennis was running late at practice and wouldn't be able to get you. I told her I would grab you, Dennis was going to meet us at the restaurant."

Erik laid a hand on her shoulder, she tensed for a moment but relaxed. "I'm just glad that I got there in time," he admitted. When he saw the man sitting next to Cassie he thought it was over. He felt true fear when he realized who it was sitting there. Then the fear of a parent as they realized they were helpless. "It's okay to be freaked, Cassie. If my hands weren't on the wheel they would be shaking right now."

"They make us take self defense classes with Alex, he teaches us as a group and then has a female officer talk with the girls about what we also need to be aware of, of what to do if we get taken," Cassie told him. "I never figured I would be in a situation where I might have to use it."

They were quiet for a few minutes. "Did you recognize him at all?" Erik asked as he made the turn onto her street. He knew who it was but he wasn't going to tell the teen that she had just met the physical embodiment of the devil. And when he told Ana she was going to completely freak out that she had placed Cassie in danger by adopting her.

"I thought maybe he could have been one of my mom's old johns," Cassie admitted. She hated thinking back to that time of her life. "She had this one that always wore expensive stuff like that guy did, he used to give me the creeps. The only motherly thing she ever did was when he was over I was sent across the hall to the neighbors."

Erik pulled into the narrow drive to the house and turned off the engine. He got out of the car then opened her door. Cassie surprised both of them when she hugged him tightly. "It's okay," he promised stroking her hair. "He isn't going to get near you again."

"Ana is going to freak out," Cassie said as she stepped back and wiped a tear away.

"She's entitled to freak out, we all are," Erik told her. He saw Ana standing in the doorway looking at them with this stunned look on her face.

It was late, close to eleven by the time they got everyone in their rooms. Martha was already upstairs with the girls and the boys said they would be alright for a bit. They were all shaken about what could have happened. Now it was just Erik, Ana, Jules, Terry, Alex, and Luke.

"Alright we have three weeks of school left," Jules said as she looked at the master schedule. "Cassie only has one more week of rehearsals before her recital. Dana, her vocal coach, is going to see what she can do about letting her rehearse during school hours after today they are going to talk to parents about being there before rehearsals end."

"If she has to have afternoon practices I can pick her up and bring her back," Erik suggested. They all looked at him. "I have meetings all this week and next near Juilliard, we're looking into buying a rundown apartment building nearby that Terry and I took a look at."

"Thanks," Ana said laying a hand over his. He turned his so they were palm to palm and squeezed hers.

"The guys at the precinct are working on a schedule to have a patrol driving by the house throughout the day and night," Alex informed them. "The sketch artist is going to go to the school tomorrow and work with Cassie and some of the teachers. We can also do some picking up if need be."

"Any updates?" Luke asked Alex.

"School is gathering up the security footage from the camera's outside," Alex replied. "We looked all over and no one matched his description. My partner left a message on her mom's parole officer's phone. As soon as we know something you will know something."

"What about Dennis?" Jules asked. The big kid had taken the news really hard, feeling like it was his fault Cassie was in danger.

"I talked to his coach," Ana answered. "He is going to drive Dennis home after school each day, he also said he can get Cassie too if need be."

"The question right now is: was Cassie the target or was it random?" Alex asked. "I know she is pretty certain that he looked her mom's last boyfriend but this also could be a random attack, the guy saw the opportunity and tried to take it not knowing that people were watching."

"My stalker is back," Ana said softly. Everyone looked at her. "I really don't want to think that Cassie has become a part of my personal nightmare but we should take that into consideration."

"How do you know he's back?" Alex asked.

"He hasn't left behind anything concrete," Ana answered. "I see him out of the corner of my eye. Places he shouldn't be, but he is gone before I can get a good look."

"Mind games," Alex sighed. "Alright, we will keep that in mind."

"Yea but would he target Cassie to get to you?" Terry asked. Ana had been upfront with them when she was interviewing for the position. She wanted them to know that she had baggage, that it might be an issue down the line. But none of them expected that it could ever become real.

"He tried to rape me so who knows what he is capable of," Ana replied.

"Look, we've talked about the fact that these kids come with bad baggage," Luke reminded them. He had been quiet while they talked. "Cas could be right and this could have been one of her mom's old johns. It doesn't make the situation any better but we all know that the past doesn't always stay buried."

"So what do we do?" Jules asked.

"I have an idea," Ana replied. "What if Jules and Terry also run their appointments from here?"

Luke drummed a hand on the counter. That had been one of his ideas he had been working out in his head. "I'll have our techies come a set up two secure points for you guys to do remote satellite," Luke stated. "The problem is patients."

"I can meet mine at Alex's precinct, they have an office for us to use when working with witnesses," Jules stated. "It even has a separate entrance so they don't have to go through the precinct to get to it."

"That won't be a problem, I can call the chief and let him know," Alex told her.

"Ana and I can rotate use of her office in the carriage house," Terry replied.

"The sale goes through on Friday," Erik informed them. "So if you can get through until the first of July I can then have you guys move into one of the office suites."

"We've always said they are more important than anything else," Terry replied. "What else?"

"My wife already said that I can put in some more time here," Luke told them. "She knows what's at stake with these kids."

"I can try to make it so I am here more during the week," Alex replied.

"I can move into the guest suite for the time being," Erik added. They all looked at him in surprise. "It gives you an extra set of hands and ears. I also have a car so I can help with the transporting of teenagers. And I don't have kids like Luke does."

"You have an expensive car and teens make messes," Luke warned him. Erik was stepping into this position with all the grace and care that Carl never had. This had nothing to do with dating Ana, or trying to impress her, Erik was doing this because he cared about these kids. He also needed to be there in case Meph decided to make a visit to the house.

"I think it can survive a horde of teens," Erik replied. "Besides my car has survived worst."

"We will have to add you to the list of who can drop off and pick up," Jules informed him.

"I can take care of that tomorrow and he's already on Juilliard's list. He scared the guy away when he showed up so they love him at the moment," Ana answered. "We have the forms in the office here, Erik can fill them out and I can scan them over to the schools."

"And we'll take you on a run tomorrow so you can meet the school's staff," Terry suggested then paused remembering that Erik ran Heroes Reborn. "Wait, you have stuff to do at the Hero's. So pick a day and I'll take you through the routes."

"Scott already rescheduled my appointments that were for tomorrow, so I'm free," Erik told them.

"You had your own appointments rescheduled because one of our kids was threatened?" Terry asked amazed.

Erik looked at them. "Isn't that what the person in charge does? Look if I'm overstepping let me know."

"You're not," Jules assured him. "It's just Carl wasn't really involved with the House. The only time we heard from him was if we did something wrong in his eyes."

"That's not how I work," Erik informed them. "If I'm running something then I'm apart of it, which means being there for the good and the bad. I don't just put my name on it and then yell at people when I don't like what they are doing. Besides, Carl's an ass."

Ana let out a yawn. "I' think I'm done," she sighed as she stretched.

"We'll figure out the rest," Jules assured her. "You get some rest."

Ana smiled at her then motioned to Erik to follow her. They headed through the connecting door and went up to her bedroom. "You don't have to do this," Ana told him. "Put your life on hold to help us out."

"I'm not putting anything on hold," Erik promised her. "And you don't have to do all of this on your own."

"I am slowly realizing that," Ana said softly. She smiled as he bent down and kissed her.

"I should head back down stairs."

She shook her head and he looked at her. "I... the nightmares will be bad tonight. I don't care if all we do is sleep, I don't want to be alone."

"Are you sure?" Erik asked staring at her.

"I'm sure."

There was a soft knock on her door and then they heard Cassie saying her name. Ana got up and opened the door. Cassie stood there with her pillow and teddy bear that Toby had bought her when Ana adopted her.

"Can I sleep in here?" Cassie asked.

"Of course," Ana replied.

"Then I should really go to the guest suite," Erik stated. Cassie shook her head.

"Can you stay," Cassie whispered.

He looked at Ana who looked just as uncertain as he was. This was all new territory for Ana as well. "Erik, in the hall closet is a blow up mattress and sheets, can you get them?" Ana asked him. It would give her some time to talk to Cassie. "It's on the top shelf."

Erik nodded and slipped out of the room. Ana looked at Cassie. "You want Erik to stay in here as well?"

"I know what goes on between adults," Cassie said softly. "I know what you guys do is different than what my mother did. You guys care about each other, where she just wanted the money."

"Honey," Ana sighed. It was conversations like these where Ana found her dislike for Cassie's biological mother grow even more.

"But I get it, and just as long as you promise me you two won't do anything with me in the room I'm cool with it," Cassie added. "Besides, I feel safer around him. Like he's my protector."

Ana hugged Cassie tightly. She would never dream of doing anything with anyone when a teenager was in the same room with Cassie. But she knew that Cassie's own mother hadn't been so respectful. The door opened and Erik returned with his bundle of goods.

"So where do these go?" Erik asked.

"By the window seat," Cassie told him.

Ana watched the two of them get Cassie's spot set up while she went into her own closet and pulled out some clothes that her brother and cousin had left there. She walked out and handed Erik basketball shorts and a t-shirt. "You are a bit taller than Sam but it's better than sleeping in your clothes."

"Then while you two ladies get ready I will step into the bathroom and change," Erik stated. This would give them time to talk without him overhearing.

Ana helped Cassie get settled into her spot, she brushed a bright blue curl out of Cassie's eyes. "You're safe," Ana whispered to her.

"I know," Cassie yawned.

By the time Erik came out of the bathroom Cassie was already asleep, Ana had violin music playing from her phone. She climbed into bed and he followed pulling her close against him. He kissed the top of her head and they listened to the thirteen year old snore from her spot.

Chapter 18

AFTER THE MORNING rush of getting everyone off to school, Ana stood in the kitchen of the carriage house refilling her coffee. Erik came down the stairs dressed for work he walked over to her giving her a quick kiss then pulled her into him. She rested her head against his chest taking in the strength that he gave her.

"You'll be okay?" He asked laying a kiss on top of her head.

"I'm hanging around here for the day," Ana assured him. She had already spent the last hour on the phone with her parents and brother updating them on what had happened yesterday. Her father wanted to be there so bad but he knew the risk was too great if he came. "In the event that Cassie changes her mind I want to be here."

"I have a meeting at our soon-to-be new office," Erik told her as he kissed her goodbye. "After that I'll pack up what I need and make a few phone calls. See if my contacts know anything and if they don't then I'll be telling them he broke a major rule. He targeted a minor and that's a huge mistake."

"Alright," Ana replied. "I called my family already and told them what happened."

"Did you tell them what I am?"

She smiled. "Oh no, I have plans for how you are going to tell them."

"See that worries me," Erik admitted with a smile. He kissed her again and headed into his car.

Ana watched him pull out of the driveway before walking into the main house. Martha was in the kitchen cleaning up from breakfast. She looked up and smiled at Ana. "I like your young man," Martha stated. "He does what needs to be done, not to impress, but because he wants to help."

"He is pretty amazing," Ana agreed with a smile.

"How did the meeting go?"

"School is on high alert and several parents have offered to help with pickup and drop off, even knowing they will have to go through a background check," Ana replied. She had taken Cassie in early this morning for a quick meeting with staff about yesterday. "The faculty have even offered to help."

"And we were worrying about that last night," Martha stated. "What happens if there is an emergency somewhere else?"

"This was brought to our attention, we are spread thin if an emergency comes up," Ana replied. "Luke is working on ideas on how to handle that. I know Terry was going in today to work on that with him."

"Jules has a court meeting today on one of her cases, so the house will be quiet," Martha told Ana. "You need to rest."

"I am going for a run," Ana replied.

Thirty minutes later Ana was in her running gear and heading towards Central Park. There were a lot of people using the good weather and hanging out. For early June, the weather was warm and humidity low. After she stretched she put on her running playlist and began to run. This was one of the rare times when she was alone and she could think without someone interrupting her.

They had three weeks until her birthday and they were still no closer to figuring out how to stop the devil then they were at her last birthday. All they had found was more dead ends or more questions. But right now her main concern was Cassie, the teen had been rattled by yesterday. Ana felt sick with the knowledge that it could have been Meph and if it was then they were running out of time.

She slowed to a walk and noticed a man standing on one of the bridges. He looked out of place in a sense, like he didn't belong in this time and place. When he turned and smiled at her she stopped as if frozen to the spot. He had short cropped gray hair and a bushy white beard. Looking around she saw no one was around them as she walked over to the white haired man. SHe knew this man, had seen him in her dreams. Her blood hummed in her veins almost as it recognized him as well. He wore a dark brown suit with a pale blue shirt under the jacket, on his right middle finger he wore a gold ring with a the symbol for mercury carved into it.

"This is a beautiful park," he said in a heavy German accent. "Such tranquility."

"Are you real?" Ana asked quietly not that anyone would care if she was talking to herself. This was New York City.

He chuckled at the question. "What is real, my dear Analiese? That is a very deep question that many would think simple to answer."

"Supposedly deep thinking runs in my family. Why are you here?" She asked the alchemist who had cursed her family.

"I am here because it is time to end this conflict regarding what is rightfully mine," Johann Faust stated.

Ana laughed. "You do not believe me," Johann replied as he watched. "You think I am deceiving you?"

"For all I know, your old buddy asked you to come play some mind games with me," Ana confessed. She looked at him, then back at the water. "After all these years, all the deaths, you choose now to appear. Not the night he had me chained to his bed, but now. Why?"

"Because he is changing the rules," Johann answered. "Mind games, suggestions, disguises, they are all part of his game. He is a trickster. But with you he alters his games, changes his tricks. That, I do not like."

"What are you?" Ana inquired as she studied him. "You can't be an angel or a demon? Ghost?"

He chuckled at her question. "I am me," he said simply. "I am no spectre or tick of imagination. If you touch me your hand will not pass through me."

Raising an eyebrow, Ana did just that. She laid a hand on his then gasped as she felt warm skin. "You died five hundred years ago, how are you here?"

"I was granted absolute knowledge, part of that knowledge allows me to move between the worlds as more than just a spirit."

Ana stared at him for a moment letting that sink in. "Wait," Ana replied holding a hand up. "So you are telling me that you can pop into our world, that your deal gave you this ability, yet this is the first time you've done so?"

"As I stated earlier, our mutual acquaintance is changing the rules."

"And you never thought to intervene before, when you could have stopped one of my relatives from suicide?" Ana asked. "When he tried to rape me?"

"Some would say that only the strong survive in this world," Johann pointed out. "It is a brutal fact and one we like to ignore."

"You really are an asshole."

Johann looked at her, puzzled by her comment. "Why?"

"Why are you an asshole?" She asked and he nodded. "You wanted to know all the knowledge this world had to offer, you wanted the secrets of the heavens. The answers to all of man's questions. You claimed you were a scholar, a scientist, yet the moment you got frustrated you summoned the devil, you traded your soul for absolute knowledge. You damned your entire blood line for a selfish act and never bothered to help them."

"Your comments, they hurt," Johann stated. An just laughed bitterly at that. "If you were in my place what would you have done?"

"I would have opened my eyes and looked at the world that I was missing because I had my head buried in a book," Ana answered. "I wouldn't have put my trust in him."

"You think I am weaker than your uncle," Johann realized angrily, amazed that someone would view him as weak. "I survived the Devil's temptation!"

"Did you really survive?" Ana inquired. "You gave in to what he offered."

Johann just stared at her, so Ana continued. "Do I think my uncle was stronger than you? My answer is yes, because he refused to join the Devil. Because he fought until he could no longer fight. He made sure that everything, all earthly matters, were settled. His suicide wasn't a whim, it wasn't out of frustration, it was the only way to save his soul."

"Mephistopheles took me to places that no one has ever seen," Johann argued. She really was an infuriating child. "He showed me realms, worlds that you wouldn't believe were possible. I learned more than all the brilliant minds put together."

"And what did you do with that knowledge?" Ana asked him. "I'll tell you what you did with that knowledge. You did nothing with it, you locked it away in a forgotten place. You didn't use it to better the world, to fight back against disease or injustices. You kept it to yourself. You wasted it, you damned your bloodline because of your selfishness."

"If I had known what he would do I would never have made the deal." Johann let out a long sigh as he stared at the angry female next to him.

She snorted at that. "Really? You really thought he was going to hold up his end of the bargain?"

"I believed that he would follow the words of the contract."

Ana couldn't believe what she was hearing. "Are the stories true?" She asked him.

"What stories?" Johan inquired.

"About Gretchen, Helen of Troy?"

"I always did like that tale of Helen," He replied. "But if we went by the tales, then you know all my children died. Gretchen drowned our child, the child I had with Helen was killed as well. Sometime the truth is hidden within the tales."

"That doesn't answer my question," Ana pointed out realizing it was pointless trying to get anything out of him.

"No it doesn't," he agreed. "I will tell you that Helen was not as beautiful as people thought she was."

"Wow, that is just going to keep me up all night," Ana said sarcastically.

Johann watched as tourists took-in the beauty of the park. He watched a young family laugh at something their toddler did. "What is it that you want?"

"I want a lot of things," Ana stated, in truth most of what she wanted seemed out of reach. "But I'm not telling you what they are."

"You think I will go tell them to our dear friend don't you?"

"I don't trust most people, don't be offended."

Johann turned and looked a her. "And what of your new boss? You have seemed to have confided in him for someone you just met. You have feelings for him, don't you," Johann pointed out. Ana took a step back from him. "Is he all he appears to be? Perhaps I am real and he is the illusion."

Ana didn't wait for him to continue instead she turned and headed away from him, away from the bridge. She didn't turn around to see if he was still there or if he had vanished. She quickened her pace and began to run again.

Turning on her music she ignored the sensation of being watched and just focused on her pace, on getting away from her ancestors.

Erik packed a large duffle bag with what he would need for the next few weeks. He put a few suits in a garment bag then tossed his toiletry bag in his well worn rucksack. Bringing them all down to the main floor he went through his mental list making sure that he had grabbed everything he would need. Once he double checked, he headed into the study and walked over to the antique desk that held an old rotary phone. Picking up the phone he dialed the number.

Michael picked up on the first ring. "I was going to call you," Michael replied.

"Something happened yesterday," Erik stated. "He made contact with Cassie."

"Cassie? As in the young girl that Ana adopted last year?"

"Yes," Erik replied. "The mortals around her noticed him as well, to the point that one of the teachers was calling the police when I arrived."

"He brought attention to mortals and targeted an innocent?" Michael repeated stunned.

Erik could hear Michael getting up and closing his office door before returning to the phone. "This is serious," Michael stated.

"It's always been serious," Erik corrected. "It's just now he is finally breaking the rules of the mortal world."

"I am going to notify the High Court. There is no denying what he is doing."

"Mike, it get's worse," Erik warned.

"How much worse?"

"Cassie is convinced that the man who showed up yesterday is one of her mom's former boyfriends," Erik informed his friend. "Her mom would make her go across the hall when he would come because she didn't like how he looked at Cassie. He dressed in a similar style as he did yesterday. Always in shades of white, black, and red."

There was silence on the other end for a few moments. "How are the mortals taking this?"

"The cops are involved," Erik replied. "And unless I wipe or alter everyone's memory there is nothing I can do about it. Meph alerted a school to his presence, he could have endangered Cassie from a young age. There is no way I can keep the police out of this."

"I don't want you to," Michael stated. "I am done covering up for his actions. He needs to learn that he also has to follow our laws, that there are punishments for those who don't."

"You know I am all for that," Erik answered. "He drives all of us crazy thinking that because he is the voice of the Devil he is above us."

"I know it came up at the last poker game," Michael informed him. "So how's Ana?"

Erik raised an eyebrow. "She's fine. Stressed, but she's handling all this amazingly well."

"And?"

"I have no idea what you are trying to ask," Erik said in a dry voice pretending there was nothing else to tell.

"You lie horribly," Michael pointed out. It was something that always amused him about Erik, the Prince of Hell was the worst liar ever.

"Not all of us can be a natural like you."

"I don't lie, I omit things from statements," Michael corrected him.

"Uh, huh."

Michael couldn't help but laugh. It had been a while since Erik was this laid back on the phone. "You sound happy."

"I am," Erik realized. "She gives me a sense of peace that I haven't know. She sees me for who I am not what has been said about me. Mike, she's amazing. She's it."

"Then we will keep her safe and help ensure that she wins."

"I can't ask you to break any of our laws," Erik argued.

"You aren't asking me," Michael answered. "I'm telling you this is what we are doing. I don't care if you don't agree to it. You are not alone in this world."

Erik went to say something but his cell phone vibrated. He glanced at the text and cursed under his breath. "Ana ran into Johann Faust in Central Park."

"What?" Michael exclaimed. "How the hell, did he get there?"

"I don't know but she said it was him, not a spirit, or a ghost. That he can move between the realms because of his agreement with Meph," Erik answered as he read the message. "He knew about Meph contacting Cassie yesterday and wants to help because he has broken the law about innocents."

"How does he know about our laws?" Michael inquired. It was a question more for himself that for Erik to answer. "You are going to be staying at the house, correct?"

"We are worried that he might try to approach Cassie again, or maybe one of the other kids, so I'm going stay at least until school's out to help with drop off and pick up," Erik explained. "I know this whole situation is breaking a lot of rules."

"First. We wrote the rulebook so I'm not really worried about that," Michael informed him. "Second: the moment he exposed himself to Cassie he threw the rulebook out. Which means you do whatever it takes to keep the two of them safe. The cycle has to end, Erik. I'm tired of it. Tired of adding another notch in his belt."

"I know," Erik agreed. "I just worry about how much more we can all take before it's too late."

"And I'm tired of people not telling me things because it involves Meph," Michael replied. "I've looked over the file that she gave you and I have to tell you that they have more information than I do. I'm done not asking questions, I don't care who I piss of anymore. When did we allow him to have all this power?"

"I don't know," Erik said honestly. "But we need to put an end to it."

"We will find a way, even if I have to call in every favor we have."

Chapter 19

Slowly, things began to go back to normal. With the help of Alex and his partner, all the schools the kids attended had a composite sketch of the man that had made contact with Cassie. Having Erik in the house also helped, he was able to calm the kids down with his laid back style. Terry and him bonded over basketball in the back, often taken on the kids or each leading a group against the other. By his third day, it felt as if Erik had always been there, had always been a part of all of their lives.

Ana felt like she had the most adjusting to do, she had never lived with a lover before. It was a bit odd to wake up and find their things mixed together, but she liked that he was there. Cassie thought it was great and the bond she was forming with Erik was strong. Ana would find the two of them together going over history or science. She couldn't help but smile when she saw two of them together. His first weekend at the house was her weekend in the main house. Which was perfect because it gave everyone the time to adjust to him being around, got the kids used to him there.

A routine was forming, one that blended with the routine of the house, by Monday morning things were good. Ana was drinking her coffee with Martha at the counter while the first wave of breakfast was in process. They were going over the schedule for the week, Cassie's recital was Friday. Martha was not going to miss the recital so she was staying through Saturday.

"Erik is taking the first group," Ana reminded Martha. "I have to meet with Luke at the office, then Terry, Jules, and I are meeting Erik after lunch at what will be our offices. If we are not here before school is out it means we went right from the office to grab the kids."

"Alright," Martha replied. "I am doing casserole cooking today so I will be here all day if there are any emergencies."

"If you are running low on supplies, text one of us and we'll pick them up while we are running around," Ana told her.

Erik came through the connecting door and took his mug of coffee before kissing Ana good morning. He then kissed Martha on the cheek before he noted the schedule. "I'm leaving my car here," Erik told Martha handing her the keys. "I want it to look like someone is here with you. If you need to head out, take my car."

Martha smiled broadly. "I get to drive your car?"

"I'm going to regret this aren't I," Erik sighed as he sipped his coffee. Ana just laughed as she finished the list.

Ana saw the time and groaned. "Alright, I have to head out," Ana replied. "Hopefully this whole drama with Jenna is finished after today."

"What is the point of this meeting?" Martha asked as Ana filled a to-go mug with coffee.

"To show how there is no point to all of this, it's a waste of time and money, no laws were broken by us, we followed protocol," Ana answered. "I know Luke has the report on what was found out about Carl, but he isn't saying a word about what is in it. I think he is saving that for today."

Cassie came skipping into the kitchen with Jules and the rest of the girls behind her. She gave Ana a hug. "Erik is dropping you off, Alex is picking you up," Ana reminded her.

"I remember," Cassie replied as she popped a grape from the kitchen island in her mouth. "Good luck."

"Thanks," Ana said and quickly kissed Erik goodbye before heading outside.

Luke was just pulling up to the curve when Ana stepped out of the front door. She climbed into his car and they headed to the offices. "Matt is meeting us there," Luke told her. "He just had to grab some things from his office. He'll debrief us, then at nine o'clock Harrison and James will come."

"The judge is coming?" Ana asked, surprised.

"He also wants this done and over with and after what James pulled last time Matt is glad to have Harrison there if only to keep James in line," Luke stated.

"That would be good," Ana agreed.

With traffic it took a good forty five minutes to get to the office. They were the first one's in since most didn't start until nine. Unlocking the office door, Luke headed to reception, turning on the computers and lights, while Ana went to the kitchen area and turned on their coffee machine. She followed Luke into the large conference room and pulled out her binder from her bag. It contained everything that dealt with Jenna, Luke got out a similar binder then heard the doorbell.

A few minutes later he returned with their lawyer Matt Zele. "First," Matt began. "Carl has been advised not to come to the meeting by James. I am hoping he listens."

"If he doesn't?" Luke asked.

"We let Judge Harrison deal with him," Matt answered. "He has heard the recording of our last meeting and is aware of what happened."

"So where are we?"Luke asked Matt.

"We are solid," Matt assured him. "There are no grounds for any of their claims. In fact if you had kept Jenna at the house then you would have been endangering minors. She violated her probation on her own accord, so the charges that the house was responsible will also be dropped. As well as, the competency hearing on Ana."

Ana let out a long shaky breath at that. Luke squeezed her hand and let her have that moment. "You are well loved amongst your clients," Matt informed her. "The amount of testimonies we have about how you worked with teens, their parents, it's inspiring."

"Now what if this continues," Luke inquired. "I mean we can hope it ends today but if it doesn't?"

"I file a harassment charge against Carl, as well as, a few other charges," Matt told him. "It ends today."

There was a knock on the door and Rose led in James, Judge Harrison, and Carl. Ana felt her stomach flip at the sight of Carl. Carl was not a tall man, he stood at about 5'8", he had light blonde hair, and dark brown eyes. He always stayed with browns and tans when it came to clothing and he kept with that theme as he entered in a dark brown suit.

"Mr. Phillips wanted to be here as well," James explained.

"When I heard what was at stake, I felt I must attend," Carl said in a smooth voice. He didn't bother to make eye contact with Luke or Ana as he took a seat next to James.

Judge Harrison took the seat at the head of the table. He pulled out a tape recorder and set it in the center of the room where they all gave their consent for it to be recorded. "I am going to state my reason for being here," he began. "I am here to act as a mediator and am authorized to make decisions as if in a courtroom. If I feel that this needs to be heard in a courtroom then we will stop and set a date. Let us hope that will not be needed."

It had been agreed earlier that Matt would start the proceedings. "As his Honor stated, we are here to close the book on this matter," Matt explained. "There were three main charges that were brought against Bohlander House: child endangerment, failure to help youth meet terms of probation, and a competency claim against those that live in the house."

James and Carl both agreed that those were the charges. "From day one no evidence was presented to support any of the three complaints," Matt began. "To the contrary, when you look through the files of evidence, the interviews, written statements, videos, recordings, you find that those employed by Second Chance went above and beyond what they were to do. If you may, your Honor, I would to discuss each claim and what the evidence shows."

"You may, and a rebuttal may be made when you are done," Judge Harrison stated.

"We will start with the Child Endangerment," Matt replied. He let James have a few moments to get the file on that particular complaint. "According to police, child services, and other experts, if Jenna was to remain in the house then perhaps that charge would be correct but it would be for placing the other fifteen children at risk, not Jenna. She knowingly brought drugs into the home which was a violation of the policies of Bohlander House and of her parole. As for when she was in the house there is no evidence of her being neglected, placed in danger, or ignored. In fact she was given clothes, food, a room, and ample opportunity to partake in house events. She was treated just like the rest of the residents, a welcome dinner, chores, rewards and consequences. From what we have heard and seen it was, once again, her choice to ignore what was given to her."

"Counselor?" Judge Harrison asked James. "Do you want to add something?"

"If I could wait until the end I would appreciate it."

"You can have until after the next point," the judge stated. "Mr. Zele, you may continue."

"The next is the claim that Bohlander House failed to provide Jenna with opportunity to adhere to her terms of her parole," Matt stated. He pulled out copies of her parole detail. "Her terms were: once a week to attend a Narcotics Anonymous meeting, a therapy session, and a meeting with her parole officer."

Matt then pulled out copies of Ana's house schedule to show the detail of those arrangements. Other names had been blacked out. "As you can see those conditions were adhered to, I also have copies of the logs from her NA meetings, her therapists, as well as, her parole officer. Each confirm that she attended each meeting and session. However, she refused to partake in the discussions, refused to discuss things with her therapists, and was even silent when checking in with her parole officer. If Bohlander House failed to bring her to these appointments then I could understand the complaint, but they didn't fail to bring her there. She went but refused to cooperate. Bohlander House is not and should not be responsible for a sixteen year old giving the silent treatment to everyone."

"I see you failed to mention her school attendance," James stated. He pulled out a copy of her attendance record and set it on the table. "Another part of her parole was that she attend school on a regular basis and keep her grades up. However, as you can see she cut school nearly everyday."

"And Bohlander House is responsible how?" Matt asked.

"They should have ensured she attended the school."

"We did," Ana said almost groaning.

"So you say," James replied.

"I would like Dr. Gerfallen to re-explain the school procedure with the young girl in question," Judge Harrison interrupted. Ana had already explained the procedure when they were in court.

"We were aware from previous school records that she was a frequent truant," Ana explained. "Her reason for failing classes was due to her attendance more than her grades. When she actually did apply herself she would get B's and A's. Knowing that we worked with the school she would be attending. One of the three of us would drive her to school where we would be met with a security guard. We would then go to the main office where we would sign her in while the security guard escorted her to homeroom."

"What happened if she vanished after that?" Judge Harrison inquired. He knew he had asked the question before but wanted her to repeat the answer.

"The school would notify one of us," Ana answered. "Then we would notify her parole officer and the search would start to find her. In the two months with us she cut twenty times, twenty times we would stop what we were doing to find her."

"That seems like a very entailed system you had going to ensure she stayed put," Judge Harrison admitted.

"It is one of the more detailed plans we have come up with," Luke agreed.

Judge Harrison turned and looked at James and Carl. "And what would have been a better solution?"

James was surprised by the question and looked at Carl for some ideas. He got no help from the older man. "Perhaps to have had an adult follow her to each class and sit with her during the class," James suggested.

"And when she had to go to the bathroom?" Ana inquired. "Would they have to follow her into the bathroom as well? Would they have to go into the locker room to ensure she didn't sneak out during gym?"

"When we come up with these plans, your honor, we also have to consider the other students," Luke explained. "We considered an adult but even the school agreed that at sixteen Jenna was old enough to know where she needed to be. She had no impairment that made it difficult to remember where she needed to be or how to get there. Also, adults are not permitted in the locker room, so having an adult with her would still leave times when she could sneak out."

"Mr. Lloyd any other comments?" Harrison asked James.

"I'm good for the moment," James answered.

"Very well, then Mr. Zele continue."

"The last complaint was that Drs. Gerfallen, Vijelens, and Wyles were unqualified for their positions within the house," Matt went on. "That this contributed to the failure in helping Jenna."

"And what was found?"

"That the three are a huge and integral part of why the house works," Matt replied. He pulled out an extremely thick three inch binder. "This is filled with all the interviews conducted. You will find nothing but glowing testaments to the House, it's program, and the three that live there. I was even able to track down one of the students that failed the program, he is now in his late twenties."

"What did he have to say about being kicked out?" James asked.

"He stated that he wished he had taken up the opportunity the program would have given him," Matt answered. "Instead he was more focused on himself, on his pain, that he wouldn't let anyone help him. You will find letters from the head of Family Services explaining how vital Bohlander House has become to them. The police precincts have the House number on the board with all the other service numbers. Other states are thinking of adopting the program's structure, understanding that it only works with the right people in charge. If the testimonies don't show they are competent then I have their psych evaluations, academic history, and publications they have written."

"And what of the red flag I brought up last time?" James inquired. "Did you include that or did you leave it out?"

"I find your red flag invalid," Judge Harrison informed him. "My brother was arrested when I was sixteen. He was smug teen who thought he knew better than anyone. He got involved with a gang and killed three people. He is currently serving three life sentences. Now, I could have followed his path, instead I watched how his lawyers worked, watched the Judge try to reach through to him, and I wanted to be that. But if we went by your theory then I should never have become a lawyer or a judge because I have a brother in jail. Our family does not dictate who we become, only we can dictate who we become."

There was silence for a moment as he words hung in the air. "Now, Mr. Lloyd what do you have to say about all of this?" Harrison inquired.

"That it appalls me the law is able to allow this to happen, that this young female will be sent into the juvenile correction system because no one will take responsibility for her and help her," James began. "But since there seems to be little evidence to back up our complaints I will withdraw them from the court, as long as, Mr. Phillip agrees."

"What is the fate of the young girl?" Carl inquired. "Where will she go?"

"She will stay in the Juvenile center she is in until she is eighteen," Judge Harrison explained. "Her sentence can be shortened if she shows good behavior otherwise she will serve the remaining two years of her sentence. "

"And what of Bohlander House?"

"Nothing," Judge Harrison answered. "There is no evidence to support your complaints, so the case is dismissed."

"So those who failed her will continue to work and fail others?"

Ana felt anger rise through her but it was the judge that spoke. "The only reason that I can see that they failed the young woman is because she refused to let them help," Judge Harrison stated. "Therefore, they cannot fail when one does not allow them to help. She is sixteen, she knows the difference between right and wrong. You say no one took responsibility for her, well what of her own responsibility? There are consequences to show what happens when we do not listen, when we break the laws."

"And this is acceptable?" Carl argued.

"From the moment you showed up with Jenna at Bohlander House I wondered what your motivations were," Luke spoke up. "She is the only teen who you showed any interest in. You were head of the house in name only, never going there, barely looking over the cases. Yet with Jenna you argued, fought, and ignored our entire process and I wondered why? Tell me Carl, why Jenna? Why after all this time you finally decided to become involved."

Carl said nothing. He leaned back in his chair folding his arms across his chest and stayed silent. It was James who spoke. "My client does not have to listen to this nor does he have to answer the question."

"No, but he will have to answer some questions," Matt said taking out a thick sealed envelope. "As the court is aware, an investigation was started as to Mr. Phillip's involvement with Jenna, his refusal to follow protocol."

"I am aware," Judge Harrison answered. He spoke to the recorder that he was now opening a sealed envelope and took out the paperwork and photo's that were inside. "Does Mr. Lloyd have a copy?"

"It was sent to his office on Friday and the receipt was signed by him," Matt stated.

Harrison nodded and began to go over what was found. The pictures had him losing his appetite, as did some of the emails that had been sent between Carl and the judge who had originally signed-off allowing Jenna to go to the House.

"These are quite incriminating," Judge Harrison began.

"We are aware of the contents," James stated. "We would like to make a deal."

"What is it?" Harrison asked before Matt could comment.

"That Carl pleads guilty on lesser charges, if Dr. Gerfallen resigns from Second Chances and Bohlander House," James answered.

"No," Matt and Luke said at the same time.

"Then I suggest you file your complaints with criminal court immediately, Mr. Zele," Judge Harrison stated. "I would like to have a moment to speak to the rest of those present, while you make the call."

Matt nodded and left the room with his evidence. Judge Harrison turned to Carl and James. "This ends today," he warned. "You have tried to destroy an amazing non-profit, ruin those who work there, and for what? I'm not sure. You are going to want to focus your time and energy on the criminal charges about to be brought before your client, Mr. Lloyd. And you will both leave Dr. Gerfallen alone or I will suggest harassment charges be added to the list."

He then turned and smiled at Ana. "Ana, it has been a true honor," Harrison informed. "You have shown grace above your years as you have been dragged through a senseless ordeal. I look forward to our future interactions and watching you blossom. Luke, you need to keep her, she is a rare creature."

"I have no intentions of letting her go," Luke promised him.

"Then I declare all charges are dismissed, this case is over," Harrison declared.

Chapter 20

JEREMY ENTERED ANA'S office at the house and smiled at her. They were finally meeting for his regular session. It was their first one since Ana had seen him talk. She could see how proud of himself he was, there was more confidence there. A lot of the doubt was gone.

"You were amazing," Ana said walking over and giving him a hug.

"The Board wants me to come to their July meeting and give the same talk," Jeremy told her. "They want the parents to hear it now."

"You should," Ana replied.

"I'm going to," Jeremy said. "I'm also re-thinking my major. I think I want to be a drug counselor or a school crisis counselor. I didn't really think how my story could help others. And it's really overwhelming, in a way, to have people think I'm this hero because I'm talking about it."

"What do you think about it?" Ana asked.

"I'm not a hero," Jeremy replied. "My parents, my brother, they are for forgiving me and giving me a second shot. What I am is lucky. I had people in my corner and not everyone has that, so I want to be that guy in the corner that helps them."

Ana was speechless for a moment. "You amaze me," Ana stated. "You utterly amaze me at times."

Jeremy blushed and looked away for a moment. When he did, he spotted a sketch hanging up on the bulletin board he froze. He didn't even hear Ana call out his name as he got up and walked over to it. All he could hear was the guy telling him that he got a new product and wanted Jeremy to try it, that the stuff was better than crack or heroin. He was only giving it to his favorite clients.

"Jeremy!" Ana yelled.

It finally snapped him out of his thoughts. "I…"

He heard his name yelled again and then the sounding of feet running. When he woke he was laying on a couch. A guy was kneeling in front of him checking his pulse while Laurie sat in the chair next to the couch. Ana was standing up watching him with fear in her eyes.

"Don't sit right up," the guy advised Jeremey when he tried to move. "Take it slow."

Ana handed Jeremy a glass of water from the coffee table. Erik got up and looked at Laurie. "His heart rate is back to normal, but keep an eye on it," Erik advised.

"I have my emergency kit with me all the time," Laurie told him. She then looked at Jeremy who was looking normal. "Honey, what happened?"

"I saw the sketch in Ana's office and it brought back memories and then it went black," Jeremy recalled.

"The composite sketch?" Ana asked sitting on the edge of the coffee table. Erik had caught Jeremy before he had hit the floor and brought him into the living room. Laurie had followed, ready to take control until Ana told her Erik had been a Medic in the military, then Laurie went into mom mode, letting Erik tend to Jeremy.

"Yea," Jeremy answered, he looked away not wanting to see how any of them reacted. "He was my dealer."

Erik looked at Ana and they both closed their eyes for a moment. "I'll call Alex," Erik told her as he left the room.

"What's wrong?" Laurie asked Ana.

"The composite sketch is of a man that targeted one of our students," Ana began. "Actually it was Cassie he targeted. She thinks it's one of her mom's former boyfriends. The police had her describe him to their sketch artist and now he's hanging up wherever the kids go."

"He didn't hurt her?" Jeremy asked. He had never liked the vibes he got from the guy but then his thought was all dealers were shady people.

"No, Erik arrived in time and the school was already alerting the cops and ready to intervene," Ana assured him. "It shook us all up."

"Look if I can help, I will," Jeremy told her. "I'll talk to the cops about what I remember. Where I met him, our meeting spots."

Laurie took his hand and smiled at him. "You keep amazing me," Laurie told him.

"Ana said the same thing," Jeremy blushed.

"Well it's true," Laurie replied. "Most people keep the past in the past. But you, you have embraced it, and use it to help others."

He blushed even deeper as Erik entered with a can of Soda. Erik handed him the soda and sat next to Ana then handed Laurie a business card. "This is Alex's business card, he's a detective and working the case," Erik explained. "He said to call when it's convenient."

"I'll write up what I remember then call him," Jeremy replied as he drank the soda. While he drank, Erik took his pulse again and nodded with approval.

"Red meat, some sugar, and lot's of fluids," Erik told Laurie. "Between the assembly and the shock of seeing his dealer it probably just overwhelmed him. So just monitor him for the next two days and if it doesn't happen again I think he'll be good."

"Thanks," Laurie said. She hugged Ana then shook hands with Erik. "Come on, let's get you that burger."

Jeremy nodded and followed his step-mom out of the house. Ana collapsed on the couch as Erik sat next to her. They were both silent for a moment, Erik took her hand and held it tightly. With her free hand she ran it over her face not even sure what to think.

"I want you to go over all our notes," Ana finally said. "Maybe you will see something we're missing. I know Sam and Toby are stuck at the moment because of technical difficulty they can't explain."

"Alright," Erik agreed. "I'm going to have to call this in, let Mike know he's selling unknown drugs to minors."

"It's when shit like this happens I start doubting my sanity," Ana laughed.

"You aren't crazy," Erik assured her lightly kissing her.

They heard a gentle cough and both looked up to see Jules there. She smiled and took the seat that Laurie had vacated. "So what's up?" Jules asked.

"The creep is also Jeremy's former dealer," Ana answered.

Jules raised an eyebrow and stared at both of them. "Are you serious?"

"I wish I wasn't," Ana replied.

Erik kissed the top of her head. "I need to go call Mike."

Ana nodded and watched him walk out of the room. "I'm going to have him look at everything we have," Ana told Jules. "This is just getting crazy. I talked to mom earlier and she wants to be up here with us to help but knows she can't because it will just make the dreams worst."

Jules took Ana's hand and held it tight. The curse wasn't just Ana's, it affected her entire family. The more family she was around or the closer they got to her birthday, the worst the nightmares became, the stronger Meph became. It was as if their blood gave him more power. But Jules and Luke could be by her because they weren't blood.

I'm going to tell Cassie," Ana continued. "She needs to know. She needs to be aware of what could be a danger to her."

"I think you're right," Jules agreed. "After this happening, I think she should know."

"Will she believe it?"

"Have Erik change into an Angel if she doesn't," Jules suggested.

"You just want to know what he looks like as an angel," Ana laughed.

"And you don't?" Jules teased.

"I've seen him in his form in the painting," Ana reminded her.

It was close to nine before Ana had a chance to talk to Cassie. They sat with their legs crossed on Cassie's bed in the carriage house. For an hour, Ana filled Cassie in on what it meant to be a Gerfallen, the curse, who Meph and Erik were, and all the crazy theories that her family had come up with over the years. Ana's tablet laid between them open to the shared folder that contained everything in it. Cassie was going through the hundreds of photo's that Sam had taken of the room they had discovered. Even the one's that didn't develop where on there. When Ana was done she watched Cassie as the teen went through the information on the tablet.

"So he broke one of their big rules when he approached me," Cassie stated. She was referring to Meph.

"Yes, and another because he alerted the others to his presence," Ana replied.

"You said that he could have been the dealer to one of your patients," Cassie realized. "Do you think he picked us in order to send us into your life? I mean, I know he started messing with me before you even started at Second Chances but maybe after you did he started aiming toward your path."

"Then the only good thing he has done is pushing you to me," Ana answered pulling the teen in for a hug.

"And Erik too," Cassie pointed out.

"Possibly, but he was still friends with Luke and might have ended up as my boss anyway," Ana replied. "But you are right in a way he has given me two precious gifts."

"You are such a sap," Cassie laughed but she liked these moments with Ana.

There was a gentle knock on Cassie's bedroom door. Cassie told them to come in and Erik poked his head into the room. "How are my two favorite girls doing?" Erik inquired.

"So you're an angel?" Cassie inquired studying him. "So does that give you like superhuman senses?"

"I know when people I'm close to are in trouble," Erik answered leaning against the door frame. "Before Ana called me that day, I did have a feeling you might have been in trouble. It was weak but the closer we get the stronger it gets."

"Wow," Cassie whispered. Then she beamed. "That's so cool. So who else knows about who you are?"

"Luke," Erik answered. He saw the surprise look on Ana's face. "The night his friend was about to jump from the ledge. I couldn't let it happen he was a good guy, deserved a second shot. So I jumped with him and transformed to catch him. Luke saw the whole thing, when I tried to erase it from his mind the attempts failed. It became our secret and we started to talk about things, him about the curse and me about what I do."

"And now you have us," Cassie replied with a huge smile.

"That I do," Erik agreed with a smile. He walked over and joined them on the bed.

Chapter 21

ANA AND ERIK had dropped Cassie off at Lincoln Center at 4. Before they left, Erik surprised Cassie with a silver necklace that had a pearl drop. She cried hugging him tightly before skipping off to the back doors. Tonight was her recital, Alex was already at the center and would stay back stage the entire night so no one had to worry about any unwanted visitors. Ana and Erik headed back to the house where they tried to get fifteen teenagers dressed and ready for Lincoln Center. Ties, collars, and pants had been checked over, as were the lengths of skirts and dresses.

Cassie's recital was the mark of the end of the school year, which also meant Ana's birthday was around the corner and Meph would start up again, and soon. Erik and Ana went back and forth over telling Terry, Martha, and the teens what was going on. They were both torn about if the teens should know and what would they believe. Helen and Luke met them at the house helping to load up all the kids in the vans and cars. Jill and her husband would be waiting at the center to help get them all organized. Terry, Jules, and Ana read off the list of who was going with which adult and that the adult named was their guide for the night. After what seemed like forever, they all piled into vehicles.

Erik parked the first van and Ana got out helping to open the doors on the side of the van. Five teens got out, all trying to act like this was just another boring activity but were actually impressed they were going to the famous music hall. Terry pulled up next and ushered the teens toward Jill. While he and Erik double checked everything she walked to the entrance where several of the faculty were standing as greeters.

"You got them all here?" Dana stated as she greeted Ana. "You need to write a book on how to deal with teens."

Ana laughed. "We had extra hands on call tonight," Ana replied.

"Your group is in the orchestra, center section, we roped out four rows with six seats in each," she told Ana.

She stared at Dana. "You didn't have to give us top seats."

"Ana, what you all have down with these kids, with Cassie, we wanted to do this," she assured her. "It was decided by a unanimous vote that they should get this experience, so enjoy the evening."

Ana passed the information on the adults as they began to herd the kids inside. They heard the comments about how young they all were to have kids that old, and how many, and belonged to who. The comments were ones that they had all heard before and were generally ignored. Ana, Jules, Terry, and Luke each took a row and began getting the teens into their seats. Erik and Martha each took seats on the ends so that adults flanked the teens on either side.

The teens were all excited as they looked through the playbill they were given. Luke looked at Ana and they both let out a sigh of relief. They had all feared tonight and what it would take to get the horde here in one piece.

"She's going to be so pumped," Ana told them.

"We'll get our seats then meet up at the house afterwards?" Helen suggested.

"Yes," Ana agreed.

Ana began her famous speech. "No cellphones, no snickering, no booing, no thumbs down," Ana reminded them. "You don't like something keep it to yourself until we're home. When Cassie comes on you better be the most well behaved people in this room or you will have a very long summer vacation."

She heard several parents tell their kids that the same rules applied to them as well. When she was done, Ana took her seat by Erik. He took her hand and squeezed it, he had been with Ana when they dropped off Cassie. You would have no idea that the girl was going to be singing her first end-of-the-year recital with how she was just skipping around. Ana was nervous enough for the both of them. Ana glanced at the program, tonight there would be five and she noted that Cassie would be last. Each student would be singing three to four songs of their choosing. Music accompaniment would be provided by other students from the school.

Before each student would go on, their coach would tell the audience a little bit about the student, about the selections they had chosen and then would thank the family for support. Most of the speeches contained the same themes, hard work, musical prodigy, and glowing words about the parents. When it was Cassie's turn Ana got nervous. Cassie didn't have a normal back story, and definitely not one fit for this audience.

"Last summer we received the most unusual phone call," Dana began. "A Judge that deals with families and adolescents called to tell us that he just signed-off on an adoption. The reason he was calling was when the young girl was asked why she chose her new mom, the girl simply said, 'because she will let me follow my heart,'. He asked what that was and she said opera. So he asked her to sing for him and she did, belting out Musetta's Waltz without any music. That young girl turned 13 in October and is our youngest student. She is also one of our happiest students, always skipping, we never know what hair color she is going to have. And when when you hear her sing, it's like hearing Angels. So please enjoy Cassandra Gerfallen."

The curtains parted and Ana thought that Cassie never looked more beautiful. Her curly blue hair was done up in a twist that left curls surrounding her face. The makeup was perfect for a young girl. The dress was tea length and done in a soft cream with pale blue brocading over it. The dress and makeup complimented her light coffee skin and reflected her innocence and charm. Cassie spotted her and gave her a quick smile before taking a deep breath.

Then her voice rang out in perfect clarity as she began to sing "Un Bel Di Verdrema" from Madame Butterfly. The aria began with no music, Ana knew that Cassie had nailed the first note when the famous music hall went silent. Erik looked at Cassie then at Ana with utter amazement in his eyes. Cassie had refused to sing to him, wanting to surprise him at the recital. Her voice was not like anything he expected.

The audience had been told to hold all applause until the end of each performance, but there was this hushed silence that was in awe of her. When Cassie finished her first aria, she waited for the musicians to come and start her second choice. Ana froze when she heard the quick tempo of the music. Erik looked at her when he recognized the song as well. For her second aria, Cassie had chosen "Faites-lui Mes Aveux" or the Flower song from Faust.

As the aria came to an end Cassie did a quick curtsey then smiled at the audience. "I asked Ms. Dana if I could explain why I chose the last song," Cassie told the audience. "You see my biological mom sold herself to pay our bills. When I was ten one of the guys beat her and held a knife to me, the cops brought me to this place where I would be safe. It wasn't a kids shelter but a house, one where we could get this second chance. I met this woman named Ana. She showed me what it was like to be loved, to be cared for, she taught me how to trust. Last summer I asked her to become my legal guardian, when I explained to the judge why her. I told him because she would push me, she would be hard, and she would make me try out to this school. He wanted to know how good I was at singing so I sang this next aria. And for me it now reminds me of the day that I finally got a family of my own. So thank you Ana."

Ana was biting her lip not to cry but it was all over when Cassie began to sing *Musetta's Waltz* from La Boheme. Ana couldn't help but smile watching her perform and made a mental note to send a video of the performance to the judge that had signed the papers. Erik squeezed her hand as they watched in wonder. The girl loved it, she loved to sing, to perform, to her it wasn't work. This was her joy.

He had arrived late yet no one seemed to notice him as he walked through the doors that should have been locked. He took a program from the counter then followed the directions to the upper mezzanine. Everyone was focused on the performance, he was able to walk to the back wall without anyone making a comment. Of course, if someone had noticed him he would have made sure that they had forgotten him.

From his spot he could see the entire theatre and found the section that the whelps from Bohlander House were sitting. Ana was in the first row of students with Erik Astrium. He watched the two of them interact, though when young Cassie appeared on stage his focus was drawn to her.

He was quite impressed with the talent coming from the young girl. Music had always been his one pleasure and hearing her sing was truly amazing. He couldn't help but smile when the young girl had selected a piece from the opera *Faust.* Perhaps his whispers had found their way into her mind after all. How would dear Ana react to knowing he was influencing her ward? He let the music flow through him as he hummed along with the angelic voice coming from the stage. He had thought tonight would be torture hearing young children trying to sing pieces meant for their elders. But this young girl, her voice was truly a surprise and refreshing to see someone so young enjoy the masterworks from long ago.

Chapter 23

THE FINAL WEEKS of June were hot and sticky. The weather was not helping Ana's migraine that had been coming and going for the last two days. Only Jules and Erik knew that this was no normal migraine, that this was one caused by Mephistopheles trying to get into her mind. The only time she got any freedom from it was when she was near Erik. Even with the migraine there was still work she had to do, helping run the house was just a small part. While she was only seeing Jeremy at the carriage house, she was still helping Luke go through intakes of new patients at one of their drug rehab facilities.

She also couldn't be glued to Erik twenty four hours a day, he had his own job and responsibilities to handle. The teens had handled the fact that Erik was living in the carriage house and sleeping in her bed with little problems. There were a few questions that were directed at Erik and mostly along the lines of if he hurt her he would be dead. Erik handled it all with warmth and assurances.

Ana sent him and Jules a text as she headed out of the house. With Cassie's recital over it was just normal pick-up at the end of the day. Rush hour had started, so the streets were filled with people starting to head home. Ignoring the pounding in her head she made a mental list of things that needed to be done between now and the last day of the school. They had two seniors graduating but invitations had gone out last week. So it was just going over finals schedules.

Dana and Cassie were waiting for Ana outside the school entrance. Dana smiled at Ana. "She did amazing," Dana informed Ana. "Tea and have her rest her voice. Her only finals are now paper finals."

"Martha put the kettle on as I was leaving," Ana assured the vocal coach.

Dana laughed. Cassie came skipping down the stairs and sailed past her vocal coach. She pushed her backpack up on her shoulders and beamed at Ana. "I rocked it," Cassie told her.

"That is what I heard," Ana replied. "Bye Dana."

Ana smiled as Cassie skipped alongside her. They joined the horde of people going on their way. Cassie was telling her all about the school day and how she had done on the history paper. She wanted to know if Erik was going to be at dinner or did he have another meeting. "He has meetings, they're finalizing the demo of the building he bought," Ana told her. They stopped at the red light and waited. "He'll base his office at of this new building while Rich will still be at the house on Long Island. Jules, Terry, and I are also going to have an office there so we are closer to you guys."

"Is Erik staying at the house?" Cassie asked. "Or, is he going to move out when things calm down?"

Ana put an arm around the teenager. "It's still a bit new for Erik and me," Ana answered. "We weren't planning on things to move as they have. But I do like having him around. Would it be okay with you if he stuck around?"

Cassie shrugged and was quiet for a few moments. The light turned green and they headed across the street. "We all like him," Cassie told Ana. "He's cool. He isn't fake and he has his limits, so he doesn't let us walk over him."

"Is there a but?" Ana inquired.

"Mom had all these guys coming and going, none of them stuck around," Cassie explained. "There might be a guy at the breakfast table but most likely he wouldn't be there when I got back from school."

"I know, which is why I wanted to do this slowly," Ana confessed. "I didn't want to throw him on you."

"I liked how he came rushing to my aid, that he stayed because it would mean another person to help keep us safe," Cassie replied. "Like he didn't come to sleep at the house just because of you. He came because he wanted us to be secure, and you are like a bonus."

Ana chuckled at the analogy. "So you are good with this?"

"As long as I still get time with you, then yeah, I am good with it," Cassie stated.

Ana ruffled her curly hair as they continued walking. As they made a turn Ana slowed until she came to a stop. Quickly she moved Cassie so that the young girl was behind her. In a low voice Ana spoke to her. "Don't say any names, do whatever I tell you, and don't scream."

Cassie nodded as they just looked around and stared at the scene in front of them. The jammed packed street and sidewalks of the Upper West Side were silent. It was as if time had just stopped, pedestrian's were frozen in their stride while taxi's were stopped in mid-turn. There were no voices, no car engines, not even the sound of dogs barking.

"You follow me, you stay holding my hand," Ana instructed her in a low voice. "You do not let go unless I tell you too."

"I won't," Cassie whispered. With her free hand she looped a few fingers through Ana's belt loops.

Ana took a deep breath and began to walk slowly, making sure that Cassie stayed behind her. Cassie knew how to make herself invisible from her years of hiding from her mom's men. She looked everywhere, as they walked at a snail's pace, waiting for him to come out of nowhere. This was like the night at the bar but only this time she wasn't drugged. And this time she had Cassie with her.

When they rounded the next corner, Ana stopped keeping both hands on Cassie. Mist was beginning to form out of nowhere. A faint burning smell filtered through the air as mist swirled around Ana and Cassie. Ana watched as a form began to appear out of the mist. He was tall, wearing a suit of all black, even the shirt under the jacket was black. The only color was the gray tie he wore. His hair was the color of embers and flowed in waves past his shoulders. His eyes were the color of coal and his smile sent chills up Ana's spine.

"So you are the whore that the realms are fighting for," the demon stated. "I was expecting a great beauty, like Helen of Troy."

"I heard she wasn't that pretty," Ana said dryly making the demon laughed.

"They are right about your wit though, it is impressive." He walked closer toward her.

As the demon got closer the smell of frankincense became stronger, he walked around her and Cassie, smiling as he studied Ana from head to toe. "I truly do not understand the realms' obsession with mortals. You are on this earth for such a brief time, the amount of energy we put into you is mind boggling."

"So stop," Cassie suggested ducking her head out from Ana's side.

"I see the kitten has claws as well," the demon stated. "You are raising her well."

"She is a minor, her soul is not yours," Ana informed him. She saw anger flash in his eyes. "Who are you?"

"Her name first," he hissed.

"No," Ana answered. "You let her walk away."

He laughed at that. "There is no walking away from this, my dear. There is no answer to find, no clue to uncover that will end this without blood being spilled."

Ana turned her back on the demon and looked at Cassie. "Go to the safe place," Ana whispered.

Cassie nodded. Ana turned and looked at the Demon. "She is a minor, she can not be manipulated or touched, nor can she be harmed in anyway," Ana stated clearly. "She walks free."

"How do you know of our Law?" he asked her. Though really he shouldn't be surprised that a descendant of Faust knew their ways.

Ana said nothing and gently squeezed Cassie's hand letting the girl know it was time to run. "What do you want?" Ana asked keeping him focused on her.

"I want nothing," the demon replied. "I just came to see what the fuss was all about."

"Well you saw, now can we go back to our lives," Ana inquired.

He laughed at that, a laugh that brought fear to Ana. Cassie bolted while the demon focused on Ana. "There is no getting back to your life," the demon informed Ana. "This is to warn you. War is coming. And your soul is the prize."

"Thanks for the warning," Ana answered, she kept her eyes on Cassie as the girl made it to the next corner.

The Demon stepped in front of Ana and smiled slowly. Then Ana heard Cassie scream and it almost brought her to her knees. Ana ran but was grabbed around her waist by the demon.

"You aren't going anywhere," he hissed in her ear. "How you know our Law, I don't know, but know this mortal. You are easy to break, easy to kill..." "Beelzebub!" A deep voice roared. The voice seemed to be all around them.

Pulling her tighter against him, Beelzebub whirled around looking for the owner of the voice. "Too afraid that you must hide from me?"

Ana gasped as she watched Erik appear. He was up in the air, his wings spread out as he hovered above them. He no longer looked like the man she knew, this was Lucifer, the Prince of Darkness as they called him. Erik had explained once that the Seraphim had four faces, or four forms. Erik was his mortal shell, in Heaven he was the Morning Star, the first to greet the dawn as it rose.

The being that was here now was Lucifer, the guardian of souls, the protector of Earth. His wings started-out white, where they met his shoulder blades but darkened to black at the tips. He wore a gray t-shirt and jeans, his brown hair was now long and black with piercing blue eyes. Beelzebub tightened his grip on her arm, she hissed as she felt her skin burn under his touch.

"Release her," Lucifer stated as he landed in front of them.

"I'm surprised you went for her and didn't save the innocent," Beelzebub stated.

"That is because Michael is getting her to safety," Lucifer answered and smiled when he saw fear flash in the demon's eyes. "The Guard is here, Beez. I would let go of her now unless you want it to be known that you started the war."

"Take the whore," Beelzebub stated. He then smiled as he shoved a claw through her torso then shoved her toward Lucifer. "Satan will hear of this."

"I hope so, if I were you, I would be afraid of who else will hear of this," Lucifer answered.

In a whirl of mist the demon was gone and Lucifer caught Ana as she fell to her knees. The blood was already soaking through her shirt as she looked at him with glassy eyes. "I have you," he assured her scooping her up into his arms.

Surging into the air, he soared toward the house, where Michael and Gabriel both were. He felt Ana slowly slipping away from him as the poison from the demon began to spread through her body. He landed in the back courtyard of the house to a speechless Terry who had been talking to Cassie. They turned when he landed.

Michael was the first to act and took Ana from Lucifer's arms. Once she was out of his arms, he transformed back into Erik causing Terry to let out a string of curses. "Which one?" Michael asked as he rushed her into the house.

"Beelzebub," Erik stated as he transformed back into his human form.

Martha let out a gasp when the Archangel laid Ana on the island. Terry began to get the kids out of the kitchen and upstairs. Gabriel, who had arrived with Michael, helped get the kids out of the room. He promised to watch over them as Terry called Alex.

"Ma'am, I am going to need bandages, hot water, and wine," Michael informed the house keeper. Martha nodded and quickly went to get the items. He then looked at Erik. "Shit, it had to be him."

"Is that bad?" Martha asked trying to keep her mind busy.

"Demons, like Beez, are born from chaos," Michael answered. "It means that his touch, his blood was poisonous to humans.

Jules came barreling into the room but Terry caught her around the waist as he returned to the room to get Cassie. "Jules, take Cassie and get her with the other kids," Terry instructed.

"She's…" Jules whispered.

"Juliana," Terry said gently. "Take Cassie and go be with the kids."

Jules nodded as she wrapped her arms around Cassie guiding the teen out of the room to go be with the others. Jules had never been good with lots of blood.

"Terry, go to Ana's room," Erik instructed as he began to think again. "You will see a green duffel bag. In it is my Medic Bag, get that and the black leather case under it."

"Anything else? A bible? Torah? Qu'uaran?"

"All three if possible," Michael suggested as he took one of the rags Martha brought him. "What do you need me to do?" Martha asked.

"How good are you with blood and gore?" Michael asked, as Erik cut through the shirt.

"I was an ER doctor for twenty years, and I saw my son overdose and die from it," Martha informed both of them. The two angels stared at her. "I've seen it all."

Terry came back through the connecting door with the two items. "Got them."

Michael began to give instructions while Erik took Ana's vitals. Her color was bad, her breathing was thready, and her pulse was weak. "The poison is in her system," Erik informed Michael.

"Terry, in the black case you are going to find a large vial," said Michael. "I need you to get it out and open the top. Martha you need to fill a syringe with the solution."

The two nodded while Erik began to examine the wound, Michael helped roll her on her side. "It didn't go all the way through," Erik noted. "That's a positive."

"If it went through?" Terry asked as he opened the bottle and handed it to Martha.

"Then we would be calling the morgue," Michael answered for Erik.

Alex came rushing in through the back door and stared at the scene in front of him. He then went for Ana's feet and placed a hand on the ankles as if he knew they would need to hold her down. Terry joined him at his end and they waited silently for instructions.

Martha filled the syringe. "Okay, what now?"

"Terry, hold her feet down with Alex, Michael take her waist, and I'll get her shoulders," Erik told them. "Martha you are going to inject the liquid into the wound. She is going to react and it will be violent. So the minute the last drop is out of the syringe - move! The four of us will hold her down until she passes out. Alex, Terry, if any of the foam starts running toward you don't touch it."

Martha looked at Erik and nodded. Taking a deep breath she walked to the island and studied the wound. It looked as if the skin had melted around the edge of the wound, there were char marks on the internal skin, you could see the bones and part of organs. Martha found a path that led to the deepest part and said a quick prayer before placing the tip of the needle into the worst part. The minute she began to release the liquid the blood began to bubble and smoke. Ana began to thrash but the three men held her down as Martha continued to release the liquid, when it was empty she took several steps back and watched.

Erik was pushing down on Ana's shoulders but he was also whispering to her. Martha knew he was speaking Hebrew and it calmed a part of her to hear the words. It had been a long time since she had heard Hebrew. She noted that it was also calming Ana down as the young girl struggled on the island.

"Tell me that wasn't Holy Water," Terry asked as he let go of her ankles.

"Not entirely," Michael answered. He looked at Erik. "You good?"

"Just have to clean it and stitch her up," Erik replied in a neutral voice. He had to think like a doctor, ignoring every emotion that was surging through him. "She survived the initial injection so she should make it through the night."

Chapter 24

ANA FELT AS though she had been run over at least a dozen times before being dragged throughout the city and all of it's boroughs. She had never felt so exhausted and drained before. She heard someone yell that she was awake and then she tried to move and pain washed over her. Another voice told her to stay still, not to move. Then a familiar and gentle hand touched her forehead before taking her hand.

"Shhh," Erik whispered. "Open your eyes slowly."

Ana listened and slowly let her eyes get adjusted to the light of her bedroom. Erik was smiling down at her and she swore she saw a tear roll down his face. "Hey," she croaked out.

"Hey, yourself," Erik answered with a smile. He brushed some hair out of her face and kissed her gently.

Erik heard movement in the hallway then moved aside as Cassie came running into the room. She stopped short at the side of the bed then smiled at Ana as she kissed her on the cheek.

"What happened?" Ana asked as she tried to sit up. Erik moved and helped her get into a more upright positions with the use of pillows.

"A lot," Toby answered from the doorway.

Ana stared at her brother who looked exhausted. Toby walked into the room and laid a gentle hand on Cassie's shoulder. "Go let Luke, Jules and Sam know, their in the main kitchen," Toby whispered to her.

"Alright," Cassie said. She squeezed Ana's hand before leaving the room.

"What do you remember?" Erik asked her as he sat gently on the edge of the bed. He took one of her hands in his, needing to touch her.

"I had picked Cassie up from her practice," Ana recalled. "We were walking back, then all of a sudden it was like time had frozen. A demon, you called him Beez, showed up."

"Anything else?"

"Cassie ran but I heard her scream, then you showed up, then I felt like I was on fire, then nothing," Ana answered.

"Cassie is fine," Erik promised her. "He used a few harmless minions to scare her. We got to her before any damage could be done. As for feeling like you were on fire that is because Beez stabbed you with his claw, thereby poisoning you."

"How long have I been out?"

"Well in reality, you have only missed a day," Toby replied.

Ana stared at him. "If you want detail into angel time travel stuff than you need to talk to Angel boy over here," Toby answered. "I don't do time travel."

"Beez broke many laws in what he did," Erik explained. "We utilized the fact he stopped time to our benefit. Gabriel went to Austria and brought Sam and Toby back while Michael and I made sure that your wounds were taken care of. When you were out of the woods, I took a trip to your parents to let them know what happened and brought them to your Aunt's where they will stay for the time being. Then, when it was all in order, we put time back in it's place."

"How long was time frozen?" Ana asked, though she was a little afraid of the answer.

"A day. No one noticed because we reset it at the exact moment before Beez froze it, so no one knows they missed a day."

"If you think about it, it makes sense," Toby replied.

"I'm okay though?" Ana inquired.

"Yes, you are perfect," Erik answered his words shakily as he touched her face again. He didn't tell her that the poison could still be in her body, that they weren't sure how long the antidote would work for. They didn't know what the long term effects of it would be on her.

Ana laid back on the pillows feeling drained already. Toby leaned over and kissed her forehead. "Rest," he commanded. He then looked at Erik. "You too. I'll hold down the fort, but you both need some real rest."

"Are you sure?" Erik asked.

"Dude, you've been up for like two days straight, you need to rest," Toby told him. "Besides, I can call our parents and let them know she's awake."

"Thanks," Erik replied.

"You saved my sister's life, you don't ever have to thank me," Tony said.

Erik said nothing as Toby headed out of the bedroom closing the door after him. Erik looked at Ana and kissed the hand he was holding before resting it against his heart. He thought he lost her, he had been afraid that in the moment she was gone he wouldn't be able to save her.

"I love you," he whispered.

"I know," Ana answered with a smile. "I love you too."

Erik kicked off his shoes then climbed into the bed next to her, carefully he pulled her into his arms and just held her. "I have never been this scared in my life," Erik informed her. "When he stabbed you, when I saw your face as he did, I thought he had killed me as well."

"He wanted to tell me that war was coming and I will never have a moment's peace," Ana recalled. "I don't think I was scared until I heard Cassie scream. And it wasn't for me, it was all for her. How did you get there so fast?"

"Michael," Erik replied.

"Oh."

"He knew the moment it happened and was here in a blink of an eye, as well as Gabriel," Erik told her. "I knew something was wrong, I had this feeling I couldn't describe. We found Cassie just as she got caught, Mike and Gabe took her back here and I went after you. You know, Martha is pretty handy to have around. Luke is giving her a raise."

"Why, how does she fit into this?"

"Because this house has officially become Angel Central and Marhta is in complete control of everything. She also helped flush your body of the poison," Erik informed her. She went to open her mouth but he silenced her with a kiss. "Go to sleep."

The following morning, Ana sat on the back porch with Luke, Toby, and Sam. She couldn't remember the last time the four of them had been together like this.

When she had stepped into the kitchen for breakfast she got a lot of hugs, no one looked at Erik any differently. Erik, Terry, Martha and Jules herded the kids off to school leaving Ana alone with Luke, her brother and her cousin.

"How you doing?" Toby asked as he looked at her.

"I just feel stiff more than anything," Ana stated. "The wound is nearly closed, and the area around it feels tight. But otherwise I feel better."

"Never do that again," Toby suggested. He ran a hand over his face. "Having an Angel show up out of nowhere to transport you to NYC because your sister might be dead is not something I want to relive."

"I don't plan on getting stabbed by a demon any time soon," Ana promised. "Mom seemed to be more relieved after we Facetimed."

"Seeing you helped calm them down," Toby agreed. He looked at Luke. "They like Erik, though are a bit surprised by his other name. But as dad said, nothing with this family should surprise him."

"Amen to that," Sam chuckled. "We both thought we were hallucinating when Gabriel descended into the lab. He just like melted through the ceiling."

"Sam actually commented that maybe we should invest in an industrial vent fan because the fumes must have been getting to us," Toby recalled and got elbowed by Sam. "I gotta say travel by Angel Air definitely has it's perks. No jet lag, no security checks."

Ana rolled her eyes. "I love how you all can keep to what is important," Luke stated.

"So what happens now?" Sam asked. "I mean what do we do?"

"With you guys here we'll sit down and talk about everything that we know. What Erik might know, Luke can listen and see if he can bring in any new ideas that we have not thought of. Then go from there," Ana answered. "Erik has been reading through everything we have gathered including what our parents found."

"Any idea what Beez wanted?" Toby asked.

"To shake me up, scare me," Ana guessed. "I honestly don't know."

They were all silent for a moment. "So you're dating the Morning Star?" Toby began.

"Really, this is what you want to talk about now?" Ana groaned.

"He's thirty eight in mortal years," Luke pointed out.

"I would like to know how you know who is," Sam asked, looking at Luke.

Luke sighed as he sipped his coffee. "Short story, I watched him go all angel to save a suicidal man," Luke answered.

Ana was about to say something but stopped as she became calm and centered. Erik was back. "He's back," Sam noted. He had felt the calm go over Ana.

"Wait, they can still do that weird mental link thing?" Luke asked Toby. No one could ever explain it but Sam and Ana had this connection where they could pick up on the other's feelings and even thoughts.

"Only it's more annoying now, they will just have entire conversations without saying a word," Toby stated. He studied his sister and his cousin. "Like right now, they are totally discussing who's going to make a fresh pot of coffee."

Ana turned and looked at her brother. "No we were not," Ana informed him.

"We were talking about how to talk you into re-filling our cups," Sam added and jumped off the step before Toby could hit him.

"I see we've returned back to normal," Jules stated as she came outside. Sam slid behind her as if using her as a human shield.

"Are you all back?" Luke asked Jules.

"Yea and we are calling for an all adult meeting in the library," Jules informed them. She walked over to Ana as she stood and pulled her into a tight hug. "You need to learn to trust more people with this, you don't have to keep protecting everyone."

Toby snorted. "Good luck getting her to listen."

Ana flipped-off her brother and headed into the main house. Erik was filling his coffee mug as she walked by him. He grabbed her around the waist and backed her up to the counter, smiling he bent down and kissed her. They ignored the comments from her brother and cousin. When they parted, Erik rested his forehead against hers.

"I needed to remind myself that you are here," Erik said softly. "That you didn't die."

"Still here," Ana smiled. "But whatever reminding you need I'll be happy to help."

"And now I just lost my appetite,"Toby groaned, as he walked back out of the kitchen.

Ana laughed as she walked with Erik to the library. The library was one of the few rooms where the history of the place was completely intact, the only modernization were the four computer tables that were placed in each corner of the room. Terry was bringing out one of the huge white boards that they had on wheels while Jules was at one of the computers.

"What's up?" Ana asked as she flopped into one of the overstuffed chairs. Her body still felt exhausted from what happened yesterday.

"This is a war summit meeting," Martha informed them. "Terry, Alex, and I had a conversation last night about how you guys need some new perspective so we are going to go over everything that is known whether it is fact or theory."

"We will also warn you that the kids want in on this," Terry added as he grabbed some dry erase markers.

"No innocents," Erik stated as he took a seat on the ottoman next to Ana's chair.

"No offense to your rules, but the other side took Cassie," Alex reminded them. "So clearly they are ignoring them."

Ana laid a hand on Erik's knee. "They're right," Ana replied. "If it keeps them safe then they need to know."

"Alright, but you all have to follow what I say because this can get out of hand real fast," Erik warned. "There are going to be certain things that don't leave this room, and the kids can not hear."

"That sounds fair," Jules agreed.

"So where do you want us to start?" Ana asked Martha and Terry.

"This curse," Martha suggested as she found her seat. "What is it and why were Angels in my house?"

Sam, Toby, Ana, and Luke all looked at each other. It was Ana that spoke. "Our family is descended from Johann Faust," Ana stated. She waited to see if the name was familiar.

"Wait, as in the magician from the Marlowe play?" Terry asked, it was one of the few plays that he liked from college. "He made a deal with the devil for ultimate knowledge."

"That would be him," Ana answered.

"He's real?" Terry couldn't believe this, the curse was based on some guy who was supposed to be fiction. "Shit, my high school English Teacher would be all over this."

"Yes," Ana replied. "The play, opera, novel, they are all based on legends of him."

"So how does this tie into what happened?" Martha inquired.

"Faust doesn't go to hell, God takes pity on him, feels that Mephistopheles or the Devil had tricked him, so his soul was saved and he was sent to Heaven," Ana explained summing up the ending of the tale. "The problem is that Meph, as we call him, believes he is owed a soul and because my charming ancestor signed in blood it has cursed all who come from him."

"Does it apply to all of you or just specific members?"

"The first born of each generation," Sam answered. "It was my father and now it's Ana."

"Kind of like the Slayer, but worst," Terry noted.

"Yea, except I don't get any cool powers or a stake," Ana pointed out.

"How does the curse last for 500 years?" Martha asked before they lost track of the conversation.

"The contract was signed in blood by a willing participant," Erik explained. "Which means that the soul to replace the one lost has to be willing as well. Needless to say, none of Ana's ancestors have been as eager as Johann was to sign away their soul. Instead, they've been running from it or trying to end it."

"What does it entail?"

"When the first born reaches adulthood Meph begins the torment," Ana explained. "He haunts your dreams at first. Then he starts showing up in the reflection of mirrors, just a quick glimpse so that when you look again he isn't there. He whispers to you, taunts you with your fears, promises you your heart's desire."

"What about those that came before you?" Terry asked already afraid of the answer.

"They either committed suicide to end the torment or died in accidents or from illness," Toby answered. "And before you ask: they committed suicide to get away from Meph not to join him. Which makes their soul ineligible to be held to the contract."

"I am going to take a large guess here and say that Ana is different," Martha noted.

"For a variety of reasons," Erik replied. "Ana is the first born for this generation. In her family line, she is also one of the few females to survive to adulthood, and the first to make it to thirty. The other few either died in childbirth or from disease. Because she is not male, Meph altered some of his usual tactics."

"Why?" Terry inquired.

"Because, in his mind, the female mind is weaker, not as strong as a male's," Erik answered. Ana narrowed her eyes at him and he saw Toby coughing into his coffee. "I said he thinks that way, not me. Trust me, babe, if I thought that way I wouldn't be here."

"Nice save," Sam commented.

"Back to why Meph changed tactics," Jules suggested.

"First, we have rules on what is and not allowed with specific genders," Erik explained. "You can seduce but not coerce, or force. Which we know he broke that rule with Ana. Meph underestimated her and by the time he realized this she had identified his pattern. As a result, her mind was able to build walls against him."

"Okay, so Meph feels he is owed a soul because God took Johann from him," Terry summed up. "And for over five hundred years he has been having this huge temper tantrum because he want's what he was promised."

"Pretty much," Toby stated.

"So why did God intervene to begin with? Why redeem Faust?" Martha asked as she reminded herself to go see her rabbi.

"That's a good question and one you will have to ask him," Erik answered. "I honestly don't know. There were the rumors that God favored Johann above all other mortals for some reason. I've met Johann a few times and was never impressed with him."

"The play mentions your involvement in this," Terry recalled. "That you and Beelzebub helped Meph with his tricks." Terry left out the part about having a secret crush on Lucifer.

Erik chuckled. "The play mentions a lot of things," Erik replied. "During the fifteen hundreds, I was down in the underworld doing my Prince of Darkness thing and dealing with the chaos that both Meph and Johann had caused. With Meph and Beeze up here toying with Johann, someone had to help manage the souls."

"Is there a reason we are shortening their names?" Martha wondered out loud.

"Names of Angels and Demons have power," Erik explained. "If we say their full name they will know we are talking about them. If you shorten them then they can't know for sure and there is the side benefit of pissing them off."

"Does that go for the ancestor?" Terry asked

"Don't use his last name and we're fine," Erik answered. "I don't trust him, so I don't want him knowing what we are talking about. With mortals, you have to use their full birth name for them to know."

"Ok, so we know why Meph wants Ana," Martha stated. "The question is, what are we doing about it? I mean how does this whole cycle end?"

"Usually, with a contract on a soul, it ends when the soul is delivered to the Devil," Erik informed them. "Meph is claiming that because no soul was given the contract is still good."

"How does he obtain a soul?"

"It has to be willingly given," Erik answered. "Suicide, coercion, deceit, those will make the contract void."

"God claimed that Jo was deceived so wouldn't it make the contract void?" Alex inquired trying to remember the play and what Ana had said about using full names.

"Meph claims otherwise and God has been mute up to this point," Erik told them all.

"So what do we do?" Terry asked running a hand through his hair. "I mean, Ana is not giving up her soul."

"We all agree on that point," Toby stated. "Since the night that he almost raped her we, as in the Gerfallens, made a promise that we would end this battle. The monastery I bought in Austria, it was Johann's old work shop. We have each read everything ever written on Johann and the tales around him. We've also read countless books on demonology, on angels."

"I have a contact in the Vatican that helps with information from time to time," Sam added.

"Brother Thomas?" Erik inquired.

"Bald guy who is the church's demon expert," Sam asked.

"That's him," Erik said with a chuckle. "He's good."

Terry took a moment while Erik and Sam discussed the brother and began to make columns on the whiteboard for the information that they knew. "Ok, so you've done research, what has that told us?" Terry asked as Alex walked over to the whiteboard to start making more columns.

"In a dream with Meph we learned that he is not an angel," Ana told Terry.

Erik stopped Terry before he wrote fallen Angel. "He is a half demon not a Fallen Angel," Erik corrected him. "Let's have this conversation now. Demons are born from chaos and hate. They have never been an angel, never had wings, and cannot be redeemed. Fallen Angels are Angels, they were born out of order, peace, and love."

"So what makes them a Fallen Angel?" Martha asked.

"They chose Chaos over Order," Erik said simply. "They believe that humans should be controlled, herded. The only way to do that is with fear of damnation. So they chose to leave the heavens."

"Does that mean you believe we should be controlled?" Terry inquired

"I fell for another reason entirely. I fell so that humanity would not suffer from my pridefulness, so that consequences of me disobeying orders would be mine and mine alone."

Ana held up her hand before they got off topic. "Are you sure Meph is a half demon?" Ana asked Erik and he just raised his eyebrows at her. "He took me to his home or whatever. We were in this dining room, a mix of modern and antiques. It's where I saw the painting of you, which drew my attention away from him."

"I bet he had to love that," Terry noted.

"He was annoyed," Ana agreed. "But he was also distracted by it. I at first thought the painting was of him, he then informed that he was born with no wings. He told me he was born damned."

Erik stared at her for a moment, he had read that line in her notes and wondered what it meant. "Repeat that again, for me."

"He said that he was born without wings, that he was born damned."

"Those were his exact words, 'he was born damned'?"

Ana nodded. Erik stood up and began to pace. Erik snapped a finger and they all got quiet. "I need to run this by Mike, this could be huge," Erik realized.

"Why?" Toby asked.

"In the beginning, there were strict rules over who we could mate with," Erik explained. "And there were reasons for that. Angels could only be born from peace, hope, love. Whereas, true demons could only be born from chaos and hate. Even if you had one parent who was an angel you wouldn't have wings. If one parent was demon your poison wouldn't be lethal to mortals. It has always been believed that Meph was half demon. That his other parent was divine, that this was the reason Satan chose him to be his voice and physical embodiment."

"Would he have certain abilities that other demons wouldn't have?" Martha asked.

"Meph can appear as a human," Erik answered. "You can see why this would be an advantage for Satan. You can also see why such a pairing would be outlawed. Even the most powerful of Demons, like Beez, can't fully transform into humans. Beez eyes give him away. Asyriel, another powerful demon, can never hide his horns unless he wears a hat. But Meph, he has none of these problems unless you are sensitive to vibes then he will make you uncomfortable."

"Demons that could walk amongst humans without being recognized for what they are," Terry summed up. "That would be terrifying."

"You are wondering if Meph is something else aren't you?" Sam realized. "Why?"

"No one, creature or human, is borned damned," Erik stated. "Regardless of the type of baby, they are born innocent. There are some demons that aren't bad, they hover over the line of good and evil. Just like some angels chose to fall because they believed people should be herded, because they were jealous of human free will."

"Is that why you fell?" Alex asked. "So we could have free will."

"I have free will," Erik stated. "I believed all should have it as well.";

The room was silent. Erik let out a long sigh. "My father has Three sons," he began. "I am the first born, born of God. I am his left hand, his enforcer of his will. Jay is the middle and is the Right hand. He is the peacekeeper, the teacher. Azza, he is the youngest, his role is to watch over all but can not interfere with the will of man."

"Being the enforcer you saw the good and the bad," Alex noted.

Erik nodded. "I believe that no one should be herded, that all should be free," he answered. "My father likes order, he likes knowing all the outcomes, and free will can interfere with that."

"If Meph isn't an Angel, demon, or a mix of both, then what is he?" Ana asked trying to get them back on task. She knew how off topic these conversations could get."

"That is the million dollar question," Erik answered. He was wishing he had paid more attention to Ana's dream at this point. "Mike will have more resources than we do."

"Ana said something about there being more than one painting," Sam realized.

"Yes, it belongs to a series, I believe there is one maybe two more in the series," Erik tried to recall. "Why?"

"Perhaps they will give us clues," Sam answered. "When I talk to Brother Thomas I'll see if he'll let me into the Archives."

"A trip to the vatican?" Ana asked.

"Where else will I find them."

"If they aren't there, I might have a few suggestions as to where they could be," Erik told him.

"What do we do with all this information?" Martha asked. "I mean, we keep coming up with theories but what do we do with this?"

"If we can find away to show that Meph is in the wrong, that he is breaking laws that have kept all of us safe for millennia, then the central authority would declare the contract null and void, and/old remove Meph's powers would be voided," Erik explained. "Which means Ana and those that come after her would be safe from him. If he starts a war over this, his punishment would also be the loss of soul and the contract would be ripped up. The more information, the more questions, the more theories, means all the more we have to show the High Court that he is breaking the laws of the spiritual world."

"The High Court?" Alex asked.

"It's exactly what you think it is," Erik told him. "The major heads of all the world religions. And by heads I don't mean religious leaders like the Pope."

"Oh," Alex whispered understanding that Erik was talking about divine beings.

"I'll make arrangements to go to the Vatican," Sam said getting up.

"I'm going to stay here and work with Erik on research," Toby decided.

"What do we tell the kids?" Terry asked.

"Let me think about that," Erik replied. "I'll field the questions."

"This should be fun," Ana sighed.

Chapter 24

THE FOLLOWING DAY, Erik found Cassie on a bench in Central Park. The teen had managed to slip out at dismissal without anyone noticing. The only thing that was keeping Ana from calling the National Guard was that Erik sensed Cassie was okay. So he left Ana for Toby and Jules to handle, while he went to find her. Erik shoved his hands in his jeans as he headed toward where the young girl sat. When she looked at him she knew she was in trouble but said nothing as she made room for him to sit down with her.

Cassie waited for him to say something but he didn't. He just relaxed against the bench watching the people who were walking through the park.

"There was this older woman who had the apartment across from my mom's," Cassie began. Erik looked at her when she spoke. "She loved opera and classical music. Her place always smelled of cookies, cigarettes, and lavender. All the kids in the building, we called her grandma. She was always watching some kid when a parent worked late, or schedules got crossed. She never took any money for it either. You would think some would take advantage of the kind old woman who watched kids for free. But no one did."

"They respected her," Erik stated. "They knew she understood their situations, that she didn't judge, ask questions."

"She never pried into anyone's lives," Cassie said agreeing with what he has said. "She knew Harlem. Knew if we were left alone what would become of us. She wanted better for each one of us."

"Did she get you into opera?"

Cassie nodded. "It started out one night a week when my mother's usual spot was booked and she had to 'entertain' at our apartment," Cassie replied.

"We would have hot dogs, mac and cheese, and baked cookies. I would fall asleep to whatever opera recording she had on and then in the morning mom would pick me up and we would get pancakes at the corner diner. When mom was sober it was great. She could actually get work as a cleaning lady, she would sing, we would go to the library and the park."

"She tried."

"Until she stopped trying," Cassie said bitterly. "I was seven when she stopped caring. When Grandma slid me a spare key to her apartment to use when I got scared or I needed a place to be alone. I thought I would never need it, but I hid it in my backpack because I didn't want my mom to find it. The last place she would ever look was the backpack."

"You ended up using it," Erik commented. Cassie nodded. "You don't have to tell me this."

"I do, because you need to hear about how Meph came into my life and tried to destroy my world," Cassie answered. "My mom fell in love. Most likely it was lust and the fact that he gave her an unlimited supply of alcohol, but to mom it was love. She told me things were going to change, that he was going to be our ticket out of scratching out a living. I just needed to be a good girl and do what he said. Not be the troublemaker that she thought I was."

Cassie paused taking a deep breath. She was telling Erik things that she had never told anyone before. "The moment he entered our apartment I knew he was evil," Cassie recalled. "He wore this pristine black suit, with a white suit shirt, and red tie. His hat matched. His eyes were this weird hazel like they were every color in the world but were still just hazel. When he would smile at me it would be slow, like he was trying to creep me out. That night was the first night I ever used the key. Every time he stayed over I would wait until they were fighting or in her bedroom and slip out, always to return before breakfast, not that either would have noticed by that point."

She didn't realize that Erik had gotten her water until the water bottle was pressed into her hand. "The night I arrived at Bohlander House, Alex lied about what happened," Cassie stated. Erik stared at her, surprised by her admission. "I don't even know if Luke has read the full police report because it was sealed immediately."

Erik didn't want to ask what happened, instead he waited, knowing if she had come this far she would tell him. He watched her drink the water bottle, she was thirteen years old but you forgot that when she talked at times. She seemed so much older, like she had already lived a half a dozen lifetimes and in a way he felt like she had.

"He referred to himself as Lou," Cassie remembered as she looked at Erik. "He would bring expensive things for us. Take her out places, pay our bills as long as she wasn't being trouble. I had just turned eight, I was doing homework at the table when he walked in the room. He sat down and watched me do homework, it was so creepy having him just watch as I worked. I finished my homework and put it in my bag when I noticed the key was missing. In that moment I knew. He just smiled when I turned around and stared at him. He didn't like that I was leaving the apartment, a young girl should know better than to be sneaking out at night. I asked him for the key, told him it was for a friend who always lost hers. He laughed and said he knew where I went and that if I kept going there he would ensure that I would never be safe again."

"So you agreed?"

Cassie laughed. "I was eight and I thought I could take on this large man," Cassie answered. "I told him that it was mine, he didn't have a right to take things from me. He told me I should be careful how I spoke to him, so I turned to walk to my bedroom and he grabbed me. He might have been stronger but I was little and nimble. When my mom walked in the door she saw him draw a knife on me. And all she said was that she needed to take a nap and we should keep it down. The man had a knife to my neck and she asked that we kept it quiet."

She stood up and walked to the tree, leaning against it. Needing to feel something that was alive. "He assured her that she wouldn't hear a sound from us. She went to the bedroom and shut the door. He told me he could cut out my tongue if I wasn't quiet and just to reassure me that he could, and would, he ran the blade over my tongue. Not hard enough to draw blood but enough to let me know he was serious. He dragged me by the hair to my bedroom and tossed me on my bed. When you're eight you don't think of rape, of being molested. You are more worried about staying in the lines, how many broken crayons you have. You don't think about the dark stuff other than the typical monster under the bed."

"He's not a typical monster under the bed," Erik stated as he clenched and unclenched his fist. "Did he?"

"He tried," Cassie whispered. "I clawed, kicked, squirmed, screamed, not caring if he cut my tongue out, or if I woke my mom up. He was too busy trying to keep me still to finish the deal, as he would say. I managed to roll off the bed and grabbed the knife I had kicked out of his hand. He lunged for me just as I pointed it at him. I stabbed him in the heart, Erik. Thankfully a neighbor had called the police about the noise, and Detective Alex came through the door at that moment, he saw me naked, saw him half dress, standing by the bed. Meph was staring at the knife in his chest and do you know what Meph did? He laughed and said 'you little bitch'. He didn't fall down dead, he wasn't even bleeding. Alex shot at him, unloading a clip, he didn't die. He ran off, leaving no blood behind. Alex wrapped me in a blanket and ran me across the hall to Grandma."

She took a moment to breath before finishing. "The EMT's were already there waiting while Alex's partner arrested my mom. It was all a blur and then Alex brought me to Bohlander House, I slept with a knife under my pillow that night. The next morning I handed it to Ana and told her I didn't need it anymore."

Erik was speechless. He didn't know what to say, getting up he walked over and gently pulled her into a hug. He rested his chin on top of her head and just held her. "I will destroy him if he ever touches you or speaks to you again," Erik whispered.

Cassie knew he meant it too. "He told me that I had a destiny to fulfill, that I was ruining his plans," Cassie remembered. "I forgot about it until all this came up. Until Jeremey recognized him as his former dealer, until I met his asshole buddy in the streets. Then I remembered that he told me I was a pawn in his game. I have a feeling Jeremey was a pawn in his game as well. That he pushed at Jeremy and me so that one day our paths would cross with Ana. I bet if you look at Jenna you will find him there as well."

"The thing is Cassie, he underestimates what a pawn can do," Erik told her, making her look him in the eye. "He sees a pawn as weak, a way to get him into position to win. But a pawn can also block, giving the other players time to mount a defense. Maybe you started out as a pawn in his game, but now you are far from just a weak player."

"I'm thirteen, what can I do?"

"Well for starters you can start by listening to rules," Erik suggested and she groaned. "A simple text saying: "Hey, I needed some down time," would have been enough."

"And would Ana have let me go?"

"By not telling her, you never gave her the choice," he pointed out. "

"I am in so much trouble aren't I?" Cassie sighed.

"You are," Erik agreed. He put an arm around her shoulder. "Let's go home. The three of us are going to have a good family conversation, you are going to tell Ana what you told me. Then we will have another 'war meeting' as Terry likes to call them, and then I am going to hug Alex and thank him for saving you."

"Terry might get jealous," Cassie pointed out as they started to walk toward home.

"I think he'll survive," Erik informed her.

It was after eleven when all the teens were in their rooms and the house was quiet. Erik filled them in on what he and Cassie had talked about. He also told them about Cassie's theory, that perhaps Jeremy and herself were pushed toward Ana. That they were pawns in Meph's game as well, tools to control Ana. Now, Erik wanted to know who else was here that had a tie to Ana.

"Alright Terry, how'd you end up here?" Erik asked.

"I was interning at Second Chances," Terry answered. "Luke and the others wanted to expand into family therapy. The program was close to my dorm, and it would pay for my transportation when I worked over the suggested hours for the internship. It was win/win. I didn't know any of them, just that they were on the list of internships for my masters program. I read up on them, liked what they were doing and didn't care that it wasn't a full-paying internship, like some of my other classmates got."

"Why psychology?"

Terry leaned back in his chair and sipped his wine. "My parents are Catholic. Went to mass and confession every week," Terry replied. "My three siblings and I went through CCD, my older two went to Catholic school from first grade all the way through."

"Why not you?" Erik asked.

"New board of trustees for the school came in, wanted to be more selective, raised the tuition costs and lowered the sibling discount," Terry said. "My parents couldn't afford the four of us to go, since my two older siblings were in high school they kept them in so they could finish with their friend. My younger sister and I went to Public School. We like to brag that we got the better end of the deal. Anyway, I always had questions. Drove my CCD teacher and parents crazy. It wasn't just about faith, but everything. Why are some people bullies, why are other people the bullied, why do some people not want to help others, while others would. Dad figured I'd become a lawyer or a philosopher."

"And you became neither," Alex chuckled.

"He is very happy about that too," Terry replied with a smile. "I took psych as an elective in high school. And that was it. I could ask all my questions and not be told to be quiet, I was encouraged to ask and come up with answers. I knew it's what I wanted. Then when I came out to my parents regarding my orientation, which of course they already had figured it out, I learned they had been seeing a therapist. They were conflicted between their faith and who I was. The therapists helped find a balance between the two important things in their life. Their faith and their family. They had done this before I came out, so that when I was comfortable with who I was, they would have all the answers they needed for their church friends. It blew me away."

"Do they still go to church?" Jules asked. It was important but she was curious.

"They left their church, dad got in a fight with the priest when the guy went on a rant that 'my kind' would go to hell. Dad told him that in the bible it says to love thy neighbor not hate them. They now go to a methodist church a few blocks from their apartment, have a new group of friends and are happier. They have accepted Alex since I brought him home, treat him like they do my sister-in-law and my other brother's girlfriend."

"So no connection to Luke prior to internship or with Ana or Jules," Toby noted.

"None," Terry agreed. "Trust me, Alex and I have been trying to figure out if I somehow ended up because it was part of some plan. And I didn't meet Jules or Ana until they interviewed for Second Chances."

"What about you?" Toby asked Alex.

Alex took a long sigh before he began. He looked at Erik when he did. "The guy you dove off the roof for, when you showed Luke your other side," Alex began. "He's my uncle. He told us how some angel saved him and we went along with it because it woke him up to get the help he needed. I had heard him talk about his friend Luke but we never met, not until that day. We talked over bad hospital coffee while we waited for word on my uncle, I was staying until my aunt showed up. I was a foot cop working to becoming a detective. Luke wanted to work with cops so that the kids in this new project of his would learn that we aren't all bad. We exchanged cards and began helping each other out."

"How is your uncle doing?" Erik asked.

"Amazing," Alex replied with a smile. "He took that second chance you gave him and embraced it. It forced both of them to take a good look at their lives, they realized that the stress wasn't worth it. They moved to northern NJ, it's a cute town with mountains and lakes. My aunt is the town lawyer basically, and Uncle Don is a high school gym teacher. He holds workshops during sports seasons for parents and kids on not getting carried away, not putting added stress onto students. My cousins like it, so it's all good."

"For being a fallen angel you tend to do more good than evil," Toby joked and got smacked upside the head by Ana.

"Well you know what they say about us," Erik replied with a grin. "Angel on the street, demon in the sheets."

Toby groaned as the rest laughed. "I deserve that," Toby admitted.

"Any word from Sam?" Jules asked Toby.

"He landed and checked into the hotel where he is staying in Italy," Toby answered. "He's tired and cranky."

There was a knock on the swing door of the kitchen and Martha entered. "How's six degrees of separation from the asshole going?" Martha asked as she put a kettle on the stove to boil.

"As of right now, Terry is our only outlier," Toby stated. "So come join us so we can now drill you with questions."

Martha laughed as she got her tea mug ready then, leaned against the counter. "What do you want to know?" Martha asked.

"How did a former ER doctor end up here?" Erik asked.

"That is more complicated than you would think," Martha sighed. "I worked in Hell's Kitchen, or whatever they are trying to call it now. I got all the crazy things, I could calm down someone high on anything, get them to let us do our jobs. I loved it. I worked two twenty four hour shifts and then was on call for one 12 hour shift. That gave me four days of doing nothing but being a mom to my three boys and a wife to my husband. We lived in a small middle class neighborhood on Long Island. My husband was a public school principal. We had our problems, but what family doesn't. My youngest, Miles, he never seemed to fit in. He tried to following whatever trend there was. We would tell him to be himself but I don't think he knew who he was. He was always trying so hard to be whatever everyone else wanted."

"A lost soul," Erik whispered. Martha looked at him. "Sorry. Souls are judged, not as harshly as some would think or like. But they are judged. Actions and the reasons for that action are all considered. For example, if you killed someone. Why? Was it out of revenge? In cold blood? Or self defense? We take it all into consideration. The dad who killed his daughter's rapist isn't necessarily going to be thrown into the pit of despair."

"Wait, you really have a pit of despair?" Toby asked, almost bouncing with glee. He also caught the movie reference.

"No, but we joke that we should because a lot of souls are disappointed that we don't," Erik admitted.

"And the lost souls?" Martha asked as she poured the water into her cup.

"They could never find their place on earth and when they come to be weighed the balance never moves," Erik replied. "It's rare. We don't cast them aside, instead we let them choose, they are one of the few groups that can move between the areas until they find where they belong."

"So they finally find it?" Martha asked with a soft voice.

"Yes," Erik said. "How did he die?"

"Drugs," Martha answered. Terry squeezed her hand when she sat down next to him. "I knew the signs, my husband didn't want to believe me. But I saw it enough at work that I knew what the dark circles meant, the erratic behavior. He wore long sleeve shirts in the summer, would be depressed and withdrawn one day and the next he would clean the whole house from top to bottom. I knew that he needed to want treatment for it to work but I still made him go. Three rehabs, countless therapists. He told me once that he liked the high because it made him forget who he was. As I mother, it killed me. What could I say to that?"

Jules got up and handed her a tissue, then got one for herself and Ana. Martha wiped the tears before continuing. "I got a call at work, a cop I knew. He was called to a party, a non- responsive male. He knew it was my son, he wanted to tell me so that I wouldn't be on the floor when they wheeled him in, he wanted him to be cleaned up first before I saw him. I called our Rabbi, my husband, his brothers. I wanted us all to be there. My husband refused, he had a school board meeting, he couldn't make it. My older two boys, one with a six day old newborn, the other was in the middle of a meeting with a judge, they dropped everything to be at the hospital. The hospital made sure that his body was released so he could be buried the next day. I waited until we were done with our five days of mourning, then I filed for divorce. I didn't ask him for a cent, I didn't want any of his money. I just wanted to be away from the man who couldn't come say goodbye to our son."

"You are an amazing woman," Erik whispered laying a hand on hers.

Martha smiled and sipped her tea. "On the anniversary of his death, my Rabbi contacted me, he knew that I needed to do something with my life instead of just going through the motions," Martha replied. "He heard about Bohlander House, that they were in need of a house keeper. He researched it, called Luke for information, informing him he might have a candidate. He thought that with what I went through, what my sons went through watching their brother spiral out of control, that I would do good here. So I researched it and I realized I needed this place as much as it needed me. I told Luke and Terry that. I didn't interview with them, I interviewed them."

"She blew us away," Terry admitted with a chuckle. "She came in told us she would work Monday to Friday morning, she would spend Friday to Sunday in Long Island with her sons. She would cook, help keep some semblance of order, and she would bake cookies, teach them how to cook, bake, and clean. She would be their shoulder to cry on when the world was cruel and kick them in the butt when they were being dumb. Luke told her he would call her with our decision, she told him there was no decision. She wasn't applying for the job, she was taking it. I think Luke might still be afraid of her."

They all had to laugh at that. Martha just blushed as she sipped her tea. Erik looked at her. "So you never had contact with anyone from Second Chances?"

"No, I heard of their drug program, we had talked about it when Miles checked out of the third one," Martha admitted. "I didn't realize the program was connected to the house until I researched the house. But we never applied, I didn't meet anyone until I went in for my interview."

"Alright, so two with no previous connections to anyone who is part of this drama," Toby noted. "The rest of us had some sort of contact with at least one player."

"Then you have Cassie and Jeremy," Jules reminded Toby. "I doubt we are going to find that every kid who went through these doors is somehow touched by Meph. But it is interesting that the two she is closest too were. While she is not close with Jenna, Jenna has caused major drama for her."

"I'll talk to her parole officer and advocate tomorrow, show them Meph's picture see if they recognize him," Alex replied. He felt his work phone vibrate. "I have to head out."

"I'll fill you in later," Terry told him.

Alex nodded after a quick kiss headed out of the room. Terry rolled his neck. "Well to bring some good news to the table, I got a call from the zoning board and the city. The city approved the construction for the attic."

"So the apartment is a go?" Jules inquired with a beam.

"Not just one but two apartments," Terry answered. "Our contractor drew up plans for two amazing apartments. Luke thought that one would be the best because then it's done."

"You mean I won't have to play third wheel to the love birds?" Jules teased looking at Ana and Erik.

"It becomes an option to everyone," Terry answered. "Alex is probably going to spend more time here. He may not fully move in until upstairs is done. We both agree living out of a suite would be a bit much."

"The fact that he's a cop and the kids not only love him but trust him should tell you that he's awesome," Ana pointed out. "I'm just glad some good is happening right now."

Toby squeezed her hand. "Only a week until your birthday," Toby assured her. "We can beat this. We have angels on our side this time."

"And a house full of teens who know how to fight," Martha added. "Trust me, the whole 'fighting your demons' thing has taken on a new measure with them."

Erik ran a hand through his hair and looked at his watch. "I need to make a call," he told them. No one asked.

"I'll keep an eye on her," Toby promised.

"I'm right here," Ana pointed out.

"And your point?" Toby asked looking at her.

Sighing, Ana laid her head on the kitchen island. Martha just patted her hand telling everything would be alright.

Chapter 25

IN THE MORNINGS, once the teens were off to school, Toby would run with his sister. At first he groaned and complained about it, but at the same time he enjoyed it because it was one of the few times it was just the two of them. Between being a mom to Cassie, helping raise fifteen teens, dating an angel, and handling the curse, Ana didn't get a lot of down time. In addition, running through New York was not a hardship either. The historian in him loved it as he wondered what happened on the street corner they just crossed, or wondered what was the original plan behind an ornate building.

They neared the park and he followed her as she headed across the road. Several people waved as they ran and he realized they knew her, they probably wondered who he was, but no one stopped to ask. This was New York, they didn't need to hear your life story. He knew Ana took pity on him because she slowed her pace down to a jog and he was breathing easier.

"Thanks," he mumbled as they neared one of the quieter sections of the pond.

She just rolled her eyes at him and kept going. He stopped first when he saw the man sitting on the bench feeding the ducks in the pond. Toby grabbed Ana's arm and pointed.

"People get mugged when they point," Ana sighed taking her earbuds out. She looked at where he was pointing and sighed. "Let's go talk to him. He'll be annoying if we don't."

"You realize who he is?" Toby asked, his voice filled with excitement.

"Yea, I told you that I met him right?" Ana inquired.

"But that's... I mean... holy shit," Toby stammered fumbling for words.

"You are totally geeking out on me aren't you," Ana realized and sighed as she put her hands on her hips. Rolling her eyes again she headed to the bench where the old man sat. "We need to talk," Johann Faust stated.

"Then we'll talk," Ana replied. She motioned to her brother. "That is my brother..."

"Tobias Johan Gerfallen," Johann finished for her. "Don't look so surprise, I have read up on my family, Analiese Gretchen Gerfallen."

Ana winced at her full name. It was only used when she was in trouble. Johann stood up looking around the busy park. "Not here," he informed her. "Too many ears."

"The house," Toby stated. "Mike, uh, he increased security."

Johann raised a white eyebrow at him. Ana nodded. "Just follow us and don't freak out by ..."

"Your advancement in technology?" Johann supplied.

"And stop finishing my sentences," Ana suggested.

Turning, she headed back in the direction from which they had just come. She could hear Toby and Johann talking, she wondered if either of them realized they were speaking Austrian. Which was probably a good thing since they were discussing alchemy theories and experiments. Ana shot out an arm to keep Johann from walking straight into the busy street, he stumbled but steadied himself as he watched the traffic lights and the cars. Thankfully, the one good thing about New York was that people were use to crazy, so no one paid much attention to him looking around with wild eyes.

Toby filled him in on the traffic light, cars, and other advancements that had occurred over the last five hundred years. "And we thought the printing press was a big deal," Johann mumbled as they approached the house.

Ana jogged up the stairs and opened the large double front doors. She let them in before setting the alarm again. Martha was on errands with Terry while Jules met with the contractor over their office space. This was the last week of school so the kids were all gone for most of the mornings and afternoons. They let their ancestor walk around the space as he mumbled to himself about all the wonders he was seeing. Toby talked to him at times answering the questions he asked. Ana headed into the main kitchen and put the tea kettle onto boil. Then poured herself and Toby more coffee.

When the two entered the kitchen her ancestor just shook his head as he walked to the table by the windows. "I have watched as the world changed, but to see it up close," he whispered.

"I doubt you came here to talk about progress," Ana replied.

"Ah yes," Johann replied. He wiped his eye glass lenses on his shirt then placed them back on his face. "When I met you in the park the first time, Analiese, I was skeptical of all of it. The curse, you, even young Erik. How could something I did five hundred years ago still be causing chaos now? To me, our contract was simple. The Devil would get my soul if God deemed my soul unworthy when I died. God deemed me worthy and my soul was spared. To me that was the end of it."

"You didn't know that because it was signed in blood it would go to the next person in your family," Toby theorized. "And I doubt Meph would explain that little catch."

"It was my name on the contract why would I think of such a thing?"

"Because you were dealing with the Devil," Ana suggested and poured the hot water into a mug. She added a tea bag to it and brought it to Johann. "Just let it steep for a few minutes. When it gets to the color you like then pull the bag out. Like a strainer but it can be thrown away." "Ah, I see," Johann said as he studied his tea. Once it was too his liking he took the bag out and Toby handed him a small plate for it. Taking a sip he sighed at it. "Such a simple thing and it brings back so many memories."

The connecting door between the main house and the carriage house opened and Erik walked in. He stop short when he spotted the three of them at the table. Ana stood up. "Johann Faust this is Erik Astrium," she introduced them.

"Your wings are stunning," Johann stated as he went to reach for what Ana and Toby didn't see. Johann stopped himself from touching. "Sorry, I did not mean to offend."

"Johann sees my angel form because he is deceased," Erik explained. "He sees my wings whereas you can not."

"That makes sense in an odd way," Toby realized.

"Can we get back to why he is here," Ana sighed before she lost control of the conversation. Erik sat down next to her. "We met him in the park on our run," she informed Erik.

"Ah," Erik answered.

"You said you wanted to talk to us, that it needed to be somewhere safe away from prying ears," Toby stated to his ancestor.

The old man nodded and stared at the steam rising from his tea. "On October 31st of the year 1501 I made a deal that I believed would bring me great knowledge, joy, and happiness," he began. "I thought that all my questions would be answered, that I alone would have absolute knowledge. I was young, naive, foolish, and those ideals have brought more harm than any of the good I had dreamed of."

"What did you hope for?" Toby inquired.

"What every young genius wants: to be recognized for their accomplishments, to cure disease, leave a legacy of knowledge. The only legacy I have left behind is one of blood."

"And now you want to change that?" Ana stated. She wasn't sure what to think of the old man sitting before them. Whether she could believe him on not, she rubbed her temples as a headache formed. Erik laid a hand on her thigh giving her comfort, letting her know he was there.

"I do, whether you choose to believe my intentions that is up to you," Johann replied.

"We've read all the stories about you and the curse, but as for actual records there isn't much from the 1500's," Toby explained. "We believe that our blood ties are through a nephew of yours."

"Fredrick Faust?" Johann asked, Toby nodded. "He was my son, not nephew. My brother and his wife raised him as their own child."

"In all the stories, they never spoke of a surviving child," Erik pointed out.

"According to stories you were part of my fall," Johann reminded him. "As we all know, stories don't always tell the truth, they sometimes hide it amongst the words."

"Gretchen," Ana realized all of a sudden. "Her infant she killed, she didn't really kill it, did she?"

Johann closed his eyes at her name then nodded slowly. "My first victim," Johann replied. "She was the younger sister of a dear friend. We fell in love, but her mother and brother disapproved of our match. To show his loyalty to me, Meph as you call him, whispered to Gretchen. Supplied her with sleeping tonics to give her mother for us to be together. We talked of running away together, I could get a position at any university. We could be together. The last night we were together, the potion Gretchen was given killed her mother. It destroyed Gretchen. To everyone else it appeared her mother had died in her sleep, but Gretchen knew it was the potions that Meph had been giving her. I watched helpless as she began to lose her mind."

"Did you know Meph was involved?" Toby inquired as he refilled all their mugs.

"Deep down I did, I didn't want to believe it fully," Johann admitted. "I was too obsessed with my studies and stolen moments with Gretchen to think he was involved. I only learned of her pregnancy when her brother confronted me. He informed me that he had sent her to a convent to live, where she would be cared for, where she could live away from the gossip. We fought and I killed my best friend. The news that I killed her brother, it shattered Gretchen."

"The story tells of her drowning her infant," Ana said gently.

"It does, and I was told that as well," Johann replied, there was sorrow in his voice. "The truth is a bit more amazing than the story. Gretchen attempted to drown Frederick and believed she had. A nun found her in the courtyard with Frederick in the fountain. Frederick gave out a shuddering breath, the nun acted fast. My brother's name had been given if Gretchen could not care for the child. The nun told everyone the child had died, but in truth arranged for him to be brought to my brother and his wife. My brother never approved of my thirst for knowledge, he was a farmer and blacksmith. He lived on the outskirts of Salzburg with his family."

"The abbey?" Toby asked excitedly as if it was coming full circle now.

"I purchased it later in life as a place to study," Johann confirmed. "I left it to my brother and my son. That is getting ahead of ourselves though." Johann paused and sipped his tea before going on. "When I learned of my son's apparent death I went to Gretchen. Begged her to let me rescue her from death, she had already been tried and convicted. Meph had kept me busy so that I could not be at her trial. She refused, I think it was the first time that she had a moment of clarity since her mother's death. I think in Gretchen's mind death meant peace. No more guilt over the deaths she caused. I watched her execution feeling numb and hopeless. I went on a several night and day drinking binge. When I woke up I was in a different place, Meph decided I needed away from my mortal realm."

Toby and Ana stared at him not sure what to say or think. "So we're direct descendants," Ana stated. "Not through your brother but from you."

"Did you know?" Toby asked Erik.

"There was a theory that the infant had been saved, but no it is not mentioned in the files that I have read that Frederick is Johann son's," Erik answered. "If Michael knows, which I am sure he does, then he never shared that information with me. When Gretchen appeared before me to be judged, I didn't press her mind, you could see how fragile she was."

"Where was she placed?" Johann inquired. "I never found her."

"She lives among the angels as one of their handmaidens," Erik answered. "She is at peace and cherished for her kindness and gentle nature."

"She deserves all the peace that she can get," Johann whispered. He sipped his tea before starting again. "I learned the truth in my old age, after I bought the abbey. My brother knew I lived there and would visit, he would mend what needed to be mended, and would bring me surplus from his fields. I knew his children, his wife. Frederick always had questions, wanted to know of my latest theories. My brother and his wife would always watch with trepidation when we talked."

"Did they know about your deal?" Ana asked.

Johann shook his head. "No. No one knew what I had done. I think my brother feared the truth, feared that his son was following in my steps for absolute knowledge," Johann admitted. "That perhaps he would go too far in the search."

"When did you learn the truth?" Toby inquired. "That Frederick was your son."

"I was old, rambling about in the abbey," Johann remembered. "I didn't want doctors or nurses looking after me, I wanted to finish my work. Frederick and his siblings would check on me from time to time. My brother had died already, their mother lived with Frederick's sister. She always worried about me, no wife or children to look after me, so she made sure her children did. Frederick was a lawyer by then, a brilliant one at that. He came to me one night, it was winter. He made sure the fire was going in the hearth, that there were no drafts in my rooms. And he told me the truth."

"Did he always know?"

"No," Johann answered. "My brother told him on his deathbed. He explained how ill Gretchen had been, that I knew only after it was too late to do anything. That all this time I still had not known that he was my son. I expected resentment, hatred from the lad when he told me. Instead he gave me forgiveness, understanding of the way things were. He would have been denied so much if it was known he was a bastard. Even after I told him of the deal I had made when I was younger than him he still looked at me with forgiveness. He told me that he could think of several people he knew that would sign away their soul for the chance to know everything."

"That's how you were redeemed," Erik whispered. "No wonder Meph is so furious."

"What do you mean?" Toby asked turning to look at him.

"Frederick is a victim of Meph and Johann," Erik said looking at the old man. "His death has been told inso many different ways. His mother tried to drown him as an infant, he is rescued by a nun and raised by family without knowing. When he learns the truth instead of hatred and rage, he offers forgiveness. Real forgiveness, he didn't blame Johann or Gretchen for what could have been. Instead, he understood the reasons for it, he didn't harbor ill will. Because of that, because in a sense, he was the most wronged that was still alive, he redeemed Johann. We always wondered why he was able to pass through the gates without a trial, but now it makes sense."

"What about Gretchen?" Ana asked.

"She accepted what she had done, while she didn't totally blame Johann, she accepted her part as well, she didn't offer redemption, she offered acceptance for herself," Erik replied. "That is different."

"Alright, so now that we know our family history, what do we do with it?" Toby asked. "None of this tells us how to break the curse."

"Meph's connection is stronger because it's direct," Erik explained. "Which is why he can hold so much power over you. He would also be furious that a human screwed him out of soul. Because Frederick offered forgiveness to Johann it allowed God to offer redemption to him. This isn't about being tricked out of a soul, like it has always been thought, this is revenge against the bloodline that he thought he would have control over."

"But he does have control over us," Ana pointed out. "It's in a roundabout way."

"Not the way he wants, he want's servants to do his bidding, to increase his range," Erik answered. "You, and those before you, have not been willing participants to his plans. It's why suicides don't count. Your uncle killed himself to get away from Meph not to join him. And at this point I'm not sure if a soul would satisfy him."

"You think he is after something more?" Toby asked.

"Five hundred years to plot and plan revenge could lead to him wanting more than what he feels is his just due," Erik pointed out.

"You said that he would want servants, people to do his bidding," Ana recalled. "Johann being forgiven had taken this from him."

"Each soul we collect is ours," Erik answered. "Like our own army and we are the general with the Devil being in charge of all Demon's and Fallen Angel. While numbers are important so is the individual. In this case, Johann would be considered a prize for any army. He is willing to do whatever it takes, he was willing to sell his soul for knowledge. That could be twisted, garnished, abused. He could have been a commander of his own unit."

"So Meph want's someone who could replace Johann or increase his position," Ana theorized.

Toby drummed his fingers on the table. "We've been looking at the deaths as a sign of Meph pushing them too far," Toby stated. "You know, he wanted to see how far he could push them before they would agree and give his soul."

"You are now wondering if there is more to it," Ana realized. She recognized the look on her brother's face.

"He was seeing how strong they were," Johann answered for Toby as he realized what his descendant was thinking. "If they were strong enough to keep him at bay then they would become a strong leader. The more the individual pushed back the harder he would push. And the more fragile they became the more fun he would have."

"Exactly," Toby said hitting the table with his hand. "If they are no use to him then he is going to push them over the edge so he can move on to the next candidate. I'm guessing there is a rule somewhere that he can't mess with more than one generation at a time?"

"In a sense," Erik replied. "If you were allowed to go after multiple generations at one time, think of the chaos. So limit it to one and it reduces the strain on the line."

"So he is pushing harder at me because I'm able to block him better?" Ana inquired.

"You also got away from him," Erik replied gently. "So he wants you even more."

"Lucky me," Ana sighed.

"You are also female," Johann stated. They all looked at her. "You can do something that your male relatives can not. You can carry life. Not only would you be a cunning warrior but you could bear him his own army of half demons-half humans."

"An army that could walk the earth without being noticed," Erik whispered.

Chapter 26

ERIK WALKED JOHANN back to Central Park. Night had fallen and while the park might be technically closed Erik knew they would be allowed to pass through. They walked in silence, Erik watched as the older man took in everything as they walked. The world had changed so much since Johann was alive. The twentieth century had seen a huge advancement in technology, trying to grasp it all was daunting.

"The formula that I was working on," Johann began. "Meph wanted it."

"Why?" Erik asked as they neared the entrance of the park.

"What do you know of him?"

Erik shoved his hands in his pockets as they walked. "He is the physical incarnation of Satan. He is his voice, he is no angel, but he is not all demon, he can hide elements of himself that other demons cannot. He is thought to be more myth, a literary creation more than an actual being."

"A fact that always drove him crazy," Johann replied. "You received the credit he believed he deserved."

"I never asked to be mistaken for Satan," Erik stated annoyed. "I never asked to be portrayed as the devil, to be feared."

"And you think he understands that?" Johann asked. "He hates you, because in his mind you have taken everything from him. He should be the Prince of Darkness, the one all fear, that was his role, his destiny. You have taken that from him and now you have taken Ana from him."

Erik went to argue but saw the look on Johann's face and kept his mouth closed. "Our mutual acquaintance was meant to be an angel," Johann informed the angel. He held up a hand before Erik could interrupt. "I said he was meant to be, not that he was born one. His mother was an angel and at first it was believed so was his father."

"Believed?"

"She lied," Johann said simply. He watched the shock of understanding flash over Erik's face. "She had fallen in love with a mid-level demon. When she learned she was with child she lied, she was ashamed of her lover, of how weak she was to have fallen for a demon. If she had told the truth there would have been forgiveness, choices for both of them. But she lied to your Father, she also lied to her lover telling him she had been raped by another. Her lies damned the child even before it was born."

"How do you know this?" Erik inquired.

Johann smiled sadly. "Absolute knowledge. It allows me access to information that others do not have."

"Does he know that you know?"

"I have not spoken to him since the moment my soul was judged," Johann admitted.

They stopped at the spot Johann used as a gateway to the spiritual realm. "How do we end this?" asked Erik.

"A soul, willingly given to save her, one out of love, honor, and understanding," Johann stated. "A soul so pure that when offered has no other ulterior motive."

"Is that the only way?"

"There are always other ways," Johann pointed out. "Find his reason for doing this, bring forth strong evidence of his wrongdoings and it would end with a trial and judgement. Either way a war is coming, Meph is bringing it and he does not care how many are lost in the process."

"He thrives on chaos and grief."

"He does," Johann agreed. "Keep my descendants safe."

"She is my salvation, my future, she is my heart," Erik admitted. "She has seen all there is of me and accepted it all. She is unlike any human I have ever met."

"It is why he fears her," Johann answered. "I believe that this will be the last time I am permitted to cross the barrier until after this is settled. I will send word through Michael, if I think of anything else that will help."

"Thank you," Erik replied.

"Do not thank me," Johann warned. "If not for me this would not be. I created this with my foolish thirst for knowledge. Keep them safe."

Johann paused and looked back at the Morning Star. "The poison is still inside of her," Johann noted. "You have contained it but…"

"A demon's poison can never be fully removed," Erik finished for him. "I know."

"She is a fighter," Johann replied.

Erik nodded and watched as the old man slowly vanished. He headed back to the house thinking over what Johann had told him. Michael would need to know some of it so that he could fact check the information. Erik didn't want to take any chances and his thoughts on trusting Johann were completely mixed.

"I see he has learned how to use the gateways," a voice stated behind Erik.

Erik had felt him a second before he spoke. "You aren't going to be able to talk your way out of the mess this time," Erik informed Mep.

"I don't plan on talking my way out of it," the demon stated. "I plan on showing everyone how foolish they are."

"I have no time for this," Erik said. He turned and began heading back toward the house.

"Yes, go back to the little woman," Meph taunted. "Assure her that all will be right, that she isn't an abomination like her ancestor. Promise her you will keep her safe when you know that you can't."

Erik said nothing. "You know I am right," Meph continued. "You know that when I have her, when I make her mine, she will realize that you failed her in every way possible. And I will cause her more pain than I did your precious Lilith."

Meph laughed when he saw Erik's body become rigid. "Does she know how you failed your first love? Or have you spared her from that, knowing it will destroy her? That you almost tore the world apart for another? What would your precious mortal think when she learns that you couldn't even protect your own kind?"

Meph walked toward Erik. Circling him as he grinned, each word was hitting Erik harder than any physical blow. "I cannot wait to have Analiese all to myself," Meph whispered in his ear. "Breaking her is going to be the greatest thing I have ever done."

Erik whirled and grabbed Meph by the throat. The move was so fast that Meph couldn't defend himself against Erik. Smoke billowed from where Erik's hands gripped his neck, the sandy blonde hair of Erik began to lengthen and turn black. His eyes changed to the color of the midnight sky as his raised Meph off the ground. Meph tried to break the hold but he couldn't even move a finger. Of the two, Erik in his true form was the stronger. And the being holding him by the neck was Lucifer.

"Do not forget your place, half breed," Lucifer snarled as his wings took shape leaving his mortal shell behind. His wings carried them into the night sky. "I am the Prince of Hell, my name brings fear to those who believe, I am everything you wished to be, but I am more than you could ever be. You are a mere errand boy for the Devil. I am the first born of God. I am the Morning Star! You are trivial!"

They soared high above the buildings. "This is my realm now," Lucifer continued. "And you are wreaking havoc up here when you have no authority. So this is your official warning: leave this realm, leave those under my protection alone. The slightest whisper, a glimpse in the mirror, and it will mean you are officially breaking our laws."

"And you'll do what? Declare war?" Meph spat as he tried to break the hold.

"I will bring the heavens down upon you, I will raise the fires of hell, and I will destroy you."

For a moment fear ran through Meph's blood. "You would never."

Lucifer laughed and it caused every hair on Meph's body to stand on edge. "I was young and foolish when you first challenged me," Lucifer reminded him. "I am no longer young and foolish. I act now with the power that is bestowed upon me. This is your one and only warning."

"Lu, buddy," Meph scrambled, using an old nickname. "Let's talk about this. We can come to an understanding. We can do the Persephone thing, I get her for six months, and you get her for... agh!"

Lucifer tightened his grip. "There is no talking, you agree and accept my warning and conditions, or it's war."

Before Meph could even speak Lucifer dropped him from his grip. He was plummeting to the ground below and quickly summoned his own powers to slow his fall. When he looked up to the sky he saw that Lucifer was already gone.

Ana sat on the back step with Dennis. He was graduating tomorrow and was nervous, his speech was chosen to be read at the ceremony. While the rest of the house was getting ready for bed, Ana sat with Dennis trying to help calm his nerves. When they heard the faint sound of wings flapping over their heads they looked up to watch as Erik landed before them. He was already transforming back to his mortal form when his feet touched the ground.

"That is so cool," Dennis whispered.

"Nerves?" Erik asked as he sat down on the other side of Ana.

"Stomach is in knots," Dennis admitted and sipped the tea that Martha had made for him.

"It's only human to be nervous before a speech," Erik assured him. "You see it as weakness, that you shouldn't be nervous when speaking to a large audience. When in fact, it takes a great deal of courage to stand up before people, to tell them something personal, knowing that some won't hear it. Some might snicker, and some might fall asleep. It is those that do not care for others that are able to do such a thing with no nerves. Even the greatest orator will admit to nerves just before they take the stage. Being nervous isn't a sign of weakness, Dennis. It is a sign that you care, that you want to inspire those before you. You will do great tomorrow."

"Wow," Dennis replied. "That was… thanks. I think I can sleep now or attempt to sleep."

"Terry is going to wake you at eight because you have to be there for nine," Ana reminded him as Dennis got up to go inside.

"Joe is sleeping in with Chad," Dennis told her. "Because he knows I had to set my alarm for eight."

"Ok," Ana replied. She waited until Dennis was inside before looking at Erik. "What happened?"

"I ran into Meph on my way back," Erik answered running a hand through his hair. Adrenaline was rushing through his body. "I gave him an official warning. Which means the moment he breaks it we can act."

"Is that good?"

"It is, we will be justified in acting," Erik explained. "Since this is my dominion while I am here I can warn other demons away, if they ignore it then I can act. So by him showing up and threatening you and your family's bloodline it actually benefited us."

"Because now he knows that if he breaks the warning you can go after him," Ana realized. "We know he won't listen. I also don't want you getting into trouble because you are helping me."

"You are worth the trouble," Erik whispered, kissing her softly. "The kids are worth the trouble. I do not regret anything that involves you, Cassie, or the teens."

Chapter 27

Vatican City

SAM WAS EXHAUSTED. His eyes were bloodshot from countless hours of reading, his hands ached from all the transcribing he had done. He was no closer to the second painting here than he was back in New York City. Running a hand through his hair he let out a frustrated sigh, he was suppose to call them with a progress report, but he had nothing to give them. How was he going to tell Ana that he had nothing?

Sam nodded to the other scholars as he walked the halls of the Vatican library. He was never one to give up but right now he wasn't sure how much more he had left in him. Taking the stairs down toward the restricted area, he handed the guard his pass then went through security. Once he was cleared, he headed toward a narrow corridor moving past an old gilded mirror.

"I wonder if he thought he was really helping you out by killing himself," a voice said from behind him.

Sam froze for a moment. There was no one else in this section but the guard. "Maybe he didn't care," the voice went on. "I mean, I got to be honest, your father has some pretty disturbing thoughts."

"If he had them then it was because you put them there," Sam answered. He turned and stared at his reflection in the mirror.

This was the first time that he had ever seen Mephistopheles without Ana being around. He wore a red suit with a white shirt under it, a black tie and pocket square, and a black hat with a red band. There was an arrogance to him which didn't surprise Sam. Sam noted that you couldn't really make out any features of Meph's face, as if the creature kept that hidden for reasons unknown to him.

"Am I as impressive as you thought?" Meph inquired.

"Actually, no, you're not," Sam answered as he folded his arms across his chest. "I mean, I figured you would have horns or something, but really the look, it's kind of lacking."

Rage flashed in Meph's eyes. For a moment Sam thought the creature was going to lash out, but he watched as Meph calmed himself. "You would have been a worthy opponent," Meph declared. "You know, I honestly thought, after your dad dumped you by his suicide, you were going to be my next soul. I think I was surprised as all of you when it turned out to be your cousin."

"You thought it passed onto to the males as well?"

"She's only the fourth female to be born first in your family, there hasn't been a lot of testing of the theory," Meph pointed out. "God, the first two females were so weak. I thought they were going to turn themselves in for witch-craft when I first showed myself to them. Which would have not done me any favors. The third had potential. However, between plagues and childbearing, none of them lived long enough for me to sink my claws into them."

"While this conversation is so engaging," Sam began dryly. "There are things I need to do, so what do you want?"

"Ana at least lets me prattle on for a bit longer," Meph noted. Letting out a long and dramatic sigh. "Fine, I will get to the point. I have a deal to offer you."

"Oh this is going to be good," Sam sighed.

"Hear me out before you say no," Meph stated. "Your family is so quick to say no."

"Gee, I wonder why," Sam replied. "But I'll listen."

"See, not so hard," Meph said. "Here is my deal. It's a one time deal, expires at midnight, it will never be offered again."

"Just tell me it already."

Meph smiled slowly. "I offer you an exchange," Meph began. "I forget about Ana's soul and she can lead a boring mortal life with no interference from me."

Sam waited for the second part. "And what do I have to do?"

"Well you will have two options," Meph informed him. "First, you sign your soul over to me and you will receive the painting. The second option is: your first born child in exchange for the entire series of paintings."

"And if I don't?"

"Then I will take your soul after my victory over Lucifer and his pals. Therefore, your soul will still be mine."

Sam ran a hand through his hair as he thought over what Meph had just offered. It wasn't a deal at all and Ana would kill him if he offered his soul in exchange for hers.

"Does the first born child option ever get chosen?" Sam asked more out of curiosity than anything else.

"You would be surprised."

"I'm not accepting the terms," Sam finally said.

He went to walk away but a hand grabbed his arm. Pain radiated down it, he turned and saw Meph's arm coming out of the mirror.

"You are all fools!" Meph yelled. "You think you can honestly defeat me, that you can actually win!"

"We must have you scared and desperate if you are showing yourself in the Vatican," Sam stated.

He was flung into the wall across from him. Sam watched as the creature emerged from the mirror. Smoke billowed around him as he walked toward Sam. "The paintings will tell you nothing," Meph informed him. His voice echoing off the walls and vaulted ceilings. "There are truths that no mortal can dare understand. Secrets that would shake your core of understanding. This is a game you will not win."

"This isn't a game!" Sam yelled. "These are lives that you are messing with!"

Meph went to strike him but his arm froze as another voice began a chant in Latin. Meph whirled around and saw a monk standing there, hissing as he slid back into the mirror, vanishing in it. Brother Thomas ran to where Sam lay on the floor and helped him stand up.

"Did he touch your skin?" Thomas asked as he guided Sam to a chair.

"No, he touched my sleeves," Sam answered. "I've been wearing long sleeves since Ana's attack."

"Smart," Thomas replied. "I'm still going to check."

Sam nodded as he pushed his sleeves up so that the Brother could examine his arms. They were both quiet while the monk examined him. "How did you know?" Sam finally asked.

"A mutual friend of ours called me, told me to be aware that Mephistopheles might try to get to you," Thomas explained. He stood up and took a seat next to Sam. "You are clear of any poison or wounds. Anyway, I informed the guards to alert me at the slightest disturbance. Our sensors picked up a heat change in the mirror."

"He's always moved through mirrors," Sam sighed. "It's one of the ways that he torments my cousin."

"There were old superstitions that mirrors were gateways to the soul," Thomas recalled. "It seems our enemy uses that as a literal means to target people."

"We have him worried."

"I would agreed with that," Thomas nodded. He then stood up, motioning for Sam to follow him.

Thomas took out an old ring of keys which surprised Sam because most of the the library had changed over to digital key cards or thumb prints and retinal scanners. They were silent as they walked toward the back of the large room. This was where relics, rare artifacts of the early church, and art, not on display, were kept. It was where Sam had hoped to find mention of the paintings.

There was a door that blended in with the wall around it. He inserted an ancient old key that unlocked a hidden panel. Thomas stepped in front of it and touched his hand to the scanner. Then a retinal scanner. Sam watched as Thomas pressed a button on the panel than spoke into the panel. "Admit also Samuel Faust."

Sam was startled at the use of his old family name. The door swung open only long enough for the two of them to quickly move through it. They headed down a dimly lit hall before coming before another door. Thomas took the key ring out again and inserted three keys turning them each one at a time. Pushing the door open, Thomas let Sam enter first. Sam knew that he had not seen less than half of what the Vatican held, but this room was like anything he had ever seen before.

"What is this room?" Sam asked, as he stepped farther into it.

"The Faust archives," Thomas answered.

It took a moment for the words to sink in. Sam turned slowly to the man he had called friend. "I'm sorry, what?"

"Let me explain," Thomas started, knowing Sam was uncertain. "I had no clue that this room even existed until a year ago when the keys were handed to me."

"You mean that this archives has existed for years?" Sam asked trying to keep his temper in check. "Does my family know?"

"You are the first to learn of it's existence," Thomas admitted. "Look, I wasn't even told what this vault contained when I was given the keys. It took me six months going through what was in here to realize what it contained."

"Could this have saved my father?" Sam asked quietly. "The church has had this for how long?"

"Early 1600's is my earliest guess," Thomas answered.

Sam whirled and looked at him stunned. "And we are only being told about this now?"

"This was not my choice, Sam you must understand," Thomas began. "Bringing you here, showing you this, it could cost me everything."

"Then why show me?"

"Because if we can save your cousin's life and soul, save your family, then I will risk it all."

All the anger vanished in Sam as he realized what Thomas was willing to risk. He ran a hand through his hair then looked at his friend. "Do you know why this archive has been hidden away?"

"Nothing official, just that our role is to observe, to gather information, to watch," Thomas replied. "That their historical value to the church and the laity may not understand the importance of the archives."

"And just let all of this sit here when it could possibly help us?"

"That was my thought as well," Thomas agreed. "I had a fight with my superiors earlier today. They did not want you being allowed access. But I told them that when there is battle in New York City, when a demon comes and freezes time, attacks mortals, we can't sit and observe anymore."

"I doubt they liked that."

"Not too much," Thomas chuckled. He walked over to an old filing cabinet. "I also know where we can begin. A month ago I came across a receipt of donations from 1939. A crate of paintings for us to protect during the war. They were never collected after the end of the war."

"A lot of art was displaced after World War Two," Sam pointed out.

"Yes, but in the inventory two paintings caught my interest," Thomas explained. "They sound very similar to the one from your cousin's dream. What is even more interesting is that I can not find any other description of them anywhere else."

"They're here," Sam realized.

Thomas nodded and searched for the file he was looking for. He found it and pulled it out laying it on the table in the center of the room. "Thankfully, my predecessor believed in organization and created a filing system for everything in here."

"So we don't have to look through everything in here," Sam replied as he stood next to Thomas.

"As long as no one has messed with his system, we should be good," Thomas agreed. "Get your sketch out and your notes so we can compare them."

Two hours later the two of them were pulling out a large roll-out cabinet. Once it was fully out of the wall unit, Thomas grabbed his keys and began to see if he could find one that fit the locks. Sam studied it while Thomas went through the large ring. It was made of metal, and looked as if it should be impossible to move. Thomas was struggling with finding the right key for the lock.

Sam ran a hand down the metal expecting it to be cool but surprised when he found it warm. An idea came to him and he walked to where Thomas stood. "Let me try," Sam suggested.

Thomas handed him the keys, watching to see if Sam had better luck than he. Sam looked at the keys before choosing one that Thomas had already tried. He watched as the key slid into the lock and turned. They both looked at each other and then at the lock before Sam slowly opened it. Inside were two large paintings still in their frames. The two paintings were both already on carts, so they pulled the first draped painting out and moved it into the better light. The second one followed shortly after.

"You can unveil them," Thomas told Sam.

Sam knew his hands were shaking as he touched the old velvet cloth. "I'm terrified they will vanish the moment I take the drapes off," Sam admitted.

"I don't blame you."

Taking a deep breath, he pulled the drape off the first one and stared. "This is the painting from the dream," Sam realized. He took a step back. "My god, it's stunning."

Brother Thomas took it all in as they stood side-by-side studying it. "She's right," Thomas realized. "The injury wasn't self inflicted."

Sam noted the cut where the wing met the shoulder, studied how Lucifer was standing, and where the knife had fallen. "At a quick glance, you would think he had done it," Sam stated. He walked around the painting, taking it all in from different angles. "In one of the darker storm clouds a figure is hidden. You can see a smirk on his face as if he ran before he was caught."

Thomas noticed the figure as well. "There are so many hidden meanings in this painting," he whispered. "You could spend years studying each of them."

"We don't have years," Sam reminded him.

Walking to the second painting he pulled off the drape and gasped at the scene before them. Unlike the clouds of heaven, this was a dungeon in hell. Laying on a stone altar was a female that looked so much like Ana it was startling. Her gaze was toward the front of the painting where a large male stood. Smoke seemed to swirl around him making it hard to see any of his features clearly. Sam knew that this was Meph in his demon form.

"What is that lying just out of her reach?" Thomas asked as he moved closer to the painting.

"A sword," Sam noted. Then he noticed there was writing on it. "Do you have a magnifying lens?"

"I will get one," Thomas answered.

Sam focused on the painting while Thomas rummaged around. This was a work of a true master. Yet both paintings remained unsigned and no date could be found anywhere. They were unlike any painting he had ever seen before.

The artist wasn't capturing a scene that had happened or would happen, he was capturing a moment as it happened. In the first painting it was the moment after Meph had struck, when Lucifer is wounded and weak. In the second, it was Meph getting ready to perform a ritual while his victim still struggled to escape.

"Here," Thomas said handing him a magnifying glass.

Using it, Sam went scanned the sword as his mind translated the wording. As he stood upright he noticed something with the glass that couldn't be seen by the naked eye. A hidden scene outside the windows. He felt his whole body go numb as it all made sense now.

"I have to call Ana," Sam whispered.

"I will step out so you can talk in private," Thomas suggested noticing that Sam had gone pale. This wasn't good news that Sam would be delivering.

Chapter 28

THE LIBRARY OF Bohlander House was quiet. All the teens were upstairs for the night, allowing the adults to meet and talk about everything that had been learned in the last few days. Between Sam's discovery and what Toby had learned about Jules and her family they were all shocked. Now it was time to take that new information and figure out how they could use it. Martha entered with a tray of tea.

"Have we missed anything?" Martha asked as Erik helped her set the tray down.

"Just added quick notes to the whiteboard," Terry answered.

Eric came into the room sliding his cell phone into his back pocket as he walked over to where Ana was sitting. He kissed her before joining her on the couch. Jules sat in the arm chair next to them accepting the cup of tea hat Alex offered her. He handed one to Ana next then sat next to Terry at the small table. Toby was getting his notes in order, Martha slid him a tea cup.

He took a sip before speaking. "Alright, we are starting with Jules," Toby told them. "After the attack on Cassie and Ana, Michael and I thought it would be a good idea to look into all of our backgrounds. Not just immediate family but full genealogies. We focused on Jules because she always knew when Meph was around."

"That makes sense," Alex agreed. "She has also the longest history with Ana so starting with her would make the most sense."

"Throw-in what she can do around angels and it's hard to argue," Terry added. Jules had shown them earlier what she could do if an angel was near her. The kids were now calling her Sparkler.

"And you learned a lot," Jules surmised.

"We learned things that could rewrite history," Toby admitted. He ran a hand through his hair for he was still in disbelief of what they had learned. "Before he was Emperor, Charlemagne ruled a section of the Franks, along with his brother. Even then, his goal was to unite all the Germanic Tribes."

"I should warn you I hated history," Terry informed Toby.

The door to the library opened and Luke entered. "Sorry," he replied.

"I just got started," Toby assured him.

Luke found a seat and Toby picked-up where he was. "Charles did not rule all of the Franks until his brother, who he didn't get along with, died," Toby continued. "It is after his brother's death that he starts on his goal to unite all the tribes and convert them to Christianity. Now I should note, and this is where Jules comes in, Charles had numerous wives and mistresses throughout his life."

"Go me, for being a cheater," Jules said, jokingly pumping her fist in the air.

"And people ask me why I hate teaching," Toby sighed. "Alright, so needless to say, he has to fight a lot of battles to unite the tribes. Remember these battles are taking place in north-western Europe. In the areas that worshiped the Norse Gods and Goddesses."

They all looked at each other then back at Toby. "In his countless battles he came across the Valkyries. They are female warriors who attend to the fallen of war and bring them to Valhalla. I don't know if he realized what they were, regardless, he fell in love, or lusted, with one. They started a relationship. She, fearing that one day she would be sent to recover his body on the battlefield, bestowed upon him a blade said to have been forged by the Gods. She also would bear him a child."

"Your family line goes into hiding after Charlemagne's death," Toby told her. "When his son ascended the throne he was worried about your family because only your line could wield the power of Joyeuse. Charlemagne had also realized this and had another more elaborate sword made. That is the one that was used for coronations and ceremonies."

"Is that why Jules can do what she can? That because she comes from a Valkyrie she can manipulate your energy?"

"That's complicated," Toby admitted.

"Throughout history there have always been individuals that can see Angels," Erik answered for Toby. "Prophets, saints, others as well. But Jules is unique, she can wield our energy and use it as a weapon. That has never been seen before. It is a power that an Arch Angel has but since the four of us have never sired an offspring with a mortal there is no other explanation for how she can do it."

"And this sword," Martha inquired. "You said that only a descendant of Charlemagne could use it's power? That would mean Jules could use it."

"This is all theory," Toby reminded them. "But the sword in the second painting had the name Joyeuse carved into the hilt. That clue confirmed some of our findings on Jules family tree."

"How so?" Ana asked as she held Jules' hand. Finding out you descendent from a legendary king a mythological creature was a lot to take in.

"When her family flees to what is modern day France, it is there that we first see the use of Vijelens." Toby walked over to the whiteboard and wrote out her last name. "Which if you look at it you will realize what has been staring at us for our entire lives," Toby stated. "Her last name is the phonetic pronunciation of Vigilance."

They were all silent for several minutes, then Ana finally spoke. "In the second painting the victim is reaching for the sword Joyeuse, which you are saying only Jule's line can wield. Her last name is literally Vigilance, what if we take it a step further and say that the only way this curse could be broken is if the line of Faust and the line of the Valkyrie crossed. That whatever power this sword holds would hold the power to defeat Meph."

"It's why he didn't want the second painting found," Alex observed, picking up on her theory. "It's why he went after Sam. He might not know exactly what was in the painting but he might have known that the key to his destruction was in it."

"Okay, it all sounds great," Jules stated. "But how the hell do we get a mythical sword to me, and then to wherever the battle takes place? That sword is either lost...."

"It's in a locked vault deep within the Louvre," Toby informed her.

"What!? So we break into the Louvre?" Jules inquired. There was silence once again and she looked at everyone in the room. "You guys can't be serious?"

"It's not on the top of my list of ways to obtain it," Toby admitted. "But we are short on time. I have asked for a private look at it with one of my contacts. Only a very few people know that there are two swords called Joyeuse. The one on display was a replica made by Charlemagne to be used for ceremonial use. I should hear about my request by tomorrow."

"In the meantime what do we do?" Martha asked. "I know the kids were joking about covering every mirror at dinner, but it might not be a bad idea."

"We could send the ones we use decoration out for cleaning," Terry suggested. "It would limit Mephistopheles' access, the one's in the bathroom are a different story."

"Covering them isn't going to prevent him from entering," Erik reminded them. "It just prevents us from seeing him. But removing the one's we can might not be a bad idea."

"What if we covered a few, let him think that we are trying to block him," Alex suggested. "We take down some of the heavier ones and send them out. Then cover some of the rest so that not all of them are covered."

"Lure him into a sense of safety, that we don't know what he's up to," Erik stated. "That isn't a bad idea."

"I have a question," Luke replied. "Can he hear us on the other side of a mirror? I mean what if he has been listening in on this entire conversation and knows what we are planning."

"If he could hear we wouldn't be talking in rooms that have mirrors," Eric pointed out. "Mirrors can act as a portal, or a window to this world. We can see what is going on but unless we are in a direct conversation with the person on the other side we can not hear what is being said. If we hear anything it's a faint muffled noise, and the more people in a room the more annoying the noise."

"So he could see us all sitting here talking but not know what we are talking about," Luke repeated just to clarify.

"Exactly. In this case he will have an idea of what we are talking about but not what we are actually saying."

"Like a one way mirror," Alex pointed out. "We can only hear what is being said on the other side by the mic in the room and the speaker in our room. Otherwise, we are just watching what is happening in the interrogation room."

"Correct," Erik replied. He noticed that Ana was rubbing her temple. "You okay?"

"Headache," She mumbled. Ana didn't add that the scar from where Beez had stabbed her was also bothering her. Something was going to happen and it was going to happen soon.

"Do you want to go to bed?" Toby asked her with concern in his voice.

"I'm good," Ana promised. "I'm going to have some tea and see if that helps."

Standing up she went to walk to the table but felt the world spin around her. Voices called out her name but she couldn't focus as the pain in her head seemed to explode all around her. The voices were now screams and laughs were heard as glass shattered and smoke filled her head. Then it all went still and she saw blackness.

Chapter 29

ANA GROANED AS she slowly sat up from where she was lying. As she sat up, she opened her eyes and for a quick moment she thought she was in a nightmare. Ana sat up straighter as she realized where she was, making fear turn her blood cold. The screams now made sense. Meph had come to the house, not only had he grabbed her but he had brought her somewhere.

Slowly, Ana got to her feet and looked around. This was not the Boston penthouse that was furnished with antiques, nor was it the place where Ana was brought in the dream realm. This was the actual lair of Mephistopheles and it invoked feelings of fear and doom. Hearing a groan from behind her, Ana turned and saw that Jules was laying in a heap. Ana rushed to her side, kneeling down she turned Jules over onto her back. Meph had captured both of them.

"I feel sick," Jules groaned not wanting to open her eyes.

"Your body and mind need to adjust to where we are," Ana said, gently helping Jules sit up. "Open your eyes slowly and take deep breaths."

"Where are we?" Jules asked as she followed Ana's instructions.

"If I have to make a guess, we are in Mephistopheles' lair," Ana answered, as she helped Jules stand up. Jules, legs trembled for a minute. "He brought us physically into the realm of the dead."

"I take it that this is very bad," Jules replied, as she looked at the black walls with torches hanging from them. The floor was pitch black and smooth, she rubbed her arms as a cool wind chilled her.

"Mortals can't enter this realm physically," Ana answered. "Not without making some sort of payment. Also don't eat or drink anything."

"Afraid I'll end up like Persephone?" Jules joked trying to lighten the mood. She was referring to the greek demi goddess who Hades had taken into the underworld. Persephone ate six seeds from a pomegranate, as a result she would end up spending six months of the year in Hades and six months on earth.

Ana looked at her. "It's called the Persephone rule for a reason."

"Wait, that is true?" Jule knew she shouldn't be surprised by anything. Not with everything that she had just learned about her own family.

"The amount you drink or eat dictates how long you stay," Ana replied. "But I'm more worried about the payment."

"What do you mean?" Jules asked. She began to hear faint voices and wondered if that was a side effect. Ignoring them she focused on Ana and where they were.

"For a mortal to be granted permission to enter they must give an offering, make a payment, or provide a trade," Ana explained. "You see examples throughout ancient Literature. Odysseus slaughtered a bull to enter the realm of Hades. Even in Dante's inferno the hero had to make a payment."

"Why?"

"Because this is the world of the dead, Jules," Ana reminded her. "It leaves its mark on you permanently if you enter and leave."

"You said 'if'," Jules realized.

"Not every mortal who enters leaves," Ana replied. "How you feeling?"

"Cold," Jules admitted. "Figured it would be a lot warmer."

"It is for the souls, not for the living."

Jules nodded that somehow it made sense. "So what do we do?"

"I have no clue," Ana answered. "Meph brought us here for a reason and that reason isn't a good one."

"You have such little faith in me," a deep voice stated.

Jules turned and froze before Ana could tell her not to look. Jules had only ever seen Meph in the form he took in the mortal realm. Here in his domain there was no disguise, it was him in his true demonic form. There were human features to him even still, his face and body structure was similar to a human. But he towered over seven feet and black like smoke covered him from head to toe. His eyes glowed orange.

"Welcome to my home," Mephistopheles greeted them. "This has been a long time coming. I can't believe it is finally here."

Ana positioned Jules behind her, not caring that Jules was taller. She kept a hand on Jules, needing the contact to find courage. This place was supposed to suck all hope from you, it was supposed to make you not want to return to your life.

"You brought both of us," Ana stated. "You only needed to have brought me."

"Then how would I have paid the price for bringing you?" Meph inquired, smiling slowly as Jules trembled and Ana just glared at him. "Unless of course you have something else to offer me?"

"Don't," Jules whispered as an idea began to form in her head. "Do not give up your soul or your life to spare me."

Ana didn't give any indication that Jules had spoken. "We both knew, Ana," Jules whispered. "Deep down we knew the ending."

"I could offer my soul in exchange," Ana stated. "But that isn't what you are after, is it?"

Mephistopheles cocked his head chuckling as he looked at her with glowing eyes. "Enlighten me as to why your soul isn't the only thing that I am after?"

"The same reason you have killed every firstborn male when they have become of age," Ana answered. "Men can't carry children."

"That is true," Mephistopheles agreed, impressed with her. "I need a female to bear my children. But not any female can do that, otherwise I would take dear Miss Julianna here and use her as my broodmother."

Jules screamed as a hand of smoke pulled her from Ana carrying her to where Mephistopheles stood. Being so close to him she was able to make out his features better. From a distance, he looked almost human but now she saw that wasn't the case. Mixed in with his human features were the black scales of a demon. It was if someone had woven together a human and a demon's face with a jagged line running down where the two met. Bone-like spikes jutted up from his right shoulder and his hand was elongated with claws at the ends of them. While she hovered in the air he ran a claw-like finger down the front of her.

"I could make her bow to my will," Mephistopheles stated. His voice sounding like gravel as it rumbled through the room. "This is my domain, where I make the rules and all those here whether mortal or not are bound to my will, to my word."

"I would never submit," Jules protested.

He smiled slowly. "You wouldn't even know you were submitting," he whispered making sure that his voice skated around her like a breeze. "I am the Voice of Satan himself, I am the bearer of his will. That title was not bestowed upon me on a mere whim, it was given to me because of my gift. A simple thought, the slightest nudge and I can undo a person's convictions, do away with their morals without a moment of hesitation. You would serve me on your knees without the slightest bit of fight."

"But it can't be just any mortal woman, can it?" Ana began to fully understand his obsession with her family. Her voice breaking the spell that had fallen over the room.

The question brought Mephistopheles back to focusing on Ana. "My parent's cursed me with my creation," Mephistopheles explained as he tossed Jules through the air. A thousand ghost like hands caught her and moved her into a cell that appeared out of nowhere. "No demon, angel, or mere mortal can bear my children. It kills them and the child. I need a soul strong enough to endure life in the afterworld. A bloodline that is tainted by Satan, but pure of demonic or angelic ancestry. And there is only one line that meets all three requirements."

"So you hunted my line, waiting for the perfect candidate," Ana stated, trying to keep his focus off of Jules. She knew that her friend was up to something.

"Your mortal mind cannot possibly comprehend what it is that I seek," Mephistopheles answered, as he walked toward her. "There are things, entire worlds you do not know that exists. You grasp at straws hoping it will unlock some hidden secret that will save you and all you care about. But there is no hidden secret, your bloodline is mine. It was created by me and I have waited five hundred years for a vessel to serve my needs."

Ana went to protest but was flung against a wall, chains wrapping around her arms and legs. Hands emerged from the wall covering her mouth and holding her body still as she protested against the restraints. She watched helplessly as Mephistopheles floated across the floor to the cage that held Jules. Unlocking the cage he held out a hand to help Jules out of the cage, her sweatpants and t-shirt had changed into a stunning gown of silver, her hair was swept up in twist, diamonds dangled from her ears and encircled her throat.

"You are a true vision," Mephistopheles whispered in Jules' ear. A mirror appeared on the wall and Ana gasped for it matched the one she had seen in Austria and in Boston. "My gateway to your world is this simple mirror. Yet it has never gazed upon a beauty such as you."

Ana watched noting that Jules' eyes looked glazed as if she was under a trance. Which she was. Jules gazed at herself in the mirror running her hand over the intricate bead work in the bodice of the gown. In the reflection, Mephistopheles wore a tux and looked as he did in the mortal realm.

"You see the luxury that I can bestow upon you," he whispered in Jule's ear. "A snap of my finger and I can give you anything you want. The finest gowns, jewels, it can all be yours."

"Anything?" Jules whispered, her eyes glowing with excitement at the prospect.

"Anything," Mephistophiles grinned looking directly at Ana as he ran a finger down the face of Jule's. "Skin so beautiful should be worshipped, perhaps I will frame it as a reminder to all who dare deceive me."

Jules turned, wrapping her arms around Mephistopheles, the meaning of his words lost on her. "What if what I want is locked away in a museum?" She asked all but purring as she played with the lapel of the of his tux jacket. "Could you still get it?"

"There is no place that can keep me out," Mephistopheles informed her. He was surprised at how he reacted to her touch, how she reacted to his. "Your reaction to my touch is quite enjoyable. Perhaps I will keep you around for longer than planned."

Jules smiled at him with absolute trust and adoration. "In the vault of the Louvre is a sword, I don't mean it's more flamboyant twin, I want the one that looks like a sword carried into battle."

"Darling, I could deliver the crown jewels at your feet if you ask, but if it is a sword, I will get it," Mephistopheles informed her with a chuckle. "And what is this sword?"

"It is the one that was once owned by Charlemagne."

Mephistopheles stilled and looked at her startled by her request. Jules ran a finger down the side of his face and across his lips allowing her thumb to slide in-between his lips. He closed his eyes as she went on. "The jewel encrusted one that was used for coronation of kings is on display, that is not the one I speak of. I want the one they hide deep within the bowels of the Louvre."

He was curious now. "Why do they hide it?"

"For it is more than just a sword meant for power," Jules whispered as she licked under his jaw. "It holds powers that most can not fathom. For the power that comes from it can blind a person if they do not bow to it, it can let the masses fall at your feet, so they lock it away. Just think of what we could do with such a tool?"

"Perhaps I need to rethink who I keep at my side," Mephistopheles admitted as he groaned under her touch. "I will obtain Joyeuse for you."

"And I will reward you for giving it to me," Jules whispered seductively.

Her back was to her best friend, she did not see the tears running down Ana's face. For Jules, the only person that seemed to exist was Mephistopheles. She was no longer freezing, her mind no longer screaming, she had found an inner peace. For the first time in her life she knew what her purpose was and it felt glorious.

"I will go and get you your prize," Mephistopheles informed her bending down to kiss her. "My servants are at your disposal while I am gone."

"Do not be long," Jules whispered as he stepped away. "For I have plans for you."

"I will be as quick as I can," he promised. He kissed her before vanishing.

Smiling, Jules looked around the room and clapped her hands. The swirling mists swirled into forms that had once been human but were now cursed as the lost souls. Here they were ruled mercilessly by Mephistopheles.

"I need a bed, an ornate one, with dark sheets," Jules began to give them orders. Tugging at her clothes, she commanded: "And something a little less than this. Perhaps white?"

The souls milled about ensuring that her requests were filled, not wanting to trouble their master. Ana was helpless as she watched. She couldn't even yell or talk to Jules, to remind her of who she was and why they here. The control of Mephistophiles was so strong that it had taken only moments for Jules to fall under it. Ana understood his intentions. He would play with Jules forcing Ana to watch and then he would kill Jules as an offering for Ana's passage. Watching it unfold while being helpless was worst than death for Ana and Mephistopheles knew that. Their only hope of surviving this was that Erik would somehow come and rescue them. But there was still payment that would have to be given, there was no getting around that, no matter who Erik was and where he stood in the hierarchy.

Chapter 30

THE LIBRARY LOOKED as if an explosion had gone off. Mirror shards were scattered across the room. Black soot covered the wall where the mirror had once sat above the mantle. Furniture laid overturned or broken. It was after midnight as Erik stood in the center of the room with Alex and Michael. Luke, Toby, and Martha had taken the younger kids to Jill's, Helen's, and Luke's places. Leaving only the seventeen and eighteen year olds, and Cassie at the house. Terry was keeping them calm and informed of what was going on in the library. The smell of brimstone and sulfur still hung in the air, but it wasn't any of this that had caught his attention. It was the remains of the gilded mirror that still hung above the mantle. The mirror had been shattered laying on the floor as glittering dust.

"He destroyed the mirror so we couldn't follow," Erik stated as he stared at the sparkling dust on the floor.

"If he hadn't?" Alex asked.

"Even with the smallest of shards I would have been able to find him directly," Erik answered. "But with nothing but dust there is nothing to send us through with."

"Why take both of them?" Alex asked. His arm was bandaged from where a piece of the mirror had sliced him.

"The Afterlife was solely created for non-mortals," Erik explained. "Demons, angels, and other creatures, we can move through the realms with ease. Our minds and bodies were made to adapt to those realms. Mortals were never created to adapt to those realms; the horrors, the peace, it is beyond mortal comprehension. For mortals to enter while alive, their purpose must be great and their offering must be just as great."

"You mean like an offering, like in the Odyssey," Alex recalled from high school literature. Erik nodded. "Okay. But Odysseus willingly went to the afterlife so I understand him having to make an offering. Ana and Jules weren't abducted, that has to mean something."

"We are forbidden to force any mortal into the afterlife," Erik began. "A mortal must enter on their own free will."

"He's declaring war on everyone."

"He is," Erik agreed.

Terry came through the doorway. "Alright, they are all settled in the dining room. All the mirrors in there have been locked in the basement. We pushed a huge hutch in front of the basement door."

"Good," Erik replied. "How's Cassie?"

"Holding up," Terry answered. "So what are we talking about?"

"Why the two were grabbed," Alex answered. A loud clap of thunder shook the house causing all the lights to flicker. "There wasn't supposed to be a storm."

"This isn't a normal storm," Erik informed him. "It's going to get worst."

"You've seen this before?"

"Only once," Erik admitted.

"Let me guess, the great flood?"

Erik snorted at that. "No," he answered as they hurried to one of the supply closets to grab emergency gear for everyone.

"So when?" Terry asked.

"When I brought a mortal into the afterlife," Erik answered. He didn't say anything else as he grabbed a bag and headed into the dining room.

Cassie went right to him and he hugged her tightly before laying a gentle kiss on top of her head. "It will be fine," Erik assured her.

They heard the rain begin to pour as the lights flickered again. Terry took out the radio and got it on a radio station. The front door flung open and Toby appeared in the doorway to the dining room. He took in the scene and then looked at Erik. He walked over and punched Erik in the jaw. Everyone took a step back and waited for Erik's reaction.

"My sister is gone and you are still here"!" Toby yelled.

"My lover is missing and I'm trying to keep my dark side from erupting," Erik corrected. "You failed to notice I have been clenching my fists since we found her room."

To prove his point, he held up his hands where his nails had dug so hard into his skin that he drew blood. "Before we can get her back we need to make sure that Martha and the teens will be protected," Erik continued. "Trust me, I want to rush off and find her and Jules, but the afterlife is a large place with countless realms. We need to assemble our team and figure out a plan of battle."

"Look," Toby began and Erik stopped him with an understanding look.

"Your sister and Jules are both missing," Erik replied. "Lashing out at me is understandable. You don't need to apologize for being afraid."

"You said you brought a mortal into the afterlife?" Terry reminded Erik. "That you saw a storm like this after you had done it."

"Lilith," Erik answered. He saw the shocked looks around him "And no, she is not the mother of vampires or children of the dark."

"So we are talking about that Lilith," Alex clarified. "Adam's first wife."

Erik nodded. Many believed that Eve had been the first woman created but there had been one before her. Lilith. She was cast out of the garden because she believed that women should be equal to men.

"She was a gentle soul, carefree," Erik recalled. "She was also confident and believed she was equal to the males around her. When she was cast out of her society, rejected for believing women were equal, Meph tried to get her to join him. She refused, seeing him for what he was. He raped, tortured, and left her for dead. I found her. This annoyed our friend even more so he tried to attack again but I summoned us both to my realm. Thus breaking the rule first."

"That's why you fell," Toby realized.

"I fell because I challenged my father on his decision to cast out Lilith, his first daughter, like those of her society did," Erik corrected. "While we were arguing it gave Meph the chance to enter my father's kingdom. At the end of the battle I was given a choice because it was believed that I was at fault for the attack, that if I hadn't doubted my father's plans Meph would not have entered. So I was told that I fall from the heavens and become a fallen Angel, the first one at that, or all that fought alongside me would be punished with me in Hell."

They all just stared at him for a few moments. It was Cassie who spoke. "Is that why your wings aren't all black? Because you took the responsibility of all of your actions so that others wouldn't be punished?"

"Don't make me into a hero," Erik warned. "I am not my brother. I fell to prove my father wrong."

Toby looked at him as he began to organize what they had. The Morning Star was prideful but he was also humble and would take the blame and the punishment to protect those who called him friend. This was a person you wanted on your side when things literally went to hell.

Chapter 31

ANA WATCHED HELPLESSLY as Jules worked to make the room more appealing. She couldn't move, she couldn't speak, the hands and chains had no give to them. All she could do was watch her friend be manipulated and controlled by a living nightmare. Before her, Jules hummed as she lit candles surrounding the room in soft candle light. The large four poster bed was draped with black and silver material that pooled onto the floor. Jules had changed out of the elaborate gown and into a cream silk nightgown with lace around the edges. She let her hair down out of the twist so that blonde hair spilled over one shoulder.

Not once had Jules looked at Ana, it was as if Ana did not exist in Jules' world. Ana felt a cool breeze and noted the form of a lost soul had moved past her. She noticed something different about this soul, it's form had become more human. It's body wasn't as twisted, it was standing more erect as if something was changing it. Ana began to study each of the soul-forms as they wandered the room waiting for orders. Each one was standing up straighter, there was more form to them, they looked more human than they had when Ana first awoke in this nightmare.

Ana's attention was brought to a door that appeared, there were voices on the other side. She knew better than to hope that it was Erik. When the door opened and Mephistopheles entered she couldn't help but feel disappointed. Ana watched as the demon like creature studied the transformation of the room, as his eyes found Jules and ogle at her current attire.

"I thought you couldn't look anymore beautiful than you did in that gown," Mephistopheles stated. "But it appears I was wrong."

Jules ran a hand down the front of Mephistopheles and smiled slowly. "You know how to charm a female," she replied. "I hope you don't mind that I made some changes."

"My dear, I want you to feel at home," he assured her. "And to show you that I am serious I have brought you two gifts."

"You shouldn't have," Jules giggled.

"Nonsense, you deserve to be spoiled," Mephistopheles informed her as a diamond and sapphire necklace appeared out of the air. "I found this on my way to get your gift."

"It's stunning," Jules replied as he fastened it around her neck. She touched the large jewels then turned kissing him on his cheek.

Mephistopheles ran his own finger along her collar bones watching in fascination as her body shuddered from desire and not from fear. "You respond to my touch like no other," he whispered laying a kiss under her chin. "Why did I bother with your friend?"

"Why did you?" Jules asked on a breathy sigh as his mouth traced a line of kisses along her jaw line.

"She is of no importance any more," Mephistopheles stated. Reluctantly he pulled himself back. "Before we lose ourselves in each other I believe I have another gift, the token you asked for me to retrieve."

Jules eyes were full of desire as she let out a groan of protest when his body moved away from hers. "Hmmm," she hummed as she tried to pull him back to her.

"You are a sensual creature," Mephistopheles observed. "But we have all the time to explore each other."

He walked to a table that appeared suddenly, laying on it was a long and slender box. "Your prize."

Jules refocused and walked toward the table in the center of the room. She ran her hand along the ordinary looking box and felt her fingers tingle from excitement. They trembled as she undid the locks of the box and slowly she lifted the lid. There, nestled in velvety material, was a long broadsword that had once been wielded by a great warrior and ruler.

"It is said that when the true bearer holds it, all will bow to them," Jules said softly as her finger traced the blade. "It is a modest blade, no one would think it belonged to a king."

"It is rather plain," Mephistopheles agreed. "I must admit I was tempted to bring the one used for coronations but you were so specific that I was afraid to disappoint."

"The jewel encrusted one was made to draw attention away from the original, it was to look like a sword that one would expect of a king. This is the sword of a warrior," Jules stated. She looked up at the monster before her and smiled. "Thank you. You do not understand how much this means to me."

"It is my pleasure."

He watched in fascination as Jules ran her hand over the blade and couldn't help but imagine those hands exploring his body with the same amount of fascination. Her hands wrapped around the hilt and for a moment he thought he saw a ripple in in his realm.

Jules wrapped her second hand around the hilt and heard the whispers that seemed to swirl around her as she lifted the sword out of the case. For a moment, she felt light-headed as she held the sword, then she looked at Ana who was chained to the wall. She saw the pleading look in Ana's eyes and Jules made eye contact with her for a moment.

"O soul be chang'd into little waterdrops, and fall into the ocean and never be found," Jules whispered. It was a line from Marlow's *Doctor Faust*.

"I know that line," Mephistopheles realized and for the first time he stared at the blonde before him with uncertainty. It was impossible for her to still have her own mind, she was in his realm, he controlled her.

Jules smiled slowly, this time it wasn't a seductive smile. "You brought me into your realm as payment," Jules began. "You brought us here to declare war, to rip down the boundaries of the realms."

"You know not of what you speak," Mephistopheles growled as he took a step back from her. She was glowing, something no mortal should be able to do. "I do not like being tricked, little girl."

"No, you like doing the tricking," Jules replied.

Ana gasped when Jenna appeared before them. "Like you tricked Jenna into believing you could give her the world if she listened to you," Jules replied.

"How did you bring her here?" Mephistopheles demanded. She wielded power he had never seen before.

Jules said nothing as an image of Carl appeared. "You promised him Jenna and that his past misdeeds would be erased," Jules continued. "Yet your promises were nothing but tricks to get their help to defeat a foe you could not defeat on your own."

"How do you know this!"

"You know all that is to know of the bloodline of Faust, but yet you never once looked into my line did you?" Jules inquired with a smile.

"Your mother was a drug addict who chose drugs over her children," Mephistopheles reminded her. "If this is your attempt to stall so that help can find you I promise you there is no help."

Jules took a step toward him. "For someone trusted with the voice of Satan himself you really are stupid."

"You dare!"

He stormed toward her but with a flick of her wrist she sent him flying through the air. Jules looked at Ana and kept eye contact. "I do this of my own free will," Jules swore. She was now looking at Ana as if the room and Mephistopheles no longer existed. "I was born to protect, to ensure that this day would come. I lived so that I could be vigilant against harm and evil, to bring light when there was dark. I die to free those bound by hate, chaos, and betrayal. May my blood heal the sick, my bones strengthen the weak, and my soul be free to stay vigilant to those who are wronged."

Mephistopheles screamed as Jules took the sword and ran it through herself. The hands and chains that bound Ana to the wall vanished letting Ana fall to the floor. She ignored the hands that this time tried to help her stand as she ran to where Jules sank to the floor. The white gown was now turning a deep red. Ana sunk to the floor next to Jules and wrapped her arms around her.

"You are such a moron," Ana whispered holding Jules.

Jules chuckled. "I am," she agreed. "I had to."

"I know," Ana answered, kissing her friend on the forehead.

Jules lifted her bloody hand and laid Ana's hand on the hilt. "It's yours now."

"No!" Mephistopheles yelled. He then looked at his slaves. "Get her body out of here!"

None of them moved instead they looked at Ana and Jules. "I said remove her body!" Mephistopheles repeated.

When they again refused he flew toward Ana and pulled her away from Jules. Holding her by the throat he raised her high above his head. "You bitch!" he roared. "Did the two of you plan this?"

"Even if we had we still got the best of you," Ana replied.

He threw her through the air. But instead of crashing into the wall hands caught her and gently lowered her to the floor.

"It seems you no longer control the lost souls," Ana stated as she gripped the sword tighter. "Now what?"

Chapter 32

ANA WATCHED AS the lost souls gently picked Jules up from her lap and brought her over to the bed. They gently laid her body on it, then pulled a sheet up over her, they formed a circle around the bed as if to protect Jules from further trauma. Ana turned and stared at the being before her. Her friend's blood stained her hands and clothes, and the demon responsible stood before her with a smile on his face.

"You asshole!" Ana screamed launching herself at him.

She punched him in the jaw. Ana had wrapped herself around him in such away that he couldn't get her off of him. "She killed herself," Mephistopheles reminded Ana.

Grabbing a hold of her hair, he was able to dislodge her and dangled her above the floor by the back of her neck. "I am not some mere mortal you can pummel," Mephistopheles growled. "I am a god, I am fear, I am your worst nightmare come to life. And yet you think you can decieve me, that her death has brought you some advantage. You are alone in my world. There is no hope, no rescue. I am your fate. And your time has run out."

Dragging her from the room, Mephistopheles threw open a large oak door and tossed her across the cold stone floor. Before she could act skeleton like hands came up from the ground and held her in place. Mephistopheles walked to a large cabinet and unlocked it, he took out a large bowl made of smooth stone then brought it to a wooden pedestal near a window. Outside of the window was a landscape straight from a horror film.

He filled the bowl with a clear liquid then took a silver chalice off of a shelf. It was a simple chalice with no decoration on it, no gems, just smooth metal. Dipping it into the water he smiled as he walked toward Ana.

"Her death has insured your torture for all eternity," Mephistopheles warned her as he knelt down next to her. "In this cup is the key to my victory and your defeat."

Ana tried to turn her head away but the skeleton hands that held her prevented her from doing so. Two creeped up to her mouth and forced it open so that he could pour the liquid down her throat. At first it was cool and then it began to burn. Ana tried to scream but she was so overcome with pain that no sound came out of her mouth. The whole word began to spin and flashes of her life slammed into her as blackness began to creep into her mind.

Slowly, Ana began to wake up. At first, her vision was blurry, as if nothing could focus, but as she woke up more of the room came into view. The walls were done in pale yellow, french doors were opened to a balcony allowing the tropical air to flow into room. She was laying in a large four poster bed, a pile of pillows surrounded her. Moving to the edge of the bed she looked around the room waiting for something to feel familiar. Part of her felt like she should know this place, yet another part felt like this was a dream. A dream that she should wake up from.

Standing up, Ana walked to the balcony and stared at the impossibly blue water before her. Tranquility came over her as she brushed a strand of hair out of her face. Stretching, she looked down and saw she was in a white tank top and pale pink pajama pants. Smiling, she looked around at the grounds below her, at the water lapping at the private beach. Heading out of the bedroom she took the stairs. Fresh coffee filled the air and she followed its scent, she entered the kitchen and poured a cup of coffee for herself then walked to the open doors. Leaning against the door frame she sipped her coffee and watched him as he finished with his workout on the deck.

God, he was beautiful. His black hair was cut short, his broad shoulders and back rippled with muscles. He had removed his shirt after his run and was just in basketball shorts. Ana smiled as he slowly turned and noticed she was there. His amber color eyes twinkled with mischief as he walked toward her. And he was all hers, that thought came loud and clear into her mind.

"You finally woke up," he stated as he bent down and gave her a kiss.

Meg Castro

"I did," Ana answered. "Someone kept me busy late into the night last night."
"I wonder who that would be," he laughed. He took her coffee and stole a sip. "Well, you said you were ready for a family so I am all about fulfilling that wish."

Ana watched him walk into the house and for a moment she felt like someone had whispered her name. That was impossible, this was their private getaway. Not even the press knew about this place. The beach was private, making it a perfect spot for them to come and get away from the craziness of their lives. She had just finished a huge international book tour and needed some time to unwind. The minute she had landed in JFK, he was there waiting to take her away from her agent and publisher.

"Pancakes or waffles?" he asked as he headed to the refrigerator.

Ana's stomach rolled at the mention of the choices. She set her coffee down and slid into the stool in front of the island. "Nothing," she whispered.

He turned and looked at her. "Are you alright?"

"I think jet lag is setting in hard," Ana replied as she started to feel odd. "I think I'm going to have some yogurt and then take a bath."

"Are you sure?" Concern flashed in his eyes. "Eating something would most likely help."

"Perhaps after the bath I will be in the mood for something to eat," Ana said. She squeezed his hand then headed back upstairs.

Walking into their large master bathroom she smiled at the large tub that was set before a large window. From here she could soak in her tub and watch the ocean waves crash against the beach. Turning the water to hot, she stripped out of her pjs and began to hum as she poured some bubble bath into the water. While the tub filled she walked to the mirror above her vanity and studied herself in the mirror. Her black hair was cut in a sleek bob but she could see the black circles under her eyes. It was funny how they both had amber eyes. Another wave a nausea came to her, something about that seemed wrong.

Turning the water off, she stepped into the almost blistering hot water and sighed as she sank down so only her head was above the water. This made all the sacrifices, travel, and long hours at the computer worth it. The stress and fatigue of travel and the long press tour seemed to melt away. Her mind began to relax and she started to hum again. Her fingers played with the bubbles as she hummed an aria. It was odd, they never really listened to opera or classical music so to have it stuck in her head now was weird. Perhaps she had heard it while on tour. An image began to form in her mind of a young girl standing in the center of a stage singing the aria she was humming. The girl seemed impossibly young to have a voice that was so beautiful and haunting.

The girl had been looking down as she sung, as if she was unsure of herself, but then suddenly she looked up, as if she was staring right into Ana's soul. Dark eyes framed by blue hair, the eyes seemed to be pleading with Ana. But Ana couldn't figure out what the girl was trying to tell her. The knock on the door brought her out of the dream.

"I brought you your coffee," he told her as he set on the edge of the tub. "Are you alright?"

"I would feel better if you joined me," Ana said with a smile.

"My lady's wish is mine to grant," he chuckled as he stripped out of clothes and joined her in the large tub.

Later they were back in bed, the sheets having dried them off from the bath. Ana laid curled against his strong chest as he fingers seemed to draw imaginary patterns along her skin. She smiled as the sun seemed to rise higher in the sky.

"Do you ever wish we could just leave it all behind," Ana sighed. "Just live here forever."

"We can do whatever you want," he told her as he kissed her shoulder.

She let out a content sigh. "It's a nice dream."

"We can make it real."

"I would miss my family, the kids," she answered. The thought came out of nowhere.

"What kids?" He asked sitting up on his elbows.

There was an edge to his voice. Ana looked at him and the concern was there in his eyes. "Did I say kids? I meant fans. I was probably thinking about our conversation from last night."

He watched her with what looked like more uncertainty than concern. She laid a hand on his arm. "I'm fine," she promised him. "This tour was longer than the others, and we crammed in more stops. I just need a few days to unwind, catch up on my sleep and I'll be back to normal."

"I am sure you are right," he agreed. "I will let you rest."

Ana watched as he dressed and slowly walked out of the room. When she heard him descend the stairs she knew something was wrong. None of this felt right, some small voice in her head was telling her this wasn't real. Yet she could feel the sheets, the floor, her skin. But she couldn't shake the feeling that maybe the voice was right. That maybe this wasn't real. At that thought a pain radiated through her head and she suddenly felt as if she was drowning. Trying to cry out for help she instead fell into darkness.

Chapter 33

TERRY AND ALEX had volunteered to go with Michael and Erik into the underworld. There had been arguments over it, with Luke and Toby both saying it should be them, it should be someone of Faustian blood to enter. But it was Erik who said that was the reason it shouldn't be Luke or Toby. Meph would use their link, their blood, to trick them. It was the reason that Alex and Terry should be the one's to go in because it would not be expected. And so with Gabriel agreeing to stay with the house, to protect Martha and the kids, Luke went to his house, and Toby went to Jill's. Angels were also watching the places where the kids were, especially now that all of Manhattan was out of power.

The preparation had taken less time than they planned when they received word that no payment would be needed because of what Mephistopheles done. This allowed the two angels to take them directly into Hell without an offering. And Hell was unlike anything the two mortals could expect.

Hell smelled of sulfur, rotting flesh, and boiling blood. It robbed you of every good thought that ever entered your mind, it tried to steal your humanity with each step you took. The renaissance painters got it wrong, it looked more like a Edvard Munch painting than anything else. Terry knelt to the side as his stomach protested against their trip. Alex lay on his back next to him while Erik and Michael were both checking their pulses.

"This is why mortals are forbidden," Michael explained as he helped Alex to sit up. "The mortal mind was not created to handle what is outside your realm." "Why?" Terry asked as he slowly stood up. If you say it's because we're stupid I have some words about that."

"No, nothing like that," Erik assured him. "With the exception of those creatures who live in your realm, all other creatures are touched by a divine being. This enables them to handle going from realm to realm without suffering."

"And those in the human realm, how are we created?" Alex asked.

"Procreation without divine intervention," Michael answered. "There are some that have been touched and they either became great heroes or villains. Seers are the crazy homeless person on the street corner that sees armageddon whenever he closes his eyes."

"So armageddon is real?"

"Just one of the possible outcomes when your realm was created," Michael replied. He looked at Erik. "Can we move?"

"They've stabilized," Erik told him. "Much faster than I thought."

Michael nodded then looked at Terry and Alex. "This realm, it will play tricks on you, force you to see things no mortal should," Michael warned. "You must remember who you are, and believe in what your heart tells you. Ignore your mind, it will be played with."

"Your connection to each other can also be used against you," Erik added. "So be careful."

"Is that why you didn't want her brother or cousin to come?" Terry inquired. They had been warned about saying names.

"One of the many reasons," Erik answered. He turned and looked out on the landscape. "Those mountains, that is where we are headed. Remember do not accept any food or drink from anyone including Michael and myself. You need no sustenance while in these realms so any feeling of hunger or thirst is fake."

The two nodded. "Lead on," Terry suggested.

"We're ready," Alex agreed. He slipped his hand into Terry's, giving it a squeeze they looked at each other and smiled. If they could make it through this than they could handle anything else that life threw at them.

As they walked down a path, Alex looked all around taking everything in. He used his detective mind to catalogue, find the detail, hoping that it would help him know what was true and was fake. Their footprints would appear for a few feet behind them but then slowly fade away by an unknown breeze. There was no movement of air, no sense of being hot or cold, it was all neutral.

"Where's your place?" Terry asked Erik. Erik was following them while Michael led the way to the black colored mountains.

"Not here," Erik answered. "I'm closer to the entrance by the river."

"His place is nicer," Michael added. "Each domain takes on the persona of their ruler."

"Who has the nicest?"

Michael and Erik looked at each other smiling slightly. "Hades."

"Though Osiris' isn't far behind," Erik replied.

Alex stopped walking for a moment. "If they exist, but there is the belief in one god, doesn't it mean monotheistic are wrong?" he asked.

"When it comes to religion, no one is wrong," Erik stated and motioned for Alex to keep walking. "Religion is an idea, a structure of beliefs that a person can choose to believe in or not. There is no one religion, no one right path, because each person is different. It should never be forced upon a person because then it becomes weapon."

"But…"

"To believe means you accept the truth, you accept that it is real, that it exists," Erik continued. "It can be simple, like Michael believes Rocky Road is the best ice cream flavor ever. To him that is true. Or it can be more complexed like believing in things that you cannot prove exist."

"And what about faith?" Terry inquired.

"That is trickier," Erik admitted. "It is easy to believe in yourself, to believe in what we see, feel, or know to be true. To have faith in something or someone means you have no doubt, you have complete trust. You can believe that god exists but still have doubts, to have faith means there is no doubt, no one can talk you out of your faith."

"So faith is better," Alex answered.

"There is no correct answer," Erik replied. "Faith is the hardest thing to have and often is misunderstood. Believing in something is just as good as having faith. The issue is when we force our beliefs onto other people."

"So what's the perfect answer?"

"There is no perfect answer because religion is for the individual," Michael replied. "Just as having doubts isn't a bad thing either because it means you are thinking about what you are being told. It means you have questions, and while there might not always be answers questions are how we grow."

"My priest when I was growing up should hear this," Terry mumbled.

"But would he actually hear what was said?" Erik inquired. "Because, for some, it is hard to point out how their beliefs are harming others."

They walked in silence for awhile. For Alex, it seemed as if the mountains were never going to appear closer. In fact, it felt like the longer they walked the farther away they seemed. He knew it was impossible but he also knew that nothing he was seeing would be possible anywhere else.

"When we get there, what happens?" Terry asked.

"Depends on how fortified he has his place," Eric admitted. "He isn't going to be planning on mortals coming with us. He also might not be expecting us at all."

"How is that even possible?"

"Because technically we are breaking at least a dozen laws by entering his realm without invitation or declaring our presence," Michael answered.

"And despite what people say about me, I really don't like breaking the rules," Erik added.

"What would he expect?" Alex asked.

"That we follow the rules we created," Michael replied. "That we wouldn't risk a war for the soul of a single human."

"We could start a war for being here?" Alex asked.

"Our reasons for being here are justified," Erik assured them.

"And the prodigal son returns it seems," a deep voice stated.

Without thinking or talking, both Michael and Erik shoved the humans behind them ready to defend if need be. There was no one around them, all there was were upside down barren trees, red sand, and a heavy gray sky. They were the only four souls on the road to the dwelling of Mephistopheles.

"I wonder if perhaps this has to deal with the chaos that the Voice has brought upon us," the deep voice continued. "For to bring the Prince to this realm with the greatest of all Archangels and two mortals, one can only wonder what would be the cause of this."

"Roth," Erik realized as he let himself relax a bit.

The demon appeared before them, long black hair fell to his waist, he wore a long gray trench coat over gray pants and a black shirt. A black mask with a long beak nose, reminiscent of the old plague masks, covered his face. He was a few inches shorter than Eric but broader in build. The figure bowed before Erik then to Michael.

"Relax, he does not know you are here," Astaroth informed them.

"Then why are you here," Erik inquired, while he knew that Roth would not attack, he was also unsure of why the demon was here. "You don't normally hang around his domain."

"No, I prefer Hades to being here," Astaroth agreed. "He has lost control of the lost souls. They are no longer bound to him, something happened that broke their ties to him."

"You have a Brooklyn accent," Alex noted a bit shocked by that fact.

Astaroth chuckled as he studied the two mortals. "I govern over all the spirits of the Americas," he informed them. "I have spent much time in your great city, I am particularly fond of Coney Island."

"You said that he has lost control of the Lost Souls," Erik inquired, bringing them back to what Astaroth had said a moment ago. "What do you mean?"

"I don't know any more than that," Astaroth admitted. "I was sent here to find out more."

"It does makes sense to send Roth to figure out why," Michael said to Erik.

"Why?" Terry asked.

"He controls the minds that link the realms together," Erik answered. "So he can move freely between the realms without suspicion. What else can you tell me?"

"He kicked out most of his army and has sealed himself away in his castle," Astaroth informed them. "We all know he is up to something, the question is what."

Erik looked at the mountains then at Roth. "He has a member of the Faust line with him, brought her and another against their will."

"Well I'll be damned," Astaroth whispered. "Does he realize he could destroy all we know with his stupidity?"

"He has Beez in on this as well," Michael informed him. "Beez showed up in the city and froze time."

"That explains why our one boss said he would throw him in the pit if he stepped out of line again," Astaroth realized. He looked at Erik. "What do you need me to do?"

"Keep him from seeing us," Erik answered.

"That I can do," Astaroth agreed. "You know where my loyalty is, my Prince."

Erik nodded and watched the demon vanish. Terry stepped up next to Erik. "Can we trust him?" Terry asked Erik.

"We can," Erik replied. "Roth is one of the other reasons I fell from Grace."

"I thought that was over a woman," Alex recalled as they continued moving.

"Roth was once female, an old female god," Michael explained so that Erik did not have to. "She went up against the early Israelites and was defiled in such an atrocious way that there were those of us who stood up for her. It was much later that Meph and Beez were involved with what happened with her, and later still when we learned their involvement with other females who fell."

"How did she become a he?" Alex asked.

"She was so shamed by what had been done to her," Michael began. "That she begged for death, for mercy. Instead she was changed into a male. The Roth you saw remembers very little of what his life was like before the transformation which is both a blessing and a curse."

"You are appalled about what happened to her," Terry realized, looking at Erik.

"It wasn't just what happened to her, there were other injustices that were occurring," Erik answered. "Injustices that I refused to clean up for my father, that I refused to pretend didn't happen. Roth was the last straw, my father and I are both proud men. We said many things in anger, things that can never be taken back. I was given a choice and I made that choice."

"Bull shit," Michael stated. Erik glared at him. "You were given two impossible punishments and you chose a third option. We all told you that we would stand with you."

"And your punishments would have been worst," Erik reminded him. He knew that the two mortals were watching, in part amusement, as the two angels argued. "It doesn't matter now. What Meph started all those years ago, placing the seed of doubt, he has now watched it grow into something we never thought possible."

Terry stopped them when he pointed off into the horizon. "Is it me or did the mountains just move?"

Michael, Erik, and Alex turned and looked at where Terry was pointing. Michael and Erik both took a step forward telling the other two not to move. The whole world seemed to have changed in some way, now the mountains that had been in front of them were to the west. There were oases in the distant but they were more haunting than a place to go to refresh. The waters were a deep gray, with black trees surrounding the water, headless birds wandered around the edges of the small lakes. What loomed in front of them now was a grand estate with high stone walls, a gated entrance, and watch towers to see who was approaching.

Erik turned to warn Terry and Alex but stared. The two men were gone. "This is not good," Michael stated.

"That's an understatement," Erik replied. He looked at the estate. "I guess we knock."

Chapter 34

ANA AWOKE TO find herself in a circular room with no windows and no doors. She was chained to the wall of the room. Shaking the fogginess from her mind she looked around studying every inch of the room. In the center was a fountain of sorts, it was rather plain being made of stones. There was no ornamentation, no gold inlays, nothing to show that it was of any importance. The fact that an entire room was built around it worried Ana more than if it had been an elaborate piece of art. Nothing was here by chance, there was a purpose to everything.

Forcing herself to look away from the clear waters of the well, Ana took in the rest of the room. Mirrors of all kinds covered the walls of the room, at the moment there were no reflections in them. Their surfaces all black. Hearing a groan that sounding familiar Ana turned to the left and gasped when she saw two cages. Alex and Terry were in them, she didn't notice any injuries but that didn't mean anything in this realm.

A door appeared out of nowhere and Mephistopheles walked through it wearing a long gray cloak. He smiled sinisterly at Ana as he entered the room. "I see you have awoken," Mephistopheles stated. "While you slept we had two guests join us."

Ana said nothing as she watched him. A table emerged from the mists that covered the floor and four chalices sat upon. In the center of the table was a decanter that was currently empty. Mephistopheles produced a long dagger from the folds of the cloak, he bathed the blade in the fountain than laid it on the table. Once it was placed he turned and walked toward Ana.

"You are amazing, strong-willed and stubborn," Mephistopheles informed her.

"I have been told that before," Ana answered.

"Every false memory I tried to implant in you, you were able to see through it," Mephistopheles explained. "I gave you everything you wanted and you still were able to get through it."

"Then you didn't give me everything I wanted," Ana replied. He narrowed his eyes at her as if he wanted to hit her. "Why bring them here?"

"I didn't," he answered. "Your lover and his foolish friend brought them. They trespassed so I had no choice but to bring the two mortals here."

"What are you doing to them?"

"I am doing nothing to them," Mephistopheles replied, acting as he was offended by such a question. "I cannot help it if they are reliving their worst memories. I cannot help it if they are being mentally tortured for any transgression they have committed over their lives. This is all on them."

"They are innocent!"

Mephistopheles laughed at her comment. "You mortals throw that term around as if it is a justification for everything," he stated. "No one is innocent, no one is free of judgement or ridicule. Your detective, he has killed people, but it is in the name of the law so he is clear of guilt. Your housemate, he has given up on patients, on people, sending them away. They are far from innocent."

"And you are making them relive those moments aren't you," Ana realized.

"I am forcing them to accept their sins," Mephistopheles stated. He then smiled as he walked closer to her. He ran a claw down the side of her face drawing a trickle of blood. "You could help them, though. Ease their torment."

"And the catch?" Ana asked. as the chains came off of her, she fell to the ground.

"You are a suspicious creature, aren't you?"

"Gee, I wonder why," Ana retorted as she stood up.

He ignored her comment as he walked to the table. "This is no ordinary fountain," Mephistopheles explained. "This is a spring that is part of the River Gjoil. It is the river that separates…"

"The living from the dead," Ana finished for him.

"You know your Norse mythology," Mephistopheles noted. "While the river Styx brings the souls to us, the Gjoil is to prevent anyone from stumbling into our realm."

Ana approached the fountain and thought she saw swords flowing in the waters of the deep recess of the well. She felt a chill as she got closer to the fountain, rubbing her arms as she approached. Mephistopheles took the decanter and filled it with the water from the well then set it on the table with the four chalices.

"Here is how you can save your friends' souls from eternal damnation," Mephistopheles began. "You drink the water from the well and survive."

"And the catch?" Ana repeated her question from earlier.

He chuckled at the question. "There are four goblets here on this table, each one different, each one unique. If you choose the correct one and drink from it, then your friends will be released, their souls saved, they will be able to leave this place without the torment that they would experience."

"If I choose the wrong one?"

"See that's where the fun is," he answered. "The four represent four different elements, virtues, and sins. You have to choose the one that will offer forgiveness, while being able to overcome the negative side of that element."

"If I chose wrong?" Ana inquired.

"Then you will be tortured by that element you chose," Mephistopheles replied. "And so will your friends. So let's say you chose the goblet that was forged from fire and that was the wrong one, you will all be placed in a pit of fire. You will be forced to watch everything you love be destroyed by violence, hate and anger. If it was Air, and that was wrong, then you will feel as if you are suffocating, while watching as everyone you love believe the lies that are told about you. As they quarrel with themselves and each other."

"So the elements represent the way we will be tortured," Ana stated. "The negative side of that element is how those around us will be affected."

"Yes."

"But if I chose the right one then my friends walk free, their souls untouched, their minds able to handle all that they have experienced while here," Ana clarified.

"Yes," Mephistopheles replied.

"I agree to the terms," Ana stated.

"Then all you have to do is select the correct chalice, pour the water into it, and drink the contents," Mephistopheles answered her.

Ana walked to the table where the goblets sat. Each one was different, made of different metals, with their own unique designs. Some were encrusted with jewels while others were etched with detailed patterns. There was one though that was plain, it was made of copper. Parts of it had turned green but other parts were shiny. There was no design on it, no gems on it, no engravings of any kind. It didn't seem to fit in with the other three goblets. Ana ran a finger around the rim of the glass, it felt warm to her touch. Touching the other's they were cool under her fingertip.

Looking around, she saw Alex and Terry cringing with whatever they were being forced to experience. She looked over at where Mephistopheles stood and saw him watching her with curiosity. Ana looked at the goblets again and selected the plain copper cup. Pouring the water into the cup she held it to her mouth and goblet to her lips.

The liquid burned as it went down her throat. Ana could hear her heart beating in her ears, she could feel it speeding up in her chest. Her veins felt like they were on fire. The pain which radiated through her body brought her to her knees. Gasping for air she tried to focus on everything around her but all she could hear were screams and voices filling her head. Images flashed through her mind as she tried to gain control of her body. There was fear that she had chosen wrong.

"Embrace the fire," Mephistopheles whispered close to her ear. "Let it consume you, let it take control."

Ana struggled, refusing to listen to him. "You will only truly live once you accept the fire that burns within you," he continued. "Your refusal to accept it has brought us here. You were born to be one of us, born to live in the flames that burn the souls of the damned. You were never for the regular world, you were never supposed to be ordinary."

She refused to listen to him, refused to let his words mean anything to her. Instead, she focused on everything that she had to lose if she caved. She thought of Cassie, of Jeremy, the other teens, of Eric, and her family.

"Why do you fight against what you know is true?" Mephistopheles asked her. "Embrace your destiny."

Ana snorted at the last line which brought her out of the fog that had taken over her mind. "Next you are going to tell me you're my father," Ana replied as she slowly got up on one knee.

Mephistopheles gave her a strange look not understanding the statement. He watched as she slowly began to stand up on her own. "You are only postponing the inevitable."

"No, I'm not," Ana answered. "You can't have my soul. You can't have the souls of my friends or loved ones. You thought I would choose the wrong goblet, but I didn't, it's why you tried to take over my mind. But you couldn't because I am stronger than you think I am. And I will never submit."

"How could you even know the right one?"

"I saw it in a movie once," Ana stated.

Meph just stared at her. "I highly doubt that."

"Seriously, the guy was in the room full of Chalices, and he had to pick the Holy Grail," Ana explained. "Instead of choosing the most expensive one he chose the one that was a battered plane cup. He was right."

She lied. She wasn't going to tell him that she heard a voice whisper when she touched the plain one. She wasn't going to tell him that the voice sounded like her ancestor telling her that cup would save her friends. Instead she would piss him off with the movie reference.

Outside, the world seemed to be changing as black rain began to fall from the sky. Erik and Michael followed the overgrown path that they knew led directly to Mephistopheles' lair. Neither had spoken since they realized that Terry and Alex had vanished. They longer they stayed in Mephistopheles domain the higher risk they ran of losing track of time in the mortal realm and why they were here. The path they took wasn't filled with illusions, so they didn't have to worry about traps or the feeling that they were never getting close. Instead, the building was getting closer and closer.

They both came to a stop as they heard a loud explosion that shook the ground. Erik grabbed Michael and pulled them both behind a large boulder as fireballs seemed to rain down from the sky. Critters scurried around them trying to find a safe place to hide. A fire ball landed nearby them scorching the ground, they both moved as the heat from it singed their skin.

"Shit," Michael yelled as they both dodged in opposite directions from another.

"He's losing his temper, which means he is losing control of his powers," Erik realized. "Ana must not be cooperating the way he wanted."

"Go girl," Michael said with pride. Not many divine beings could ignore Mephistopheles, the fact that this could be a sign that Ana might be was impressive.

"She's tough," Erik agreed with a smile.

He pushed himself up off the ground and walked to help Michael get up. The whole ground shook violently and cracks started to form in the ground around where they stood.

"He's ripping his own realm apart!" Michael yelled over the noise.

"I noticed," Erick said dryly.

They both sprouted their wings without going into full Angelic form and hovered over the ground.

"We need to hurry," Eric stated.

"This isn't going to go unnoticed," Michael added. "And that might be good for us."

"Let's hope."

Chapter 35

ANA GAGGED AS she vomited up foul tasting water. Her hair was soaked as water ran down her back, neck, and front. She lay shivering on the cold stone floor curled up as tight as she could as air began to fill her lungs again. Whatever Mephistopheles was trying to do was not working and his temper was starting to show. She gasped for air as her tormentor paced across the floor in front of her. His fury at her picking the correct the goblet knew no bounds. Terry and Alex had vanished with the snap of his fingers, deep down Ana knew it wasn't because he had freed them. All she knew was that he broke a vow he made.

"No one can resist!" Mephistopheles yelled. "No one should be able to withstand the force of my mind."

Ana tried to crawl away from him but he grabbed her hair like it was ropes pulling her back toward him. "What do you see?" Mephistopheles demanded. "When you are submerged, what do you see?"

There was no lying to him, she knew that. He would be able to find out anyway even if she didn't tell him. "Everything is cloudy," she began, her voice no more than a whisper. "There is movement around me and muffled voices but nothing is clear."

"And then?" He shook her. "Do not hold back from me!"

"And then it clears for a moment and I see my memories, then I see what you want to change," Ana continued. "Then I wake up on the ground."

He dropped her from his grasp and threw a fireball at the wall behind her out of anger. Ana screamed, scrambling away as the room shook from his losing control. A piece of the ceiling came crashing down, Ana jumped out of the way as it shattered on the ground.

"You are unmaking your own world!" Ana yelled as she dove behind a piece of furniture as more of the ceiling came down. "You are letting this obsession with me, with my family, ruin everything you have!"

Mephistopheles didn't listen as he filled the chalice with more water. He turned and looked at her. "You will bend to my will!"

"If I haven't yet, what makes you think I am going to?" Ana asked. She moved around the rubble, using the large chunks of ceiling to conceal herself from Mephistopheles.

Outside the window she watched the fire rain down from the sky as the earth trembled. Her fear was for those who would try to rescue her. Ana always knew that this would happen, Mephistopheles would bring her here. What she had never planned was to have people so loyal to her that they would risk their own mortality to free her from her hell. That is what kept her fighting, what kept her breaking free of Mephistopheles' control. Knowing that there were people who were fighting with her.

"I do not know how you keep resisting me," Mephistopheles stated. "But you will tire, you will make a mistake. In that moment I will bring upon you such torture that you will beg for a death that will never come."

"This realm will be destroyed before I cave to you," Ana informed him as she stepped out from behind the rubble. "Am I worth this?"

"You do not understand," Mephistopheles replied as he brought her to him with a snap of his fingers. "This has been thousands of years in the making. The search for a worthy candidate, the line that can undo all their rules, all their perfect intentions. This is a path where there is no going back and I knew that when I started this journey."

"This isn't all about my family," Ana realized. She looked at the creature before her. "This is revenge."

Mephistopheles cackled at that as he ran a long fingernail down her arm. He drew a slow trickle of blood from her and smiled. Taking a drop of the dark red liquid he licked it off his finger and smiled.

"Blood holds so much magic and power," Mephistopheles whispered. "It can unlock all of person's secrets. It can bind us, control us, and unite us. I wonder what your blood will tell me? Will it tell me how I can bend you to my will?"

Meg Castro

Ana struggled against him as he smiled at her. She had to survive, even if it was just to find what he did to Terry and Alex, so she could get them out of here. She would make sure that they brought Jules back with them so she could be buried properly. Once they were gone she would end this game. Grief slammed into Ana as she thought of Jules, she was not going to let her down. Then a thought occurred to her, something that Jules had said before she died. Then she saw a figure appear in the shadows. Johann stood there out of Mephistopheles view holding the sword.

"The sword," she whispered.

As she whispered the words the sword appeared in her hands. She knew what she had to do now. Wielding it she caught Mephistopheles with the blade catching him in surprise. His hand dropped the chalice she had chosen, she grabbed it as it fell to the ground. Instead of filling it with water, she filled it with some of his blood and drank it. He laughed waiting for the poison that was his blood to take hold, but it didn't. Ana ran for the door. Seeing her. Mephistopheles tried to close it with his power. Taking a running dive, Ana slid through it as it slammed behind her. Now they were connected and she knew where her friends were.

Running as fast as she could go she followed the force that was pulling and guiding her to the dungeon. Those that got in her way perished by the blade of the sword. The walls trembled and groaned as Mephistopheles' temper soared to new heights. When she came to the locked doors of the dungeon she cut her palm and laid it on the locks. They snapped undone and she entered. Terry and Alex were chained to the far wall with hoods over their heads. Shadow people were floating throughout the room. But when they saw Ana carrying the sword they parted, almost bowing as she walked to the wall. Using the cut on her palm she undid each of the chains then pulled the hoods off of them.

"Shit," Terry said as he looked around. Ana helped him stand up, then she went to Alex to help free him. Terry tried to catch his bearings before he went over to pull Alex into a hug.

"Shit is right," Alex agreed. He reached out pulling Ana into their hug. "If anyone ever told me I would go through hell for a girl I would have told them they were crazy."

252

Ana chuckled slowly as she held onto both of them for another moment. When she finally pulled away she looked at them with sorrow. "Jules is dead."

"We know," Terry whispered squeezing her hand. "What do you need us to do?"

"Before he finds us," Alex added.

"He won't," Ana promised and used the sword to cut her palm. She placed her palm on both of their foreheads. "This will protect you from his games, his creatures, and their poison."

"We don't want to know, do we," Terry stated.

"No, you really don't," Ana answered. "Is…"

"We got separated," Alex told her. "They were talking about a plan when these winged demons came and grabbed us."

They heard the great roar that brought more stone down around them. "Jules is in the north tower," Ana informed them. "The lost souls are guarding her body, tell them I give you permission. Stay there until you get the feeling it's time to go."

"None of this makes any sense, but we'll go," Terry assured her. He kissed her on the forehead. "Promise me you will be joining us in our world."

"I promise," Ana lied as she pushed them out of the dungeon. Once they were heading in the right direction she went back to deal with Mephistopheles.

Erik ducked around the corner holding onto his side as he did. The demons were pouring out of the walls. Roth had secured them weapons when they met up with him at the gates to Mephistopheles' home. Between the walls breaking apart and the demons they were all beat up and bleeding. When they heard the roar that echoed throughout the building they knew Mephistopheles was losing total control.

"When do you think his army is going to show up?" Michael called to Erik. He had just taken down a gallath who had come out of a mirror.

"I felt the call of his horn a moment ago," Roth stated as he ducked from a rock falling. "We need to hurry."

They headed up the stairs and Michael almost ran right into Terry and Alex. Michael grabbed Alex to keep him from tumbling down the stairs. "You are free?"

"Ana just freed us," Alex stated. "She told us where to go."

"There is blood on your forehead," Roth noted. He touched the marks, closing his eyes he understood what Ana had done. "They are protected."

"Then go to where she instructed you," Michael replied. "Which way did she go?"

"Toward the south tower," Terry recalled. "She has a huge sword with her."

"What did it look like?" Erik asked as comprehension began to dawn as to what Ana was doing.

"Huge, almost as big as Ana," Alex replied. "It was very plain, no ornamentation on it, no jewels. It was old, you could tell by the color of the metals."

Michael looked at Erik. "Do you know?"

"If I'm right then it's the true Joyeuse," Erik replied. There was only one reason that Ana would be able to wield it. "Jules is dead?"

"She wants us to get her body so Jules can come back with us," Terry said softly.

Roth took a dagger from his belt and handed it to Alex. "Take this. Any demon or being that hinders your path show them the blade and they will let you pass," Roth instructed. "If they refuse say my name."

"Alright," Alex agreed as he slid the dagger into his belt.

Erik watched as the two mortals headed to the north tower, he then pointed toward their destination. Michael waited until it was just the three of them. "You know this sword?"

"It can only be wielded by those descended of Charlemagne, those that show his strength, courage, and fearlessness," Erik explained. "It protects the bearer from poison, corruption, and gives them the power to lead others."

"How did it end up here?" Roth inquired. He then paused holding up his hand to stop them. A group of demons came down the stairs, Roth and Erik both did away with the demons.

"Because Jules comes from a legendary line of the great king," Erik answered. "He had a child with a Valkyrie. Jules comes from that line. It was hidden, erased from the records and legends. It took Sam and Toby some work to find it and realize who Jules was. It's why she could hold the sword and not go crazy."

"But how can Ana hold it?" Michael asked. "We know her entire family tree."

"Because the true bearer of the sword can pass it on to someone else upon their death," Erik said softly. "All the power and protection would pass on to that person as well."

"So she brought the sword here in order to protect Ana, knowing that she would have to die in order to do so," Michael realized. "Well shit, that is more honorable than anything I have ever witnessed."

Roth stared at both of them. "Then we finish this once and for all, and we honor Jules in a way that is fitting of her legacy."

Chapter 36

His laughter filled the entire room. Ana winced in pain as she tried to move but the pain was so great it robbed her of breath. His anger at her freeing the two mortals had left her very nearly broken. But she noticed that with each injury she received she watched him wince slightly as well. He wasn't aware of it though, for all he craved now was her blood on his hands.

"Your lover will be here soon," Mephistopheles informed her. "He has brought friends with him. All the more witnesses to your destruction!"

Ana was tired. She had watched her best friend sacrifice herself so that Ana would have the tool she needed to win. Her memories, her reality, had been altered and manipulated. And then he tried to force his way into her mind by using the chalice to change her mind. None of it had worked, but each thing had left its mark on her. The realm was also starting to bear it's weight on her. It wasn't changing her but she was growing more tired with each blow and with each moment that past.

"There is no freeing your blood," Mephistopheles continued. "You cannot win this, Analiese! You are mine, you have always been mine. Let this end and I will not punish you."

As tempting as the offer was she knew he lied. She could feel it ringing in her blood as the whispers told her not to listen. Wisps whirled around her limbs as if soothing her injuries as they cooled her off. Whispers told her not to give up, she could do this. She needed to believe or it was already lost. All Ana knew was that she was tired of all of it. Closing her eyes she smiled at the faces that came to her. Cassie with her vibrant hair and angelic voice, Jeremy with his determination to beat his own demons. They both had seen so much bad in this world yet each day they got up and found their peace, found their will to keep going.

Strength seemed to bloom inside of her and the weariness began to fade away as he slowly began to sit up. The pains that had made it hard to breath had faded and as she stood up she didn't feel any broken bones. The bleeding stopped, wounds healed. The sword no longer felt heavy in her hands, instead it felt lighter, was easier to wield.

Mephistopheles watched her as she got to her feet and Ana noticed a slight look of fear flashing in his glowing eyes. "This is impossible," he stated.

"Nothing is impossible," Ana replied. "So we can keep this up all day or you could just give up."

Mephistopheles laughed at that. "You humans are so amusing," Mephistopheles noted. "You think that you are indestructible, you can walk away from battling your better. There is no coming away from this, my dear. You either submit to my will or I kill you."

It was Ana's turn to laugh. "You think I don't realize that."

Her statement confused him as he looked at her with a look of total confusion on his face. Ana took that moment and ran with the sword held high. She caught him off guard, caught his minions off guard. She used that moment of confusion. Sprinting toward him she raised the sword, leaping into the air as she plunged the blade through his middle. He screamed, Ana twisted the blade as she shoved it all the way to the hilt so that the blade came out the other side. Ana gasped as they sunk to the floor.

Black blood boiled from the wound as it ran down the front and back of Mephistopheles. He tried to yank the sword from him but it wouldn't budge from him, his minions whirled around them as blood began to pool around Ana and Mephistopheles. Ana heard the pounding of three sets of feet coming up the stairs then sliding to a halt at the doorway that now appeared.

"My God," Michael whispered as he took in the sight before them. Roth kept him from running into the room.

"The blood will darken you," Roth warned. "It won't harm Lucifer, for he fell from grace."

Erik ran to Ana. Kneeling down, he gently gathered her in his arms. She rested her head against his chest as they stared at the monster before them. Mephistopheles began to shrivel up the more he bled, he was trying to stand to move but his body was just contorting into different directions. As he died, white wisps started to emerge from him and fly into the ceiling as if the souls he had trapped were finally being released.

"You did good," Erik whispered to Ana laying a kiss on her head. "You did good."

Terry and Alex stood guard in front of the bed with weapons at the ready. They had already fought off some creatures as they tried to get to Jules. The dagger that the demon had given Alex had worked allowing them some ease. A lull in activity allowed them both to take a much needed breath of air. Terry pulled Alex to him and they just stood there leaning against each other, reassuring each other they were okay.

Terry looked at the bed. "She looks like she is sleeping," he noted. "She's so peaceful."

"It's like one of the paintings of a fairy tale," Alex realized. "The princess sleeping for eternity."

"We will make sure that she is remembered," Terry stated. "Her sacrifice will not be for nothing."

They heard a rumble, gentle hands began to push them towards the bed quickly so that they were on either side of Jules. They weren't sure what the sign would be but they each grabbed Jules' hand and waited. They heard the scream that seemed to rip through the building. The rooms shook with such violence that the floor around them began to break away. They climbed onto the bed holding onto Jules not sure what they were supposed to do.

"I love you," Alex told Terry. "I love you too, but we are getting out of this," Terry told him.

"When we do, you're marrying me," Alex informed him.

"I'm holding you to that proposal," Terry replied.

They felt the floor give way, felt the bed shake and they held on with everything ounce of strength they had. There was a flash of blinding light. They couldn't seeing anything but they heard crying as they seemed to fall for eternity. A whisper told them to open their eyes.

When they did they were in the family room of Bohlander-Gerfallen house. Jules was no longer with them nor was the bed. They looked down and saw they were covered in blood and grime but they didn't care, they were back, they hugged each other. It was only then they heard a name being repeated over and over again. Then they watched Toby and Sam running through the door with the look of horror. Then they heard Jules yelling "no" over and over again, Then they heard Erik's yell of pain. They realized two things. The first: Jules was alive. The second: Ana was not.

Chapter 37

ERIK SAT IN the living room of the Carriage House. A steaming cup of tea sat in front of him, he felt a hand on his shoulder. Smiling sadly he looked to see Jules standing there with Sam behind her. Toby followed them in with Luke, Alex, and Terry. Jill and Helen were helping Martha with the teenagers. They were all still in shock, reality had not fully set in yet. No one spoke as they sat around the coffee table. Martha's usual steady hand trembled a bit as she poured them each tea, refilling Erik's before sitting down.

"Mom and Dad will be here tonight," Toby stated in a thick voice. "They made the identification and signed off on the paperwork to transfer her."

Erik was silent as Jules laid a hand on his. He knew she felt guilty, that she should have been the one dead. "I don't blame you," Erik told her, squeezing her hand. "Ana feared that her death might have to occur to end it all. We talked about it in private, we knew the risks, knew what could happen."

Sam took a seat on the arm of the couch, his hand was on Jules' shoulder offering her comfort. The moment he had seen the series of paintings in their entirety he was on a plane to New York to warn them. Only to be delayed by the storm that knocked out power to all of Manhattan. Meteorologist were still talking about the freak storm that had brought the city a stand still.

"What now?" Alex asked.

"Michael is trying to get answers to our many questions," Erik admitted. "The High Court is meeting reviewing everything that has happened, so we wait and see what will happen."

"Will you get in trouble?" Sam asked.

"I could, I broke several laws as well so I could face punishment," Erik answered.

"That's bull shit!" Terry exclaimed standing up from his spot on the sofa. "I mean you and Michael were the only two that did something. The rest should be punished for standing back and doing nothing."

"That's not how it always works, though," Erik replied. "There is very little gray area where I come from."

"I agree with Terry," Toby stated. "You did nothing wrong, you should not be punished."

"He won't," a soft voice said from behind them.

They all turned and saw Cassie standing there. She was wearing ripped jeans, a blue t-shirt, her hair was currently back to it's normal color of raven black. Yet there was something about her that was different. Erik stood immediately walking to the thirteen year old.

"You should be resting," he said gently.

She smiled at him and he felt peace wash over him. Erik took a step back as his eyes went wide. "Why did I never notice before?" Erik whispered.

"Because it wasn't time for you to know," Cassie answered. She laid a gentle hand on his before walking into the room. "Erik will not be punished, nor will any of his forms. Neither will Michael or any other beings that assisted them."

"What the hell is going on?" Terry asked. "Why is Cassie glowing?"

"Cass, how do you know all this?" Toby asked carefully as he watched his niece stand before them.

"I know many things," Cassie admitted. "You see Joseph Gerfallen was supposed to have ended the curse. It had been seen by many that he would bring redemption to the line of Faust."

"But he didn't," Sam pointed out. "He was another victim of Meph."

"You can say his name," Cassie informed them. "He is no more, Ana saw to that."

"Wait," Erik said holding up a hand. "How is that possible? Who are you exactly?"

"I am the contingency plan," Cassie answered. "I was created to ensure that Mephistopheles would be stopped. Of course I wasn't even aware of that until Ana and Jules were taken, then everything made sense."

"We need to start over," Alex suggested before more questions were asked. "Cassie, I want to say start at the beginning but I mean start with Joe's death. Start with your creation."

"As I said, it was foretold that Joe would be the end of the curse," Cassie explained. "He would defeat Mephistopheles but not giving into the mind tricks. Joe was so well guarded by Angels. We couldn't completely block out Mephistopheles mind games but we could weaken the damage."

"How did he die?" Sam asked. Jules took his hand in hers and held it tight knowing this was not easy. "If my dad was so well protected by Angels than how did Meph get through to him?"

"Distraction," Cassie answered simply. "Even Angels can be caught off guard. Mephistopheles created a distraction that required everyone's attention and help. He took that moment to weaken Joe's resolve. To show him images of what he would do to his family. When he was killed, when we heard the screams of Ana, we all knew what happened."

"You said you were a contingency plan," Terry replied. "What do you mean?"

"There was no proof the Meph had broken any laws," Cassie explained. "But many in the High Court believed that he had broken laws. They believed things were being overlooked because he was the Voice of Satan, consequently, events and his actions were being brushed aside."

"The court was in disagreement causing tension?" Sam clarified.

"Yes," Cassie agreed. "Those in the High Court who believed Meph was guilty watched both Sam and Ana closely. No one was sure who the curse would pass to or if it would even continue. While they were watched plans were discussed."

"Without anyone knowing?" Erik asked. "How could Michael not know?"

"Because it never left the High Court," Cassie answered. "No one was to know that there was suspicion of Meph. It was agreed upon that it would stay within the court."

"So what was agreed upon?" Toby asked.

"Ana began having nightmares not at eighteen but at seventeen," Cassie replied. "They were much milder than the ones she would later have. Because of how soon he acted, because he confirmed their worst fears, they decided on me. A soul that was pure and innocent would be born, no one would know who the soul was. This soul would even be unknown to the High Court. The soul would be guided to Ana somehow. The soul would live a normal life with no knowledge of who they were until the time that Meph's attack occurred."

"It would explain why he was in a way attracted to you," Erik realized. "He picked up on something about you without knowing what it was and it drew him in. It explains our connection as well."

"It does," Cassie agreed.

"What was your purpose?" Toby asked. "I mean what were you supposed to be able to do that no one else could do?"

"The knowledge of who I am would come the moment that Ana was taken by Meph. Because he broke the laws about bringing an unwilling victim into the afterlife, this other part of me was awakened.," Cassie explained. "Though I had some suspicion. The day when time froze due to Beez I started becoming aware of this other part of me. I could hear Erik's phone ring when no one else but an angel could. I could see what Michael and Erik looked like in their angel form without them being in them."

"What would your role be?" Erik asked studying her.

"If Ana failed in destroying Meph, I would have been summoned to his realm to complete her task," Cassie answered. "Since Ana did not fail I did not have to do that. Now I just know who I am."

"Then she succeeded?" Toby asked with a sense of relief. If her death meant that it was over, that she was at peace finally, then it made the grief a bit easier.

"The next generation of your family will know nothing of the curse," Cassie answered. "Meph's soul is imprisoned in one of the fire pits for the rest of time. He will be a reminder to all about what happens "

"And my sister?" Toby whispered, his voice breaking at the question.

Cassie bit her lip as a tear ran down her face. "She's not coming back," Cassie replied knowing what he was hoping for. "The poison from Beez was killing her. The headaches, the fatigue, it was because of her body's struggle to fight the poison. The tonic that was used contained it to give her more time but it wasn't going to prolong her life for more than a year."

"Instead of dying slowly she chose to go out in a way that would ensure we were all safe," Jules realized. "If she took down Meph then she could rest easy knowing we would all be safe."

"She's always trying to protect us," Sam agreed with a choked up laugh. "Cassie, how did Jules survive?"

"That would be Ana as well," Cassie admitted.

"Holy shit, the promise," Terry remembered. They all looked at him not sure what he meant. "The three of us were in this room with Meph. Alex and I were in individual cells, Ana was free. There was a well, and a table of goblets. Meph told her that if she chose the right goblet then we would go free."

"I know the well you are talking about," Erik replied. "It's part of the World Tree. It connects our realm to the realm of Hela, she is the Norse Goddess of the dead. Whatever promise was made at the well would have to be fulfilled."

"When Meph presented her the deal he stated both mine and Alex's name," Terry continued. "Yet when Ana repeated it to clarify what he meant she changed it. She asked that any of us who came into his realm be able to leave unharmed. And Meph agreed to it, re-stating what she had said."

"He had already forgotten about Jules so he didn't think anything of it," Erik realized. "And that would do it. She outsmarted him."

"But wouldn't that have worked on her?" Sam asked.

"No, mortals can't kill divine beings without consequences," Erik answered. "To kill one is to sacrifice yourself as well."

"And if you had done it?" Terry asked Erik.

"The contract would have passed onto Satan and he would decide if the terms were fulfilled or not. And he really isn't the kind of guy you want to decide on something like that."

"In the end it had to be Faust blood to end the curse," Cassie stated. "Ana knew that if another killed him there was a chance that Satan would have the final say.

"And if she failed then you would have been the one to kill Meph," Toby restated. Cassie nodded. "What if you failed?"

"There was a second," Cassie admitted. "He is older than me by a few years, but if I had failed then he would have been alerted."

"How could he be older than you if you were the first?" Luke inquired.

"When he was four, his mother had fallen asleep, he was a precocious child and made his way outside where he fell into the pool," Cassie explained. Luke looked up at her sharply. "He technically died and was revived in the ambulance. When he was revived he had become the backup. However, it was not an easy thing, for his soul and body had known a time when he was a normal being. He has struggled throughout the last few years of finding his place. Ana helped him find it, helped him learn what his calling is."

"Jeremy," Luke whispered knowing deep down that it had to be Jeremy. "He's the second."

"Explaining yet again why Meph was most likely drawn to him as well," Alex realized.

There was silence for a few moments. It was Martha who spoke. "Is it over now?"

Cassie nodded. "Well yes, in the sense that the curse is over. The Gerfallen and Faust lines have been redeemed." Cassie looked at Erik when she spoke again. "Erik and I have a decision that we need to make."

"What's that?" Erik asked.

"Well, we can leave this world, for our job is done," Cassie answered. "We can return to the heavens and be with Ana."

"Or?" Toby asked. His heart constricted at the idea of losing another person he cared about.

"Or we finish out our mortal lives," Cassie finished.

"My punishment?" Erik inquired. "If I return now or later, what punishment awaits me?"

"There is none," Cassie replied.

"How do you know that?" Erik asked. "I get that you are the contingency plan but how do you know that there is no punishment waiting for me? Unless you are on the High Court, which you aren't, you would have to be the..."

Erik looked at her again as he realized just who this young woman was. "A voice like the angels," he mumbled. "You are the Voice of God."

Cassie beamed at him as she nodded. "Not expecting a thirteen year old girl?"

"More like Alan Rickman," Toby admitted and got an elbow by Sam.

"You have no punishment," Cassie informed Erik. "In fact when you return, it will not be as the Duke of Hell but as the Morning Star."

Erik was speechless for a few moments as he realized what she was saying. "You were right in some of your arguments," Cassie added.

He ran a hand through his hair as he stood up and walked to the window. "So what do you want to do, kid?"

"Ana will be there for whenever we are ready to return," Cassie pointed out.

"She'll probably kick both of our butts if you don't see what you can do with that voice of yours," Erik added.

"Plus you have a bunch of teens and Vets that count on you," Cassie reminded him.

"Do we get a say?" Toby asked. "Because I'm not ready to lose my niece. I would like to keep her around for a bit longer if that's alright."

"We stay," Cassie said.

"We stay," Erik agreed.

Epilogue

Ten Years Later…

THE FAUST ABBEY, as it was called by locals and tour books, was filled with people. Music was coming from the courtyard, kids were running around laughing, while food seemed to be everywhere. The May Pole was wrapped in bright ribbons while promises of a bonfire later for May Day were announced. There were a few media trucks and reporters, all having been invited to be at the event. Today was the official dedication for the completed Abbey. It was going to be a center for Refugees, where they could live, work, go to school, and just live. They named it *Ana's Hope*, away to keep Ana's legacy alive. The program would take in families from war torn countries and give them a safe place to live while they worked on their next chapter.

Toby was laughing at something that Luke was saying to him. They were all here at the dedication. Terry arrived a few days earlier with Dennis, Jill, and his adopted son Joe. Alex had to remain in the states because of a case he was working on. Sam, Jules, and their ten year old son Freddie and five year old daughter Grace had been here since the beginning of April to help Toby with last minute details. Toby's parents, Sam's family, and Luke all arrived yesterday with two surprise guests: Erik and Cassie. The New York Metropolitan Opera had given Cassie time off to come to the dedication, she might have been their new soloist but they also understood the impact that Ana had on Cassie's life.

Toby smiled as Erik walked over to him. "This is amazing," Erik stated looking around at everything. "She would be honored."

"Yea, she would," Toby agreed.

He noted that Erik was still wearing a silver band on his left hand. Erik had started wearing it a few months after Ana's death. Toby had asked him about that first Christmas. Erik knew Ana was his one and only love, so the ring was to keep women from trying to pick him up, he got tired of saying not interested. Toby also learned that Erik had slipped an engagement ring into Ana's coffin before the burial. After that he introduced Erik as his brother to anyone who didn't know him.

"How's our own diva doing?" Toby asked. Erik stayed in New York to support Cassie, he legally adopted her a year after Ana died.

"Silencing critics, charming the audiences, and ignoring the boys who think they are good enough for her," Erik commented.

Toby had to laugh at the last part. "She's twenty three."

"And still too young to date," Erik pointed out.

"How is Jeremy doing?" Toby asked.

"He keeps sniffing around her, I don't like it," Erik answered which had Toby laughing even harder. "But he's doing great at Bohlander House. Terry is impressed with how he is doing with the teens."

"Do you think he's attracted to her because of who they are?" Toby asked.

"It's why I want them to go slow," Erik admitted. They had told Jeremy the truth after Ana's death, about what a part of him was. It took Erik transforming into an Angel and Jules doing her thing to show Jeremy that they weren't crazy.

They both jumped back as Freddie came running past them. Sam was laughing as he tried to catch his son. "He never stops moving," Sam chuckled. He gave Erik a hug. "You're getting gray."

"You should see my wings," Erik joked making the three of them laugh.

Jules joined them. "Grace is with your mom," Jules told Sam. Then looked at Toby. "And being spoiled by yours."

"It's been awhile since we've all been together," Toby pointed out.

Jules leaned against Sam and smiled at the sign with Ana's name on it. "So what happens now?"

"We start the next chapter," Toby stated. "We finished Ana's with this place. Now we can look at the next generation and focus on them."

"That sounds like a good plan," Jules agreed.

Acknowledgements

THIS BOOK STARTED over ten years ago when I met my husband's best friend, Mark Lieberman. Little did either of us know where this friendship would take us but over many coffee cups at a local diner we discussed our fascination with Faust and Mephistopheles. We always talked about doing a project together but never delved into it. Fast forward to February of 2016 where Mark decided we should do this. What was going to be a short ten thousand word story that would go with a short video he would make exploded into something more. This novel. That simple short story became so much larger than we originally planned. Without him this book would still be an idea tossed around in my head.

Resources

IN THE WRITING of this book the following resources were used to help with the
building of the characters and the story that we told.

1. *The Complete Works* of Christopher Marlowe
2. *Faust* by Johann Wolfgang von Goethe
3. *The Encyclopedia of Demons and Demonology* By Rosemary Ellen Guiley
4. *The Dictionary of Demons* By Michelle Belanger
5. *A Dictionary of Angels- including the Fallen Angels* by Gustav Davidson

www.ingramcontent.com/pod-product-compliance
Lightning Source LLC
Chambersburg PA
CBHW070852180626

46817CB00003B/751